7/98

Vincent Murano
Richard Hammer

SIMON & SCHUSTER

New York ▪ London ▪ Toronto
Sydney ▪ Tokyo ▪ Singapore

The
THURSDAY
CLUB

A NOVEL

SIMON & SCHUSTER
Simon & Schuster Building
Rockefeller Center
1230 Avenue of the Americas
New York, New York 10020

SIMON & SCHUSTER and colophon are registered trademarks of Simon & Schuster Inc.

Designed by Levavi & Levavi
Manufactured in the United States of America

10 9 8 7 6 5 4 3 2 1
Library of Congress Cataloging-in-Publication Data

Murano, Vincent.
The Thursday club : a novel / Vincent Murano, Richard Hammer.
p.   cm.
I. Hammer, Richard, 1928-   . II. Title.
PS3563.U717T48   1992
813'.54—dc20   92-1635
                                                        CIP

ISBN: 0-671-73448-2

ACKNOWLEDGMENTS

FOR THEIR EDITORIAL GUIDANCE in shaping this manuscript, we wish to thank Michael Korda and Chuck Adams of Simon & Schuster. And for their continued support and considerable best efforts on our behalf, we express our deep gratitude to two fine agents, Robert Gottlieb and Mel Berger, both of the William Morris Agency.

FOR ROBERT GOTTLIEB
AND
MEL BERGER

Prologue
SEPTEMBER

1

It was the smell that got Wilbur Evans. From his high perch in the cab on the bulldozer, he shoved the levers that burrowed the blade deep into the Arthur Kill landfill, a vast, ugly mountain of garbage-filled plastic bags bursting at the seams. Most people called it the Staten Island dump. It was the biggest rubbish heap there was. Evans wasn't paying much attention, his mind wandering, his eyes peering now and then toward the dim shape of the Outerbridge Crossing in the distance. Along the parkway that ran beside the dump toward the bridge raced an occasional bus, car, or limousine filled with high rollers and suckers heading for a killing, or, more likely, bankruptcy in the pleasure palaces at Atlantic City. Overhead, wheeling and soaring through the sky, a squadron of gulls cawed angrily, the sound even louder than the muffled roar of the bulldozer. Occasionally, one would make a sudden swoop to scavenge the refuse.

The blade edge of Evans's bulldozer caught a thick black bag, buried for nobody knew how long. The plastic split. Heat, trapped and building for years, turned to steam and burst out. Whatever was in the bag wasn't garbage. After ten years, he'd become immune to the smell of garbage. This was something else.

He jammed on the brakes and stared down at the torn plastic. He could make out what looked like a pile of smoldering brown leaves. He climbed down from the cab, a crowbar in one hand, and approached cautiously. He poked into the pile, stirring it, probing until the crowbar caught on something. He yanked. The crowbar exploded out of the heap, the force propelling him backward, sending him sprawling. Then he saw it. Caught on the end of the crowbar, shreds of skin and matted hair clinging to it, was a head.

Detective Jan Polanska and two uniformed cops from the 123rd Precinct were the first to arrive. They threaded their way carefully over the garbage, but still stumbling and nearly falling into it. Approaching the torn plastic bag, they got a glimpse of its contents, caught the odor. Polanska had smelled death before; it was a stench he would never forget.

An emergency service crew reached the scene, parked at the edge of the dump, and started toward the small group of men gathered across the field of plastic, toward the hastily strung yellow ribbon with the black lettering "Police—Crime Scene" that ringed the place. As they got close enough to see and smell, one of them said, "Oh, shit," and turned away, trying not to be sick. "This ain't for us. I'm gonna call the meat wagon." He stumbled back across the field.

The morgue wagon arrived. The attendants in it had been warned what to expect and were dressed accordingly: thick white coveralls, sealed at wrists and ankles; thick double gloves with a weave to protect their hands from any penetrating contamination; surgical masks covering their faces; goggles over their eyes. They looked like something out of a nuclear nightmare. Carrying body bags, they advanced steadily, then turned away momentarily when they got close. Then, reluctantly, they set about carefully loading one of the body bags. They did not touch the thing that lay inside the ripped black plastic. Instead, they took the bag itself by the corners and eased it, and its contents, into the waiting container. They zipped the body bag shut, carried it back to the morgue wagon, shoved it into the back, and drove away, across the island, across the Verrazano Narrows Bridge, through Brooklyn, across its bridge, up the FDR Drive, to the morgue at Bellevue Hospital.

Dr. George Kaplan, the Medical Examiner, was a meticulous man. Ever since his graduation from New York University Medical School, thirty years before, he had worked for the city, a specialist in pathology. Over those years, he had seen everything through the thick black-framed glasses that usually rested low on the bridge of his nose. He had grown impervious to even the most grotesque sights. But what lay on the table before him and his assistant was a thing even he had trouble facing. He wanted to hurry, to rush through the examination and be out of that room, to wash away even the memory of it with the strongest antiseptics, and then drown its memory in strong drink. Yet he took his time, carefully sifting through the body bag and the garbage bag that lay inside. A switchblade knife clattered across the tile floor. He picked it up between two gloved fingers and placed it in a sterile plastic evidence bag that he set on a table. A cardboard bar coaster, faded letters barely legible after all the years, Piel's Beer, a vanished brew, adhered to the plastic. He removed it gently, carefully, and placed it in another evidence bag. He took a scalpel, clamps, picks, the other tools of his trade, and bent over the decaying corpse, moving slowly and painstakingly section by section, noting everything, dictating into a tape recorder in clear, dry, precise medical terms what he observed.

Hours later, when he was finished, he dictated another report, more concise, less medically specific, summarizing his findings and his conclusion for whoever happened to draw the case, the investigators and, if it ever came to that, the prosecutors. They couldn't care less for medical terminology.

"The body, discovered in a garbage bag in the Arthur Kill Landfill on Staten Island and presented for examination, was in an advanced state of decomposition, decay having progressed rapidly once the bag was opened and the body exposed to the air. However, it was possible to determine that the corpse was that of a well-developed Negroid female about five feet three inches tall and one hundred and ten pounds, approximately twenty to twenty-four years of age at the time of death. Hair discovered with the body, some attached to the scalp, was, on drying, of light color, though the roots were dark. The pubic hair was black. It was determined that the hair from the head had been bleached. Examination of the mouth revealed a number of badly made silver amalgam fillings. It is not likely that dental records can be obtained easily at this late date, as I would estimate the parameters of death as between twenty and twenty-five years. Further analysis will be necessary to determine, within some limits, a more precise time frame. Identification may prove difficult since decomposition is so far advanced that fingerprints could no longer be taken nor were any remarkable distinguishing features noted. On preliminary examination, it appeared that cause of death was multiple stab wounds inflicted by a sharp blade in the area of the chest and lungs, some superficial, a number penetrating the lobar and pleural regions and the ventricles (see autopsy report, with diagrams, for precise locations), any one of which could have been fatal. A knife, whose blade upon examination corresponded to the wounds, was discovered in close proximity to the body. The knife has been placed in a sterile evidence receptacle and will be sent to the police laboratories for further analysis, together with the remains of the clothing—a short leather skirt, light-colored blouse of some cheap synthetic material, spike-heeled shoes made of plastic rather than leather, all of extremely poor quality (no undergarments were found)—and a cardboard bar coaster labeled Piel's Beer, also found within the bag. While the initial supposition was death by one or more stab wounds, further examination revealed that actual cause of death was a bullet that pierced the left ventricle and lodged against the spine in the region of the cervical vertebrae. It was determined that the shot was fired at very close range. The bullet was removed, packed in an appropriate container, and will be sent to the police ballistics laboratory for analysis and comparison. While the ballistics laboratory will offer a more precise judgment, the bullet appeared to be of a soft flat-nosed lead variety that exploded and shattered on impact, leaving a massive spreading wound. An interesting sidelight: one of the knife wounds penetrated precisely over the point of the bullet's entry so that initially that entry was difficult to discern."

*   *   *

One copy of Dr. Kaplan's report and summary was placed in his
files. Another was dispatched to Jan Polanska, the Staten Island
detective who had been first on the scene; he filed it and tried to
put it, and the entire episode, out of his mind; the case was no
longer his, having been turned over to Central Homicide. Besides, he was retiring at the end of the month after twenty years
on the force, and moving to Florida; he was very happy that he
would never hear of the case again, except perhaps to read
about it in the newspapers. A third copy of the report found its
way into department channels; eventually it would reach the
desk of a deputy police commissioner, a Detective Division–5,
commonly called a DD–5, with an attached UF–49, the classifi-
cation for homicides and other major crimes. Yet another was
forwarded to Central Homicide at One Police Plaza in Manhattan, the seat of the New York City Police Department nestled
beneath the Brooklyn Bridge. There it came to rest on the desk
of Detective Felix Palmieri, a gray-haired, bull-like man, a cop
for twenty-five years, a detective with a gold shield for twenty,
most of them in Homicide. It joined the stack of a half-dozen
other homicides Palmieri was then in the middle of investigating. It would be days, though, before he got to take a look at
that report. He was temporarily on assignment out of the office,
stolen from his normal routine by a onetime partner and still one
of his closest friends, acting as a backup for that friend in a case
that was drawing to its conclusion.

2

The convoy, two trucks led by a black Cadillac, left the Lufthansa cargo hangars at Kennedy Airport just after midnight. On the passenger side in the lead truck, hand resting on the revolver in his belt, sat Phil O'Connell. He was riding shotgun. During the day, he was a New York City detective, assigned to the Brooklyn North narcotics division. His occupation was no secret to the guys in the trucks or the Cadillac. He was moonlighting now, something he had been doing for months. His job was to protect this cargo, his gun for use against anyone who might want to hijack it, the shield in his pocket against any New York cops who might be curious and try to stop them. Flashing the shield and snapping "On the job" would be enough to send them on their way without checking the manifests, bills of lading or other documents. It had happened—twice—and the shield had done its work.

On the passenger seat in the second truck, relaxed, but his hand never very far from the revolver nestled in a shoulder holster, sat the Jersey shotgun, ready to take over when the convoy passed through the tunnel under the Hudson River. His name was Ben Rogers. He was a lieutenant assigned to the Self-Initiating Unit of the New York City Police Department's

Internal Affairs Division. To the guys in the first truck, O'Connell included, and to the guys in the Cadillac, his name was Jimmy Carbone. They believed he was a Jersey City cop on their payroll. The driver next to him, however, knew better, knew his true identity.

That driver was Dominick Vitelli. Six weeks earlier, he had turned, had become an informant. It wasn't because he minded driving a truck from the Kennedy cargo area across the city to the plant in Jersey City in the middle of the night. It didn't bother him, either, that the cargo he carried, like the cargo in the truck ahead, was steel drums filled with volatile chemicals. The people who knew how were going to take those chemicals and turn them into speed. Nobody had ever told him that those chemicals were unstable, that under certain conditions they might explode, and if they did, there wouldn't be enough of him left to have a decent funeral. What bothered him was that he knew what those chemicals were being used for, and if he got busted carrying them he was facing twenty years in the slammer. That was the risk he was willing to take, for the right price. Except that he was sure the price wasn't right, and when he'd complained, they refused to raise the ante. They told him that was the going price, and if he didn't like it, they'd get somebody else, and they'd remember him in the future.

So Dominick stewed for a while, then decided, screw them. He found out the right people to go to, and he went. What he had to say interested those people, the federal drug enforcement people in New York and New Jersey. And when he mentioned Phil O'Connell, they contacted Ben Rogers, who had a particular interest in bad cops.

Vitelli brought Rogers in and introduced him as Jimmy Carbone, a Jersey City cop with an itchy palm. They were glad to have him, glad to have his shield on the west side of the river. O'Connell was particularly glad. He'd been feeling kind of lonely, an outcast, he said, in the middle of all those scumbags. He sure as hell wouldn't be there if he didn't need the bread. You couldn't raise a family, not a wife and five kids, on what the NYPD paid. The only way to make out was to grab the brass ring when somebody offered it.

Rogers agreed. It wasn't much different in Jersey, maybe a lot worse. Cops from the Big Apple got paid more.

Bullshit, O'Connell said. Maybe a few bucks, but life in the Apple cost a hell of a lot more. So now that there were two of them, they could handle the slime if they had to.

Rogers had heard that song, or variations on it, so many times since he'd been with IAD he could have sung it by heart. It was like those guys really thought they were better than the people who were using them, who were paying them off. It was pathetic. The red-faced, beer-bellied O'Connell, who had all the signs of an oiler, Rogers was sure, was no different.

Now it was six weeks later and Rogers was in the cab of the second truck, next to Dominick Vitelli. The convoy moved out of Kennedy at moderate speed, making sure to break no traffic laws. At the Lufthansa cargo area, they had loaded drums filled with liquid chemicals straight off the plane from Germany. Two hours later, if all went well, those drums would be dropped off at the lab in Jersey City. There was little traffic at this hour, and they wended their careful way through Queens and into Brooklyn, crossed the Brooklyn Bridge, moved through the dark streets of lower Manhattan, passed through the Holland Tunnel and into New Jersey.

In the dark sky overhead, a helicopter kept pace. No one in the convoy noticed or paid any attention. Nobody but Rogers. Taped inside his pants, nestled against his groin, was a small transmitter, emitting a steady signal marking his location. Fastened to the panel in the chopper's cockpit, a location finder picked up that pulse, knew precisely where the convoy was at every moment; if nothing went wrong, the trucks below would be followed right to their destination by the chopper overhead and by a dozen cars lagging well behind and out of sight, cars filled with federal agents from the Drug Enforcement Administration, and New York and New Jersey cops, among them Felix Palmieri, someone Rogers knew he could depend on and trust to back him up all the way.

It was an easy trip. There had been no trouble or delays. There had been just one tense moment as the convoy was passing City Hall. Vitelli's truck hit a pothole, bounced and swerved until Vitelli got it back under control. The sweat beaded on Rogers's forehead. "For chrissake, Dominick," he said, "watch it."

Vitelli grinned over at him. "No sweat. I know how to drive this fucker."

"Yeah, sure," Rogers said. "Only hit another one of them and there won't be enough pieces left to pick up. And the mayor's gonna need a new place to hang out."

Vitelli turned a little and stared at him. "What the fuck you talkin' about?"

"Don't you know what's in the back?"

"Fuckin' A. Piss to make shit."

"Yeah? You hit another one of those potholes and that shit will make dynamite look like a ladyfinger."

Vitelli turned a little pale. "They never told me nothin' like that."

"They wouldn't."

"Jesus H." Vitelli slowed practically to a crawl the rest of the way across the city, forcing the truck ahead and the Cadillac in the lead to slow so as not to lose him.

It was after two by the time they reached the plant in Jersey City, a cinderblock building nestled among auto-repair shops on a dark street. The Cadillac sounded its horn, then pulled a few feet away and parked on the street. The double doors at the front of the building swung up and open. The trucks edged inside.

The Cadillac's door opened and the two men got out, walked quickly into the plant, approached Vitelli's truck. "What the fuck's the matter with you?" one of them demanded.

"Nothin'," Vitelli said. "Why?"

"Back there in the city. I coulda walked faster."

"The gas pedal, it stuck. I had to pump it to get it going. That's all."

"Shit," the man said.

Four men in coveralls appeared out of the dim interior, moved toward the trucks, opened the backs and began unloading the steel drums.

Rogers waited.

"Hey, you, Carbone," one of the Cadillac's passengers shouted, "What're you waitin' for? We ain't got all night. What 're ya on, a fuckin' vacation? Move your ass."

Rogers moved slowly. Where the hell was the chopper? Where were the cars? Where was Felix? Had they lost the signal? Had his transmitter malfunctioned? Maybe he was going to have to take them himself. He took another step.

Then he heard the sound, the cacophonous shattering of the air overhead as the helicopter began to descend. Its searchlights suddenly beamed down, illuminating the street outside, bathing the cinderblock building in a blinding light. The wailing of police sirens rebounded, echoing through the street, approaching rapidly, a half-dozen cars screeching to a stop outside, their doors already open. Men, some in uniform, some plainclothes, wearing dark zippered jackets, iridescent letters on the backs, DEA and POLICE, glowing in the night, leaped out, guns drawn. Those inside the cinderblock building began to scatter.

"Hold it! Right there! Freeze!"

The movement inside stopped. The police and federal agents moved in.

"Against the wall! Spread 'em!"

O'Connell emerged from the passenger seat of the first truck. He looked sick. Rogers watched him. O'Connell reached into his belt. His hand was shaking. It came out, holding his gun.

Rogers thought, Jesus, I'm going to have to kill this bastard. He drew his own gun and started to move toward O'Connell. Palmieri was suddenly right beside him, his own gun drawn.

O'Connell's gun came up, turned and the barrel went into his mouth.

"Oh, you stupid son of a bitch!" Rogers shouted. He and Palmieri leaped across the space between them. Rogers reached O'Connell first, grabbed his arm, twisting it, struggling to force the gun free. Palmieri wrapped his arms around the cop's waist, trying to wrestle him to the ground. The sound of the shot was muffled inside O'Connell's mouth, as the bullet tore through his cheek, carrying with it teeth and flesh, leaving a gaping, bleeding wound.

Rogers and Palmieri supported the bent cop, lowered him to the ground. "Oh, you stupid son of a bitch," Rogers said again. He looked at Palmieri and shook his head.

At that moment, he didn't know whether he hated O'Connell because he'd been corrupted or because he'd tried to kill himself. Maybe, he thought, the guy would have been better off dead. For O'Connell, it wasn't going to be just a slap on the wrist, a case of turn in your shield and gun, and goodbye Charlie, see you later. Where he was going, there would be no blue wall to hide behind. There'd be a posse waiting at the gates, and he'd have a bull's-eye etched on the back of his prison-issue grays.

Rogers turned away. Then he and Palmieri, not talking, for there was no need for words, walked slowly out of the cinder-block garage toward Palmieri's car for the long ride back into the city.

OCTOBER

3

A couple of days later, Palmieri walked back into his office at Central Homicide at One Police Plaza, sat down at his desk, looked at the pile of paperwork that had gathered and grown in his absence, sighed, and began to skim through the files, looking to see if there was anything new on the old cases, anything new that had been thrown his way.

What was new was the body from the garbage dump. As he read Dr. George Kaplan's notes, there was a sense of relief that, thank God, he'd never come any closer to this corpse than the description on paper. He could visualize it without even closing his eyes. The remembered smell of decaying bodies crept up his nose. He sneezed, shook his head, and bent over the report. He began to make his own notes. There was a body, dead a very long time, a woman in her twenties, stabbed and shot. The clothes, the hair, and other things—especially his intuition, which he relied on implicitly—said to him, hooker. Hookers, dozens of them, scores of them, got killed or disappeared every year. Most of the time the disappearances weren't even reported, and nobody worked very hard trying to solve the murders. She could have come from anywhere garbage was picked up and carted out to the Staten

Island landfill. Maybe ballistics would turn up something when it checked out the bullet. With all the guns in the city, most of them unregistered and their bullets never tested, Palmieri doubted it. No matter—this case would go to the bottom of his list; it had a very low priority. Palmieri had a dozen other things to occupy his time.

But Felix Palmieri loved puzzles. Over the next days, whenever he had time, he would pause to think about the case, looking at it from a dozen angles. He drove out to Staten Island. Detective Polanska was not happy to see him. He was even less happy when Palmieri insisted on a guided tour of the dump. Polanska had trouble steering him to the right spot, and when they found it, still ringed by shredding yellow ribbons, there was nothing to see, just mounds of bulging black plastic scattered everywhere. Still, Palmieri took his time, turned over the plastic, searching and finding nothing.

He called the coroner, spoke to Dr. Kaplan. "It's all in my report," Kaplan said. "She was a mess."

"You didn't leave anything out?" Palmieri asked.

"I never leave anything out," Kaplan said. "Read the goddamn report. It's all there."

Palmieri called his friend Harold Fassman in Ballistics. "Who's handling the slug from the body in the Staten Island dump?"

"I am, personally," Fassman said.

"And . . . ?"

"It's not priority one," Fassman said. "People are getting shot and killed right now, today, dozens of them. This one's twenty-five years old. When I get to it, I'll let you know."

Everything seemed to end in blind alleys. But Palmieri believed, and he had often said, every alley, even a blind one, has an exit.

A week later, he found a message on his desk to call Harold Fassman in Ballistics. He called.

"Felix, on the stiff from the Staten Island dump. She's yours, right?"

"Who else?"

"The slug. I think I have a possible." There was something in the way Fassman said that.

"You don't sound happy," Palmieri said.

"Can we get together?"

"Sure." Palmieri looked at the ceiling, at the smoke-stained yellowing paint. Harold Fassman had a tendency to see conspiracies lurking behind every filing cabinet, hidden in the grooves of every bullet under his microscope. "When and where?"

"Lunch tomorrow. How about that Dim Sum place just up Mott? Twelve-thirty."

Just before twelve-thirty the next day, Palmieri walked out the back door of police headquarters, strolled a block north, and was in Chinatown. Except for a few signs in both English and Chinese, he could have been in any city in mainland China, surrounded by street peddlers chattering away in dialects he couldn't understand, their carts packed high with clothing, exotic foods, jewelry, all sorts of objects, many of them unfamiliar, most of them straight off the boat, a lot of them illegal or fake.

By twelve-thirty, Palmieri was seated at a small table toward the rear of the restaurant, his eyes on the door. By quarter to one, Fassman still hadn't appeared. Harold Fassman was never late. They ate lunch together every couple of weeks, and Fassman was always early. Maybe, Palmieri thought, he meant a different Dim Sum place, though that was hardly likely. Fassman invariably chose this one. Fassman was a man of rigid habits who did not like change, resented the unexpected.

Palmieri left the restaurant, wandered up and down Mott Street looking into the restaurants as he passed. The tables were filled with a mixture of people from the courthouses and offices nearby and Asians from the neighborhood, all out for a quick, cheap lunch. He did not expect to find Fassman in any of them.

By one-thirty, Palmieri gave up. Back at his desk, he dialed Fassman's exchange. The phone rang several times before someone picked up. Palmieri asked for Fassman.

There was a long pause. Then the voice, low and lugubrious, said, "Haven't you heard? Mr. Fassman committed suicide last night."

Palmieri sat at his desk for a while, then got up and went over to ballistics. Fassman's desk was unoccupied. He went over to the next desk. "I'm Palmieri, from Homicide," he said.

"Oh," the man said. "You're the one who called." The man didn't introduce himself. "Terrible thing," he said. "Totally unexpected. "Everybody here is pretty shaken up."

"I imagine."

"I mean, we didn't know Fassman was sick or depressed or anything. Not so he'd do something like that. Now people are saying he musta had cancer or some incurable disease. I mean, he just jumped out the window. But I don't know. I never detected any signs of anything being wrong."

"Sometimes you can't," Palmieri said. "People do strange things. Harold said he was working on something."

The man nodded. "Oh, yes, for a week or more. I must say, he seemed upset about something yesterday. I asked what it was, but he wouldn't say, just that he wanted to run some more tests. I don't know what it was, but I figured it must have had something to do with what he found."

"Did he make notes?"

"They'd be in his desk."

"Mind if I look?" Palmieri sat down at Fassman's desk and started to go through the drawers. Harold Fassman was an orderly man, everything neatly arranged by date in file folders. Palmieri took his time, reading each file carefully. Everything there was routine. There was nothing in them that could have upset Fassman. One thing was puzzling, however. He found nothing about the bullet found in the body in the Staten Island dump—no matches, no record of tests, nothing at all about that particular bullet. Fassman had said he had a possible. There should have been something.

He looked over at the man at the next desk. "Hey," he said, "what's your name?"

"Anderson. Philip Anderson."

"Look, Anderson, where else would Fassman have filed what he was working on?"

"You didn't find anything in his desk?"

"Would I be asking if I did?"

"I don't know. Doesn't make sense." He looked around. "Maybe over there." He waved toward a row of filing cabinets.

Anderson pointed out the cabinets with Fassman's name on them. He stood beside Palmieri as he opened the drawers and went through them. There were records of ballistics tests dating back years. There was nothing that would interest Palmieri. He looked at Anderson. "Anyplace else?"

"Not that I can think of."

"Did he send a report upstairs?"

"I don't think so. I don't think he'd reached that stage yet."

It didn't make sense. Things vanished all the time, sure. But this was something else. Harold Fassman had come upon something that shook him up, enough so he wouldn't talk about it on the phone, had to talk to Palmieri about in private, at lunch. Then he jumped out a window and the records of whatever he was working on vanished. It was crazy.

Over the next days, when he had a spare minute, Palmieri worried it, trying to find a hold. He went back over the autopsy report, studied it, tried to find something there, especially about the bullet. How the ME described it. It took him a while. And then it came to him. "What the hell's wrong with me?" he muttered. "I must be getting old."

The next day, he decided to take a long shot. He made a trip up to the building at Hudson and Varick, went down into the basement, to Old Records, and asked Charlie, the ageless gnome who ran the place and somehow knew where everything was, to dig out some old missing persons files.

4

The ringing of the telephone beside the bed woke Rogers. He glanced at the clock. It was two in the afternoon. Melissa was up already. He'd fallen into bed just as the sun was breaking over the city. Exhausted from the long night, he still had not slept well. Weeks after the night in the New Jersey garage, he was still having bad dreams, about bad cops trying to commit suicide.

Rogers shook away the image and reached for the phone, muttering a groggy hello.

"Hey, *paisan*, don't you rat fink shooflies in IAD ever go to work?"

"Not so you'd know it." He recognized the voice. Felix Palmieri. They'd known each other for a decade, had been partners for a time when Rogers went to the detective bureau and before he got his gold shield; they stopped being partners when Rogers went to Internal Affairs, though in the years since, they'd remained good friends, something a lot of people couldn't understand. Cops who worked Internal Affairs usually had no friends.

Palmieri was an old-time cop. He could have retired anytime over the last five years. He wouldn't. He loved the job too much. It gave him a sense that his life had meaning, that he was worth something. It ranked right up there with his wife and family. Other cops viewed Palmieri as a friend—as one of them.

Rogers, on the other hand, was an IAD rat, out to get cops; he was an outcast in the department.

"I've been calling you at the office since ten. How's your girl?"

Rogers looked at the rumpled sheets beside him. He heard movements out in the other room. "She's fine, just fine."

"I got a thing. I want to talk to you."

"So talk."

"Let's meet. It could be your kind of thing. *Capeesh?* Only you got to be an old hairbag like me to get it."

"The phone won't do?"

"No. What about tonight?"

"No can do. This is my night with Nonna."

"Okay, so enjoy her pasta fazool. She makes the best, like from the old country. Next time, invite me. What about tomorrow? Make the time." They settled on a bar they both knew near Rogers's apartment in the Village.

Rogers got out of bed and walked into the living room. Melissa Redburn was standing in the middle of the room, dressed in old, tight faded jeans with one knee ripped out. She wore no makeup and her long, fair hair was pulled back. Her jacket was half on, one arm in its sleeve. She looked like she was posing, not like a model, more like an actress onstage. Not surprising, since that's what she was trying to be, when she wasn't working part time at One Police Plaza. She was the blond and beautiful kind of girl that men looked at without seeing anything beyond the face and the body. They never stopped to think she might have a brain; if they did, they'd dismiss the idea as irrelevant or impossible. Beautiful blondes aren't supposed to be smart, too. It had taken Rogers weeks to realize that the mind behind those blue eyes never stopped working, and what it came up with was more often than not a surprise, the unexpected.

Her eyes were on the television set, on the figures moving across the screen, a tally board totting up a count, yeas and nays. She always did that when she had time, turning to C-SPAN. She was not just a news junkie, she was a Congress junkie. She knew the names of every congressman and senator, knew how they stood on every issue, could predict how they would vote on any bill. She claimed you could learn a lot about those guys watching them in action. Not just the words, but the body language. Actors ought to watch that kind of thing more, she said, watch the act the politicians put on; they could learn a lot, and not just about the world. She was a cynic.

Rogers stood for a moment watching her, watching the screen. Congress was voting on military appropriations, and the nays seemed to be having their day. Melissa looked pleased. It was a thing they argued about. She was sure the world would be better off without armies, that the money could be spent on worthier things, and, besides, with the cold war coming to an end, who needed armies anyway? Rogers believed just the opposite—for him, armies were essential, a protection against the unexpected. She was forever accusing him of being the last of the cold warriors, like their congressman, Michael Benedetto.

After a few moments, she sensed his presence, turned around, and looked toward him. "Good morning," she said. "What time did you get home?"

"Late," he said.

"I know that. Who was on the phone?"

"Felix. He wants to meet for drinks tomorrow."

"Am I invited?"

"Not this time."

"Oh," she said. She asked no more questions. She flicked the remote control and the screen went dark. She shrugged the rest of the way into her coat and started for the door.

"Come back to bed," he said.

"Can't," she said. "I'm late as it is." Then she was gone.

Rogers heard the news on the radio the next morning. A cop investigating the murder of an upper-level mob guy had been gunned down in an alley in Little Italy. The cop was a homicide detective. The cop's name was Felix Palmieri, a twenty-five-year veteran of the department. The police had few clues to the identity of the killer or the reasons for the murder, though Palmieri was known to have been investigating the slaying of a major Mafia capo. Palmieri, the radio said, was survived by his wife, four children, and seven grandchildren. The entire resources of the department were being mobilized, and a citywide search was under way for the gunman. Police expected an arrest momentarily. All of which meant, Rogers understood, that the cops hadn't a clue.

For a long time he sat by the radio, hardly hearing the words or the music that followed. Melissa woke in the middle of the bulletin. She shook her head, stared at the radio with disbelief, and put her arms around him, holding him against her. He thought about Felix Palmieri, a good cop who had once been his partner and who had remained his friend. Felix had been around too long to go wandering up blind alleys, and especially to be doing it without a backup. He knew better. It was one of the things Palmieri had tried to drum into Rogers: never go anywhere, even if you don't expect trouble, without a backup. When the two men had worked together, they always backed each other up.

Since they split, Rogers had been working on his own without that backup, except when now and then he'd steal Felix from homicide. He didn't trust most guys to be at his back where he couldn't watch them. It came from working with IAD, from feeling like an outcast. Maybe Felix had come to feel the same way. Felix should have retired years ago like his wife wanted him to. Only Felix loved the job too much. Felix was the best. Rogers would miss Felix Palmieri.

The next afternoon, Rogers went to the funeral home. The casket rested on a stand in front of the altar. There were flags around it—the country's, the city's, the department's. There were banks of flowers, the aroma scenting the air, though not completely washing away that odor that always permeates a funeral parlor. For a few moments he stood over the open casket and gazed down at the body of Felix Palmieri. It looked like something made out of wax; there wasn't much resemblance to the man he'd known so long.

He turned and walked down the stairs, through the blue-gray smoke that drifted upward, and into the mourners' lounge. Along the walls there were rows of folding metal chairs. In the center of one wall was a group of upholstered chairs, reserved for the family. Mary Palmieri sat there, her body erect. She was dressed in black. Her ashen face was stricken, her eyes uncomprehending, unaccepting. A handkerchief was clutched tightly in her hands. Deputy Police Commissioner William Dolan was sitting next to her, holding her hands, talking softly to her. He and Palmieri had been in the same class at the Police Academy, and had remained friends through all the years as each worked his way up in the department.

Rogers went to Mary Palmieri, bent and kissed her cheek, mumbled a few words. She looked up at him. Dolan released her hand after pressing it one more time. He nodded at Rogers sorrowfully, then got up to make way for him and walked away.

"Ben," she said.

"Mary. Jesus."

"It didn't happen that way," she said. "Not the way they said. Why are they saying that? What are they trying to hide? I told Bill that. He said I was just upset. But it's not that. He got a call. He was getting ready for bed and he got a call."

He nodded, waiting. Something was coming.

"He hung up and he got dressed and he said he had to go out—right then."

"Who called?" Rogers asked.

"I don't know," she said. "He just told me it was important and he had to go. He told me not to wait up. He said he'd be home in a couple of hours. Only he never came home. And then they came and told me. They said he was in an alley, in Little Italy, and somebody came up and shot him. They said he came right up to Felix and shot him and there were powder burns on Felix's coat." She looked at him, pleading. "Ben, how could that be? Felix would never let one of them get that close to him. How could it have happened?" She began to cry, the tears scarring her cheeks. She didn't wipe them away.

Rogers sat down beside her and put his arm around her. She leaned her head against his chest, the tears staining his jacket. He stared over her head, at the cigarette smoking drifting toward the ceiling, at nothing. He'd already seen the preliminary report on the shooting, so he knew the basics. Who, he wondered, had called Felix Palmieri in the middle of the night, summoned him to a fatal rendezvous? Who could have gotten that close to Felix, close enough to put a gun against him? One of Felix's informants? Maybe. Or somebody else? A lot of losers

must have had it in for Felix. But would he have let one of them
come at him from the front, get close to him without reacting? It
just didn't seem like Felix. Whatever happened, there was no
way of knowing for sure. But there was this: Felix never even
got his gun out of the holster.

Rogers sat with Mary until her tears abated. He said a few
more comforting things, meaningless, he knew, slowly rose and
started out. Dolan was just outside the door, smoking. The two
men nodded. They'd known each other since Rogers had teamed
up with Palmieri. Through Palmieri, Rogers had come to know
Dolan well, had come to look on him as one of the few men of
power in the department he could turn to in time of trouble, one
of his few allies. Rogers liked the deputy commissioner and
respected him. Everybody did. He was a cop's cop, a big burly
Irishman with red hair and a complexion to match. He towered
over almost everybody. He exuded an aura of power and confi-
dence. For the guys in the department, the most important
thing was that he backed them all the way. He had been one of
them, a cop on the beat back in the early days. Guys said he had
kissed the Blarney Stone, that he was living proof that the stories
of the luck of Irish were really true, that maybe he even had a
pipeline to Someone Up There. All through the years he seemed
always to be in the right place at the right time; he made more
collars than almost anybody else on the force, and the collars he
made were good ones, the best, and he seemed to have the nose
and eye to find the convicting evidence that had escaped everyone
else. Though he had risen to become a super chief, he had never
lost the touch or the memory of what it was like on the streets.
If Palmieri had been something of a father to Rogers in the department, then Dolan had been an uncle, or maybe his rabbi. His
door was always open. Rogers was forever getting into trouble
with the brass, because too often he went his own way; even the
IAD people considered him a loner, a renegade who didn't always
follow the rules. But Dolan supported him all the way.

Dolan held out the cigarette pack. Rogers took one and bent
for a light. "Terrible thing," Dolan said.

"You know it, chief."

"Felix. He was the best. We go back a long way. But you
know that. Poor Mary. I don't know how she's going to get
through this. It's hit her hard."

"The life of a cop," Rogers said. "Every time you hit the streets."

"And the wives wait home and hope the phone won't ring, or the priest isn't knocking at the front door."

"Yeah."

"Still not married, Ben?"

"No."

"Lucky in a way. Unlucky, too. Something to come home to." He shook his head. "I'm worried about Mary. She was talking wild in there."

Rogers nodded. "You know what she's talking about?"

Dolan shook his head. "No idea. I checked it out myself. It happened just the way the reports said. Felix had to be crazy going into that alley alone. Not like him. He was asking for trouble. Mary, she's distraught. It's to be expected."

"I guess so. I keep wondering who called Felix out."

"No idea. One of his stoolies, more than likely. He'll surface. Don't worry, we'll find the bastard. Look after her, Ben. She needs somebody to lean on."

The city gave Felix Palmieri an inspector's funeral. The mayor ordered the city's flags flown at half-mast. The mayor ordered Fifth Avenue around St. Patrick's closed to traffic from midmorning until after the cortege left the church. The mayor, taking time out from his increasingly bitter campaign for reelection to lead the mourners, sat in the front row across from the family. He was seated with the Police Commissioner, the Deputy Commissioners and all the high brass, two rows in front of his opponent, John Morrison, the patrician reformer. With tears streaming from his eyes, the mayor eulogized Felix Palmieri with more eloquence than he usually displayed, and with a hot rage condemned those who would shoot down in cold blood a man who had devoted his life to protecting the people of the city. Those who had done this awful deed, he promised, would be brought to justice swiftly and would be shown no more mercy than they had shown Felix Palmieri. The cardinal himself conducted the service. There were eulogies filled with personal recollections from Police Commissioner Warren Wilson, from Deputy Police Commissioner Dolan, from others who had known and worked with Felix. More than five thousand cops filled the church, lined the sidewalks outside, and spilled out into the avenue. There were forty honorary pallbearers, guys who had worked with Felix over the years. Rogers was one of the pallbearers who carried the coffin. Dolan was another. Cops everywhere placed black bands across their shields.

5

A couple of days later, Rogers made the trip by subway from his apartment in the Village down to One Police Plaza. He came up out of the subway onto the triangle facing the Greek-colonnaded Federal Courthouse, crossed the narrow street and turned alongside the courthouse into St. Andrew's Plaza, lined with now shuttered fast-food stands. In warmer weather, the area was a lunchtime food bazaar, alive with exotic smells, bustling with customers. Today, Rogers was virtually alone in the big open space.

He skirted St. Andrew's, the small church that gave the place its name, passed the United States Attorney's office, and approached the sprawling plaza with its rusted steel formless sculpture. In its center loomed the massive brick block house, One Police Plaza, some architect's distorted vision of a medieval fortress, a discordant, jarring image juxtaposed against the graceful classic structures nearby.

In offices and squad rooms inside One Police Plaza, the war on crime was planned and executed, the verdict on success or failure to be handed down in those nearby courthouses. Maybe the building was an improvement over the rat-and-roach-infested, ramshackle old 84th Precinct station house in Brooklyn that had been given to IAD for its headquarters, but Rogers didn't like it. It was too antiseptic. Over in Brooklyn, roaches and rats became familiar, had names, were almost friends. Over in Brooklyn, when the city sent in exterminators, all they did was give the rats and roaches white coats. Here, the rats and roaches were exterminated.

Rogers flashed his shield, went through the opening designed only for cops and civilians who worked there, and took the elevator up to Central Homicide. When he walked in, a couple of detectives who recognized him gave him that strange look he had grown used to, like they wanted to spit, or maybe worse. It happened when you were with IAD. When they saw you, they thought maybe you were about to make them a target. He ignored them, going straight to the desk Felix Palmieri had used for so many years. The top was clean, which it never used to be. In the center there was a rose in a small vase.

Somebody he didn't know came over and stood next to him. "Something I can do for you?" There was no welcome in the tone—it said he had no business there and to get the hell out.

Rogers looked at him. "Rogers. Lieutenant. IAD," he said. "I want to take a look at Felix's stuff, what he was working on. If it's still here. You got a problem with that?"

"I don't know." The guy froze for a second, then said, "I'll have to check."

"Do that." He waited. The guy walked away, went into an office at the end of the room and closed the door behind him. After a few minutes the door opened again. The guy came out and went in a different direction. An older man in plainclothes followed and started toward Rogers. Rogers knew him. Captain George Donaldson.

"Hello, Ben," he said.

"Captain." Rogers nodded.

"Terrible thing about Felix. He was a friend of yours, right? Everybody's all broken up."

"That figures."

"Any special reason you want to go through his things?"

"What was he working on?"

"Six, seven different cases. You looking for anything in particular?"

"He called me. The day before. Said he'd come onto something that might be in my ballpark. We were supposed to meet."

The captain examined him closely. "He never mentioned anything to me. But go ahead, take a look. You find anything, let me know. You want to copy anything, the Xerox is over there," he gestured. He turned away abruptly and strode back across the room to his office.

Rogers sat down in Palmieri's chair. The cushion still bore his imprint. He opened the drawers and began to go through the folders. For the next three hours, he read, made notes, made trips to the Xerox. The files were all neat, all arranged—not at all like Felix. Somebody had gone through his stuff and organized and straightened it out.

According to the files, Felix had six open cases: the murder of the mob big shot, the knifing of a teenage girl in an East Village bar, a dead baby found smothered in a trash can, a nurse raped and garroted in a hospital basement, a Middle Eastern diplomat shot when he left his East Side residence, a jewelry dealer on 47th Street shot during a holdup. Some were just at the beginning of investigation, some about ready to close. There was nothing that looked like a job for Internal Affairs. But you never knew.

He turned back to the desk, opening the drawers, searching. Felix was always making notes on little scraps of paper and then squirreling them away where sometimes even Felix couldn't find them. Way back in the top drawer, stuck between the edge of the drawer and the underside of the desk, Rogers found a few. Some of them were notations, cryptic scrawls in Felix's nearly undecipherable writing about things Rogers had read about in the six cases. Several other notes, however, didn't seem to relate to anything in any of the files—just scribbles about a hooker, and twenty, twenty-five years ago, and a knife and a bullet, and some more.

Rogers got up, walked across the room and knocked on Captain Donaldson's door, and, at a bark from inside, walked in. Donaldson looked up at him. "You find anything?"

"Who cleaned up Felix's desk?"

"One of the girls, probably."

"I found some of Felix's notes. They don't seem to relate."

"Hell, you know Felix. He was always scribbling. What kind of notes?"

Rogers told him.

Donaldson laughed. "That. Jesus. You must have seen it in

the papers. The body they found over in the Staten Island garbage dump. I tossed it at Felix. You know him, he always liked
playing around with puzzles, even if they never went anywhere."

"Wasn't there a file? ME's report, lab tests, that kind of
stuff?"

"Sure. Isn't it there?"

"No."

"He probably took it home with him. He wasn't supposed
to, but he always did. It'll turn up."

"Sure."

"You come onto anything, you'll let me know," Donaldson
said.

"Sure thing," Rogers said. He closed the door behind him
and walked back to Felix Palmieri's desk. He gathered the copies of the files, a copy of the scrawl, put the originals back in the
proper places and left Central Homicide. Going down in the
elevator he couldn't get it out of his head that something wasn't
right. The whole thing stank. When he had time, he'd begin
checking back on Felix's cases. He'd make the time. He owed
Felix Palmieri that much.

6

In the days after Palmieri's funeral, Rogers, in his spare time and in time he made, pored over the open cases Palmieri had left behind, looking for something, for anything. It was a thing he liked to do, a thing he was good at, piecing together isolated and seemingly disparate facts and coming up with a whole, finding answers where sometimes it seemed that none existed. It was one of the things that had drawn him and Palmieri together and forged the bond between them.

"You and your goddamn crossword puzzles," Felix used to say just about every day they worked together. "The ten-letter word for horseshoe crab is xiphosuran. You dumb or something?"

"For chrissakes, Felix, don't tell me. Do your own damn puzzle."

Rogers's grandmother, who had raised him from the time he was eighteen months old after his parents died in an airplane crash, recognized a special quality in him. "You have a gift," she told him often in her broken English interlarded with her native Sicilian. "Not like a priest, which would be better. But a gift. You see hidden things. Where most people see only fragments, you see the whole. What you will make of it, only God knows."

Maybe God knew, but it was a long time before Rogers did. His high school adviser told him his grades and aptitude tests showed he ought to consider law. He considered it, but he couldn't picture himself sitting in an office being suffocated by law books and briefs, and he couldn't imagine standing up in front of a judge or jury in a courtroom. Besides, even then he thought there were too many lawyers in the world as it was, and nobody needed another one. He thought about getting a job, any kind of job, when he finished high school. It didn't matter, just so long as it paid well. He mentioned it to his grandmother.

She had a fit. If she valued the old ways and the old traditions, she was not closed to the new. She had a mind that was forever reaching out and searching. She read *The New York Times* every morning, read the monthly magazines, read history, struggling with the English words. She raged at the kids loitering on the street corners doing nothing, tore comic books from her grandson's hands when she saw him poring over them. So now she screamed at him, "*Stupido.* You would be *ignorantone* all your life? You think that's why I took you into my home, why I bring you up? An education you will get. Somebody you will become."

"We could use the money," he said.

"Money enough we have. Money we don't need. Money I don't care about," she said. "You will speak of this no more."

She was right about one thing, anyway. She didn't need the money he might bring in. They lived frugally, just the two of them, in her small house in an Italian-Sicilian enclave in Queens. She always seemed to have enough for whatever they needed. The mailman delivered an envelope at the beginning of every month. Rogers saw it sometimes. The postmark was New York, which told him nothing. He never saw what was in the envelope, but when it came, she always stuffed it immediately into her large black leather carryall alongside her bankbook, rosary beads, holy cards, citizenship papers, and any number of other items and documents, and marched purposefully off to the bank. When he had asked her about it, she responded vaguely about insurance, annuities left by his parents when they were killed, and by his grandfather who had died long ago.

Rogers was sure that his grandfather must once have been there, but he had no real picture of him, just some disconnected memories. He seemed to have a faint recollection—although he was never certain if it was real or just an illusion—of a large man, to him, then, a giant, who seemed forever down in the cellar, sometimes alone, sometimes with other men, surrounded by crates filled with grapes, and with figs and peppers hanging to dry. He even remembered the big man's hand, and the way he always ruffled Rogers's hair. And he remembered a special smell, the aroma of wine and strong cigarettes. Then suddenly he was gone. Rogers couldn't remember when or why, only nights when he cowered under the blankets as the house reverberated with anger and shouts. And then there was peace and silence, but in his grandmother there was bitterness, a refusal ever to mention the giant again. When Rogers asked, she turned away, saying only that he was dead.

In high school, he had run distances, cross-country in the fall, the mile in the spring. He loved the sense of being alone out there, being in control, of depending on nobody but himself, knowing that if he won, it was his doing, and if he lost, he had nobody to fault but himself. He had won enough races to attract attention, to have a couple of colleges offer him scholarships. So he went away to school, to the hills of northern New England. He found he didn't know why he was there. He also found the people distant and cool. He felt alone, a stranger. He drifted. He stayed a year.

That spring, when the term ended, he joined the army. He needed the time, the distance. In one of those rare fortuitous military decisions, he was assigned to the Criminal Investigation Division, the C.I.D. It was a decision that paid off a dozen times during his three-year hitch. There was the chameleon about him. Without effort, he went underground, and over the next three years assumed various guises, turning himself into a drunk at a bar, giving and receiving confidences; a deserter seeking sanctuary and help; a disenchanted GI looking to turn a quick buck; a stateside drug dealer looking for a connection; an organized crime hood in the market for anything on the base that wasn't nailed down. Whatever the job called for, he was there.

The years in the C.I.D. showed him where his future lay. Eighteen months after his discharge, the day after he got his degree from Fordham, cramming three years work into a year and a half, he joined the New York City Police Department. Like every other recruit, he went through the police academy, then, without a rabbi to say a good word or a hook to put in a contract for him, found himself in a precinct nobody else wanted, in his case at the ass end of Queens, in Rockaway. He rode around in a patrol car with an old cop who spent his time shopping, who seemed to want to do nothing so much as to cadge free cups of coffee and doughnuts and to avoid trouble until he could retire. It took Rogers two Sundays to figure out why his partner loved to work on the Sabbath, to figure out what was the attraction in all those hole-in-the-wall bodegas that just happened to be open on Sunday in violation of the city's blue laws, and how come he could drink so much coffee, eat so many doughnuts, and smoke fifty packs of cigarettes a day. He found out when he happened to drop by one of the bodegas alone for a pack of cigarettes and discovered two bucks neatly folded inside the matchbook. It didn't take mathematical genius to realize that the old cop was pocketing an extra hundred a week. And then it took him another week to understand just how impenetrable the blue wall was, and how much protection it provided for those who stood behind it.

"It's one of the perks, kid," he was told. "Besides, it's us or them," the "them" he understood being the public at large.

That was the first time he found himself in trouble with the department, the first time he was on the outside looking in. It got worse the night they stumbled on a floater that had drifted up on the beach. The old cop, his partner, pulled a ring, from the floater's finger, rinsed it in the ocean to clean it and then pocketed it. The ring was worth maybe five bucks, but it was all the floater had. The old cop made sure of that. He went over the body with practiced hands, something he obviously had done many times before. When Rogers said something, his partner grinned. "Shit, kid," he said, "he ain't got no use for it anymore. Somebody's gonna get it, and it might as well be me."

Blowing the whistle just wasn't done. "We protect our own," he was told. He blew the whistle anyway. The next thing Rogers knew, he was transferred to Street Crime, working the late shift. He was made to play the decoy, dressed in rags, unshaven, dirty, a homeless drunk lolling under a Bronx El, while his partners waited in shadows to come to his rescue and make a collar. They knew about him. His reputation followed him, as it was bound to. There are no secrets in the department.

"You got a flair for it, Ben," one of the backups said late on a freezing January night, grinning as he helped him off the street a couple of minutes after three tough kids had started to work him over with a pipe. "You should have been an actor." His other partners could hardly hold back the laughs even with their revolvers drawn on the kids.

"Sure," Rogers said, trying to discover if any of his ribs was broken. "Only why the hell did you wait in the wings so long?"

His partners laughed out loud then.

Eighteen months later, after four broken ribs, three concussions, and more bruises and contusions than he could remember, he was pulled off Street Crime. He could thank Felix Palmieri for that. They had met on a winter night, the streets slick with sleet. Street Crime found a body near the bridge over the railroad just north of 96th Street. The body had a bullet in the back of the head. Palmieri drew the case. He liked the way Rogers had the facts down, how he could give them so there was no doubt what he was saying, how he could speak English and not departmentalese. There was a thing about the stiff that said pusher. Probably a welcher. He told Palmieri that, just a hunch. Palmieri liked that. Here was a guy who saw things clear, here was a guy who liked puzzles, here was a guy after Palmieri's own heart. He asked for Rogers, and got him. They worked together for two days, put together a solid case. The guy had indeed been a pusher who welched on his source, and had paid the price.

When they said goodbye, Palmieri asked, "How long you been in Street Crime, kid?"

"A year and a half," Rogers said.

"Shit," Palmieri said. "Too fuckin' long."

"You know it."

"No rabbi?"

"Not even a priest."

Palmieri studied him. "Don't tell me," he said. "You're always the pigeon. Right."

"Always."

"It figures," Palmieri said. "I checked. I heard about you. You ain't never gonna be nothin' but the decoy. There's not much future in that. One day, the backup's not gonna be there when you need 'em. What the hell are you, some kind of Goody Two-shoes?"

Rogers shrugged. "Right's right, wrong's wrong."

"You sound like a fuckin' bible-thumper."

"Not that," Rogers said. "If I wanted to be a thief, I wouldn't be wearin' blue. I figured when I got the shield, I chose up sides."

"Yeah," Palmieri said, "us against them. Only you got the wrong idea who them is."

"Maybe," Rogers said. "I don't think so."

"I like you, kid," Palmieri said. "You ain't gonna have it easy. I'll see what I can do."

Palmieri went to his friend Bill Dolan. Dolan, not yet a chief but on the way, called Rogers in, sat with him and Palmieri, talked about the department, talked about Rogers. "What would you like?" he asked.

"Not Street Crime," Rogers said.

"I want him, Bill," Palmieri said.

"We'll see what we can do," Dolan said.

A couple of weeks later, a transfer came down. His new assignment: Central Homicide. His new partner: Felix Palmieri.

They were partners for four years, the partnership, but not the bond and the friendship, ending when they busted a twisted narcotics cop, then tossed to see who would testify against him at departmental hearings. Rogers lost, or won, depending on how you looked at it.

That cop had beaten and then shot a small-time pusher in a Brooklyn alley, claiming the pusher had ignored his demand to stop, had turned instead and pulled a gun, and the cop had been forced to shoot. It didn't smell right, and the closer Palmieri and Rogers looked, the ranker the odor. People on the street said the pusher never carried a piece, that in the dozens of times the pusher had been picked up he had never resisted, had given up without a murmur.

Rogers and Palmieri dug, and the deeper they dug, the worse it got. The cop had been on the take from the neighborhood dealers, had not only been protecting them in exchange for a stipend, but had been pocketing some of the junk he seized and selling it back. They couldn't get him on murder, but they got him on corruption. The department held a hearing. Rogers was the major witness against him, and when he finished laying out the seamy story, the brass threw the crooked cop over the blue wall.

For Rogers, though, his day of testimony sent him to Siberia as far as most other cops were concerned. He was marked, a guy who had turned against one of his own. It didn't matter that the cop was a rogue, a guy who should have gone to prison instead of just getting the boot. Rogers had broken the unwritten rule that the department protects its own. He had done it in the past, to be sure, but then he had been just a rookie and, while nobody quite trusted him, there was the thought that given time he would learn just which side he was on. Now he had done the unforgivable.

Only Palmieri stood by him. "Don't worry, kid," Felix said. "It'll pass. You did what you had to. There wasn't any other way. If the coin had come down heads, it'd have been me instead of you."

It didn't pass, though. Guys he had known for a long time, guys who had been his friends, avoided him, talking to him in flat monosyllables if they talked to him at all.

A month later, he was called in by Chief Dolan. "You're being transferred," Dolan said. Rogers knew that was coming. He was at the top of the list for promotion to sergeant, which meant an automatic transfer; it was what went with a promotion. What he didn't expect were Dolan's next words. "Report to Internal Affairs on Monday."

"You've got to be joking," Rogers said. "I like what I do. I'm good at it. Felix and I are a team. Who the hell wants Internal Affairs? I've got enough trouble as it is."

"It's no joke, Ben," Dolan said. "We've talked about it. We like the way you bit the bullet when it came to that rotten apple. A lot of guys around here would have clammed up. IAD needs guys like you, guys who aren't afraid to do the right thing no matter what. No arguments. It's a done thing."

So he went to Internal Affairs. Only Felix Palmieri seemed to understand. He echoed Dolan. "I'm sorry to be losing you, kid," Palmieri said. "But what's done is done. Look, somebody's got to do that damn job, somebody who's goddamn honest. Maybe you don't believe it now, but you're the right guy for it. But, remember, you ever need anything, I'm right here, kid. I mean it. And, for chrissake, don't be a stranger."

In the years since, Felix had made sure that the bond remained. He called often, at least once a week. They had lunch when they could, had drinks together on slow evenings. Felix had Rogers to his house for dinner, tried to fix him up with girls. When Rogers made lieutenant, it was Felix and Mary Palmieri who threw the party to celebrate. And when Felix's youngest son was born, Rogers was the godfather.

Now Felix was dead and Rogers was left with a commitment to him, to follow up on the cases he had left behind. And more, to find out what had really happened in that alley, to discover who had killed Felix, and why.

On a yellow legal-sized pad, he made notes, listed names, indisputable facts, times and dates, jotted large question marks where there were uncertainties, question marks that filled the pages. At night, as he studied those files, scribbled his notes, Melissa watched him, looking up from a book, standing in a doorway, making no comment.

He began to roam the city, going wherever the cases took him. Traveling to shabby, run-down streets in East Harlem where the baby's body had been found; moving slowly through the hospital basement on the East Side; studying the fashionable East Side street outside the Arab consulate; threading his way through the 47th Street mobs; mingling with the kids at the singles bar; walking the streets and alleys of Little Italy. He knocked at doors and asked questions of bored and impatient witnesses, who told him they were getting tired of answering the same questions a hundred times, they'd already told the other cops the same things—and, besides, didn't the cops have better things to do with their time than waste the taxpayers' money by repeating themselves over and over? But now and then he asked a question that hadn't been asked before, and saw surprise, saw a light in eyes, got different answers from the ones on report sheets.

All the time he was looking for something more than just closing the book that Palmieri had left open. What Mary Palmieri had said to him in the funeral home kept gnawing at him. Of course, it could have been just her grief. But maybe it was something more. Maybe she was right, and the official line was just a line. Maybe in one of those open cases lay the reason for that midnight call. Maybe in its solution he would find Palmieri's killer.

*　　*　　*

Rogers and Melissa stopped at the Palmieri house in Queens one evening after the weekly dinner with his grandmother. He had called ahead and Mary had said they should come on over, that she'd love to see them. She was alone. The crowds who had come to comfort her in the days after her husband's death had inevitably gone back to their own lives. Now she mourned in solitude, in an empty house, the children gone, some married, some away at school. She slept in an empty bed.

When they arrived, she had coffee ready, had baked a cake, and insisted they eat. They agreed, but only if she would share it with them. She did not look well, which was to be expected. She had lost weight, and there were dark purple shadows under her eyes.

They talked a lot about Felix, remembering better times, even bringing a little laughter from Mary. At one point she got up, went into the bedroom, and returned holding Felix's gun. "I want you to have it," she said to Rogers. "Felix would have wanted that."

Gently, Rogers brought her around to talking about that last night. She didn't want to talk about it. He pressed just a little.

She studied him. "Are you looking into it, Ben?"

"Unofficially," he said. "On my own."

"I'm glad."

"Why do you think it's not according to the official line?" he asked.

"It was the way he spoke on the phone," she said.

"What do you mean?"

"Not like he was talking to one of his informers. Different. I'm not sure just how, but different."

"You're sure?"

She nodded. "I've heard him talk to those people a million times. I can always tell when it's one of them calling. This was different. And when he left, he was in a rush, not taking his time like he usually did. And then, he never would have let somebody he didn't know well get that close to him. He was always careful. He took chances, but never when the odds were too long. He always said the most important thing was to come home to us." That was all she could say.

After a while, he left her and Melissa and went to the room where Felix Palmieri had kept his private papers. Mary hadn't cleaned them up yet. They were a mess, just the way Felix had left them. It would take hours, maybe days, to go through them. She told him to take them with him; she had no use for them any longer, no one did, and her voice broke when she said that.

7

Late one morning a few days later, the weather still mild for fall, he picked up the phone, dialed Central Homicide and asked for Carlos Rodriguez. He could hear the ice in Rodriguez's voice when he identified himself. Rogers sighed. It was such a predictable response.

"I want to talk to you," Rogers said.

"So talk."

"About Felix."

"Jesus Christ," Rodriguez said. "Felix is dead. Can't you people let the dead rest in peace? Felix was clean. He was a straight arrow."

"Tell me something I don't know," Rogers said. "You were Felix's partner."

"Now and then. A time or two. Most times he worked alone, no partner. It was his way."

"Not the way I heard it. The case load dictates that you've got to have a partner. Nobody works alone. You were it. Your name was on the reports."

"I got nothin' to give you."

"I'm not looking for anything on Felix. I want to know about what he was working on."

"Go to the hall of records."

"I'll buy you lunch," Rogers said.

"I don't like cheese," Rodriguez said, "and I don't eat in no ratholes."

"One o'clock," Rogers said. He named a place in the Village where nobody was likely to see them. "Don't be late." He hung up.

Rogers was five minutes early. He took a table at the rear and watched the entrance. There was still a question in his mind whether Rodriguez would show or whether he'd put in a call to the Detective's Endowment Association that he was being hassled by a lieutenant from Internal Affairs. At precisely one, as though he had been standing in the shadows outside with his eyes on his watch, waiting for the second hand to stand straight up, Rodriguez came through the door, stood just inside and looked around. He was about forty, dark complexioned, with black hair combed straight across his head from a part just above his left ear, the kind of thing a guy does when he tries to hide the fact that he's going bald, only it never works, just makes it more obvious, which was the case with Rodriguez; and the black looked like it came out of a bottle of shoe polish. He was a small man, but husky, with muscles bulging the sleeves of his jacket. Rogers remembered that Palmieri had once told him Rodriguez was into pumping iron. He was sweating; the weather was warm, but not that warm. Felix had said Rodriguez was okay. Before he got moved to Central Homicide, he'd been a detective in a bad precinct in Brooklyn north, a real sewer where the vermin were protected and the pad was the rule. But Felix said he'd been clean, that he'd checked him out. Rogers wondered. Maybe Felix had lost the edge; going out in the middle of the night without a backup said maybe he had. Someday Rogers might want to take a good look into Detective Rodriguez. But not now. If necessary, he'd just push a little and see if there was any give.

Rodriguez spotted him, came slowly back through the restaurant; it wasn't very crowded. He stopped a few feet away, stood looking down at Rogers. "Yeah?" he said.

"Sit down," Rogers said. "I'm buying you lunch."

Rodriguez studied him. "I ain't hungry," he said.

"Sit down anyway."

Rodriguez took his time, then pulled out a chair and sat. "You got something to say, say it," he said.

"Tell me about the things Felix was working on."

"Shit," Rodriguez said, "you got it all. You come snoopin' around his desk and made copies of the files. And you been out on the street askin' dumb questions. You got everything there is."

"You were his partner. Fill me in on what I didn't get."

"What the fuck for?"

"Who called Felix out that night?"

"How the hell do I know?"

"Guess."

"What is this, Twenty Questions? I got no crystal ball." He glared at Rogers. "Besides, what the fuck do you care?"

A waiter crossed toward them. "You want something from the bar?" he asked.

"Not me," Rogers said.

"You want to see the menu?"

"No need," Rogers said. "A burger, medium. And coffee."

Rodriguez shook his head. "Nothin'," he said. "I ain't hungry."

"Order something," Rogers said.

Rodriguez looked at him, then looked up at the waiter. "You got tofu?" The waiter nodded. "Right," Rodriguez said. "Tofu and a salad, and apple juice. Not sweetened crap. Natural." The waiter shrugged and started away. Rogers tried to stifle a laugh. "Good stuff," Rodriguez said. "Keeps the weight down. Gets the muscles toned. Plenty of protein, no fat."

"You dirty, Carlos?"

Rodriguez stared. He sweated some more. "No way," he said. "I never took a dime. You check. You'll find I'm clean."

"I might do just that," Rogers said.

Rodriguez sweated some more. He took out a handkerchief and wiped his face. He started talking. He couldn't be more cooperative. He wanted to help in any way he could. Rogers should just tell him what he wanted.

"Who killed Felix?"

Rodriguez shrugged. "You know what I know. What the department says."

"His wife says no."

"What does she know?"

"Run his cases by me. The open ones."

"Help me out. I'm up to my ass in open cases."

"The baby in the trash can."

"Jesus. Fifteen-year-old kid gets herself knocked up, don't tell nobody. She's a little big anyway so nobody notices. The baby comes, she smothers it and dumps it. Only reason it got out of the precinct was she ran and they couldn't find her. Shit, we had that one in five minutes. Ask me somethin' hard."

"The nurse."

"Fuckin' hospitals," Rodriguez said. "People all over the place. Doctors, nurses, interns, handymen, patients, people come in off the street, you name it. Nurse comes down on her break, goin' to the cafeteria, which is open all night. Only she never gets there, and it's an hour before anybody misses her. But nobody thinks nothin' until some porter falls over the body in a goddamn broom closet. And nobody sees nothin'."

"Somebody saw something," Rogers said. "Somebody saw a cop walking out of the basement entrance at three o'clock in the morning."

"Big deal," Rodriguez said. "Cops are in and out all the time."

"Guy who saw him said he was alone and moving fast, faster than you'd expect from a big fat cop with a belly slopping over his gun belt. The guy didn't think anything of it then, only later. Like you said, cops are in and out."

Rodriguez sat up. "Nobody told us that."

"The guy told Felix. The guy told me."

"First I've heard of it." He reached into his pocket and pulled out a small loose-leaf notebook, opened it, thumbed through, stopped at a page already half filled with writing. He took out a pen and held it over the page and looked up at Rogers. "Who's the witness?"

Rogers gave him the name. Rodriguez wrote it. "I'll look into it first thing," he said.

"Why didn't Felix tell you?"

Rodriguez shrugged. "You know Felix. He liked to play things close, spring surprises."

The waiter moved across the room with their food. They fell silent as he put it on the table. He asked if they needed anything else, then walked away, hardly waiting for an answer.

Rodriguez ate with sudden appetite. Rogers watched him, toying with his own food. As they ate, he took Rodriguez through the other cases, listening carefully to the answers.

The girl outside the singles bar? "A teenage bimbo. One of them too-rich Upper East Side preppies. A tease. Teased the wrong guy. A million kids saw them leave together. A million kids knew both of them. They were regulars. Only a million kids won't give the guy up. He's one of them. You ask them, one says he's short, the next he's tall, one says he's skinny like a rail, the next he's fat like a hog. He wears glasses, he don't wear glasses, he's got a big nose, he's got no nose at all, he's got black hair, he's got red hair. Get it? And the guy that owns the joint, he never saw nothin', they weren't in the place, none of those kids was there, he never poured a drink for underage kids in his life, he always checks the ID. But we make the kid. We go to talk to him and he's got six Wall Street shysters sittin' on his shoulder. He don't know nothin', he didn't do nothin', he never met the broad, he wasn't there, and if we think different, prove it. And kindly vacate the premises. Shit, it's all in the report."

"Felix made a note," Rogers said, "that maybe the kid was telling the truth. He wanted to look into it more."

"Fuckin' Felix," Rodriguez said. "Him and his goddamn notes. He was never satisfied with what was starin' him in the face. The little bastard done it. You can put it in the bank and it'll earn you interest."

Most times, Rogers thought, Felix tended to be right. It was something to look into.

The diplomat? "Don't talk to me about that one," Rodriguez said. "We were told, Hands off. Somethin' about politics over there and none of our business. Only, I gotta tell you, and maybe Felix wrote somethin' about it and you picked it up, which is why you're askin', Felix thought it was somethin' else. Like junk, maybe. He never said. Only we couldn't touch it. The thing was, with Felix, he got into somethin', he didn't let go. So maybe he was workin' on it anyway. If he was, he didn't tell me."

Sal Ianucci? "Strictly a mob hit. Like, they kill their own. And who cares? Good riddance. What I can't figure is what the hell Felix was doin' lookin' into it on his own, if that was what he was doin', and goin' into a fuckin' alley down there in the middle of the night, and then lettin' some bastard come at him from the front. I always thought he had better sense. Doin' that, he was askin' for it, and he got it."

"You buy the department line?" Rogers said mildly.

"Fuckin' A," Rodriguez said. "Had to be. No two ways about it."

"Like you said, they got him from the front. Close. Powder burns on his clothes."

"So maybe he knew the guy. Felix knew everybody."

"Maybe. But he'd let a lowlife get that close without doing anything, without pullin' his piece? He'd let a lowlife take him by surprise?"

"Who knows? Felix was always full of surprises. Maybe it was one of his inside stoolies playin' both sides. Maybe it was a capo and they'd set up a meet. Maybe there was more than one, like one guy comes up behind real quiet and grabs him, and the other guy steps up and pops him. Only thing, he was where he shouldn't ought to have been." He looked at Rogers. "That do it? That's all the cases. You got what you want?"

"One more," Rogers said.

Rodriguez looked blank. "Not that I know about."

"Body in the Staten Island dump."

Rodriguez shook his head. "I heard about that one. Read it in the papers. Guys talkin'. You know. That's all. Felix got it?"

"Yeah."

"Jesus. What d'ya know." He grinned at Rogers then, relief on his face. "You know somethin'," he said. "Whatever they say, you ain't such a bad guy."

NOVEMBER

8

"I'm repeating myself," Melissa said, "but I'm impressed."

She had said it first a few days before when Rogers opened the thick vellum envelope, pulled out the stiff invitation, glanced at it, and tossed it to her. She read it, looked over at him, and said, "I'm impressed. I didn't know you even knew him."

He grinned and tried to dismiss it. "I've known him for a long time, met him when I was with the C.I.D. in the army. And I worked on a case with him a couple of years ago down in Washington, when he was at Justice. That's all. Hell," he said, "he's probably sent out a thousand of these."

"Not like this," she said.

"You want to go?"

She grinned at him. "No. I want to stay home and watch a rerun on the tube. What do you think?"

So, late on the first Tuesday after the first Monday in November, Ben Rogers put on a suit and tie, a thing he rarely did. Melissa watched him from the other side of the bedroom. "You really do look good that way. Handsome," she said, repeating something she had said earlier. "I'm impressed."

"You're not the only one," he said, his eyes moving over the designer dress she had just slipped on.

"A simple little thing." She laughed. "Your basic black."
"Sure. At around a grand."

"A mere forty-five dollars, label and all, right off the bargain table at the thrift shop around the corner," she said.

At the midtown hotel, it took them fifteen minutes to push and shove and plow their way across the sweltering, packed ballroom to the small doorway at the rear. It was too warm for the first Tuesday in November, and there were too many people in the room. Rogers wondered what a fire inspector would do if he wandered into the mob. Not a thing, probably, at least not on a night like this. It was Wall Street and Madison Avenue and the Upper East Side come together, all dark suits and ties and thousand-dollar dresses that didn't come from the neighborhood thrift shop. The reformers were having a party.

A thousand balloons in every color of the rainbow hung from the ceiling, bouncing over the heads of the mass of celebrating humanity. It was nearly impossible in the cacophonous din to hear the band off to the side frantically playing, "Happy Days Are Here Again" and "There'll Be a Hot Time in the Old Town Tonight." Somebody was standing in front of a tote board that listed the city's election districts, chalking up the numbers as they came in, shouting the returns into a microphone, every new figure bringing another loud roar. There was no need to ask. This was the winner's circle.

Finally they reached the small doorway. Rogers handed the engraved invitation to a security guard who scanned a list on a clipboard, looked back, studied Rogers for a moment, then nodded and motioned. "The elevator right through there, Mr. Rogers," he said. "Fifth floor."

"I'm impressed," Melissa said again. "You'd think we were important people."

On the fifth floor, the elevator doors opened directly onto the suite. The place was crowded, but not like the ballroom. Here there were perhaps twenty-five or thirty people, a mixture of old pols and New Wave reformers, eying each other suspiciously, meeting briefly around tables loaded with smoked salmon, caviar, and canapés of all kinds and around the table where bartenders poured liberally from bottles of the best vintage champagne, Chivas and Johnny Walker Black Label scotch—only the best and most expensive. Somebody had spent a small fortune on this little spread.

The candidate, the mayor-elect—when the old mayor finally decided to concede—was nowhere to be seen. A lot of heads were turned toward a side door, waiting, bodies poised to be the first to move in that direction when he did appear.

Rogers and Melissa walked further into the room. Melissa stared about curiously, recognizing some faces from pictures in the papers, front pages, and financial pages. She whispered a few names to Rogers. "All aboard the gravy train," she murmured.

He gazed around the room. Everybody there except them looked and smelled like money. "These guys? What for?"

"The power and the glory," she said.

Suddenly the side door opened and John Morrison appeared. Morrison was medium height, his brown hair turning gray at the temples, his face craggy, the gray eyes deep-set. He was wearing a gray pin-striped suit, tailor-made at Brooks Brothers button-down white shirt, striped tie. He looked like pure Ivy League. He was Princeton. He looked like money, like he was born to it, which happened to be true. He looked like he belonged in a wood-paneled law office high up in a Wall Street skyscraper, which also happened to be true. What he didn't look like was politics. But looks are deceiving. Rogers had found that out in Washington. John Morrison knew where the bodies were buried, and he knew how to disinter them.

For a moment, he stood in the doorway, deep in conversation with a tall muscular middle-aged man with thick gray hair, immaculately groomed. They shook hands. The tall man smiled, nodded, and started away, pausing to say a few words to some of the reformers, nodding to the old pols, and then moving toward the elevator.

"I suppose," Rogers said, "you recognize him, too."

"Of course," she said. "Eugene Donatello. Big deal banker. Economic wizard. His picture's in the papers all the time. I bet I know what they were talking about."

"You planted a bug?"

"Didn't have to," she said. "He was the big money man behind Morrison. He's probably been asked to be the big money man in City Hall."

"With the mess the city's in, he needs that?"

"The power and the glory," she said again.

People gathered quickly around Morrison, who was looking

around the room. He spotted Rogers, murmured some apologies, and started quickly toward him, holding out his hand. "Ben," he said. "Good to see you. Glad you could make it." He smiled at Melissa. Rogers introduced her.

"Congratulations," she said.

He shrugged. "Say that to me a year from now," he said.

"When the cheering stops . . ." she said.

"The real work begins." He nodded. "I like her, Ben," he said, then to Melissa, "You want a job?"

She laughed. "No, thanks. Not my thing."

His eyes passed over the room, over the hovering crowd. "Their thing," he said.

"Hogs at the trough."

He smiled. "Don't be cynical," he said.

"Just do-gooders?"

"Of course." But he laughed. His eyes went over her head toward the elevator door, which was just opening. A florid, silver-haired man with all the marks of the successful politician emerged. Morrison excused himself. "Duty calls," he said, and moved toward the elevator, calling, "Congressman."

"Another rat deserts the sinking ship," Melissa whispered.

"My, my," Rogers said. "I thought Congressman Benedetto was your hero."

"Yours," she said.

"Benedetto's all right," he said. "Everybody says he's honest, which is refreshing. Besides, he and Morrison were buddies down in Washington."

"Politics make strange bedfellows."

"We're full of clichés tonight, aren't we?"

"We're in a world of clichés," she said. Then she shook herself. "But I'm enjoying myself. It's a different world and it's fun."

Morrison and Benedetto walked toward a corner, Benedetto holding the mayor-elect's arm, his head leaning in toward him, talking in a hushed voice that carried only as far as Morrison's ear. The elevator door kept opening, and important people kept getting off, each one intent on getting his message to Morrison. He was polite to every one of them, listening, nodding, noncommittally. But he was edgy, too; his eyes kept flicking toward the door to the next room as if he were waiting for something or someone.

Rogers and Melissa wandered around the room, stopping briefly at the refreshment tables. They were not part of this crowd, of either crowd, and they knew it. Self-consciously, they stood apart, watching.

After a while the side door opened and an aide appeared. He gestured. "Mr. Mayor," he called, "the telephone."

Morrison looked up, took a deep breath, and smiled broadly. People moved toward him, hands held out, trying to be first to reach him. The victory was now his officially.

9

At ten on the Sunday morning after the election, the phone beside Rogers's bed rang. The weather had changed during the night, the unseasonable warmth, a kind of post-Indian summer, giving way to a foretaste of the winter to come. Outside, sleet drummed against the windows, turning the streets into skating rinks. Rogers reached for the phone, not yet quite awake. He heard Morrison's baritone. "Ben? I want to see you." There was urgency in the voice, a demand and not a request.

Rogers sat up, awake, alert. Melissa stirred next to him. "When?" he asked into the phone. He knew Morrison's days and nights were completely booked, Sundays not excluded. The man was trying to put together an administration to run the city, and he had only about six weeks to do it. So a call, even on a Sunday morning, was not a social pleasantry, and a call to Rogers, who in no way thought of himself as part of Morrison's grand plan, had to hold surprise, and probably not a pleasant one.

"How soon can you get up here?"

"Where?"

"My apartment." He gave the address.

Rogers looked at the clock beside the bed, did some quick calculating. "About an hour."

"Good."

Huddled into his raincoat, collar turned up, an old vinyl-coated golf hat protecting his head, Rogers skidded across the pavement from the subway onto Fifth Avenue. He struggled the few blocks to the massive apartment building that fronted the avenue, one of those places where most apartments occupy an entire floor. As he turned into the entrance, the doorman blocked his way. Rogers gave him his name, then Morrison's, and said he was expected. The doorman looked as though he didn't believe him, and told him to wait, shutting the door in his face so that he had to stand outside. At least there was a canopy, although the wind blew the sleet into his face. In a moment the doorman was back. He held the door open and with obvious reluctance gestured Rogers inside, told him what floor to go to, and motioned toward elevators to the rear.

When the elevator opened onto the foyer of Morrison's apartment, a butler immediately appeared, taking his hat and coat, then ushering Rogers through double doors into a large room. Morrison was standing in the center. He was in shirt sleeves, the cuffs turned up, no tie, suspenders across the shoulders attached to old khaki slacks. He was alone, which, given the pressures on him, was another surprise.

"Ben," he said. "I'm glad you could come. Can I get you something to drink?"

"Too early," Rogers said.

"Not till the sun's over the yardarm, right?" Morrison said. "Come on in, sit down." He motioned toward a pair of large sofas flanking a massive fireplace. Rogers followed him, sitting down beside Morrison. On a marble coffee table in front of them was a pile of file folders. Morrison looked at Rogers. "Ben," he said, "I need some help."

"Sure. Name it."

Morrison reached out, picked up one of the folders and handed it to Rogers. He opened it. Inside was a plain white envelope. Typed on the front was Morrison's name. There was no return address. No stamp. Rogers looked up.

"Hand delivered," Morrison said. "Late last night. Read it."

Rogers opened the envelope flap, pulled out a sheet of paper on which there was typewriting. The letter was brief.

DEAR MR. MORRISON:

I have read in the newspapers that you intend to appoint Eugene Donatello as deputy mayor in charge of the city's finances. To do so would place the city and your administration in grave peril. I am in possession of information that will show that Mr. Donatello is not what he seems. In offering it to you, I place myself in great danger. I am willing to take that risk for the good of the city. If you will contact me at Box 7347, Church Street Station, I will make this information available to you or your appointed representative on a confidential basis.

The letter was unsigned.

Rogers reread it. He looked up at Morrison. "You must get a hundred of these every day, every time somebody's name surfaces."

"True," Morrison said. "They're mostly from cranks. Rumors, wild charges, totally unsupported allegations. No evidence, no offer of evidence, nothing. This is different, though. It didn't come through the mail; it was hand delivered. And whoever wrote it offered to back what he's saying. I want to find out what it's all about. And I want you to find out for me."

"Why me?" Rogers asked. "You must have a dozen guys who could do it. Hell, you can have your pick."

"You're the one I want." Morrison said. "I can trust you. We worked well together down in Washington. I know what you can do."

Indeed, Morrison knew precisely what Rogers could do. A few years earlier, when Morrison had been an assistant attorney general, Rogers had been sent to Washington on special assignment to work with him on the investigation of a crooked federal judge who was being paid off by a sleazy lawyer to spring people who had been arrested and could afford to meet the price. Rogers had gone undercover, gotten himself arrested, and then come up with the evidence that was needed to send the judge and the lawyer to a place where their influence couldn't protect them.

Now Morrison wanted him for another job. Rogers looked at the mayor-elect."I don't have to spend a night in a D.C. jail this time, do I?"

Morrison smiled. "Not this time, Ben."

"I'd have to get an okay."

"You've already got it. I talked to Chief Dolan. He said he'd arrange for you to go on special assignment for me."

"You told him what you wanted me to do?"

"No. I'm not telling anybody. I don't want a word of this to get out. Only you and I know about this. I just told him that I had some important work that couldn't wait. I wanted someone I could trust, someone I knew, and you were the guy. He couldn't have been more cooperative."

"Anything the new mayor wants, the new mayor gets. Until he starts cutting the budget for the department anyway," Rogers said.

Morrison laughed. "One thing, Ben," he said, his tone sober. "Nobody's to know what you're doing. Not Chief Dolan, not a soul. You take care of this, and you report directly back to me. I don't want a word to leak."

"You must want this guy Donatello bad."

"He's good. About as good as you can get. He's at the top, and he's willing to put it aside and work for the city, for me. You don't find that kind under every tree. Yes, I want him. But what I don't want, what I can't afford and the city can't afford, is a scandal, certainly not right at the beginning. You were in Washington long enough to know that when somebody throws a little mud, it sticks like glue and the stain remains forever. It doesn't wash off. On January first, I'm going to take over City Hall, and nobody's going to be able to point a finger at anybody who comes along with me. If there's anything wrong with Gene Donatello, I want to know it before any damage is done."

"I suppose you've checked him out?"

"Damn right. He's clean."

"You have a file?"

"It's yours." Morrison reached out, flipped through several folders in the pile, plucked one and handed it to Rogers. "Read it, take it with you if you want. You won't find anything there," he said.

Rogers leaned back against the sofa, opened the folder and

read carefully through the pages. Morrison watched him impatiently.

According to the file, Donatello was in his late forties. He had been born in New York, the son of an Italian immigrant longshoreman who had died when he was still a child, and a Sicilian-born mother, also deceased. Donatello had gone to the city's public schools, graduating third in his class from the Bronx High School of Science, and though offered scholarships by a number of colleges, had gone on to Fordham, from which he graduated summa cum laude and Phi Beta Kappa. He had served in Vietnam during the early stages of the war and earned several medals. When he was discharged, he had gone to the Wharton School of Finance at the University of Pennsylvania and gotten a master's degree in international finance. He then went to work in the foreign banking department of Fidelity International Bank on Wall Street, had been promoted quickly and regularly so that now he was the bank's executive vice president in charge of both domestic and international banking. As his reputation grew, he had been called on regularly to serve on numerous financial advisory panels, and as an expert witness before Congress. He was unmarried, lived in an apartment on Fifth Avenue, and maintained a hunting lodge in the Adirondacks. He was a member of a number of clubs, all the right ones, and a benefactor and board member of all the major mainline cultural organizations. Politically he was an independent, registered in neither party, and until the Morrison campaign, he had never actively participated in political life. Among his fellow bankers he was held in the highest esteem, given credit for having rescued Fidelity Bank when it was on shaky ground, and turning it into a stable and prosperous institution. "The most often heard criticism of Donatello," the report concluded, "is that he does not always follow the usual practices and tends to rely more on his own intuition and ability to predict trends than most conservative bankers would consider wise or sound. Most of those interviewed thought the city would be fortunate if Donatello agreed to accept an appointment."

Rogers looked at Morrison. "The guy's too good to be true," he said.

"True, nevertheless," Morrison said.

"Until now."

"It's just hard to believe," Morrison said. "My guys never

heard a word, not a whisper. And then this pops out of the woodwork. I don't believe it. The problem is, I can't afford not to look into it. But, Ben, move fast. Get in touch with this guy and find out what it's all about. There's not much time."

"Like yesterday," Rogers said.

"Like yesterday," Morrison nodded.

Rogers shrugged and sighed. "You know, Jack," he said, "I once read a book by Robert Penn Warren where the guy wrote something like man was conceived in sin and born in corruption, and if you look hard enough, you're bound to find it, because there's always something on everybody. You just have to look in the right place."

"You're a damn cynic, Ben," Morrison said. "I hope you're wrong this time." He took a breath and shook his head. "I'd like to ask you to stay for lunch. Next time I will. You and that bright girl of yours. I liked her. But I'm having some people in and I'd just as soon they didn't meet you. You understand."

"Sure," Rogers said. "I'll be in touch."

10

Rogers made him as he entered the post office from Church Street and headed for the row of postal boxes along one wall. The worried, frightened expression on his pinched, sallow face; the way he looked around through thick glasses, kept glancing over his shoulder; kept peering into the corners, casting quick glances at the other patrons, at people lounging about—all these things told Rogers this was his mark. He was a small man, probably in his mid-sixties, wrapped in an overcoat at least a size too large; maybe it had once fit, and he had shrunk. Rogers was willing to bet that under that fedora the man was bald.

For two days after he sent a reply to the hand-delivered letter, Rogers had staked out the post office, eyeballing the box, waiting. Now the wait was over. The small man went to the box, fiddled, opened it and extracted a single envelope, studied it without opening it, and then started to turn away. Rogers took a couple of steps, reached him, and touched his shoulder. The man turned quickly, startled, fear in his eyes.

"I'm Morrison's guy," Rogers said.

The small man took a deep breath, looked around, searching. "How can I be sure?" he whispered.

"Open the envelope. You'll find a piece of paper. It says my name's Ben Rogers. It says I represent Morrison. It says if we don't make contact here, you should call me. It gives my number."

The man studied the envelope for a moment, then tore it open and read the sheet inside. He looked up at Rogers. "That's what it says. But how do I know you're this Rogers?"

Rogers pulled out his wallet, opened it. The man studied it. "You're a police officer?"

"Right."

"I wasn't expecting . . ."

"What were you expecting?"

"I don't know."

"This has nothing to do with the police," Rogers said. "It's unofficial, strictly for Mr. Morrison."

The man stared at him, nodded slowly, and took a breath. "My name," he said, "is Werner Rosenblatt."

"Let's go someplace and talk," Rogers said. He took the man's arm and led him through the lobby and out onto the street.

"Not here," Rosenblatt said, trying to pull himself free.

"You name it," Rogers said.

"A car's safer. You have a car? They could be watching."

"Who?"

Rosenblatt shrugged and didn't answer.

Rogers turned and silently led him the three blocks to the garage near the World Trade Center where he had parked. He unlocked the car and climbed behind the wheel. Rosenblatt got in beside him, closed the door, shrank into the seat, hugging the door as though for protection. Rogers glanced at him. "Where to?"

"Anywhere," Rosenblatt said. "Just drive anywhere."

Rogers drove out of the lot and headed for the West Side Highway. Rosenblatt said nothing until they joined the traffic flow heading uptown. He kept turning his head to look at the road behind them.

"Nobody's tailing us," Rogers said.

"I have to be sure," Rosenblatt said. They were at 34th Street, the glass walls of the Javits Center shimmering in the sunlight just ahead, before Rosenblatt relaxed even a little bit. "Is it true?" he asked finally.

"Is what true?"

"That Mr. Morrison is going to appoint Donatello deputy mayor?"

"Maybe," Rogers said.

"That would be a terrible mistake," Rosenblatt said.

"So you wrote. Why?"

"How much do you know about Donatello?"

"Not a hell of a lot. What I read."

"It's all lies," Rosenblatt exploded with fury. "I ought to know. I work for him. No, I worked for him. I don't anymore."

Rogers said nothing. He waited.

"Everybody thinks he's so wonderful, so brilliant," Rosenblatt said. "He's a fraud. He's worse than a fraud. He's a laundryman, that's what he is. You know what a laundry is?"

"Yeah. I know," Rogers said.

"You don't believe me," Rosenblatt said. "I can prove it."

"Sure."

"Only . . ."

"Only what?"

"If they find out, they'll kill me. Not just me. My wife. I'm not worried about my children. They're grown up. They've moved away, to a different part of the country." He took a deep breath. "He's a dangerous man, Donatello. He has friends everywhere. They protect him. No one can get to him."

"Nobody but you," Rogers said.

"Not even me," Rosenblatt said. "I can just show you enough so maybe you can save the new mayor. You won't get him. But you can save Mr. Morrison. And the city."

"What's in it for you?"

"Nothing. Everything. He ruined my life. He's taken everything from me."

"Okay," Rogers said, "so you can prove it. How?"

"I have documents, papers, other things. I'll give them to you. Only you have to promise to help me."

"If you deliver the goods, we'll deliver the help."

"I want to disappear. I mean, not just me. My wife. I want to start over where nobody knows me, where nobody can find me. At my age, the idea of starting over is ridiculous. But that's what I want. To know they can't reach me."

"It can be done," Rogers said. "But I have to see what you're offering."

Rosenblatt nodded. "I have to get everything organized," he said. "I'll call you tomorrow, the next day for certain, and we can arrange a meeting."

"Whatever you say. You want me to drop you someplace?" He looked out at the highway. Just ahead, looming above them to the right, he could see the bulk of Grant's Tomb.

Rosenblatt was silent, watching the road. He nodded slowly. "Ninety-sixth Street," he said. "At the subway."

"I can drive you home, wherever that is."

"No. No need. I'd rather you didn't."

Rogers took the next exit, drove east to Broadway and turned south. At the subway entrance, he stopped. Rosenblatt jumped out of the car. "I have your number," he said. "You'll hear from me tomorrow." He moved quickly, disappearing down the stairs before Rogers could answer.

A rabbit, Rogers thought. An old scared little rabbit. Maybe he had something, maybe not.

11

It was a little after two when Rogers reached Hogan Place, the memorial to one-time District Attorney Frank Hogan. He turned into the graystone building, hard by the Criminal Courthouse on Centre Street, showed his credentials, was passed through, and took the elevator to the Rackets Bureau on the sixth floor. He walked in, looked around, crossed to a desk. "Hi, Phil," he said.

Phil Carlson looked up. "Ben," he said. "Long time no see. What brings you over here? All us cops here are pure as Ivory Snow."

"I want some information," Rogers said. "You ever hear of a little guy, maybe sixty, sixty-five, maybe a banker, name of Werner Rosenblatt?"

Carlson looked at him, nodded slowly. "Have you been reading tea leaves? You came to the right fountain."

"Purely by accident," Rogers said.

"I didn't think his thing was paying off," Carlson said.

"As far as I know, it's not," Rogers said. "What is his thing?"

"Embezzlement," Carlson said. "I know because I'm working on it. The ADA's getting ready to take it to the grand jury."

"What'd he embezzle?"

"Two hundred grand, that's all."

"Who from?"

"The fuckin' bank he worked for. Where else? The bank got wise, called us in. You want to know more, I'll take you up and you can talk to the ADA."

Carlson led him up to the indictment bureau and into a small windowless office. It belonged to a thirty-year-old Assistant District Attorney named Pamela Turner. Under normal circumstances, away from the office, she was probably attractive enough, but today she looked frazzled. Her makeup was smeared. Her hair was a mess. Her desk was piled with enough papers to make the surface invisible. She did not look happy to see them.

Carlson introduced Rogers, explained why he was there. She sighed. "What," she asked, "does Internal Affairs want with Werner Rosenblatt?"

"Internal Affairs isn't interested in Rosenblatt, at least not yet," he said. "I am."

"Why?"

He considered his answer for a moment. "He could be involved in a case I'm working on."

"What case? How?"

"It's a little early. I'd rather not say until I get it nailed down some."

She leaned forward and glared at him. "Look, mister," she said, "this is not the information bureau. You want information, go to the public library. I'm busy."

"Whoa," he said. "Let's not get our back up."

"Nobody's back is up. I'm amenable to a trade, but I'm not making gifts to strangers. If you have something on Rosenblatt, I want it. Then I'll tell you what we have. Even up, all the way. Take it or leave it."

"Fair enough," Rogers said, "only I don't have anything on Rosenblatt. His name came up in a case I'm on, that's all. Nothing definite. I'm just checking him out."

"What case?"

"Strictly in house at the moment. We're handling it administratively now. We don't know yet whether it's criminal. Maybe it'll never be. Usual IAD kind of thing. Rosenblatt's name was mentioned. Also that he was a banker. Lived somewhere in upper Manhattan . . ."

"Riverdale, as it happens," she said.

"Okay, Riverdale. Anyway, it was a lead. I took a shot and came down here. And what do you know!"

She gave him a skeptical look. He met her eyes and did not change expression. He looked away, caught a glimpse of Carlson, grinning. He did not grin back.

"That's all?" she said.

"All there is," he said. "Now, what about him?"

She shook her head. "If you ever see him," she said, "you'll think he's nothing but a frightened weasel. But don't be fooled. He's a different kind of rodent. He's into embezzlement, maybe a lot more, up to his ears. The bank came to us. Fidelity International. He worked there for twenty-five years, in the international department. Trusted employee and all that. Then he started to dip into the till. He was very good at it too. He'd been at it for a couple of years and they didn't find out about it until about two or three months ago. We went up to see one of the vice presidents. Donatello. Actually, Phil saw him."

"Yeah," Carlson said. "Nice guy. He was really sorry. Said Rosenblatt was someone he trusted, and then the guy does this. Of course, it happens all the time. But you can't tell them that. Anyway, he turned over a bunch of documents, audits, that kind of thing. It was solid. No holes."

"What does Rosenblatt say?" Rogers asked.

"He doesn't," the ADA said.

"Not a word?"

"The usual. He's innocent. It's a frame. Talk to my lawyer. That kind of thing. Only we did some checking and we discovered he had an offshore bank account, and some very large deposits had been made into it."

Someone knocked on the door. Turner looked that way, said, "Come."

The door opened. A tall man, a little paunchy, streaks of gray in his black hair, walked in. "Pamela," he said, then stopped. "Sorry. I didn't know you were in conference."

"Just finishing," she said. She nodded at Rogers. "Do you know Ben Rogers? He's IAD." She looked at Rogers, motioned. "My boss," she said. "Peter McIntyre."

"I think we've met," McIntyre said.

"A time or two," Rogers said.

"What brings you this way? You got a case for us?"

"I doubt it," Rogers said.

"Mr. Rogers is interested in Werner Rosenblatt," Turner said.

"Oh," McIntyre said. "How so?"

"Peripheral," Rogers said. "His name came up in one of my cases. I was doing some exploring."

"Profitable, I hope."

"Who knows?" Rogers said.

McIntyre turned to Turner. "Look, Pamela, we can do this later if you're busy."

"We were just leaving," Rogers said. He nodded to Turner. "Thanks," he said. "If I come up with anything, I'll let you know."

"Do that," she said.

12

There was a message on the machine when Rogers reached home. Call Carlos Rodriguez at Central Homicide. He called. Rodriguez was out. He left his name. An hour later, Rodriguez called back.

"Ben," Rodriguez said. So now they were on first name basis. "Since when you guys at IAD got answering machines?"

He ignored that. He wasn't about to tell Rodriguez that since the day he'd gone on special assignment for Morrison he'd been working out of his apartment. Nobody knew it but Morrison and Chief Dolan. He still had his desk at IAD, but he wasn't using it now; it would stay deserted until he finished this job. The operator had instructions to give callers another number, an unlisted one he'd had installed at home a long time ago for special situations. It was always answered by the machine.

"What's up, Carlos?" he said.

"About the nurse. Like you asked, I been nosin' around a little. It's like old fish. Felix must have got a whiff, because they sure as hell were tryin' to keep the lid on. You know hospitals. Seems like the girl was into extracurricular. Had somethin' goin' on the side, like she was siphoning off the stock, morphine, uppers, downers, all kinds of junk. Not big hauls, which would have made the shit hit the fan, but enough so after a while they figured it wasn't just lousy bookkeeping. Had to be somebody with access, because locks weren't broken, jimmied, nothin' like that. They narrowed it down to five, maybe six nurses on the night shift. You know who one of 'em was? The broad got herself iced."

"Felix knew about it?"

"Yeah. Must have. Son of a bitch kept it in his hat."

Which was like Felix Palmieri. "What else?"

"They claim she must have been free-lancing. I think not. You don't just waltz out of the joint with the stuff. She had to be passin' it on to somebody who could come and go, you know, walk in and out of the place without nobody smellin' a rat. Pardon the expression. You know the cop the guy saw leavin'? I got a description, which fit the one he gave Felix. Somethin' else. Same cop was in two, three nights a week. So I went up to the precinct, asked around, took a look through the roll call. You know what? They got nobody fits. There's more."

"What?"

"I checked out about half a dozen other places. Goddamn Felix done the same thing. Seems like all of 'em got a leak in the drug closet. Not big. But you add 'em up and it ain't peanuts. And regular, like he got a built-in time clock, this cop, or maybe just a guy dressed like a cop, comes by in the middle of the night, and nobody never asks what he's doin' there, nobody asks nothin'. Why should they? He's a cop, right, and maybe he's got business. But they all remembered him when I put it to 'em. You know why? Because goddamn Felix already pumped them. They remembered somethin' else, too. They ain't seen him in a while. Like he just disappeared."

"In how long?"

"Since about the right time."

"You got a line on him?"

"I'm workin' on it. I'll get back when I got more. Damn Felix."

The line went dead. Rogers slowly put the phone back on the cradle. Like toothpaste, he thought; all you have to do is squeeze the tube, put a little pressure in the right place. It never failed. He wouldn't have to squeeze again; Rodriguez would just keep on flowing.

Leave it to Felix. While everybody was looking one way,

looking for the simple answer, Felix was looking around corners. That was the thing about Felix Palmieri. Everybody said the easiest, most obvious answer was the right one. Not necessarily, Felix used to say. People were complicated, and since it was people who caused things to happen, then the events were probably complicated, too, and so were the reasons behind them. So he was always looking for the hidden answers, playing hunches, and it wasn't until he ran them down, and then only if he came up empty, that he'd buy what everybody else was selling.

He had found an answer this time, or at least part of one, that nobody else had seen or been looking for. What they saw was only a nurse who got herself raped and wasted in a hospital basement in the middle of the night. These things happened, and when they did it was usually some outsider with no business there, or somebody on the inside with an itch who'd gone too far. But for some reason Felix got the feeling that there was something more to it, and so he poked around and came up with a profitable little venture, and he found out, too, that it wasn't isolated. The only problem was—and it was like him—he hadn't shared it. He must have been waiting until he had more answers, which was like him, too. And maybe, Rogers thought, Felix had come up with more, and what he'd come up with led him into an alley where somebody walked up to him and put a bullet in his heart. It didn't jibe with the official line, but that was all right; the official line was just that, something put out to satisfy the public, to hold the press at bay.

13

Rogers rode the subway uptown. He was on a hunt. It took an hour, and visits to five bars and four coffee shops, before he found the little guy he was looking for, one of Felix's stoolies. Toby. No last name. No age, either. He could have been thirty, he could have been sixty, or anywhere in between. There was no telling. He was a drifter and a grifter. There was hardly a con he hadn't played at one time or another, though never on a major scale. Strictly small-time, just trying to make a quick buck here and there. He didn't hurt people. He didn't touch junk. That was dangerous. You could get yourself killed that way. You could go to the slammer that way. And Toby had no intention of spending his time in the slammer, or ending up in Potter's Field until the last possible minute.

Toby's great gifts were eyes that could see through cement walls, ears that could hear through soundproofing, and a nose that could put a bloodhound to shame. He was on the street with a few bucks in his jeans and no fear of the cops because he had been in Felix's pocket, freedom a fair exchange. Rogers hadn't seen him in a long time—not since he stopped being Felix's partner. But he remembered Toby and he was sure Toby remembered him.

Toby was in a booth in the back, bending over black coffee, inhaling the steam, swallowed up in a ragged coat he must have picked up from some dumpster, his head swimming in a too large cloth cap. Rogers stood just inside the door, waiting. After a few minutes, Toby looked up. He noticed Rogers, recognition flickering in his eyes. Rogers gave a brief nod, turned, and walked out.

Toby took his time. Five minutes later, toothpick dangling from his mouth, he appeared. He didn't look around. He started down the street. Rogers followed half a dozen steps behind. Toby turned the corner, walked west a couple of blocks, stopping now and then to open the lids of garbage cans and rummage around inside. He turned into a fleabag of a building and went through the door. So Toby wasn't sleeping in doorways any longer. He had a roof these days. Times must be better. He must have made a few scores.

Rogers went up the stoop and through the door after him. Toby was just starting up the steps. Rogers followed him up three flights and into a tiny room, hardly bigger than a jail cell. There was only an army cot, a lopsided wooden chair, and a metal table, on which sat a ten-cent-store lamp base with a forty-watt bulb and no shade. It wasn't fancy, but it was better than a cardboard box, if not much warmer. Toby sat on the edge of the bed, huddled into his coat. He looked at Rogers, waiting.

"Hello, Toby," Rogers said. "Long time no see."

The little man stared at him. "Cop," he said. "I been around. You ain't."

"I'm around now."

"Yeah. I can see. I heard you been huntin' cops."

"Not always."

"Tough about Felix."

"Yeah. Real tough. I'll bet you've been bleeding real blood."

"I liked the guy," Toby said. "Even if he was a cop. He was straight with me. Straight guy. He never fucked me."

"Sure," Rogers said. "What'd you hear?"

"About what?" Rogers waited, staring at him. Toby shrugged. "I hear nothin'. Not a peep."

"First time in your life."

"First time for everythin'," Toby said.

"You holding out, Toby?"

"Why would I hold out?"

"How much?" Rogers said. He reached into his pocket, found some bills, crumpled one in his fist, then pulled his hand out and walked over to Toby, bent and shoved it into his coat pocket.

Toby reached into his pocket, felt. His fingers read the denomination. It was a thing Rogers had noticed in the past, something that never failed to amaze him, the grifter's ability to read bills with his fingers. He studied Rogers and shook his head. "Thanks," he said. "Every little bit helps. But I mean it. I ain't heard a word. Nobody's talkin'. Like everybody's scared to even whisper."

"Why?"

"Beats the hell out of me. He must of been a hair up somebody's ass. Somebody big, too big. Else, who's gonna waste a cop?"

"You know what they say."

"They say! Bullshit. And you know it."

"The widow agrees with you."

"The widow's got brains."

"When did you see him last?"

"Two, maybe three days before he got whacked. He asked what I heard about a couple of things, you know, what I'd been lookin' into for him."

"What things?"

Toby thought about that for a minute. He shrugged. "Like, you know, uppers, downers, pills, you name it. Not the usual crap. Good stuff. Pure. Upscale, like they say. Like from a hospital or a medical place. I mean, what you don't usually see out on the street. I mean, Palmieri's Homicide. Stiffs are what he cares about. So what's he care about that kind of crap? He don't say, but I read the papers. I figure it's got somethin' to do with that broad got herself iced up in the hospital. Right? So I put my nose to the ground." He stopped, leaned back against the wall, hands behind his head. He grinned at Rogers.

Rogers sighed. Toby would have been right at home as a dealer in a Syrian bazaar. "How much?"

"Palmieri," Toby said, "paid me a C."

"Felix never paid you a hundred in your life."

He shrugged. "All right, so fifty."

"So ten."

"No way, man. Twenty."

"What d'you think's in your coat pocket now?"

Toby grinned. "Okay. So, what I told Palmieri was, yeah, somebody was dealin' from hospital closets, pure, the best, guaranteed one hundred percent, and cheap. He was real bad news. Cop. I didn't get no name, I didn't want to get no name. I don't know what precinct, I didn't ask. I figured what I got would be enough for Palmieri. Now I figure the reason you come lookin' for me was, he must of said somethin' to you, bein' that you do what you do, and you figure it's your kind of thing."

"Yeah," Rogers said, "it's my kind of thing." Maybe, he thought, it was what Felix wanted to talk about at that meeting they never had. Maybe, but maybe not, because Felix had said some things that didn't quite fit. "What else," he asked, "were you doing for him?"

"Nothin'."

"Come off it, Toby. You said, two or three. I count one so far. Give."

"I mean it, Mr. Rogers. Just my way of talkin'. You remember that. It don't mean a fuckin' thing."

"Bullshit." Rogers took a step toward him.

Toby cowered back against the wall. The expression on Rogers's face did nothing to comfort him. Maybe Rogers had become like a lot of other cops. In the time since Toby had last seen him, maybe Rogers had gotten a little quick with his fists, or something else he carried in his pocket. Toby didn't like to be hurt. He didn't like bruises, or worse. He didn't have Blue Cross, and hospitals charged. "Okay, okay. So I did another little thing."

"Like what?"

"He asked me to nose around the East Village, which used to be my turf, like in Tompkins Square before I made a score and things got better and I moved uptown." He grinned. Rogers remembered then. Toby had been one of the homeless denizens who squatted in that East Village park. The score he was talking about was going on Felix Palmieri's payroll. "The off-hours joints and the singles bars," he continued. "You know, find out what the street guys were saying. I figured it had to do with the rich kid that ended up on a slab."

"And . . ."

"Shit. No sweat. Everybody was talkin' about it, out loud, not even whisperin'. Maybe not to the cops, but to everybody

else. Shit, everybody seen it, or they knew somebody seen it.
The cops had it down right for a change. The kid and her boy-
friend, they had a fight and the guy lost his cool, let her have it,
and then took off like he had a stick up his ass."

"What else?

Rogers could see Toby's mind start to work. He looked
scared. He looked like he was about to piss in his pants.

"Not my kind of thing, Mr. Rogers. No way."

"I thought everything was your kind of thing."

"Not this. I wouldn't touch it with a ten-foot pole. I don't
mix in no family business."

"What family business?"

"I don't wanna talk about it."

"Toby, Rikers Island beckons. A word in the right ear and
they'll find just the cell for you. I'm sure you'll just love it on the
inside with all your old friends. Why, they might even find out
what you've been up to all these years."

Toby shrank into the wall. "You wouldn't do that."

"Oh, but I most certainly would, if it came to it."

"Jesus, Mr. Rogers." He looked a plea. "You gimme your
word?"

"That depends on what I get in exchange."

"What I got. It ain't much, but it's all I got. I swear. Felix,
he wanted to know if anybody was talkin' about some Arab got
hisself hit. He says he heard it was like one of them feuds they
have over there, only it happened here. The thing was he didn't
buy it. So, I do what I do, y'know, an' I don't hear nothin', not
a whisper. So, I do some more. I figure, who gives a fuck about
some Arab? An' this day I'm where I ain't supposed to be an' I
hear some guys talkin' what they shouldn't of been talkin' out
loud in public, even in whispers. These guys, Mr. Rogers,
they're made guys, you get what I mean. They turn around an'
I'm standin' there like I ain't got no clothes on. I put on an act,
like I had ten too many, like I'm blind an' deaf an' can't hardly
stand up. It don't mean a fuck. I mean, they wasn't buyin'. They
come over an' they give me a kick in the ass an' a lot of other
places so even if I wanted to have kids I couldn't, an' they tell me
get my ass the hell out of there an' don't come back, an' if I heard
somethin' I better not have heard it. They wasn't shittin'. I
thought they was gonna do me right there. Only thing was,
there was other people around, not close enough to hear, but

close enough to see. I ran an' I ain't gone near there since, an' I ain't goin' near there long as I live."

"Who were the guys?"

"No, Mr. Rogers, not on my life. I don't know 'em from Adam. I never seen 'em before, but I knew who they was. You can smell 'em like they was old fish. You can send me to Rikers. But I don't know no more."

Rogers figured that even if Toby did know more, he wasn't going to tell it. Not tonight, and probably not anytime. With just a nod to the little man huddled on the cot, he turned and went back down the stairs to the even colder and shabbier street outside.

14

Rosenblatt didn't call when he was supposed to. But then, Rogers didn't think he would. He had the feeling that the whole thing was just a case of a guy trying to get some of his own back. Donatello had turned him in, and Rosenblatt was about to go away for a long time. Maybe he'd decided that before he went he'd pay off a debt or two.

Going through the newspapers at breakfast the following morning, he almost missed it. It was just a little item in the metropolitan section, at the bottom of the page. A former bank official had been found dead in his apartment in Riverdale. The cause seemed to be suicide. His wife had returned from an evening out to discover his body slumped across his desk, a bullet wound in his head, a pistol with one chamber empty next to him. Authorities said that Rosenblatt had apparently spent the evening burning a number of papers. The apartment fireplace was filled with ashes and charred remains. Rosenblatt, authorities said, had recently been discharged from his position at Fidelity International Bank, where he had worked for a quarter of a century. The District Attorney's office had planned to seek an indictment of Rosenblatt for embezzlement and had just begun presenting evidence to a grand jury.

Rogers read it and reread it. He looked over at Melissa. "What do you know," he said.

"What?"

"The guy who wrote the letter to Morrison. He swallowed his gun."

The building was old, with peeling brick, set on a small knoll down by the river, just north of the toll bridge. The best thing about it was the view. The Hudson spread out below like a wide curling gray ribbon, the Palisades looming along the far shore, hazy in the cold mist rising from the river. From the outside, the building didn't look like the kind of place a guy with a couple of hundred grand would willingly choose as home. The entrance-way did nothing to dispel the impression. The faded wallpaper was peeling, streaked with grime, graffiti spattered here and there. A well brought up woman wouldn't have enjoyed the words.

Rogers glanced at the tenant board beside the entrance door, found the apartment. He didn't ring for entrance, how-ever, since the door was open, which surprised him, given the current obsession with security. Inside the small lobby was an elevator. He rode it to the fifth floor.

Beside the apartment door there was a bowl of water and a hand towel on a small table. The door was ajar; from inside he could hear the murmur of voices. He knocked. Nobody an-swered. He touched the door and it swung wider. He walked in. The first thing he noticed was a sheet hung over a mirror in the front hall. He passed it, and entered the living room, a small space with too much overstuffed furniture, too many old mahog-any tables, several hard chairs. There were a couple of pictures on the wall, pretty fair reproductions of Old Masters, the kind you could pick up anywhere for twenty-five or thirty bucks. Against a wall there was a small table covered with a cloth, holding a meager assortment of cold cuts, pastries, pots of coffee and tea, bottles of soda. Not a rich man's spread, any more than this was a rich man's abode.

There were half a dozen people in the room, all middle-aged and older. Some sat on the chairs, some gathered around a woman in a black dress sitting on a low stool. She was in her sixties. In normal circumstances she would have been a handsome woman—neat white hair, strong face, tall, slim. Taller and slimmer than her husband. Now her face was raddled, streaked with tears, her expression one of shock. A woman was talking to her, softly. She was not responding, she seemed hardly to hear.

Rogers stood near the entrance, watching, thinking this was one of the lousy parts of his job, questioning a widow after her husband had blown his brains out. It had to be done, but he didn't like it; he had never liked it, had avoided it whenever he could. He took a deep breath and crossed to her.

"Mrs. Rosenblatt," he said.

She didn't look up.

"Sophie," one of the women beside her said.

She looked up then, her eyes unseeing, the pupils dilated. Slowly she began to focus.

"Mrs. Rosenblatt," he said again.

She shook her head. "Yes," she said. "I don't know you. Are you a friend of Werner's? From the bank? Nobody from the bank has come. They sent flowers, but nobody's come."

"I met him once. The other day."

"Then how nice of you to come."

"My name's Rogers. I'm not from the bank. I'm a police lieutenant."

"Oh my God," she said, and looked away.

"I'm sorry to intrude," he said. "This must be very hard for you. But I'd like to talk to you."

"Can't you people leave her alone?" one of the women next to her said. "Of all the nerve. At a time like this."

"I'm sorry," Rogers said. "It can't be helped."

"Why don't you just go away," the woman said.

"It's all right, Gert," Mrs. Rosenblatt said. "He has to do his duty." She looked back at Rogers. "You want to ask me some more questions? I've already answered so many."

He nodded. "Could we go into another room?"

"There's just the bedroom, and Werner's study," she said.

"The study would be fine."

She rose from the stool slowly, with difficulty. She had been sitting in one position for a long time, and her muscles, no longer supple, were stiff. He reached out a hand to help her, but she waved it away. She straightened, stood for a moment collecting herself. There was a natural dignity about her, even now.

She led the way into a short hall and from there into a small

room with too much furniture. There was a fireplace in one wall
with ashes still in the grate. Not a rich man's sanctuary, Rogers
thought.

Mrs. Rosenblatt sat on the sofa and looked up at him. "What
do you want? I told the other officers everything I knew." She
waited.

He sat in the desk chair, swiveled to face her. "Did your
husband mention my name to you?" he asked.

She shook her head. "No. Should he have?"

"He wrote to the new mayor. Mr. Morrison. I met him to
ask about it."

"He wrote to the mayor? I didn't know."

"He said he had important information."

"He said nothing to me. I don't understand."

"We were supposed to meet again. He was going to turn
some papers, some documents over to me."

"All his papers, everything. They were burned. Nothing
was saved. Everything in his desk, everything in the file cabinet. Everything. It must have taken all evening. From the time
I left until . . ." She looked toward the fireplace, her face crumbling. She gave a little gasp, held it back, tried to compose
herself.

"Did he talk to you about the trouble he was in?"

"Just a little," she said. "Not very much. Werner was a
very private man. He kept things to himself. He didn't want to
worry me. We were married for forty years. In all that time, he
never brought his worries home. When things were bad—and I
could always sense it—he would tell me not to worry my head,
everything would work out all right in the end. Did you ever
hear of someone called Coué? Every day in every way we get
better and better? Werner believed that. He really did. Oh,
God, I can't understand it. No matter what was wrong, everything would have worked out. He never hurt anyone. He never
did a bad thing in his life. He was a good man. He worked hard
all his life. He never made much money, but we never wanted.
We didn't have all the luxuries, we never traveled, did the things
other people do, but we had enough." She began to cry. Then
after a moment, she took a breath, wiped her eyes with the back
of her hand. "I'm sorry," she said.

"Mrs. Rosenblatt," he said, trying to be gentle, "you knew
your husband was about to be indicted."

"Yes. He told me. He said not to worry. He said it was all a mistake. He said he explained everything to his lawyer, Morton Solomon, and Morton said not to worry."

"You knew the bank fired him."

"Yes. He said the bank examiners found that money was missing, and they traced it to his department. They had to blame someone and they chose him, because some of it was from his accounts. He said they'd find out somebody else had been doing it. Morton was looking into it, and Morton's a good lawyer."

"You knew he had a very large bank account outside the country?"

"How could he? He'd never even been outside the country. He certainly didn't have any money. We couldn't even go to Israel, which was something he wanted to do more than anything. But we could never save enough. Every time we managed to put something away, there was always an emergency. The children got sick and there were doctors. The children's college. One time we almost had enough and then I had to have an operation. We never had enough."

"But he deposited over two hundred thousand dollars into that account."

"Where would he ever get that kind of money? Every penny he earned went for the rent, went to put food on our table and to get a few clothes. That and the emergencies. There was never anything left over."

Rogers said nothing.

She looked away. She looked back, anger in her face, reading his silence as an accusation. "You think he stole it? That's what you all think. It's not true."

He asked, "Did he ever mention Mr. Donatello to you?"

"Of course. Mr. Donatello is head of the bank."

"He had nothing against Mr. Donatello, no reason to be angry at him and want to do him harm?"

"Of course not. Mr. Donatello was always very nice to him. He thought Mr. Donatello was very brilliant, a wonderful man. He was a little afraid of him, I know, because Mr. Donatello never tolerated mistakes, and Werner was always afraid he would make one. Everybody makes mistakes, he used to say, everybody but Mr. Donatello. But he would never do anything to hurt Mr. Donatello. He admired him too much and he owed him too much. After all, it was Mr. Donatello who recommended him for promotions and raises."

"It was Mr. Donatello who went to the police."

"I didn't know. Werner never said anything about that. He just said it was somebody in the bank. And that they had to go to the police. If Mr. Donatello did that, it was only natural, it was something he had to do. But I'm sure Mr. Donatello never for a moment thought Werner did anything wrong."

"Did he have a lot of insurance?"

"Less than fifty thousand dollars," she said. "And we have almost nothing in the bank, I don't care what they say about all that money. We didn't have it. I don't know how I'm going to live. I don't know what I'm going to do. . . ."

"Your children . . ."

"They live far away, too far even to get here in time for the funeral. I wouldn't impose myself on them. They have enough trouble of their own. They have children. They're just beginning."

"Mrs. Rosenblatt, I have to ask you: Why do you think your husband killed himself?"

She stared at him, her eyes reddening. She shook herself. "I told the other officers. He didn't. He couldn't have. He had no reason to. Whatever trouble he was in, he would have faced it, we would have faced it together. Besides, where would he have gotten a gun? He was afraid of guns. He never fired one in all his life. He thought there ought to be laws against guns."

He hadn't expected that. He leaned forward. "Mrs. Rosenblatt, if he didn't kill himself, who killed him?"

"I don't know. Somebody. I don't know."

"Why should somebody murder your husband?"

"I don't know. I wish I did."

"Mrs. Rosenblatt, the apartment was locked. There was no sign that anybody had tampered with the locks, that anybody else had been in the apartment."

"I know," she said. "But there's no security here. People come and go. Anybody could have gotten in. And if somebody rang the bell, Werner would have answered without thinking. He always did. I used to warn him that he was asking for trouble, but it was just such a habit. In the old days, it was safe. He couldn't imagine that things had changed that much."

"When I met him, he was very frightened. He thought people were after him."

She sat up straighter, staring directly at him. "He was right then, wasn't he?"

All the way back down the West Side Highway to lower Manhattan, Rogers ran through his conversation with Mrs. Rosenblatt, going over and over his time spent with her in her home, examining not just the words but his impressions, the things he had noticed. Denial is an essential element in grief. He had seen it often enough. Especially in suicides. The widow or widower or children always look for another explanation—accident, murder, anything else.

Maybe the widow was incredibly naive, and neither asked nor knew anything about her husband's life away from their apartment, which was possible. Or maybe she was an accomplished prevaricator, hiding her knowledge behind that wall of innocence and ignorance—also a possibility. Or maybe, just maybe, she was telling the truth, to the best of her knowledge, which was also possible.

He didn't believe it, though. Everything pointed to suicide. Still, it was confusing—too many things that just didn't fit, too many holes. He had been about ready to call Morrison and tell him there was nothing to back up Rosenblatt's letter. Now he decided to wait awhile, to try to make sense of the pieces. Morrison still had time. At the very least, he would have to talk to Rosenblatt's lawyer, Morton Solomon. Morrison could wait. And in the meantime Rogers could concentrate on the Palmieri question.

15

Just as Toby had been Felix's pigeon, Sully belonged to Rogers. If you saw Sully in a crowd, you wouldn't see him. It wasn't that he was invisible; it was just that he was so nondescript that the eye passed over him without notice. It was a gift, and he made the most of it. He heard and saw things nobody else did, that nobody wanted anybody else to see or hear, and still nobody realized that he was there.

Sully had a passion for Chinese food, especially Szechuan. He had a cast-iron stomach, and whatever spices the chefs put in it agreed with him, even the hot red peppers that everyone else shoved to the side. Rogers located him in a little place just off Pell Street, across from Chatham Square, the hub of Chinatown, plying chopsticks over a heaping dish of something that Rogers couldn't begin to identify. When Sully was eating, Sully didn't like to be bothered, not even by Rogers. And it was to Rogers that he owed his freedom from the slammer, a place, so he had confided long ago, that didn't fit into his life-style. He'd tried it once, he said, and figured never again. He'd do just about anything to stay on the loose, give Rogers just about anything he asked, just so long as nobody found out about it. But don't come around while he was eating Chinese, and especially when the Chinese was Szechuan.

So Rogers walked outside, wandering down the street, studying the naked ducks that seemed to hang in every window. He stopped in front of one of those storefront stands that sell everything from watches, transistor radios, electronics of every kind to stenciled sweatshirts, all carrying famous labels.

"You interested in a good watch?" the young Chinese guy guarding the wares asked. "We got Rolex, we got Concord, we got Movado, we got Omega, we got Cartier, we got sport watches, you name, we got. Cheap. Cheap. Five, ten, fifteen, twenty, twenty-five, what you want to pay?"

Rogers picked up one as though he were going to buy. He examined it. "The real thing?" he said.

"Sure. Real from Hong Kong. Got real from Taiwan, too. What you want?" The merchant laughed loudly.

Out of the corner of his eye, Rogers saw Sully leaving the Dim Sum palace. He put the watch down, turned, and started after him. "Another time," he called back. He followed Sully for a couple of blocks through Chinatown, caught up with him, tapped him on the shoulder.

Sully turned and looked. His head swiveled, trying to see if anyone was watching. "Not here, Mr. Rogers," he whispered. "For chrissake, not here."

"Down by the river," Rogers said. "Under the bridge. The usual."

Sully moved fast, disappeared around a corner. Rogers took his time, strolling north through the crowd, toward the Manhattan Bridge. Sully was waiting for him in the shadows of the decaying graffiti-splattered superstructure. Standing there, you could smell the aroma drifting from the Fulton Fish Market a few blocks away.

"How's it going, Sully?" Rogers said.

"Fine. Just fine. Everythin's jake."

"What'd you hear?"

"This an' that. Depends."

"On what?"

"On what you're lookin' for."

"What I'm looking for," Rogers said slowly, "is what you hear about who wasted an Arab."

Sully looked at him, shook his head. "I ain't heard nothin' like that. Not around here. You lookin' for Israelis, maybe, like what they do over there?"

"Not there, here. Not Israelis. Family."

"Like that?"

"Like that. Nose around, Sully. Get back."

"That's a big favor, Mr. Rogers. I could get killed."

"You owe me, Sully."

"Yeah, I know. I owe you big. But I like to breathe the air."

"It's important. I wouldn't ask if it wasn't."

Sully sighed. He looked at Rogers with a plea. "Life and death, hunh?"

"You could say so."

"I'll see what I can do, Mr. Rogers, only, you'll see they bury me proper, okay?"

16

It was a crisp November day, sun brilliant, almost blinding. He decided to walk when he came out of the apartment. He didn't pay any attention to the car moving by him until it pulled up to the curb and the door opened out onto the sidewalk, blocking his way. He stopped, looked into the car. A young guy, mid-twenties, black hair slicked back, nicely tailored, expensive suit, a little flashy, was leaning out toward him. "You Ben Rogers?" he asked.

"That's me. So what?"

"Mr. Ruggieri would like to have a word with you."

"Not interested," he said.

"Mr. Ruggieri insists," the guy said, polite, but with an order behind the politeness.

"When I get time, I'll drop by. I know where he hangs out."

"Mr. Ruggieri is a very impatient man, Mr. Rogers. He would like to see you now. He insists. Please get in and we'll drive you. It isn't far. It will only take a few minutes. He would just like a word."

Rogers looked at the man. His right hand was playing around the lapel of his expensive suit. Rogers shrugged. There didn't seem any reason for an argument. "Whatever you say."

The rear door of the car swung open. Another guy on the rear seat shifted toward the middle to make room. Rogers examined him quickly, pausing for just a second before deciding to go along.

The car worked its way through traffic, heading south and east. They stopped in front of a small building just off Mulberry Street a couple of blocks from where the city split into Chinatown to the east and Little Italy to the west. The sign on the door read:

Parnassus Associates
Real Estate

In small letters down at the bottom of the frosted glass, there was a notation: "Checks cashed."

The guy in the expensive suit opened the door and motioned for Rogers to follow him up a flight of stairs. At the top of the stairs was another door with a frosted glass top. Again: "Parnassus Associates—Real Estate." The young guy stepped in front of him, pushed a button. A buzz sounded dimly somewhere inside. A voice came through a concealed speaker. "Who's there?"

"Gino. With the package for Mr. Ruggieri."

A click and the door swung open. Rogers entered an outer office, a room divided by a wooden rail fence, a swinging gate in the center. There were several chairs along the walls, upholstered in red plastic to look like leather, low tables in the center on which the latest magazines were neatly arrayed. Inside the gate a young, dyed-blond secretary, pretty beneath too much makeup, sat behind a receptionist's desk. She looked up. "I'll tell him you're here," she said, Brooklyn in her voice. She pressed a button on the intercom, waited, said, "Gino's here. Yes, someone's with him." She looked at Rogers. "You can go in." She motioned toward a thick mahogany-paneled door in the wall to one side. He went through the gate and started toward it. There was another click and the door swung slightly ajar. The young guy hung back. Rogers walked inside, alone.

The inner office was vast and lavishly decorated with a large plush velvet sofa, a low walnut cabinet, a coffee table of Carrara marble surrounded by low chairs covered with a tweed fabric, a small cabinet with an espresso machine on top of it, a tray of demitasse cups and a bottle of Sambuca Romana nearby.

On the walls hung paintings, modern abstract swirls. They looked like the real thing. Either Ruggieri had taste or an accomplished decorator.

Toward the center of the room was a large walnut desk. Behind it sat Generoso Ruggieri. The desk fit him. He was a big man, taller than Rogers by a couple of inches. And bulkier, not with fat, but muscle. He could have been wearing shoulder pads beneath the expertly tailored jacket. He wasn't. The face, with the large nose, bushy eyebrows, and thin lips, looked magisterial, dominating. His hair was jet black, neatly combed. If it was dyed, it was so expertly done that no one but his hairdresser would know for sure. He was, so they said, in his seventies maybe older. He could have been forty.

He let Rogers stand in the middle of the room for a moment, studying him carefully. Then he gestured toward a large chair set in front of the desk. "Sit down," he said, his voice betraying a faint trace of a Sicilian accent.

Rogers sat. "You wanted to see me? You sent your boys to fetch me."

"Yes," Ruggieri said. "I told them to invite you, to ask nicely, to be polite." Rogers wondered if at some time he'd had somebody teach him to speak well.

"They were."

"I hear nice things about you. They say you're an honest cop. Which is unusual. I should know."

"I suppose you should," Rogers agreed.

"I like an honest cop," Ruggieri said. "A honest cop is good for business. He keeps the city safe, and right now the city isn't safe for anybody. You can't turn around without some punk not dry behind the ears yet sticks a gun in your back. Guys think they can get away with anything, rob you blind, and nothing is going to happen. Junkies, hopheads on every corner, dealing right out in the open and nobody does a thing, everybody looks the other way. People pissin' in their pants they're so scared. It was better in the old days, safer. Nobody free-lanced. People took care of each other, looked after their own business. You'd like some coffee?"

"No," Rogers said.

"It isn't poisoned." Ruggieri laughed.

"It's not that," Rogers said. "I can't drink it. It gives me *agita*, you know, heartburn."

"You mind if I have a cup?" He pressed a button on his desk. "Isabella," he said, "the coffee." He waited. In a moment, the door opened. The girl from the front desk entered. She went to the espresso machine, filled a demitasse about half full. She looked at Ruggieri. "Just one," he said. "It upsets the stomach of my guest." She carried the cup and the bottle of Sambuco across the room and set it on the desk in front of Ruggieri. "Good girl," Ruggieri said. She turned and went back through the door, closing it behind her. Ruggieri uncorked the bottle, poured some into the cup, mixing it with a small spoon, adding a snippet of lemon peel. He looked at Rogers. "Sure you won't have some? Good stuff. Imported straight from the old country. You know what they say, you got the money, go out and buy, you got no money, sit home and cry."

Rogers shook his head. Ruggieri took a sip of the coffee, making a slurping sound. Rogers watched him, waiting. Ruggieri continued to sip, studying Rogers over the edge of the cup.

"You wanted to see me," Rogers said finally. "I'm sure it wasn't to give me a civics lecture."

"Forgive an old man," Ruggieri said. "I like to talk, I like to remember how it used to be."

Sure, Rogers thought, the way it used to be. Ruggieri could put on this show, act the part of the old patriarch enjoying the good things of life, a gentleman enjoying the fruits of his labor. But it was all show, all an affectation, and if you looked close enough you could see it in his eyes. This man hadn't risen to the top, to the preeminent place in his world, through good manners. He'd gotten there over a procession of bodies that probably stretched from Little Italy to the wilds of Brooklyn and beyond. In his world, he was the object not just of veneration, but perhaps more of fear. The word was, you crossed Ruggieri you'd better have made the down payment on the cemetery plot, that is, if they ever found enough of you to bury.

Ruggieri shook his head. "You've been asking questions."

"I always ask questions. That's my job."

"Your job is bad cops."

"Only part of my job."

"Stick to that part. That way, you don't stick your nose where it don't belong, you don't get hurt. That way, you need some help, you get some help. That way, everybody's happy."

"Just where am I sticking my nose?"

"In business that don't concern you."

"What happens if I keep sticking my nose in?"

Ruggieri looked at him sadly, shook his head. "I like you," he said. "I would be most sorry if anything should happen to you."

"No sale," Rogers said. "A friend of mine got killed. A goomba. I'm the godfather of his son. That's something you should understand."

"I heard. I understand. They tell me he was a good man, he was honest. It was a great misfortune what happened to him. When a friend gets hurt, we must do something. It is part of our blood. I understand that. But . . ." He spread his hands. He sighed. He looked at Rogers. He looked down at his watch. "Now," he said. "I have a lot to do. If you will excuse me."

Rogers slowly rose from the chair. "I'll bear it mind," he said.

"It would be wise if you do," Ruggieri said. Then, suddenly, he said, "Your grandmother? She is well?"

Rogers stared. "What?"

"Your grandmother. I knew her long ago. She was a beautiful lady. I have not seen her in many years. She is still well?"

"Yes," Rogers said. "She's fine."

"When you see her, tell her we met and give her my respects."

"I will." He turned. The door clicked open. The receptionist was still behind the desk. Gino was sitting stiffly in a chair against the wall. Several young men, clones of Gino, sat in other chairs. Nobody looked at him as he opened the door and went down the stairs and onto the street.

For a moment, he stood on the sidewalk in the bright sun without moving. He looked back at the building. What the hell, he wondered, was that all about?

17

A half-dozen stretch limos graced the curb in front of One Police Plaza. As he moved by them, he noted crosses and stars of David affixed to the license plates. Visitors at one of the department's briefings, probably. He went inside, flashed his shield to the guard standing sentry at the opening marked "Police Personnel Only," and passed through into the lobby. A dozen or so visitors mingled around the bulletproof glass of the information booth. Cops in uniform, some in plainclothes, wandered about. A couple glanced at him without recognition. A few did recognize him, and their expressions changed. Up on the balcony that ringed the lobby, a crowd of brass in their uniforms mingled with a crowd of civilians, some with clerical collars, some with yarmulkes. The meeting was breaking up, the clergy briefed on what the department was planning to do to make sure the upcoming holidays passed without incident, or as few incidents as possible.

He was crossing toward the elevators when a voice stopped him. "Ben Rogers." He looked around. Chief Dolan was just coming down the stairs with a priest, a short, spare, middle-aged man with an ascetic face, a fringe of graying hair circling his balding scalp. He looked like a Jesuit. Rogers turned and walked toward the chief. "What brings you around here?" Dolan asked.

"My girl," Rogers said. Dolan looked at him. "She works upstairs, in personnel," Rogers explained. "Civilian. Part-time. When she's not acting."

Dolan turned to the priest. "Dennis," he said, "have you met Ben Rogers?"

"I don't believe so," the priest said.

"Ben is one of our best people. The finest of the finest." Dolan grinned. "Ben, meet Bishop Molloy, from the power-house." Molloy reached out a hand and Rogers took it. Dolan looked back at Rogers. "How's the job going?"

"Progress comes slowly," Rogers said.

Dolan smiled. "Ninety-nine percent perspiration and one percent inspiration, right?" He laughed. "Ben," he said to Molloy, "is on special assignment with the new mayor." He looked at Rogers. "Morrison never did tell us what it was all about. Just that he wanted you."

"We worked together that year I was down in Washington," Rogers said. "We got along well which, I guess, is why he wanted me for this thing."

"Which is?" Dolan said.

"Just looking into some of the people he wants to appoint, you know, background stuff. Not much. It shouldn't take too long."

"Let's hope not," Dolan said. "We want you back. Well, I won't keep you. Go find that young lady of yours. And, for God's sake, finish that job. If you need any help, just give a holler." He gave a wave and started away, then stopped and looked back. "Have you seen Mary?"

Rogers nodded. "We dropped by a week ago."

"How is she getting along?"

Rogers shrugged. "She looks terrible," he said. "Who can blame her?"

"I've been meaning to stop by myself," Dolan said. "As soon as I have time. Damn shame, the whole thing. But we'll get the guy." He turned then and walked off with Molloy.

Rogers stared at their retreating backs for a moment, wondering if he ought to talk to Dolan in private, fill him in on what he'd learned about Felix's murder. Not just yet, he decided. Like Felix, he liked to put things in a nice package before untying the strings. He turned away and started for the elevators.

He had intended to take Melissa to dinner, but she wasn't interested. She said she had no appetite, that there was no way she could get food down. Not just before an opening. Later, maybe. All she wanted to do was go home and take a nap before she had to get to the theater.

They went home. Melissa stretched out on the bed and closed her eyes. Rogers changed into his running clothes and went out into the cold November evening. He headed for the river and ran his usual five miles, down toward the World Trade Center and back north. All the way, he had a sense that somebody was watching, following. He kept looking around, but he saw only the usual runners. It must be just a feeling. He dismissed it.

Melissa was gone when he retuned to the apartment. He showered, dressed, and headed for the small one-time garage on Jane Street that now housed an off-off-Broadway theater.

Melissa was good. She was very good. He'd seen her perform twice before, once before he knew her, once after he'd just met her, and both times she had vanished into the character she was playing so that he always had trouble putting the real Melissa together with the person onstage. If you wanted to be any good, she told him, that's what you had to do, become the character, forget about yourself.

He thought she was the best thing on that stage, but then he knew he was biased. Still, there were plenty of others in the audience that night who seemed to share his opinion, even though, this being opening night, most of them were friends or relatives of the other actors. She got laughs in all the expected places, and in a few not so expected, as she threw in a few twists of her own.

When the lights went down, and then came up again for the curtain calls, she got the loudest and most sustained applause. He could tell that she was pleased, not only with the response, but with the sense that she had accomplished at least part of what she wanted. He drifted outside with the audience, then went down an alley to the stage door. He waited just inside.

This wasn't his turf and it made him uncomfortable. People wandered in through the stage door from outside, ignored him, sought out actors, hugged, kissed, squealed inordinate praises.

After about ten minutes, Melissa emerged carrying her coat. She spotted him, waved, and started toward him. A woman of about forty in a fashionable dress, not the jeans and T-shirts that everyone else seemed to favor, intercepted her. They talked for a couple of minutes, Melissa nodding, smiling a little. The woman reached into her purse, pulled out a card, handed it to her, and then turned and walked away, straight for the exit, passing Rogers as though he were invisible.

"You've got a fan," he said when Melissa reached him. She grinned. "Besides me, I mean. Who was the dame in the expensive clothes?"

She laughed. "I've been discovered. An agent," she said. "You know, they come to see everything, hoping they'll find the new Meryl Streep or somebody."

"She found you. It's about time."

"Well, she wants me to come to her office tomorrow."

"Nice," he said.

"We'll see," she said. "But don't hold your breath."

"Home?"

"No," she said. "Not yet. Everybody's going to the Lion's Head. You know, to kind of celebrate. Or commiserate. Whichever."

He started to shake his head. "You go. It's not my kind of thing."

She took his arm. "No way. You're not getting out of this. You belong with me. Besides, everybody's bringing somebody. You wouldn't want me to go all alone."

They wandered slowly through the Village, Melissa still keyed up from her performance. By the time they reached the bar, the rest of the cast had filled the tables at the rear, crowded in with all the friends and relatives and hangers-on. There was a lot of food, and even more beer and wine. It was after two in the morning, and nobody was feeling any pain, when they finally left.

The sharp, cold air hit them and made them feel giddy. They laughed as they held each other for support and tried to walk a straight line along the nearly deserted streets.

They were just turning the corner into their block, crossing the street. It was late enough and the city quiet enough so Rogers expected nothing. If he hadn't drunk so much, perhaps his senses would have been sharper, perhaps he would have been more alert. But he had drunk too much, and he was relaxed, and he was enjoying himself, and enjoying Melissa.

Then he heard it, the sound of a car suddenly accelerating. He turned. The car screeched around the corner, its lights out. Then the lights flashed on, catching them in the high beam, freezing them for a moment. The car bore down on them. Rogers reacted, shoving Melissa as hard as he could toward the sidewalk, spinning away after her. As the car raced by, its fender clipped him, sending him spinning toward the ground. He felt himself falling, hitting the pavement. The car kept going, reached the end of the block, and started to turn. As it braked, he caught part of the license number in the glow of its lights. Then it disappeared.

He rose slowly. Already he could feel a bruise spreading on his thigh. Otherwise, he was sure he was all right. Melissa was just rising from the sidewalk; stunned and disoriented. "They tried to run us down," she said. "They didn't stop. They were trying to hit us."

"Yeah," he said as he slid his arms around her. "Probably a drunk."

"That was no drunk," she said.

He shrugged.

"Why?"

He didn't answer. "Are you all right?"

"I'm fine," she said. "You?"

"Okay," he said. "Nothing mortal."

"Why?" she said again.

"I don't know," he said. "Could be a thousand reasons."

"But, to try to kill us . . ."

"Yeah," he said. "It seemed like they were trying to do that."

18

They both slept late. But for Rogers, it was a troubled sleep. His night was filled with dreams. He kept seeing Andy Manning, a fourteen-year-old black kid he'd busted when he was just beginning on the force. Andy had been breaking into cars when Rogers had picked him up. Andy was smart and seemed like a nice kid, so Rogers let him off with a lecture. He thought he could help the kid turn his life around. He took him home, gave him a bed for a while, fed him, made him go back to school. It looked like Andy was straightening out. And then, late one night, on a stakeout, Rogers saw Andy get behind the wheel of a car thieves were using to haul away the goods. Rogers stepped out to stop him. Andy drove the car straight at him, trying to run him over. Rogers shot, the slug catching Andy in the shoulder, turning the car so it only sideswiped him. All night he dreamed about Andy, about speeding cars, screeching brakes, angry faces behind wheels.

When he finally woke, he found that the bruises on his leg had spread from hip to knee and had turned bluish black. They were painful enough so he couldn't put weight on the leg when he got out of bed.

Melissa watched him with concern. "You'd better see a doctor."

"It's not serious," he said. "Just sore. I won't be running for a week or so, that's all."

"See a doctor anyway."

He looked at her. She had bruises along her back and side. "How about you?"

"Nothing," she said. "Just from where some guy knocked me to the sidewalk. I've had worse skiing. I hardly feel them." She studied him. "Are you going to report it?"

"Maybe," he said.

"No maybes," she said. "They tried to kill you."

She was frightened. He tried to calm her, to ease that fear. "Maybe it was just an accident. Some drunk going too fast."

"Sure," she said. "With his lights out and then on, speeding up when he saw us. Some accident."

She kept at him all morning, growing more concerned each time she saw the spasm that twisted his face whenever he put weight on the leg. When it was time for her to leave to see the agent from last night, she practically ordered him to call the doctor, and to call someone downtown and report what had happened. He didn't promise.

When Melissa was gone, he limped over to the phone and placed a call. Not the one she wanted him to make. When the voice answered, he said, "Harry, do me a favor."

"Yeah, Ben. What?"

"Run a make for me."

"What'd your last slave die of?"

"No shit. Just do it. Dark-colored sedan, late model, maybe a Ford, maybe something else." He recited the partial plate numbers that had embedded themselves in his mind. "The last two I'm not sure of. It was dark and the guy was going fast. They were either threes or eights, like, you know, three-eight, three-three, eight-three, eight-eight. Got it? Call me at home. I'll be here."

"What the hell did he do?"

"I'll tell you sometime. Now, just do me the favor."

An hour later, Harry called back. "Got it." he said. "You got a three-eight that's a blue eighty-nine Honda, belongs to a Guy Borger, lives in Binghamton. You got a three-three that's a white eight-four Cougar, belongs to a Carol Winston, lives in

Levittown. Only thing is, the heap's impounded, towed away three weeks ago for illegal parking, ain't been claimed yet. You got a eight-three that's a black eighty-seven Ford, registered to a Frank Vernon, lives in Au Sable Fork, which they tell me is up in the Adirondacks. The last one, the eight-eight. I don't know what you're looking for, but you picked a winner. It's a pool car. Out of Manhattan Central Garage. You know, an available vehicle."

"What color?"

"Dark blue."

"Thanks, Harry. I'll do you one sometime."

"Sure. I'll put it in the book."

He stared at the phone for a few minutes, trying to figure which lead to pursue. Then he dialed police headquarters in Binghamton, New York, identified himself, asked about Guy Borger. The cop said he'd check and get back. Next he called Au Sable Fork. They knew Frank Vernon. He was caretaker at one of those hunting lodges in the woods. Nice guy, they said. Around fifty. Drinks too much, but who could blame him?—he has a lonely life except when the owners show up, the owners being some rich guys from the city. Was he around? Probably, he never goes anywhere. Anybody seen him recently? Nobody had been looking. Did New York want Au Sable Fork to check? Not just yet.

Binghamton called back. Guy Borger was a seventy-nine-year-old retired businessman living with his wife in Florida for the winter. Borger had hired one of those services to drive his car down so he'd have it in the south. When? The Borgers had left Binghamton in mid-October. The car left the day before they did.

Rogers hobbled over to the closet, struggled into his coat, and limped out the door and down to the street. It took him a while, and a lot of pain, to travel even to the corner. The hell with the subway. He took a cab. At Manhattan Central Garage, he flashed his shield at a bored clerk. The clerk checked the book. Nobody had checked out eight-eight in more than a week. It was gathering dust somewhere back in the garage. Rogers found it near the end of a row. It didn't have any dust on it. It had a dent in the front fender, but then, it had a lot of dents. The fender dent didn't look new, but you couldn't tell.

Rogers went to the clerk. The clerk was certain nobody had

taken out eight-eight the night before. Rogers insisted he check the books. He checked the books. He showed Rogers the list of cars that had been checked out the night before, the day before, all the previous week. A lot of them had gone in and out, but the eight-eight wasn't one of them.

"Can somebody come in here and drive away with one of these things without checking it out?" Rogers asked.

"No way, man," the clerk said. "They got to come right by here. They got to show us authorization, signed and stamped. They got to sign it out. They got to sign it in. No way a guy can just drive away without nobody knowing about it."

Rogers limped back into the garage, back to eight-eight. He limped around it, studying the car from every angle. He bent down and examined the rear plate. The screws that held it in place were shiny. There were some fresh metal splinters around the heads.

Melissa flung the door open as he was fumbling for his keys. She glared at him. "Where the hell have you been?"

"Whoa," he said.

"Have you been to the doctor? Like hell. Did you report what happened to us? Like hell. Just where were you?"

"Poking around a little," he said, limping by her into the apartment.

She followed, stood over him as he eased himself into a chair. "I made an appointment for you," she said. "For today." He started. "Not the police surgeon. My own doctor. He'll see you at six. Don't argue."

"Let's make love," he said.

"Later," she said. "Let's go to the doctor now."

He sighed. There was no sense arguing when she was like that. "Okay. Then we'll make love."

"We'll see," she said.

"No promises?"

"No promises. I also reported what happened."

"You did what?"

"When I finished, I went downtown to see your friend and I told him."

"What friend?"

"Chief Dolan. He wants you to call him as soon as you can. He tried to call you. There's a message on the machine."

He looked toward the machine, paused. "What happened with your appointment? What did the lady say?"

"She said I was good. She said I had a future. She said she'd like to send me up for things. I'll tell you more later. Now listen to the damn machine."

He did as commanded. Dolan's voice was peremptory, demanding. He sighed and picked up the phone and dialed Dolan's direct line. Dolan was away from the office, but he had left a message for Rogers. Dolan wanted to see him at ten the next morning.

Melissa's doctor looked at the X ray he had made of Rogers's leg. "Nothing broken," he said. "A bad bruise, all the way to the bone. It's going to hurt like hell for a while. What hit you? I'd say a car."

"You'd say right," Rogers said.

"Hit-and-run?"

"Hit-and-run."

"Ice it," he said. "Then, in a few days you can use heat. Stay off it as much as you can. Melissa tells me you're a runner. Don't try—not that you'll be able. Wait until there's no more pain or soreness, and then wait another week." He rummaged around in a cabinet, took a handful of sample packets and passed them to Rogers. "If you have pain, and you will, take two of these. I shouldn't need to see you again, at least not professionally." He escorted Rogers to the examining room door. They shook hands. "Melissa," the doctor said, "is a nice girl."

"She is, indeed."

"I hope you're treating her right."

Dolan kept him waiting fifteen minutes, a shorter time than usual. Dolan was a busy man, of course, but Rogers knew that one of his little power plays was to keep underlings cooling their heels outside his office.

Once inside, Rogers sat and waited for Dolan to speak. The chief leaned back, hands behind his head. He stared at Rogers, studying his face. "All right, Rogers," he said. "What the fuck is going on?" Not Ben this time.

Rogers put on an innocent face. "I don't know what you mean."

"Bullshit. Yesterday, your girl comes marching into this office and tells me some cock-and-bull story that someone's trying to kill you. She says you both got knocked down by a hit-and-run and it was deliberate."

"No. Probably an accident. It was around three in the morning and the guy must have been drunk and he didn't see us."

"Not what she says."

"Well, she was shook up, scared. You can't blame her."

"She didn't strike me as the kind that sees snowflakes in July."

"She's not. But it was late and we'd had a little too much, you know. She'd just opened in a play and we were celebrating. It was dark and it happened fast, and she knows what I do, so maybe, given everything, she thought somebody had it in for me."

"Who?"

"If I started to name them it would take the rest of the day. IAD doesn't exactly win any popularity contests."

"You didn't report it."

He put on an innocent face. He knew he ought to lay it out for the chief. Dolan was somebody he could trust, would probably offer help. But Dolan had a lot on his plate as it was. There was no sense bothering him with hunches; Rogers would rather wait until he knew something. So he said, "Report what? I didn't make the car, I didn't make the plate, I didn't get a look at the driver, whether it was a guy or a dame. What have I got? Nothing. So, what's to report? A file and forget? Waste somebody's time, that's all."

Dolan looked at him carefully. "You were hurt," he said. "She said you got banged up, and you came limping in here like a hobbled horse. You see the police surgeon?"

"No," Rogers said. "I went to a private. Melissa's family doctor."

"See the police surgeon," Dolan ordered.

"No need."

"See him anyway. Now, what's with that thing for Morrison?"

Rogers shrugged. "It's coming. Slow. It takes time." He paused, considered, thought, what the hell, open it up. "Besides," he said, "I've been doing a few other things."

Dolan stared at him. "What things?"

"Felix's things. What he left behind."

"What the fuck have we got Homicide for? Leave it to them."

"I figured I owed Felix one. There were things Homicide didn't know."

"Like what?"

Rogers laid it out—the nurse and the Arab.

"Give it to Homicide," Dolan ordered. "It's their thing, not yours."

"I gave them the nurse," Rogers said.

"Give them the other one. You lay off. You do what you're supposed to. Finish that. They'll take care of the others. That's an order. Goddammit, Ben, you know how I feel about lone wolves, about free-lancers. That's the last thing we need around here. You work on your own, you could end up in an alley like Felix. For chrissake, I don't want to see anything happen to you."

19

There were three messages on the machine this time, all of them from Morrison, demanding that Rogers call immediately. He had left a private number.

A secretary answered Rogers's call. There was a pause after he gave his name, and then Morrison was on. No preliminaries. "What the hell is going on? Ten days and I haven't heard word one from you."

"I've been working on it," Rogers said. "I need a little more time."

"Bullshit. I've heard that one before."

"I mean it, Jack. It's not as simple as it looked."

"For chrissake, Ben, I'm under the gun. Donatello called this morning. He agreed to take the job if I still wanted him. Now just what the hell do I tell him? I want him, but not unless I'm absolutely certain."

"Can you stall him?"

"Not for long. I'm trying to put this thing together. I can't have a hole at the top."

"Just a little longer and I'll have something."

"Something wrong?"

"I'm not sure." He brought him up-to-date on Rosenblatt—

their meeting, the suicide, and the visit to the widow. "Maybe it doesn't mean a thing. Maybe there's something to it. I want to see the lawyer. He's been out of town. He'll be back at the beginning of the week. I'll get to him then."

"You think there may be something to it, then?"

"At first I didn't buy it. Now I want to look at it a little more. I just need a little more time."

"Not too much more. I need to know, and I can stall Donatello only so long."

Morton Solomon's office was on the forty-sixth floor of one of those glass-and-anodized aluminum buildings on what old-timers still called Sixth Avenue and everybody else knew as the Avenue of the Americas. A horizontal brass plate affixed to a heavy mahogany door read, Solomon, Schwartz, Malcolm, Snyder, Lawrence & White. Underneath were two vertical brass plates, each containing a list of a dozen lawyers. Apparently Solomon was senior partner of a very large firm.

When Rogers had called ahead, Solomon had agreed to make time to see him when he mentioned Rosenblatt. Now the receptionist pressed a button on the console on her desk, whispered his name. "Have a seat," she said, "Mr. Solomon will be with you in a moment."

After a few minutes of thumbing through the *Bar Association Journal*, Rogers was led down a long corridor to Solomon's corner office. Even the plush carpeting couldn't absorb the pain he still felt from his badly bruised leg.

The office was large. The view was spectacular. You could catch a glimpse of the Hudson to the west, looking clean and blue, and the misty Jersey shore beyond. The furnishings were of a size and cost to match the office and the view. It was a rich lawyer's chambers.

In his late sixties, Solomon was a little paunchy. He had flowing silver hair, a ruddy complexion, and a manner that announced he knew who he was and liked it. He was wearing expensive tailor-made clothes of an Italian cut. A week in the Caribbean sun had obviously done Solomon some good. He had a deep tan and he looked rested. He looked like a rich man's lawyer.

"What can I do for you?" he said. He waved Rogers toward a brown leather chair set in front of the desk.

"You can tell me about Werner Rosenblatt," Rogers said.

"A dreadful thing," he said. "You knew him?"

"I met him once," Rogers said.

Solomon studied Rogers closely. "Police," he said. "It was a statement, not a question. "I understand you people have been at Mrs. Rosenblatt."

"Has she complained?"

"She never complains."

"I didn't think so. She seemed like a nice lady."

"A very nice lady," Solomon said. "A gentlewoman, in the best sense of the term." He paused, taking his time. "What are you looking for?"

"Information," Rogers said.

"Why? The man's dead. Case closed."

"You know it's still open," Rogers said. "There are still questions. I'm looking for answers."

"I'm afraid I can't help you."

"Look, Counselor," Rogers said, "as you said, the man's dead, which, to me, means attorney–client privilege doesn't wash."

"Who mentioned that? It's merely that I know nothing that you people don't already know. Or should know."

Rogers took his time. He looked slowly around the office, at the furniture, at the paintings on the wall, at the view, back at Solomon. "What are your fees, Counselor?"

Solomon laughed. "Too expensive for you, I'm afraid," he said.

"But not for Werner Rosenblatt."

"For Werner? Don't be ridiculous. That was strictly *pro bono*. Besides, I'm not a criminal lawyer. Werner and I were old friends. We grew up together. We both courted Sophie. Unfortunately for me at the time, he won out. But we remained friends. Whenever he needed advice, he came to me. So, naturally, when he found himself in trouble, he came to me."

"Naturally," Rogers said. "Only, for once, he could pay the going rate."

"Werner? The man never had a pot to piss in, if you'll excuse the profanity."

"I'd call a couple of hundred grand offshore a pretty big pot."

"That, my friend," Solomon said, "is arrant nonsense.

Werner Rosenblatt no more had an offshore bank account than you're the Prince of Wales."

"That's what he told you—and his wife."

"Yes, that's what he told me. And I believed him. Because I knew Werner Rosenblatt. Which you people obviously didn't."

"What else did he tell you?"

Solomon considered. He pushed a button on his desk. "Rose, bring in the Werner Rosenblatt file. Not the old ones. The latest." He leaned back in his chair. "I'm going to do this," he said, "because I think it important that, even after death, Werner's name and reputation be cleared. As you mentioned, there are unanswered questions. They probably should be answered. If he were alive, obviously this would be impossible. But since he is dead . . ." He waved a hand.

Two minutes later, the secretary appeared carrying a manila folder in her hand. She placed it in front of Solomon, turned and walked away. Reading upside down, Rogers made out the sticker across the front: State of New York v. Werner Rosenblatt. Solomon opened the folder, skimmed through the papers inside, yellow legal-sized pages covered with scrawl. He took his time. He closed it and looked back at Rogers.

"I wanted to refresh my memory," he said. Over the next fifteen minutes, he referred frequently to the notes. "Werner called me about this on October 23. He said he had to see me as soon as possible, it was urgent. I told him my calendar was full, and then I was going away for vacation, so the first opening I had was the second week of November. He said that wouldn't do. He had to see me right away. I knew from his voice that he was very upset, so I told him to come in at the end of the day and I'd make room for him after my last appointment.

"I don't know what time he arrived, but when I was through with my conference, it was about eight and he was waiting in the reception room. I don't think there was anybody else in the office then; even the associates had wrapped it up for the day. We went back to my office and I asked him what his problem was. He told me he'd just lost his job."

"Were you surprised?" Rogers asked.

Solomon shrugged. "Not particularly, at least not initially. I just assumed that he'd been retired. You'd have to know Werner to understand. He was an extremely bright, very loyal man—loyal, to his family, his friends, and his employers. He was bright enough to have gone a lot further than he did, but I think what held him back was that he lacked the kind of ambition, imagination, and drive that are necessary to rise to the top. He was satisfied to do his job, do what was expected of him, collect his paycheck at the end of the week, and then go home to Sophie and the children. He'd held only two jobs in all the years since he graduated from City College. The first was as an accountant and then comptroller of a small garment firm down on Thirty-eighth Street. When he was about forty, the company moved south, where labor was a lot cheaper. He could have moved with them, but he didn't want to leave the city. He was born here, raised his family here, and all his friends lived here. So he went looking for a new job and ended up at Fidelity Bank.

"I always assumed he did his job there well. But the truth is, he was just another cog in the machine, and like so many others, he wore out in time and became dispensable, easily replaced by younger and more ambitious men. So, when Werner told me he'd lost his job, I assumed that he'd simply reached the end of his usefulness to the bank and he was being retired. After all, he was sixty-five. It's a hard thing to accept, of course, that you may have outstayed your welcome, but it's inevitable. It happens to all of us.

"Then Werner told me that he wasn't retiring. He'd been fired. And he hadn't simply been fired; he was probably going to be arrested and indicted for embezzlement. I couldn't believe it. I'd known Werner since we were kids, and I have to tell you he was one of the most honest and incorruptible men I've ever known.

"Just after lunch that day, he said, he'd been called into the office of the bank's executive vice president."

"That would be Eugene Donatello?" Rogers said.

"Of course," Solomon said. "Donatello wasn't alone. He had a detective from the District Attorney's office with him. The detective told Werner that a quarter of a million dollars, maybe even more, was missing from the accounts Werner managed, and what was worse, they'd managed to trace most of that money to an offshore account in a private bank in the Bahamas. That account was in Werner's name. To say that Werner was stunned is to put it mildly. He denied knowing anything about the missing funds or of the bank account, and he told the detective as far as he knew his accounts were always in good order.

The detective told him he was under no obligation to answer any more questions before he consulted his attorney. And then Donatello told him that he was fired and that he should clean out his desk and be gone by three that afternoon.

"When Werner finished telling me all this, the first question I put to him was whether there was any truth to the charges. He knew he could tell me, because we now had an attorney–client relationship and so anything he said was privileged. I don't know whether he was angrier at me for asking him that or because the charges had been made in the first place, but he was outraged, vehement in his denial. He hadn't embezzled any money, he said, and he didn't know anything about an offshore account, and I ought to know him well enough to know he'd never do anything dishonest. It just wasn't in him.

"I asked why anybody would have made such allegations about him in the first place. He said at first he couldn't understand it, but as he was putting his affairs together before leaving the bank, he'd gone through the records of his accounts over the past couple of years, and the closer he looked, the more upset he became. He found, he said, indications that some very puzzling transactions had taken place, things that could have been easily missed if you didn't know how to look for them. What he did then, he said, was to print out the records of all his accounts, so he'd have time to go over them more carefully later, and then stuff them with his other papers in his briefcase. I tried to press him on just what it was that he found, but the only thing he'd say was that it looked to him like somebody he admired and respected was actually behind the whole thing and had shifted the blame in order to cover himself. No matter how hard I pressed, and let me tell you, I pressed very hard, he refused to say anything more because he said he didn't want to make a mistake and accuse someone falsely. After he'd gone over all the records, if his suspicion turned out to be true, he'd tell me the man's name and give me the details, and we could go on from there.

"We talked for hours that evening. It was after midnight before we left the office. The next morning, I called the District Attorney's office and was put through to an Assistant District Attorney, a Miss Turner. I told her I understood that her office was investigating Werner, and that he had retained me to represent him and that if they had any questions they wanted to put to him, they should contact me and I would consider whether to set up a meeting and allow them to interrogate him. I asked whether they intended to go to a grand jury and seek an indictment. She said they were in the process of making that determination. I asked if they intended to arrest Werner. She said they hadn't made a decision on that yet, but if there was any possibility that he might skip town, they would move against him without delay. I assured her that he had no intention of leaving the city and that he would certainly cooperate fully with their investigation at the proper moment. We left it there.

"After I talked to Miss Turner, I called Werner and told him what had transpired. I said we probably ought to meet again soon, when he had had a chance to go through all the records and I was back from my vacation. He agreed. That was the last time we spoke. By the time I got back, he was dead. Now I hope that answers all your questions."

"This man he admired," Rogers asked, "that would be Donatello?"

"I have no way of knowing. I might suspect as much, based on what he indicated and the things he had said in the past, but suspicion is not proof, and without proof . . ." He waved a hand.

"You know Donatello?"

Solomon chose his words carefully. "I've met him a number of times. I've seen him at various functions and meetings. We've served together on several philanthropic organizations. But, no, I don't feel like I know him."

"What's your impression of him?"

"May I inquire why you're interested?"

"I'm interested in everything."

"Come, Mr. Rogers. I wasn't born yesterday. I read the newspapers. I am aware that Mr. Donatello has been mentioned for high office in the new city administration. Therefore I assume that Werner is really only peripheral to this interview, and Donatello is central. I also assume that, in actuality, this also has little to do with the police investigation into Werner's affairs, or even his death."

"Only an assumption, Mr. Solomon."

"A good one, nevertheless. Don't be concerned. This will go no further than this office."

Rogers shrugged. "You haven't answered my question," he said. "What's your impression of Donatello?"

Solomon took his time considering his answer. "I have always found Mr. Donatello to be a brilliant, successful, and enterprising man." The way he said it caused Rogers to look closely at him.

"But?"

Solomon answered slowly, cautiously. "I'm afraid I did not take to him."

"Why?"

"Who can ever say why one likes or dislikes another person? You asked for my impression and I gave it to you. He has never offended me. He has always been pleasant. And yet I do not take to him. Perhaps it is a reaction to his oft-repeated story of his rise to prominence from poverty. Many people come from poor backgrounds and attain high station. They do not have the need to boast of it to the world at large."

"You, for instance?"

"Yes, if you will, me. Perhaps, too, it is because I have always thought he considered himself superior to the rest of mankind. It's not anything he says, it's merely that he has a way of looking down his nose at people. Do you understand what I mean?"

Rogers nodded slowly. He studied Solomon, noting a moment of hesitation in those expressionless eyes, that impassive face. "I think," Rogers said, "it's more than that."

"I don't make charges lightly, or without proof. And for this I have no proof." He paused. "I am a Jew, Mr. Rogers, and I think Mr. Donatello does not like Jews. It is nothing he says or does; it is merely an impression. Therefore, it's not something I can explain, although if you were Jewish you would understand." He spread his hands. "I think I have said enough."

"One more thing," Rogers said. "If Werner Rosenblatt was innocent, as he claimed, and as you believe, then why the hell did he kill himself?"

"On that I have no explanation or theories. Perhaps Sophie is right. Perhaps he did not kill himself."

20

Rogers spent a day in the main reading room on the third floor of the New York Public Library, finding out all he could about "Donatello, Eugene, American banker," trying to build his own portrait of the man. He found Donatello listed in the standard, banking and international editions of *Who's Who*. He pored over more than thirty years of *The New York Times Index*. There were lots of entries, from Donatello's name in a list of honors graduates at Bronx High School of Science to an account of his heroism and medals in Vietnam, on through a long profile when he was named executive vice president of Fidelity International Bank, and beyond. Rogers made notes, wrote out the call slips, handed them in three at a time at the desk and retreated with microfilm that he threaded into a viewer. He then hobbled from microfilm viewer to desk, through the late morning and on through the afternoon, until, nearly blind from staring at the fuzzy magnified print, he finished just as the library was closing. Most of the stories were on the financial pages. Most were dull, reading as though some rewrite man had merely made a few changes in press handouts before turning in his copy to the desk.

The stories were accolades—Donatello receiving awards for philanthropy, for community services, for contributions to the

banking and financial communities. There were pictures of Donatello with governors, senators, community leaders. There was
a photograph of Donatello with a priest at a banquet where he
was honored with a medal from the church for his years of
financial advice to the archdiocese. The priest was identified as
Bishop Dennis Molloy, Chief Financial Officer of the archdiocese. Rogers stared at the photograph, trying to put it and the
name together. It took him a few minutes before he remembered. That afternoon a week or so before at One Police Plaza
when Dolan had introduced them.

There was a story about Donatello testifying before a House
committee on international banking. A photograph went along
with the piece, Donatello surrounded by a half-dozen congress-
men. Next to him was Mike Benedetto of New York, chairman
of the subcommittee.

The profile, at least, had a few personal touches, though in
the main it was a dull recounting of his rise and growing renown
in the financial world. But there was more. Donatello, it seemed,
was a man of precise and regular habits. At seven-thirty every
morning he was often the first to arrive at his office in the bank
on Broad Street. Most days, unless there was an appointment
that called him elsewhere, he lunched alone. He rarely left the
office before six. A bachelor, he often dined out. At least three
times a week he had dinner at Tremanti's, the popular restaurant owned by his lifelong friend Frank Tremanti. Frequently
he dined alone. His one avocation and recreation was hunting.
He had a lodge in the Adirondacks, the story said, where he and
friends spent a week at the start of the hunting season in the
fall. There was a photograph of Donatello in a plaid hunting
jacket, a shotgun cradled in the crook of one arm, surrounded by
a pack of hunting dogs. With him were several other men. The
faces of most of them were obscured, and they were not identified. Rogers studied the faces of those that were clear and
recognizable. On one side of Donatello was Chief Dolan. On the
other was Assistant District Attorney Peter McIntyre. Like
Donatello, both were dressed for hunting, both cradled shot-
guns.

When Morrison had first shown him the file on Donatello,
Rogers thought the man too good to be true. But the portrait
that emerged from all these years of newspaper stories seemed
to confirm what the file said. The only negatives came in Rosen-

blatt's partial accusations, and in the impressions of Solomon. It sure wasn't much to go on. And weighed against the stories in the papers, it was nothing. Rogers didn't like it.

At just before six-thirty A.M. on the Monday before Thanksgiving, the temperature hovered around the freezing mark and a chill gusty wind whipped dust and paper in swirls along the streets. On a bench against the stone wall that bordered Central Park, Rogers huddled into an old down jacket; next to him, one of the myriad homeless stretched out asleep under a layer of newspaper. Rogers's eyes were fixed on the entrance to the apartment building across Fifth Avenue. He watched as a newspaper boy, collar turned up around his ears, hustled along the avenue, carring a bundle filled with yesterday's news for the morning reader. He turned into the building and disappeared. A doorman appeared and began sweeping the sidewalk in front of the building.

At about ten to seven, a black Lincoln limousine pulled to a stop in front of the building. A chauffeur jumped out and moved quickly to open the rear passenger door. Eugene Donatello, homburg perched on his head, greatcoat with fur collar wrapped around him, emerged from the building and climbed in the limo. The car started off, heading downtown.

A half-hour later, Rogers came up from the subway at Wall Street and started toward Broad. The corporate offices of Fidelity International Bank occupied the first two floors of a classic Federal-style limestone building near the corner. Rogers positioned himself in a niche in a building across the street. The spot provided a place he could lean and take some pressure off his bad leg. He had been around long enough to know that the subway is not only cheaper than a limo, but a lot faster in the city. Ten minutes later, the limo pulled up in front of the bank. The chauffeur held the rear door open for Donatello who emerged and strode into the bank, not through the main door but a smaller one nearby.

A light went on in a corner office on the second floor. The angle was not good enough for Rogers to make out for certain who was inside, but he figured that was where Donatello hung out. In the next hour, the street and the sidewalks began to fill with cars, cabs, and people, hurrying toward office buildings, banks, the Stock Exchange. They either didn't notice him or ignored him, intent on their own destinations, their own concerns. After a time, he moved away toward the corner, joining a line in front of a coffee wagon. He watched as on the north side of Wall Street, workmen were stringing Christmas lights across the front of the old Federal Building where George Washington had been sworn in as the nation's first president. Rogers bought coffee and a doughnut and stood on the corner, sipping, letting the steam warm his face. His eyes kept moving toward the front of the bank.

A little after ten, he crossed the street and walked into the bank. The main floor was marble, the ceilings high. It reminded Rogers of Grand Central Station. To one side were tellers' cages, the old-fashioned kind with grillwork across the front, not the newer and more secure Plexiglas. Along the other side were small cubicles, with desks and a couple of chairs, and to the rear, behind a wooden barricade, were more desks, people behind them working at computer stations. There was an elevator in one wall and a flight of stairs disappearing upward nearby.

A guard approached. Dressed in his down jacket and old jeans, Rogers did not look like the usual client of Fidelity International Bank. "Can I help you?" the guard asked. His voice said there was no way he was going to help Rogers because Rogers didn't belong here.

"I'd like to see an officer," Rogers said. "About opening an account."

The guard looked at him. The look said, You never can tell; even millionaires sometimes dressed like bums. "Back there." He pointed toward the wooden barrier.

Rogers waited at the barricade for a few minutes before a woman looked up from her computer terminal. "May I help you?"

"I'd like to see someone about opening an account."

"Are you sure you're in the right place?"

"This is a bank, isn't it? Someone told me it was a good one, your money was safe here."

"I think," she said, "you've been given a mistaken impression. We're not a commercial bank. Fidelity International is an international investment bank. We do offer some commercial services to our clients, but only as a courtesy. And we don't handle small accounts."

"What," Rogers asked, "do you consider a small account?"

She studied him. "Our minimum opening deposit is a hundred thousand dollars."

"That," he said, "is just a little rich for my blood."

"There are a number of banks in the area you might find suitable," she said. "Citibank, Chase Manhattan, Chemical, Manufacturers, several others. They're all within a few blocks. Why don't you try one of them?"

"Thanks," he said. "I might just do that. If I ever have a hundred grand to spare, maybe I'll be back." He turned and headed back to the street.

He returned to the niche. A cop on foot patrol moved slowly down the street. He noticed Rogers, paused, took a long look, and then went on. Fifteen minutes later, the cop appeared again, going the other way. This time he stopped in front of Rogers and stared at him. "Move along," he said. "No loitering."

Rogers sighed. He reached into his back pocket, pulled out his billfold and flashed his ID. The cop looked at it. His manner changed. "Sorry, Lieutenant," he said. "You need any help?"

"No," Rogers said. "It's okay."

The cop went on his way.

At twelve-thirty, Donatello came through the small door beside the main entrance to the bank, walked a block south and started east. Rogers followed as Donatello quickly walked a couple of blocks and then turned into a small building. A discreet brass plaque on the door said it was the Banker's Club. A smaller brass plaque said it was for members only.

An hour later, Donatello reappeared, walked quickly back the way he had come, and reentered the bank. Rogers followed and once more took up his post. Through the afternoon, trying to keep warm against the growing chill, he etched a pattern of footprints between his station and the coffee wagon up the block. It kept getting darker, more threatening, but at least the rain, or snow, held off. The people, almost all men, who went through the entrance to the bank all looked as though a hundred grand was pocket money.

By five, the streets were filling again, the buildings emptying, another day of playing games with other people's money coming to an end. Rogers kept his vigil. He couldn't feel his feet any longer, and his hands were stinging from the cold. He kept stamping to bring sensation back to the feet, but that only aggravated the pain from his bruised leg. It started to drizzle, wet and icy. He pressed deeper into the niche for some protection.

At precisely six o'clock, the black Lincoln limo pulled up in front of the bank. Almost simultaneously the light went out in the corner office. A minute later, Donatello emerged through the small door. The chauffeur was already out of the car and holding open the rear door.

Roger flagged a cab just as the limo pulled away. He told the driver to keep the black Lincoln in sight. The driver looked back at him. "What is this," he said, "some movie?"

"No movie. Just do it."

The cabbie shrugged and headed out. It wasn't hard to follow the limo. The streets were packed, so the traffic moved slowly. The inside of the cab was mercifully warm. Gradually, feeling came back to Rogers's feet and hands. Rogers watched as the meter kept turning over, the quarters flashing past. He wondered whether the driver had fixed the meter. Another time, and he might have thought about taking the number and letting the Taxi and Limousine Commission know. What the hell, he thought, it's Morrison's money.

It took more than forty-five minutes to reach midtown. The Lincoln finally pulled to a stop just west of Fifth Avenue in the fifties, outside Tremanti's. The doorman held the car door open and Donatello stepped out, nodded to him, and ducked under the canopy that stretched out to the curb. The doorman rushed to the restaurant door and pulled it open. Donatello passed through.

Rogers mumbled to himself as he paid the cabdriver. He should have saved himself the fare. He should have known from what he'd read about Donatello that this was where he'd be heading. At least he'd kept warm.

He paused just inside the restaurant's entrance and looked around. He'd heard of the place for years, but hadn't been there before. A long bar stretched down one side, with drinkers packed three deep. A maître d' guarded the entrance to the main dining room, effusively welcoming those he knew, gesturing toward an assistant to lead them to their tables, checking his reservation list for those he didn't know, blocking the way to strangers without reservations. Rogers could see into the main dining room where the tables were widely spaced, assuring a semblance of privacy. Banquettes lined the walls, which were covered with autographed sketches of the famous, in politics, sports, entertainment, their messages tributes to the generosity of the host. Rogers turned toward the bar, the only place someone dressed as he was would be even partly welcomed. He ordered scotch. The bartender looked him over and hesitated. Rogers pulled some bills from his pocket and dropped them on the bar. The bartender poured the scotch.

Donatello was being led to a banquette in the rear corner of the restaurant. Rogers had a view from his place at the bar. He sipped his drink, feeling the warmth spread through him. A big, burly man in his late forties with an open face walked quickly toward Donatello. Frank Tremanti. He knew everybody and everybody knew him. Long ago he had learned the wisdom, and the profit, of neutrality, of studiously taking no sides in battles, political or marital, forever finding the right words for all who came through his doors. He was impossible to miss. Rogers had seen his photograph often enough on the sports pages and other places. And there was his likeness, a caricature, in the center of the drawings of other celebrities lining the walls, bigger than the others, dominating the wall, just as Tremanti himself seemed to dominate the room. Donatello rose. The two shook hands, smiling. Tremanti sat down and signaled for a waiter, who brought drinks. Rogers could not, of course, hear any of the conversation between the two men, but it didn't appear to be idle chatter. Tremanti had a worried look as he listened to Donatello, who did most of the talking. Finally, Donatello leaned back; Tremanti took a deep breath and nodded. Then he rose. The two men shook hands again and the host drifted away.

Almost inexplicably, Rogers felt his attention drawn to the restaurant's entrance as a woman appeared, young, in her twenties, blond, beautiful in the way that models in a fashion magazine are beautiful. She had the look. She had the clothes and the manner. She was wearing a coat that, had the animal rights activists been nearby, would have led to the throwing of stones. She posed for a moment just inside the doorway, enjoying the eyes that swiveled in her direction. Then she moved toward the restaurant section. Tremanti appeared from wherever he had been and hurried toward her. Greeting her warmly, like an old and valued friend, he led her toward Donatello, who rose and bent, kissing her on the cheek. It didn't look like just a friendly greeting between casual acquaintances, Rogers thought. Maybe the guy's human after all. The woman sat very close to Donatello, almost snuggling. A waiter appeared with a drink. Since she hadn't ordered, Rogers figured she must be a regular, always having the same thing.

"Who's the lady?" Rogers grinned at the bartender. He gestured with his head. He didn't have to. The bartender knew whom he meant.

The bartender shrugged and gave him a look. "Too expensive for you, pal," he said.

"Just wondering," Rogers said. "It looks like she knows her way around here."

"She does." He offered no more.

Donatello and his date took their time over the dinner and wine. It was after nine before they finished. Rogers nursed his drink as he watched, envied them the leisure and the food.

When they left, Rogers followed. The limousine was waiting and they climbed in the rear. The doorman whistled a cab for Rogers. The canopy overhung the sidewalk all the way to the street so he didn't have to step out into what was falling from the sky, a mixture of snow and rain now. The cab followed the limo to the apartment house on Fifth Avenue. Rogers watched Donatello and the woman step rapidly into the building. He decided not to wait. It had been a long day, and he was sure it was going to be a long night, and he wanted to get home to Melissa and his own bed. He didn't envy Donatello. He admired the man's taste, but he didn't envy him. After all, he himself had Melissa waiting for him.

21

Tuesday was a reprise of Monday. Rogers could have set his watch by Donatello's movements. The only variance from the routine of the previous day was that instead of having dinner at Tremanti's, Donatello went to an expensive French place on the East Side. It wasn't the kind of place that would welcome a guy dressed like Rogers, not even at the bar, if they had one, so he waited outside.

The expensive-looking blonde didn't show up. This time it was Bishop Dennis Molloy who got out of a cab and walked into the restaurant, and walked out three hours later with Donatello, got into the limo with him, and rode back to Fifth Avenue. Molloy emerged an hour later and got into a cab. Rogers followed. Molloy went straight to a clerical residence over by the river and disappeared through the door.

Wednesday was more of the same, except at the end of the day it was back to Tremanti's. And this time the blonde was in evidence.

Thursday, Rogers woke with the feeling he ought to take up a park bench outside Donatello's place on Fifth Avenue. But it was Thanksgiving and he had promised his grandmother that he and Melissa would drive out and spend the day with her, and fill themselves until they couldn't move. Always pasta and turkey, a real American-style Thanksgiving, with a touch of Italy on the side.

It was a nice day. The sun was out, the temperature near fifty, and, since they started before the Macy's parade was over, the traffic heading out to Long Island was fairly light. Rogers's leg was better, the pain nearly gone, the limp almost unnoticeable. Melissa, on the seat beside him, was relaxed, her eyes half-closed. They hadn't seen much of each other over the past week, except in bed very late at night. He was out before she was up each day, trying to form his own portrait of Donatello, and, when he had a spare moment, trying to make some sense of all the unfinished business that Felix Palmieri had left behind. And when he reached home in the evening, she was at the theater, where her show was still running. Then, by the time she got home, he was usually in bed. She would crawl in beside him, and sometimes he would wake and they would make love; sometimes, exhausted, she would just hug the other side of the bed and not rouse him. Now they were finally together, sharing the day, talking quietly about nothing.

His grandmother was waiting for them when they drove up. She must have been just inside the door, for she threw it open even before they reached the stoop. "You're late," she said. "I've been up since dawn, cooking. You should have been here an hour ago. I was worried."

They laughed. It was a ritual. "Come on, Nonna," he said. "You always say that. You love to cook. Even if we weren't here, you'd have been up cooking. Put you at the stove and you drop forty years. Besides, you've probably made the time to read the papers from front to back. You always do. How big a turkey did you make this time?"

"Small," she said. "Only twenty pounds."

"For the three of us."

"So, you will take home what we don't finish. That way I'll know you have something in your house to eat. Benito, you can stay until evening?"

He shook his head. "Afraid not this time. We have to get back to the city."

"I have a performance tonight," Melissa explained. "You know, actors work when everybody else has a holiday."

The grandmother looked from Melissa to Rogers and back.

"You have a regular job," she said. "It should be enough until you marry. I do not understand why you do this other thing at night. Why is it necessary?"

Melissa smiled. "It just is," she said. "It's the way I am. It's what happens when you act."

"You should settle down," his grandmother said. She stared at the two of them. "Tell me, why you're not married?"

They looked at each other. It was not the first time she had asked them that. She had taken to Melissa the first time they met. Even though Melissa was not Sicilian, nor Italian, not even Catholic, she had come to the conclusion that Melissa was the right girl for her grandson, though most of her friends might have called such a marriage outside the church an unforgivable sin. But she made her own rules, just as she made up her own mind, and nobody could change it.

"It's not time," Melissa said.

"It is time," his grandmother said. "You should be married and begin a family."

"Times change," Rogers said. "People don't do things the way they used to when you were young."

"Benito, times they never change, not in some things," she said.

"Well," Rogers said, "maybe someday. We'll see."

"It should be soon. You do not grow younger. When I was your age, I already had a child."

Melissa looked away, then back.

Rogers carved the turkey, as he had been doing since that first Thanksgiving when he had asked his grandmother why they didn't have turkey like the other kids, and she had gone and bought one. That first one had been overcooked, so tough they could hardly eat it. Since then, she had learned. Now she made not only turkey but everything the newspapers and the American cookbooks she collected told her ought to be on the Thanksgiving table. She stuffed the turkey with oysters and bread crumbs and seasoning, though the seasoning had an Italian flavor. She candied sweet potatoes and steamed string beans. She made her own cranberry sauce and her own pumpkin pie, covered with mounds of whipped cream she had beaten with a whisk. And then there was the pasta, always with sauces she concocted, sauces he had tasted nowhere else but which she said she had learned to make from her mother, that all the women in her village in Sicily made, always with white wine because, she said, red wine brought on hives. As always, there was too much food, and as always, she insisted they eat and eat, and then eat more.

"Enough already," Rogers groaned finally, pushing himself away from the head of the table.

"You don't like my dinner?" his grandmother said.

"I love your dinner. But I couldn't eat another thing."

"A bird could not live on what you eat. And you—" she looked at Melissa—"a baby sparrow would perish in the nest if the mother brought only what you eat."

"That sparrow would grow as big as a house," Melissa said, laughing. "It was wonderful, but if I eat any more they'll have to get a truck to carry me onstage tonight."

Anything to distract her. "Nonna," Rogers said. "I ran into an old beau of yours the other day. From the old country."

She started, looked at him with surprise. *"Un corteggiatore?* From Sicily? It could not be. I was only a young girl when I married. So there were very few men that I knew. They must all be *morte* now."

"Not this one."

"Who?"

"Generoso Ruggieri."

She looked as though she were about to have a stroke, turning crimson, the veins standing out on her neck. *"Malfattore. Un malvagio nome. Un mafioso."*

"He said nice things about you, too."

"Have nothing to do with that one," she ordered. "He will bring you only *sfortuna*. He turns rotten all things he touches."

He had never seen his grandmother this angry, nearly apoplectic with rage. She could be passionate when she felt deeply about something, but this went beyond that. He stared at her. "Whoa," he said. "I know what he is. What I'd like to know is, what did he do to you?"

She shook her head rapidly several times. "Talk about it? No more. Do not speak that man's name in my house again. Ever. As long as I live, I do not want to hear it." She took a deep breath and slowly grew calmer. "Now, we talk about something else. We talk about when you marry, the two of you."

*   *   *

They left about four. On the way home, they took a detour and stopped at Mary Palmieri's. She greeted them warmly. "Come in," she said. "Stay. Have something with us. The children are here."

They walked into the house. "We can stay only a minute," Melissa said. "I've got a performance tonight."

"Of course," Mary said. "I forgot."

"And," Rogers said, "if I never see food again it will be too soon."

"You've just come from your grandmother's?"

"You know it. How are you, Mary?"

She shrugged. "Getting along. You know. Now, come in and say hello to the kids."

They followed her into the living room. The Palmieri children and grandchildren had gathered for the holiday. It was subdued. Something was missing and everyone knew it, and nobody wanted to talk about it and everybody wanted to talk about it. Rogers's godson, Tony, only ten, still in shock, still not believing, clung desperately to Rogers for a moment, then turned and fled to his old room.

Mary watched him go, sighed, then turned to Rogers and Melissa. "He's so young," she said. Then, "I guess this is my day for company."

Rogers looked around. "I can see."

"No," she said. "I mean, people dropping by. Bill Dolan was here just before you, and Felix's partner, Carlos Rodriguez. He's okay. He brought a bag full of Spanish pastries. And a lot of others. It was almost like old times." She gave a little sob at that, her voice catching in her throat. She looked at Rogers. "Are you still working on it?"

He nodded. "Yeah. As much as I can."

"Anything you can tell me?"

"I'd rather not until there's something definite." He didn't want to get her hopes up.

"You'll keep me informed, won't you?"

"You know I will."

They stayed about half an hour. Mary hugged them both when they left. "Don't be strangers," she said.

As they drove away, Melissa looked at him. "Poor Mary,"

she said. Then, "You know, if you didn't do what you do I might give some serious thought to what your grandmother said."

He looked away from the road at her, trying to catch the expression. "But I do what I do," he said.

"Yes," she said. "And I don't want to end up like Mary Palmieri."

22

There was a dirty white card stuck in the groove of the mail-box. He noticed it as he and Melissa entered their building. It looked like something picked up from the street after a thousand feet had trampled on it. He pulled it out and took a quick glance and shoved it into his pocket. There was just a single letter etched into the dirt. "S." Sully wasn't supposed to know his home address. He'd never told him and his phone wasn't listed. But Sully knew it. He'd given up trying to find out how long ago. Whenever Sully wanted to see him, whenever Sully had some-thing, he always left a card or a piece of paper like this in the mailbox groove, like those cards stuck in mail slots by the local locksmiths or cleaners or whoever. It was Sully's way of telling him he had something and they should meet at the usual place, under the Manhattan Bridge, and, when Sully left a card, it meant the appointed time would be about eleven, when the area was deserted.

Just before seven-thirty, he walked Melissa to the theater, dropped her off, and strolled east, taking his time. Thanksgiving night the streets were pretty deserted, and most of the stores were closed. He found a secondhand bookstore near Broadway, an "Open" sign dangling in the window of the door. A bell jan-

gled when he walked in. A young girl sat reading behind a desk
piled high with dusty books. She was wearing a T-shirt adver-
tising Wolfgang Amadeus Mozart, and her legs, stretched out on
top of the desk, were strictly blue jeans and ragged sneakers
with an expensive designer slash on the side. She smiled. "Can
I help you? Are you looking for something special?"

"Just browsing," he said.

"Okay," she said. "Be my guest. If you need help, I'm right
here." She went back to her book.

He was the only customer. For the next hour, he wandered
through the store, taking books off the shelves, thumbing
through them, reading a page or two, then putting them back.
They were an eclectic assortment and in no particular order, a
volume of poetry next to a book on how to fix your plumbing. On
a shelf at the rear, he found an out-of-print collection of American plays from the 1930s that Melissa had been looking for. The
price penciled inside was $3.50. He put it under one arm and
moved on. On another shelf, he came on a book he'd read in
college that had stuck with him, that he'd been meaning to read
again: *All the King's Men.* The price was a buck fifty. He took
it. For a while longer he moved about, looking, finding nothing
more that appealed to him.

He glanced at his watch. It was nearly nine. Turning from
the shelves, he walked to the front and dropped the two books
on the desk in front of the girl. She looked up. "You found
something?"

"Two," he said.

She flipped them open, looked at the prices, did some calculating in her head. "That'll be five dollars, and forty-one cents
in tax," she said. "Oh, who cares, make it five forty. The city
doesn't need the extra penny."

He dug and came up with the money. She wrapped the
books in brown paper, folding the corners neatly, tying the package with a piece of string she dug from a drawer. Whatever
happened to plastic bags?

Over on Broadway, he found a record store that was open.
A half-dozen browsers were thumbing through CDs and tapes,
but there were no records, no LPs. Nobody carried LPs anymore. What the hell were you supposed to do with the record
player? Nice music was playing in the store. The Beatles. It
brought back memories. He stood inside for a while and listened

until they changed the record and the place began to throb and reverberate.

He went back out onto the street, heading south and east. The weather was holding and he didn't hurry. It was dark and deserted by the river under the Manhattan Bridge. He looked at his watch. It was a few minutes before eleven. He looked around for Sully. The little guy was nowhere. Rogers walked slowly along the brick pilings, peering into niches, searching. Sully could be hiding anywhere, waiting. It was a thing he usually did. Sully was always cautious.

Then, deep beneath the bridge, he saw it in the dim light from a distant streetlamp, a shadow swaying slowly back and forth, above the ground, attached to nothing. He looked up. Sully was twisting slowly about six feet above the ground. At first it looked as though he were levitating. Then Rogers saw the glint in the dim light. A steel wire was wound tightly around Sully's neck, the wire strung from a pipe jutting out from the bricks higher up.

Rogers stared up at him. He took a couple of steps toward him, slipped in a dark pool beneath the body, struggled to regain his balance. He found an old packing crate, hauled it over near Sully's body, and climbed onto it. Holding Sully with one arm, he sawed away at the wire with his Swiss army knife. It parted slowly, Sully's body canting in against him. He held it, cradled it, stepped off the box, and lowered the body to the ground, trying to be careful not to disturb anything about the scene. Even in death, the stoolie was light enough so it took no effort to hold him.

From his coat pocket Rogers took a small flashlight and shone it down on the face. The steel wire had practically severed the head from the body, and most of the blood had already poured out. There was also blood all over the mouth. In the mouth was a pigeon, jammed deep inside, the broken head protruding grotesquely. Gingerly, Rogers grasped it and pulled it out. Then he saw it wasn't the pigeon's blood that had stained Sully's mouth. Somebody had cut out his tongue.

He looked away. He went back the way he had come, found a phone booth and made the call.

*   *   *

When Toby walked into his fleabag of a room at three in the morning and turned on the small lamp, he saw Rogers sitting on his cot. He didn't like what he saw in Rogers's face. He didn't like what else he saw. The front of Rogers's jacket was stained dark with dried blood. There was dried blood on Rogers's trousers. He thought he saw some smears on the face and the hands. He started to back away, started to turn and run. Rogers got up and moved toward him, reached him just as he was starting through the door. Rogers grabbed him by the neck and threw him across the room. Toby hit the wall and dropped onto the cot.

"What . . . what's the matter?" he stammered, sweat popping out all over his face.

"You little bastard," Rogers said. "I want it. I want it all. I want it now."

"I don't get it. What?"

"What you know. All of it. I don't give a shit, just don't hold anything back."

Toby started. "About what?"

"Don't give me any shit. I want it. Now." He took a step forward. "Lay it out for me. What you heard. What you know."

"I don't know nothin'."

Rogers stood over him. "Toby, don't make me . . ."

"Please, Mr. Rogers. Please. Somethin' happened? Somethin' went wrong?"

"Yeah, something went wrong. Real wrong. Now, Toby. Not tomorrow. Not when you have time to think. Now."

Looking at him, Toby understood he had no choice. "Okay, okay. You don't gimme no choice. It's you or them, and maybe you're worse." He took a deep breath. "The Arab what's you're talkin' about. Right?"

"Right."

"Okay, okay. I'll tell you. What I heard was, this fuckin' Arab had oil wells comin' out his ass, an' he goes to the wrong guys an' tells them he's got a little trouble with cash flow. Can you believe that? Bullshit. What it was, was he was into the shylocks like for over a hundred large. They wanna get paid, what he owes 'em, that an' the vigorish. They tell him, pay up or you're history. So he cuts a deal. Guaranteed, one thousand percent. They tell him, move a little package two or three times from there to here in the pouch, like what don't get searched, an' they'll put a paid in full on the marker. The bastard says, fine, no sweat. He comes an' he goes an' there ain't nothin' in his fuckin' pouch but a bunch of papers with writin' on 'em like nobody can read that ain't an Arab. He says he's a fuckin' diplomat, an' they can go shove it, an' there ain't a fuckin' thing they can do. Can you believe that? He tried to stiff them. So they showed him there was a fuckin' thing they could do."

"Which wrong guys?"

"Honest to God, Mr. Rogers, I don't know 'em. I seen 'em around is all. I know they're family, I know they're made, I know they're fuckin' trouble. Honest to God, that's what I know, that's all I heard, what I told you. I don't know no more."

"Descriptions, Toby. What did they look like?"

Toby turned that over. "One of 'em," he said, "he was like maybe he'd been in the ring, or maybe he'd been slugged one time too many. What I mean, he had a squashed-in nose an' ears like cauliflowers, an' too many lumps, an' like he was leaning to one side. The other guy, he was just a guy. I mean, nice dresser, expensive suit an' like that, face you'd forget 'cause it was like a hundred guys, black hair real neat."

"What place, Toby? Where'd you hear all this?"

"Outside a porno place, Mr. Rogers. That an' a clubhouse."

"Where?"

"Canal, right around the corner from Mulberry."

23

It was after 5 A.M. before he reached the apartment. He had walked all the way downtown from Toby's, through the cold November night, through the dark deserted streets, impervious to the pain still in his leg, trying to banish thoughts, to deal with the guilt that filled his mind.

He unlocked the door and walked in quietly. There was a light burning on a table in the living room, left on by Melissa so he wouldn't have to stumble about in the dark. Melissa was asleep. He stood over her, looking down. He had a desperate need to take her in his arms, hold her, make love to her and wash away what tore through his mind. He turned and went into the bathroom, stripped, threw his bloody clothes into a pile in the corner, stepped into the shower and scrubbed himself until he was raw.

When he returned to the bedroom, Melissa was awake, sitting up, staring at him with concern. "Are you all right?"

He shook his head. "No."

"What happened? You weren't home and you didn't come to pick me up. I wondered where you were."

Until Melissa came into his life, he had always kept things to himself, had never shared his feelings with anyone. With

Melissa, there were no secrets. He told her, not all, but enough.

She moved and went to him, held him against her and drew him back to the bed. They made love with a need and a desperation they had never felt before, a passion that surprised both of them, that left them drained, empty of everything.

Rogers slept until almost noon. When he was sufficiently awake, he looked up the number of a funeral home in the yellow pages.

"I'd like to make arrangements for a burial."

"You are a relative of the deceased?" the voice on the other end said.

"No. A . . . " he paused for a moment, then, "a friend. He didn't have any relatives." And his friends aren't anything to be too proud of either, he said to himself.

"What kind of arrangements will you require?"

"Simple," Rogers said. "Just a casket, I guess. No service. I'll come up later and pick out a box."

He made the trip across town to the morgue, down to the autopsy area.

The stench inside the autopsy room was overpowering. His stomach recoiled. No matter how much antiseptic they used, it wasn't enough, it couldn't get rid of the smell of generations of bodies that had been opened, dissected, and examined here. A couple of doctors, pathologists in lab coats, were bent over something on a table, wielding the tools of their trade. Rogers took a step toward them. What they were working on was what was left of Sully.

One of them looked up. "Hey, you," he said, "you don't belong in here."

"Police. Rogers. He was mine. Mind if I stay?"

He looked at Rogers and shrugged. "It takes all kinds. My name's Sadowsky." He motioned down at the body. "Somebody really had it in for him," he said. "Cut out his tongue, wrapped the wire around his neck, and then strung him up while he was still alive. What the hell did he do?"

"Listened too hard," Rogers said.

"And blabbed what he heard?"

"Sometimes," Rogers said.

"Well, this time I'd say he listened to the wrong people. He got a name?"

"Sullivan," Rogers said. "Sean Sullivan."

"Thanks. It's nice to know who you're cutting." Sadowsky looked around, found a form on a nearby table, took a pen and scribbled on it. "Want to know what he had for Thanksgiving dinner? Not turkey. Chinese. There were red peppers in his stomach. Not digested. He must have eaten about an hour before this happened."

"He liked Chinese. He couldn't get enough of it. The hotter the better."

"Figures. Something else," Sadowsky said. "The guy was a reader. That or somebody left something behind."

Rogers looked at him, puzzled. Sadowsky gestured with his scalpel toward a table. On it was a parcel, a brown paper wrapping torn so the contents were revealed. Two books. Rogers peered toward them. "Mine," he said. "I dropped them when I found him. Forgot all about them."

"Happy reading," Sadowsky said. "Take them with you when you leave. I doubt whether anyone else has any use for them."

"How much longer?" Rogers asked.

"Another half-hour, maybe."

"When are you going to be ready to release the body?"

"Not up to me," Sadowsky said. "Up to you guys. But I don't see any reason why we should have to hold it."

"No reason," Rogers agreed.

He stood there a while longer, watching, feeling removed. It wasn't Sully on the table being cut apart and analyzed. It was just another stiff. Then he turned, retrieved the books, and left. Outside, he made some calls, and then signed some forms. Nobody had any objections to the body being released. Nobody wanted it once Sadowsky was through with it. It would just take up space in the morgue, and then space in Potter's Field, or a cemetery somewhere if he could find one.

After a visit to the funeral home to pick out a plain pine casket, and a cemetery from a list the home maintained Rogers took a bus uptown, walked west to 43rd Street and went into the office of *The New York Times*. He explained his errand to a security guard who gave him directions to the appropriate office. There the woman in charge gave him a form. He filled it out.

"Sullivan, Sean, 41. Died suddenly on Thanksgiving. Burial Saturday, at St. Agnes's, Huntington. A Friend."

He paid the fee for the notice. A woman told him she could get it into the paper the next morning. He thanked her and left.

The casket was already in the hearse, waiting, when he and Melissa reached Maguire's Funeral Home the next morning. An hour later they stood in the deserted cemetery. A chill wind whipped across the barren, dun-colored field, biting through clothes, bringing unbidden shivers. A couple of men in dark suits lowered the casket into the ground. Rogers, his arm around Melissa, stood beside the grave and looked down. He murmured something about keeping a promise. Melissa looked at him. He shrugged. The grave diggers started to fill the grave. Rogers took a handful of dirt and dropped it on the lid of the coffin, hearing the clatter as it hit the pine.

24

They were having breakfast Sunday morning when the phone rang. It was Dolan. He wanted Rogers to get his ass down to One Police Plaza immediately. Forget it's Sunday.

He went. The blockhouse was quiet, not many people about. Dolan was in his office, but dressed in tan slacks and a plaid shirt—not his usual attire. But, then, this was Sunday. Dolan glared at him. "You fucked up my weekend," he said.

Rogers said nothing.

"I told you to keep your nose clean. I told you to do whatever the hell it is Morrison wants from you and leave other stuff alone, leave it where it belongs. I didn't tell you. I ordered you. Now, what do I find?" He reached, picked up some papers off his desk and waved them at Rogers. "I don't know what you're up to, I don't know what you think you're doing, but you got a guy killed."

"I know. You don't have to tell me."

"Sean Sullivan. Who the hell was he?"

"A stoolie."

"Working for you?"

"Yeah."

"Doing what?"

Rogers considered. "I asked him to look into a few things."

"Palmieri things?"

"Yeah. But that was before you called me off. I didn't see him around so I didn't do anything about it. Then he got in touch, asked me to meet him, and by the time I got there, somebody got to him first."

"What was he looking into?"

"That thing about the Arab."

"Dammit, that was out of our hands. That is a federal investigation. Their thing, not ours."

"Not what Felix thought."

"What did he know? He always had crazy ideas. What did he think this time?"

"He thought it might be family."

"Bullshit!"

"I don't think so. I think he was on the right road."

"Your stoolie tell you that?"

"No, but one of Felix's stoolies did."

"He's sure?"

"A-one hundred percent."

"Okay. Give it to Homicide. Let them deal with it. As for you, I ought to bust you. Maybe I ought to have my head examined, but I'm not going to. You get back to the Morrison thing and finish it up. But I'm going to watch you like a hawk, and you step out of line again and you can forget all about collecting a police pension. Now, get the hell out of here before I change my mind."

25

Rogers figured Monday was a slow night at Tremanti's, but he called ahead for a reservation anyway. Yes, they could accommodate him at seven. It was to be a kind of celebration combined with wake—a celebration of the fact that he and Melissa had been together for a year; a wake for Sully and for the closing of Melissa's show. She was sad, she said, but accepting; it was the fate of the actor. No show, not even *A Chorus Line*, ran forever. So she offered no objection to the idea of a dinner out, her only caveat, "Can we afford it?"

"On Morrison," he said.

"Like that?"

"Like that. I want a good look at Donatello—and his blonde. Just one thing. I'm Ben Roberts tonight."

"And just what does Mr. Roberts do for a living that he can afford a dinner at Tremanti's? In case we meet somebody who asks."

"Think of something," he said. "Salesman?"

"Never," she laughed. "Nobody'd believe it. You couldn't give away fire extinguishers if the house was burning down. It has to be something else. I know." She grinned. "A floorwalker at Bloomie's."

"In ladies' perfume?" he said.

"Naturally. Seriously, what about an executive?"

"Oh, sure. I'm just the type."

"You are. Dress you up and you could pass for one of those guys who rides the train in from Westchester or Connecticut every morning, rides back in the evening, and makes a million bucks in between."

"Doing what?"

"Whatever it is executives do." She thought. "I know. You work for IBM. Computer whiz, that kind of thing. Out on the far edge. You could pass."

"Sure," he said. "A hacker. Only nobody better ask me to explain CPUs and bits and bytes and all the rest."

"At least you know the terms. But don't worry, nobody's going to ask. We probably won't meet anybody who wants to know us, and we sure won't meet anybody we know."

"Wear that little black thing," he said. "You know, the thousand buck number from the thrift shop."

"Wear a suit," she said, "the blue one, and a tie."

They took a cab uptown. The doorman at Tremanti's looked them over as he opened the cab door. His eyes registered approval of Melissa, even if she wasn't wearing fur. A lot of women didn't wear fur these days. He hustled and held the restaurant's front door for her. The maître d' scanned his reservation list, checked off Roberts halfway down, and signaled an assistant who led them to a table in the back, near the kitchen. It was to be expected. Nobody knew them. They didn't rate the best treatment.

They ordered drinks. While they waited, Rogers glanced around the room. Donatello was in the same banquette as before with the same blonde next to him. "You know everybody," Rogers said. "Who's the blonde? With Donatello."

She moved her head a little, looked, and started to laugh. "You wouldn't know, would you? You ought to read the fashion magazines sometimes, Ben. She's on the cover of *Vogue*. She's been on a dozen covers. Her name's Nikki Wells, at least that's what she calls herself these days."

"You're a walking Who's Who," he said.

"Not quite," she said. "I know her."

"You what?"

"Know her. We were at Smith at the same time. We

weren't exactly friends, but we knew each other. I mean, she was Boston, Newport, and Sanibel. I was just an ordinary kid from Providence, nothing special. Like a lot of scholarship kids, I was a grind, nose in the books all the time, a double major in history and English. She managed to get by without hardly trying. I think she majored in Amherst, Harvard, MIT, Dartmouth, and a few others. She was like a pot of honey with the bees swarming for a taste. Her real name's Nicole Wellstone. Do you want to meet her?"

It was an intriguing idea. He turned it over, and then slowly shook his head. "Not now," he said. "Maybe later. But only if it's by accident."

"That," she said, "can be arranged."

"If it happens," he said, "we go back to square one." She looked puzzled. "Forget the Roberts. I turn into Ben Rogers again. Donatello knows people I know."

She nodded.

When the drinks came, they drank their first toast to Sully's memory, then put that aside. The waiter brought menus. What did the waiter recommend? He rattled off several of the Italian specialties, his voice curling around the names as though he could taste them just by saying the words. He emphasized one dish that sounded especially fattening. Rogers looked at Melissa. She grinned. "What the hell. So I'll have to diet for six months."

The sommelier, gold tasting cup on a chain dangling from a pocket in his apron, large gold key to the wine cellar on a chain around his neck, appeared with an oversized book and placed it in front of Rogers. He opened it and pretended he understood what he was reading. The average price for a bottle was more than dinner. What the hell, it was on Morrison. Rogers looked up at the wine steward and asked what he would recommend. The wine steward's recommendation was a mere eighty-nine dollars a bottle. What the hell. He nodded.

After a ritualistic sniffing of the cork the sommelier poured a little of the wine into Rogers's glass. He sipped. It was smooth and silky, and tasted better than the stuff he was used to drinking. The wine steward asked if they'd like him to pour now or let the wine breathe for a while. They'd let it breathe.

The meal, which arrived after a rather lengthy wait, proved to be a disappointment. Melissa made a little face. "Not worth the price," she said. "I cook better. There must be another reason people come here."

"Yes, you do," he said, "and, yes, there is. Look around." She looked. There were celebrity faces, familiar from the newspapers and magazines, scattered around the room.

"They don't look like they're enjoying themselves," she said. "I always wondered about people who went to the 'in' places. Now that I'm in one, I still wonder."

They were just finishing dinner when Melissa suddenly stood up. "The accident's about to happen," she said, and started away from the table. His eyes followed her. Just ahead of her, the blonde was turning into an alcove leading to the ladies' room.

They reappeared a few minutes later, walking together, smiling and nodding in a kind of happy conversation. Rogers watched as they headed for Donatello's banquette. Donatello rose as the blonde made an introduction. He nodded and said something. Melissa replied. There was a brief exchange and then Melissa, smiling, turned and walked back to their table.

"They want us to join them for coffee," she said. "And brandy, the man said. Do you want to?"

"How can I refuse?" he said. "It looked like old home week."

"You know how it is when old friends meet after long absence."

"I thought you were just acquaintances."

"Close friends, my dear. As they say, close as close can be."

The two men shook hands as Melissa introduced them. Donatello's grasp was firm, assured, held just the right length of time. Nikki gave Rogers a smile. Donatello asked them to sit down. They did.

"I was just telling Gene," Nikki said to Rogers, "that Melissa and I are old friends from college."

"She was just telling me too," Rogers said.

"Was I ever surprised to see her. I don't think we've seen each other since commencement. God, that was a long time ago." She began to prattle on to Melissa about old college friends, those she'd seen since graduation. Watching her, listening to her, Rogers was struck suddenly with the realization that she was a lonely young lady. Which surprised him. She was beautiful and, from what Melissa said, earned more in a week than he made in six months. She could have had her choice of men. But apparently she had chosen Donatello.

While Nikki talked, Donatello watched Melissa. "I've seen you before, somewhere," he said finally. "I have a memory for faces. It will come to me."

Nikki looked over at him. "Gene," she said, "are you trying to make me jealous? And with my friend?"

He smiled at her affectionately. "Don't be foolish, Nikki. I'm serious. I've seen this young lady before."

"Do you go to the theater, Mr. Donatello?" Rogers said. "Melissa just closed in a show."

"Off-off Broadway," she said.

"I don't get to the theater very often, I'm afraid," Donatello said. "I don't have much time for it. It was someplace else."

Melissa glanced at Rogers. He had been considering the question since Donatello raised it. He gave a brief, imperceptible nod.

"Election night," she said. "In the Morrison suite."

"Of course," Donatello said. "I was just leaving." He stared at her. "You were wearing the same dress."

"You're very observant," she said.

"When you're responsible for other people's money, you have to be." He glanced over at Rogers. "And you, Mr. Rogers, you were with her."

"Right again."

"Are you friends of the new mayor?"

"Not exactly," Rogers said. "I did some work with him when he was in Washington."

"At the Justice Department?"

"That's right."

"What is it you do, Mr. Rogers?"

"I'm a cop."

"Come now, Mr. Rogers," he said, "don't be modest. Not an ordinary cop, certainly. Not if you worked with Morrison in Washington. And not if you can afford an evening here."

"I'm a lieutenant, Mr. Donatello. And this place is kind of out of my league. Actually, it's the first time we've been here. We figured, what the hell, combine a wake and a celebration. Do it right."

"A wake?" Donatello asked.

"For Melissa's show closing."

"And the celebration?"

Rogers looked at Melissa. She grinned. "We've been together a year," she said.

"Congratulations," Donatello said. "That certainly is reason enough for a night out." He looked back at Rogers. "I have a close friend in the department," he said. "I don't know whether you know him, but I'm sure you know of him. Bill Dolan."

"Actually, I do know him," Rogers said.

"Interesting," Donatello said. "I'll tell him I ran into you."

Rogers could tell by her expression that Melissa was beginning to worry. She stepped in, taking over the conversation, playing up to Donatello, gushing on about the restaurant and the people there, putting on a Billie Dawn act without the dumb blonde accent. Donatello was flattered and played along, mentioning names and pedigrees.

As they were finishing coffee, Frank Tremanti made his way over to their table. Donatello and Nikki welcomed him warmly.

"Join us, Frank," Donatello said. Nikki seconded him.

"For just a minute," Tremanti said. He reached for a chair and pulled it up.

Donatello introduced Rogers and Melissa. "Mr. Rogers," he said, "works for Billy Dolan."

"That a fact?" Tremanti said. He studied Rogers. "Billy's a sweet guy," he said.

"Not precisely the word I'd use to describe him," Rogers said.

Tremanti laughed. "Yeah," he said, "Billy can be one tough nut when he wants to be. You folks enjoying yourselves?"

"Tremendously," Melissa said.

"First time in the joint?"

"Yes," she said. "We've heard about it. It certainly lives up to its reputation." She smiled at him.

Tremanti beamed. "Can I buy you guys a brandy?" Without waiting, he beckoned to a waiter. "Give these folks whatever they want," he said. He started to rise. "It's been a pleasure meeting you," he said to Rogers and Melissa. "From now on, don't be strangers." He looked toward Donatello. "Gene, before you leave, can we have a word?"

Donatello looked at his watch. "Sure, Frank," he said. "In fifteen or twenty minutes."

Tremanti strolled away.

"He's a nice man," Melissa said.

"The best," Donatello agreed.

"He's a real sweetie," Nikki said. "There isn't anything he wouldn't do for you if he likes you."

Despite the arrival of more drinks, the mood and the table seemed to have taken a downturn. Donatello appeared impatient. Their talk was desultory. After a few minutes, Rogers turned to Melissa. "It's getting late," he said, "and I think we ought to be getting home."

Donatello glanced at his watch again. "It is, isn't it," he said. "I didn't realize it had gotten to this hour."

Rogers turned to signal to a waiter. Donatello stopped him. "Forget it," he said. "You're my guests."

Rogers looked at him. "We couldn't," he said.

"Don't argue," Donatello said. "I insist. To celebrate your anniversary, and our meeting . . . for the second time. Let it not be the last."

"This is silly," Rogers said. "We couldn't impose like this."

"Nonsense, Lieutenant," Donatello said. "I can afford it. Now, no more arguments."

There was nothing but to go along. The last thing Rogers wanted to do was antagonize Donatello. He shrugged and murmured a thanks. Melissa rose and said goodbye to Nikki and Donatello.

"Call me," Nikki said. "I want to see you."

"I don't have your number," Melissa said, "and I'll bet you're not listed."

Nikki laughed, reached into Donatello's breast pocket and pulled out a pen. She took a cloth napkin, scribbled her number on it and passed it to Melissa. "Take it," she said. "Frank won't miss it. It's a souvenir, along with my very own private number."

Melissa folded it and put it into her purse. She pulled a piece of paper and scribbled on it and handed it to Nikki. "My number," she said. "Home and office." Nikki took it and shoved it into her purse.

As they turned away, Nikki called after them. "Wait a

minute. Gene's having some people in on Thursday. We'd love to have you."

Before Rogers could say anything, Melissa nodded. "Wonderful," she said. "Now that the show's closed, I'm free. What time?"

"Seven."

"We'll be there."

"You don't know where," Nikki said. "Let me have that thing again and I'll write it out." Melissa pulled out the napkin and handed it to Nikki. Nikki scribbled an address on it and handed it back.

Donatello said nothing, although Rogers could not help noticing that he didn't look pleased.

Outside on the street, the doorman flagged a cab. They got in and headed downtown. "Morrison got away cheap," Melissa remarked as she settled back on the seat.

"I wonder," Rogers said. "I don't think that guy gives anything away without a reason."

"You didn't like him."

"No. And I don't think he took to me like a long-lost brother, either. How about you?"

"He's a real sweetheart." She smiled.

"The blonde, Nikki, is she as dumb as she acts?"

"In school, when I first met her, I'd have said dumber. After a while I wasn't sure. Nobody was. Maybe it was all an act."

"What does she see in him? She could have her pick. And he's old enough to be her father."

"Uncle," she said. "Or daddy, with a sugar in front of it, if she wasn't so rich herself."

They rode the rest of the way in silence. Rogers mentally reviewed the evening, trying to put the pieces together into a whole. Donatello was suave, polite, a gentleman who gave no outward or deliberate offense. But there was something there that didn't sit well. Rogers had met him, finally, had spent an hour in his company. He had come away with the feeling that, if he had to decide right now who was telling the truth, he would go with Werner Rosenblatt.

DECEMBER

26

In midtown, the Salvation Army Santa Clauses were out on every street corner, ringing their bells, trying to get passersby to drop a dollar, a quarter, anything, into the kettles. In Little Italy, the only Santas were in store windows, along with a lot of tinsel and other decorations. The street corners had been taken over by people from upstate, and maybe from somewhere in New England or even farther away who had trucked in forests of Christmas trees overnight, lined them three deep down the blocks and then begun hawking them. Moving through them was like trying to cut a path through a dense grove of evergreens. They threatened to crowd pedestrians off the sidewalks.

Rogers threaded his way toward Canal Street. It was a little after noon, a nice time for a walk on a nice day, the sun bright, the temperature about right for late November turning into December and the Christmas season. He looked for signs of Christmas cheer, for the friendly faces, for the smiles. He didn't find any. The people looked angry and harassed.

As he neared the corner of Mulberry, he saw the porno parlor and the clubhouse with its heavy steel door. A couple of guys were standing around outside. They looked like wiseguys who were probably there on business. A couple of them could have fit Toby's description of the slick guy who looked like a hundred others. He did a quick take. He recognized one who wasn't slick. His name was Dinardo Faranulli. Some people called him Ding-Dong, which was an apt description of his upstairs, but never to his face. He looked like a wrestler, a tag team all by himself, or a weight lifter who could have pressed a quarter of a ton without breaking a sweat.

Rogers had busted him once when he was still in Homicide. Ding-Dong was a shylock's collector. A customer had been a little late with the vigorish, so Ding-Dong went out to make the collection. The customer couldn't pay. So, as people were fond of saying, Ding-Dong did what he had to do. Rogers and Palmieri brought him in. Only Ding-Dong claimed he was having dinner at Little Tony's up on Bleecker Street at the time, and the five guys he was having dinner with would back him up. They did. So did Little Tony. So Ding-Dong walked and went back on the street.

Ding-Dong glanced up and saw Rogers coming toward him. He folded his arms and glared.

"Well, hello, Ding-Dong," Rogers said. "I thought you'd be in Attica by now."

"The name's Dinardo to you, pig," he said. "Don't hassle me. I'm clean."

"Come on. You haven't been clean since your ma stopped wiping your ass. Shoulder, hip, ankle, where's the piece?"

"Get a fuckin' warrant."

Rogers laughed. He looked around. The other guys, four of them, were watching carefully. "Who're your friends, Ding-Dong?"

"Nobody you know, and nobody who wants to know you," he said. "Besides, what the fuck are you doin' here in the first place? I hear you're supposed to be after cops on the take these days."

"My, the word does get around. And I'm also after the people from whom they take."

"Don't look at me. What I'd give a cop you wouldn't want."

"I'm looking for a guy, Ding-Dong."

"You come to the wrong stand. I don't know no guys you're lookin' for."

"Big guy, big as you, fighter with all the marks. Pals around with people that look like your friends."

"Never heard of him, never saw him."

"He likes dirty movies and dirty books." Rogers nodded toward the porno shop.

"Who don't?" Ding-Dong said.

Rogers looked over at the others. They stared back with stony eyes, then looked away. "You guys hear of anything," he said, grinning, "you'll be sure to let me know."

"Up your ass, pig," Ding-Dong said.

"How you do talk," Rogers said and moved on. At the corner he paused and glanced back. Ding-Dong was talking to his friends, gesturing angrily, nodding. Rogers smiled, turned the corner onto Mulberry Street, and started walking north, through the crush of the lunch crowd that lined every block in search of authentic Italian food, perhaps in search, too, of a glimpse of somebody infamous and dangerous.

Somebody infamous and dangerous was half a block ahead of him, a tall, muscular man in a dark cashmere overcoat, ringed by other men a little smaller, striding rapidly along, oblivious of the crowds that parted to make way for him. Generoso Ruggieri was on his way to lunch at his favorite restaurant, Montenario's. He ate there almost every day, and always at the same hour. You could have clocked him and you wouldn't have been off by more than a minute. The guys who ringed him had eyes that never stopped looking, and hands out of sight, inside coat lapels. And there was backup. All those people on the street who lived in the neighborhood.

Rogers watched as a woman in a heavy, shabby overcoat, a print shawl over her head, hurried toward Ruggieri. One of the bodyguards moved to shove her to one side, but Ruggieri put up a hand and gestured to the woman to approach, the benevolent monarch granting an audience. The old woman leaned in toward Ruggieri and said something beseeching. He listened, said something back, and patted her shoulder. She took a deep breath of relief, grabbed his hand, bent and kissed it, and then stepped aside. It was like a scene from a movie, Rogers thought. If you didn't see it, if it didn't happen every day on these streets, you'd think somebody in Hollywood made it up. Francis Ford Coppola couldn't have staged it more perfectly.

As Ruggieri moved on, he looked back toward the woman and smiled. His eyes flickered over her, scanning the crowd on the street. He spotted Rogers and nodded, then started to turn away. As recognition registered, he stopped, looked back and beckoned to him.

Rogers stepped forward. "Mr. Ruggieri," he said.

"Lieutenant Rogers," Ruggieri replied, a question in his tone. "A surprise. You are here on official business?"

Rogers shook his head. "Just slumming," he said.

"Then you will join me for lunch." Before Rogers could answer, Ruggieri reached out, took him by the arm, and steered him into the restaurant. Umberto Montenario, the putative owner, rushed forward, welcoming Ruggieri as though the king had come to bestow small favors on the lowliest of his subjects. He steered them through the mob that was waiting for tables and seated them at a table in an alcove at the rear. Ruggieri's bodyguards took a table nearby.

Montenario hurried away, then returned almost immediately, carrying a bottle of wine and two glasses. "For you, Mr. Ruggieri," he said, "I have been saving this. It is the best of the best from Sicily, a Corvo di Casteldaccia. From the finest white grapes. The vintage beyond compare."

Ruggieri smiled and nodded. "*Grazie*, Umberto," he said.

Montenario uncorked it, filled each glass and stood back, waiting anxiously. Ruggieri lifted his glass, inhaled the aroma of the wine, and then took a sip. He looked at the owner and nodded. "*Bene, molto bene*," he said.

"You will have the *pesce*?" Montenario asked. "Fresh, very fresh. I pick it out myself this morning at the market. *Sogliole* I would have myself. I will cook special for you. A little lemon, a little garlic, pepper, four kinds I grind fresh myself, butter. You will also have *insalata verde di funghi*. Perhaps a little *pasta alle vongole*."

"I leave it to you," Ruggieri said. "Surprise me. My guest will have what I have."

Montenario beamed and hurried away toward the kitchen.

"You do not mind that I ordered for you, Mr. Rogers?" Ruggieri said.

"I'm your guest," Rogers said. "If he recommended it to you, it should be something. Maybe even a little too much for lunch. I'll have to skip dinner."

"Not too much. One should eat well at all meals. Not as the Americans eat, with their hamburgers dripping grease, but as the Italians eat. This will be special. I guarantee it." He studied Rogers. "So, how may I serve you?"

Rogers put on a surprised look.

"Come, Mr. Rogers," Ruggieri said, "you did not happen to be passing this place just as I arrived. My habits are well known. Do not pretend. It does not become you. How may I serve you?"

Rogers looked over at Ruggieri's bodyguards. "I don't see the guy you sent for me that time. Gino. I thought he was your A Number One gofer."

"Gino," Ruggieri said, his voice cold and hard, "is no longer in my employ. It is no longer a concern of mine where he has gone."

"I suppose he'll turn up one of these days."

"Everyone turns up, sooner or later."

"Not always, and not everybody. I saw the guy he used to hang out with, down the street. Ding-Dong. I heard they are partners in a few things these days."

"What things?" Ruggieri stared steadily at him, his face impassive.

"Maybe you didn't know. But I thought you know everything that goes on around here."

"You flatter me. My ears hear only what people want to tell me."

"Don't be modest, Mr. Ruggieri," Rogers said. "People tell you everything. One thing, though. People always said that no matter what else you did, you stayed clear of *barbana*, junk."

"Mr. Rogers, narcotics is a business only the vile of the earth would touch. Anyone can make money. Perhaps not so quickly, but there are other things than money. Anyone who deals in narcotics is a fool, or worse. I do not know who is the more wretched, the man who sells or the man who buys. No one is safe from them. But I say this from a distance, as a man who notices things that pass before his eyes, who observes the world. It is something I care about only as a good citizen. I would stop it if that was possible. But what can I do? Perhaps, once, a few Italians did this thing, but now those who do it are Colombians, Latins, Asians, people foreign to us who care for nothing but wealth. I salute those who seek them out and put an end to their ways. But I am in the real estate business. That is my occupation. That is my only interest."

"Of course," Rogers said. "Still, people do talk." What people said, Rogers knew, was that in the early days, Ruggieri had played the game a little, but not for long. It probably wasn't moral scruples that kept him clean, despite his protestations. It was more likely that he'd seen too many of his friends end up in the slammer or in their own blood in the gutter. Junk brought down the heat and the spotlight, and Ruggieri had no fondness for either. People said that in his family you didn't last long if you pushed drugs.

"Some say foolish things, some say wise things," Ruggieri said. "They invent stories. Some may be true, most are not. Our people are famous for their imagination. They pretend they know everything about everything, and they repeat what they think they know, and some even come to believe what they have invented. One can do nothing about it. Now, Mr. Rogers, let us talk about you. I hear you have not taken my advice."

Rogers shrugged. "As some of the people you know say, I do what I have to do."

"Perhaps. But you are not wise, you are courting great danger." He looked up. Montenario was approaching, plates in hand, the steam and aromas wafting up from them. A waiter trailed in his wake, carrying the salads and the pasta. "Ah," Ruggieri said. "Umberto brings our lunch. Let us enjoy it and speak of more pleasant things. I understand you have a beautiful young lady."

"Where did you hear that?"

"As you yourself said, people talk. But I hear as well that she is not Sicilian and not Catholic. When I was young, that would have been impossible."

"It's a different world and a different time," Rogers said.

Montenario was standing over them, watching, waiting. Ruggieri lifted his fork, took a small piece of the fish and tasted it. He nodded, smiled broadly. "*Bene*, Umberto. *Molto bene*."

He looked at Rogers. "Try it, Mr. Rogers. You will find it is all that Umberto promised. Now, tell me about this young lady. You care for her? You would protect her? You would not want bad things to happen to her?"

27

"Ben," the voice on the phone said, "it's Carlos. I think our baby is back in business."

"Why?"

"The good stuff is showin' up on the street again. I went up to the hospital, but it was like the last time, nobody knew nothin', nobody wanted to know nothin', nobody was sayin' nothin', nothin' was goin' on. I sniffed around a little. Nobody's seen the cop. But I'd lay odds. They just got a different system, is all. I thought you'd want to know."

"Thanks, Carlos. I'll do something for you someday."

"You gonna look into it?"

"Could be."

"Look, you come on somethin', ring me in. I could use a good collar. You know, like one hand washes the other."

"Will do."

He put on his coat and went out into a freezing afternoon, rode the subway uptown and emerged where the two worlds of New York confront each other across a wide street divided by an invisible but unbreachable wall. On one side, the affluent world of the satisfied, if terrified, whites; on the other, the blacks

and Latinos, poor, angry, hopeless, and equally frightened because they are more preyed upon and less protected.

The hospital Rogers was headed for dominated the area,
filling blocks along one side of the avenue, and facing parking
lots, deteriorating tenements, and the rubble of what had once
been tenements along the other. He identified himself to a receptionist and asked to see the nursing supervisor. She appeared a few minutes later, wearing a name tag that read:
Phyllis Abernathy, RN. She had a great smile, one that lit up
her face.

"What can I do for you, Officer?" she said.

"Is there somewhere we can talk in private?"

The smile faded. Without it, she looked harassed, tired,
overworked, grim. She nodded and spun, leading him silently to
her office.

"Is this about what I think it is?" she said.

"It depends on what you think it is."

"Jenny Mendoza," she said.

"Her, and whoever is the new Jenny Mendoza," he said.

"What makes you think there's a new one?" she said.

"Come on, Miss Abernathy. I don't think. I know."

"It's Mrs. Abernathy," she said. "And how can you be so
sure?"

"The stuff's out there again. Your damn closets are leaking
and you people are afraid to put even a Band-Aid over the leak,
for chrissake."

"It could be another hospital," she said.

"It could be a dozen other hospitals," he said. "Only it starts
right here."

"I'm not supposed to talk about it," she said. "Not to anyone. They're all so afraid that if anything gets out, the hospital
will be hurt."

"The hospital's going to get burned a lot worse if this thing
doesn't stop," he said.

"I know," she said. She looked away, closed her eyes, and
put her head in her hands. She stayed that way for a moment,
then looked up. She had decided to chance it. "We're not sure,"
she said. "It could be one of four nurses."

"Why them?"

"How do you people put it? Opportunity, isn't that right?
They've all been with us long enough since this thing began.

They all work the night shift, and that means that they take a break sometime in the early hours and go down to the cafeteria. And they've all been on duty the nights when things were taken."

"They've all got a motive, a reason to do it?"

"I wouldn't know about that. How could I? I don't know about their personal lives."

"I want to talk to them," he said.

She nodded. "It can be arranged. Will you let them know they're suspected?"

"Probably not," he said.

"They all work at night," she said. "They won't be here until about eleven."

"I think it might be better if I talked to them at home. It would spare the hospital any extra embarrassment."

"And they wouldn't be prepared for you if you just knocked at their door. You'd catch them by surprise and one of them might say something. Isn't that it?"

"You're a bright lady, Mrs. Abernathy."

"Not bright enough," she said angrily, "or this wouldn't be going on—or I'd have caught it and stopped it a long time ago."

"Nobody's blaming you. How many nurses do you have on your staff?" he asked gently. "A couple of hundred? More? And they work three shifts. You can't be everywhere, and there's no way you can know everything that goes on."

"I'm supposed to. It's my job."

"Sure."

"I'm responsible for the lives of all the patients in this hospital. If one of my nurses is doing something like that . . ." She shook her head. "You'd like their names and addresses?"

He nodded.

She swiveled on her chair and faced a computer console on a table behind her. After about thirty seconds of punching buttons she reached and ripped a sheet of paper off the computer's printer. She handed it to Rogers. There were four names on it, along with addresses, telephone numbers, and a few vital statistics.

"God," she said, "I hope you can do something. This has got to stop. Right how, I don't care what the people in Administration say. It just has to stop."

"It will," he said. "You can count on it."

*　　*　　*

Thelma Rutledge, the first name on the list, lived in a project about ten blocks to the north of the hospital. She was, according to the sheet, thirty-four, and she'd been a night nurse at the hospital for eight years. She worked on the pediatrics floor.

Rogers walked the half mile. At the edge of the project some black kids, teenagers, were playing basketball on a court surrounded by a wire fence. It looked like there were ten to a side, at least, and a lot more on the edges shouting obscenities at some and encouragement at others. All the kids had their coats off, were down to T-shirts despite the cold, and the sweat was dripping off them. One kid towered over the rest. He kept dunking while the others clawed at his legs. It didn't seem fair. The tall kid was too good. He was maybe sixteen, and if he kept growing and improving, he had a future, maybe another Patrick Ewing. Maybe not. Maybe what he was now was all he'd ever be, or maybe the scumbag leaning against the fence, watching, would slip him a little crack as a treat. Then the kid wouldn't have a chance. The scumbag spotted Rogers. He grinned, knowing exactly what Rogers was. What other white guys came up to the project? He gave Rogers the finger.

Rogers went by, the object of a certain level of attention from the adults as well as from the kids. Everybody made him, and everybody wondered what the hell he was doing there. A couple of kids took off, fast. They were sure they knew. Eventually, he found the building he wanted and went in. There was no guard, nobody to stop him.

One elevator wasn't working. The other was occupied by two kids who apparently had mistaken it for a bedroom. The boy looked up when the door slid open, grinned, and said, "Hey, my man, what you doin' here? This be private." He reached up, pressed the "Door Close" button and he and his girl vanished from sight. Rogers decided to walk the five flights, stepping over and around the litter that filled the stairwell, ignoring the sentiments that had been spray-painted on the walls, trying to close his nose to the stench of urine that seemed to leak from the walls. He rang the bell at 5D. Inside, a baby started to cry. A woman's voice called, "Freddy, will you see who that is?"

The door opened as far as the chain lock on the inside would permit. A dark face peered through the crack.

"I'd like to speak with Mrs. Rutledge," Rogers said to the face. He displayed his shield to the eyes.

The door closed. A male voice inside said, "Thelma, there's a cop outside, wants to talk with you."

The woman's voice answered. "A cop? You sure?"

"He got a vanilla face. And he got a shield."

"Damn. Let him in."

Rogers heard the chain lock slip from its housing. The door swung open, held by a man wearing a mailman's uniform. He looked at Rogers. "Well," he said, "you might as well come in. She's just tendin' to the baby. She'll be out in a minute."

The apartment was small, as project apartments always are. There wasn't much furniture, but everything looked neat and orderly, like these people took care of what they had. A door in the far wall opened, and a woman, nearly as wide as she was tall, with a broad, open face, came through, cradling a baby in her arms. The baby looked contented, its eyes closed. The way she held the baby, everything about her said she was the kind of nurse you'd want to have take care of your kid if your kid happened to wind up in a hospital. He was sure that he could write her off.

She stood in the doorway and looked at Rogers. "I suppose," she said, "you've come about Jenny Mendoza. Couldn't be anything else. I already told the other officers all I know."

"I understand that," he said. "I'd just like to go over a few things, if you don't mind."

She sighed. "Like I already told them more times than I can remember, I didn't know her very well. I take care of the sick children and she was in the building with the surgical patients. I used to see her now and then, down in the cafeteria at night when we was on our break. Maybe I had coffee with her a time or two. But that's all."

"What was she like, what sort of person?"

"She was okay. Nothin' special. Let me tell you, we were all real surprised and upset when that thing happened to her."

"You knew she was in some trouble?"

"People talk. I don't listen."

"What do people say?"

"Like I said, I don't listen. Maybe somethin' about drugs or the like. It didn't mean nothin' to me."

"At night, when you went down to the cafeteria on your break, did you ever notice a policeman wandering around?"

"Police are always wanderin' around. I don't pay no attention."

"Did you ever see Jenny Mendoza in conversation with a policeman?"

"Maybe I did, maybe I didn't. If I did, it wouldn't have made no matter, and I would have forgot it." The baby started to stir restlessly. She bent over it, crooning a little, caressing its back. The baby nestled against her.

"What's his name?" Rogers asked.

"Him is a her and her name is Tamara. She's a little fretful with the colic. Nothin' to be concerned. She'll be fine."

He asked her a few more questions, thanked her for her cooperation and left.

Next on the list was Victoria McPherson. She lived on Park Avenue in the eighties, an odd address for a nurse. According to the print-out she was thirty and had worked in the hospital for five years. Her building was like most of the rest along that part of the avenue, about twelve stories, brick, built in the 1920s and well tended, a little patch of small evergreen shrubs along the front. A doorman stood just inside the entrance. He held the door as Rogers turned in under the canopy. There was a desk in the lobby with a small sign on it saying that all guests must be announced. A concierge stood behind it ready to do the announcing.

Rogers went through the routine. The concierge called up, got the okay, and pointed Rogers to the elevators at the back of the lobby. The elevator operator took him up to six, pointed to one of the two doors on the floor and waited before closing the elevator and descending until Rogers pressed the bell and the door opened.

Victoria McPherson opened the door herself. She had red hair, hanging loose down past her shoulders, a parchment complexion, dark blue eyes, a few light freckles across a small nose. Except for the dark circles under her eyes and a sag of fatigue in her slim body, she might have passed for a decade younger than her thirty. She was dressed in dark slacks and a white silk blouse which Rogers bet didn't come off a thrift shop table.

She looked at Rogers. "It's not about that damn Mendoza again, is it?"

"I'm afraid so."

"Christ," she said, "haven't I answered enough questions already from you people? Well, you might as well come in. Only let's make it quick, shall we? I've had a tough night and I've got another one coming up."

He followed her through a large entry foyer and into the living room. It was about forty feet long and thirty wide. Some of the furniture came straight from an antique store, the rest from a decorator's showroom catalogue. He wasn't an expert, but he'd been to enough museums to know that the paintings on the wall were the real thing. Two of them he recognized from a show he'd seen the year before at the Metropolitan; the tag beneath them had said they were on loan from a private collector.

Victoria McPherson perched on a sofa and motioned him into a nearby chair. She reached down and shook a cigarette from a pack on the table and lit it. "Don't tell me," she said. "I know, it's not good for your health. They can give you cancer or emphysema. Christ, I get that lecture a dozen times a day, at the hospital and here. My father's the worst. He gave up five years ago. Let me tell you, there's nothing to equal a reformed sinner." She inhaled deeply. "Okay, let's get this over with. What do you want to know that I haven't said already?"

"How well did you know Jenny Mendoza?"

"I knew her. We worked on the same floor, in post-op. She was a little tramp. Does that surprise you? Are you shocked that I'd say it? Never speak ill of the dead and all that crap? I mean, you must have heard it before. At least rumors. Well, they're all true. She couldn't keep her panties on, if she even bothered to wear any, which I sincerely doubt. She had the hots for every guy—doctors, orderlies, patients if they had the strength to get it up—anyone. So, was I surprised when she got herself raped and killed? Like hell I was. I was sure she came on to the wrong guy, and that was that." She leaned back, took another puff of the cigarette, and glared at him, as though offering a challenge.

"I read your original statement," he said. "There's nothing like that in it."

She shrugged and flicked her cigarette in the ashtray.

"Were you surprised when you found out what really happened?" he asked.

"You mean, with the drug closet? Nobody ever said it

straight out, but there was talk. And no, I wasn't surprised. Nothing Jenny Mendoza did would ever have surprised me."

"Did you ever hear anything about who was helping her? Somebody on the inside?"

She stared at him. "Oh my God," she said, "don't tell me it's started again." He didn't answer. "You bastard," she said. "You've ruined my day."

"Can you think of anyone who was close to her?"

"What am I, a fortune teller with a crystal ball? I told you, I walked a hundred yards in the opposite direction so I wouldn't have to run into her."

"Anyone who might have been working with her?" he asked again.

"There are a dozen nurses on our floor on the night shift. Am I supposed to suspect one of them?"

"Or someone else in the hospital."

"I don't have much to do with the other nurses once I'm outside the hospital. Except for nursing, we don't have that much in common. I live my own life. I'm a nurse because that's what I chose to be. Believe it or not, I want to help people. I wanted to be a doctor, but my father wouldn't hear of it. He thinks only men are fit to be doctors, and so he wouldn't foot the bill. Do you know what medical school costs? He thought I ought to get married and raise children. Someday, maybe, but not yet. When the right guy comes along. Don't laugh. I believe in love. I believe marriage is for keeps. So I'm a nurse. I was a nurse in El Salvador for a year, which was about all anyone can take, and now I'm a nurse here. I like what I do. I'm not running around spending Daddy's ill-gotten millions like some of the people I grew up with. I think I'm doing something worthwhile with my life. And no, goddammit, I'm not going to point a finger at somebody."

"Even somebody who may be screwing up everything you believe in?"

"Not without proof," she said. "I won't be part of a witch hunt."

"Not witches," he said. "Somebody real, and a hell of a lot worse. Go out on the street. Not Park Avenue, but a block over, to Lex. Go downtown, uptown, anywhere in the city. Take a look at the street corners. Take a look around the schools, look at the slime hanging around. Look at the people nodding out in the doorways, in the subway entrances, everywhere. They're not just the homeless. And walk down to your emergency room any damn night and take a good look at the people they bring in who've OD'd. Then tell me we're on a witch hunt."

"One nurse rifling the drug closet for a handful of pills?"

"Multiply it by a hundred, by a thousand. And it's not just a handful of pills."

She turned that over. He watched her face change. She looked at him, shaking her head slowly. "Janice Palmer," she said. It was a name on the list. "She's in general medicine, on the night shift. I used to see her and Mendoza together in the cafeteria at break. It didn't mean anything. Nurses don't like to be alone in the middle of the night. Maybe I couldn't understand why anyone would want to hang around Mendoza, but it didn't mean anything then. Maybe it still doesn't. And if it doesn't, then what the hell have I done?"

J anice Palmer lived on Manhattan's West Side in a renovated brownstone. According to the hospital list, she was twenty-eight and had been with the hospital for four years. Early the next afternoon, Rogers headed in that direction. He carried a heavy, bulging briefcase with him. The brownstone was in the middle of a gentrified block, most of the buildings already renovated, the rest in the process. This had been an inexpensive area, but no more. The rents here weren't much lower than across the park on the East Side. Unless you were lucky and had been able to hold onto a rent stabilized apartment, you had to be earning near the six-figure range to be able to afford it. Nurses don't make in the six figures, and Rogers didn't think Janice Palmer had a rich daddy like Victoria McPherson.

He went up the steps and through the heavy door to the foyer. On the wall, next to a row of mailboxes, was a rack of bell buttons with the tenants' names in slots. Janice Palmer was in 3R. Since there were only Fs and Rs, he figured the R stood for rear. He punched a couple of buttons. He didn't punch 3R. Some incautious soul shouted into the intercom, "Yes, who's there?" and then pushed the door open without waiting to find out.

Rogers didn't answer. He shoved the door open and walked into the downstairs hall. The door to the basement was halfway along the hall. He tried it. It wasn't locked. He went down into the dim, dank cellar, a shaft of light through a dusty window at street level spreading a trail along the floor. At the end of the trail, he found the telephone terminal box. He unscrewed the lid and opened it, trying not to think about what he was going to do. He was going to break the law. He was going to commit a federal crime, and if somebody caught wise, he could go to prison. He'd thought about it all through the sleepless night. He'd gotten out of bed so as not to wake Melissa with his tossing. Often enough he'd heard that when a cop breaks the law, even when he's sure it's the only way to solve a worse crime, society, everybody, suffers. Cops were supposed to play by the rules. If you wanted to wiretap, go to court, persuade the judge and get a legal order. He believed that, even though more cops than he wanted to think about laughed at it, pretended they didn't have to worry about it, went ahead and tapped and then made up a story to cover what they'd done. The best he could do was rationalize, which he had done the first time he'd planted an illegal wiretap; that time it had been for Morrison, with Morrison's secret blessing, on the federal case they were working together. Then, as now, he wasn't going to tap the line to get evidence that would find its way into court. Then, as now, it was to get a lead that might not come any other way, or if it came, might take forever and put some people in jeopardy. It was the best he could come up with, but he still didn't like it. Just stop thinking and do it, he told himself. Don't think about the consequences.

He studied the interior of the phone box and found the terminal posts. Opening his briefcase, he took out a jack with a dialing handset like the kind telephone company repairmen use, and clipped it to the terminals. Any would do. They didn't have to be the right ones just yet. He dialed a number, and as it began to ring, he spit on his fingers and began to rub them along the pairs of wires. The phone was answered upstairs. "Hello?"

He didn't respond, his fingers moving rapidly along the wires. He got a shock. He'd found the right ones.

"Hello?" the voice said again. "Who's there?"

He hung up. The line went dead. It didn't matter. He had what he wanted. He clipped a pair of wires from a spool in the briefcase to the line, laid out the wire from the terminal box along the wall toward a wooden door. The door was padlocked, the lock the kind that would open if you stared at it hard enough. He took out his knife, snapped up the pick, and had the lock

sprung in about ten seconds. He took out his flashlight, turned
it on, and the beam spread across a pile of old trunks, luggage,
straw boxes, cardboard cartons, and other junk.

He spooled the wires into the storage closet, then turned
and followed them back to the terminal box, taping them to the
base of the wall where they'd be invisible as he moved along.
From his briefcase, he removed an old voice-activated reel-to-
reel tape recorder with an inked pen register, carried it to the
closet, and hooked it up to the wires. Now, whenever Janice
Palmer dialed her phone upstairs, he'd not only have a recording
of both ends of the conversation, but he'd be able to count ac-
curately the clicks of her dialing, and so know precisely the
number she had called. He checked to make sure the connections
were set, then closed the closet door, replaced the padlock,
locked it, and then went up from the basement.

Now he pushed the button for 3R. A voice came through the
intercom. "Yes?"

"Miss Palmer?"

"Yes."

"Police. I'd like a word with you."

There was a hesitation, then, a hint of fear edging the voice,
"Police?"

"My name's Lieutenant Rogers. Please let me up."

Another hesitation, then the clicking in the door sounded
and he pushed his way into the building. He took the tiny elevator to the third floor. Her door was to the right. It was open
a little way and she was standing in that gap, watching. She
couldn't have been more than five feet tall, with short black hair,
brown eyes, a snub nose, and about fifteen or twenty pounds
more than she needed. She was trying to conceal those extra
pounds in a designer outfit. She was also trying to control her
face, to keep it blank, but her eyes radiated terror.

"Miss Palmer?" he said.

She nodded.

"Could I come in? I'd like to talk with you."

"How did you get my address?" she asked.

"From the hospital," he said.

That upset her. "They're not supposed to give it out," she
said.

"They wouldn't ordinarily," he said. "But this isn't ordinary. This is serious police business."

She stood there, blocking the way for another moment, then reluctantly stepped back into the apartment. An exposed brick hallway led to a large living room. It was a nice room, nicely done. Expensively done, in fact. Very modern. A coffee table held the latest magazines; a small bookcase was filled with current best-sellers. The television set across from the sofa was a thirty-inch monitor. The stereo system, set into a satiny black rack near the television, had a separate matching amplifier, preamplifier, tuner, tape deck, CD player, record turntable, and equalizer, the floor-standing speakers set a little distance on either side. He'd seen ads for the rig, so he knew this stuff wasn't cheap. No, somebody had put some money into this place. And recently—it had that new, store-bought smell. He'd like to get a look at her bank balance, although he'd probably find nothing there. More likely he'd strike the mother lode in a safe-deposit box, or perhaps even a shoe box under the bed.

She walked to the sofa, sat stiffly on the edge, and stared at him. "What do you want?" she asked.

"You were a close friend of Jenny Mendoza," he said. His voice was sharp, even accusing. He'd made the decision even before he saw her, made it on his way to her place after he'd listened to Victoria McPherson, to play the heavy, to shake her up, let panic eat away at her until she thought she had no choice but to make a call.

"I knew her," she said. "I've already said that a million times to other police."

"Okay, then let's run it through for the million and first."

"What else do you want me to say? She was another nurse in the hospital. We both worked the same shift. So I knew her."

"More than knew her from what I've been told. Friends, real close friends, bosom buddies as a matter of fact. Right?"

"I liked her. She was all right," Janice Palmer said. "It was terrible what happened to her."

"It was terrible, I agree," he said. "But she wasn't all right."

Her mouth fell open. She stared at him.

"She was a thief," he said. "She was worse than a thief. She was stealing drugs from the hospital and dealing them with a guy on the outside."

"I didn't know," she whispered, looking away.

"You didn't know? Come on, Janice, it's been all over the hospital. Are you deaf as well as blind?" She didn't like that, he could tell. He knew she also didn't like it that he called her Janice and not Miss Palmer. He'd bet all the other cops had called her Miss Palmer.

Rogers remained silent for a while, letting his eyes march deliberately around that living room, focusing on each piece before moving on. When he finished the inventory, he looked back at her and made a further inventory. "Nice apartment you have here, Janice," he said.

She didn't answer.

"Nice furniture, nice accessories, nice everything. Nice clothes, too. The best that money can buy. Rent to go with it. I keep asking myself, where does a dame on a nurse's pay get that kind of bread?"

He could practically see her mind working frantically. There was panic behind the eyes. "I . . ." she started, stopped, began again, "I spend everything I make. I don't save a penny."

"I'd say you spend more than you make. At least what you make on the up and up."

He held his breath for a moment. This is when she ought to throw him out, get mad as hell and tell him if he was going to make any accusations, she wanted to talk to a lawyer before she said another word. She didn't. She swallowed a few times, looked away, then looked back. "I'm very deep in debt," she said finally.

"I'll bet you are," he said, exhaling slowly. "I should be so deep in debt."

"I owe everybody," she insisted.

"The habit comes high," he said.

"What do you mean?"

"Come off it. You know exactly what I mean. It's easy to get hooked. It ain't so easy to get unhooked."

At last he got her mad. She sat straight up and glared at him. "I am not a user," she said.

He nodded. "Maybe not," he said. "Users spend everything on the garbage. I guess you couldn't be a user and afford all this. How about pusher? That ring a bell?"

He got to her then. She rose stiffly from the sofa. "Get out!" she said. "Get out of here! Right now! I don't have to listen to any more of this."

He ignored her. "Who's the connection?" he said. "Or are you the inside source, just like your dead little friend? Come on,

Janice, who are you working with? The same guy, right? Think about it. You don't want to end up like poor little Jenny Mendoza."

"Get out!" she shouted. "I'm going to call my lawyer! He'll have your badge!"

He got up slowly. He grinned at her. "Don't bother to show me out," he said. "I'll find my way. But I'll be back, little Janice. Never fear. I'll be back."

He turned and started down the long brick-walled hallway. She followed him, stopped at the entrance to the living room and watched as he opened the door and left, closing it behind him.

He rode the elevator down. She would think about what had just happened and the panic with which he had left her would grow and intensify. Maybe it wouldn't happen right away, maybe she'd take some time to think about it and consider, but pretty soon she'd reach out and contact her guy. And when she did, the little box in the storage room in the basement would be all that Rogers would need. He'd give it a few days before he returned to retrieve it, and then, in privacy and at his leisure, he would listen. She probably wouldn't say much. She wouldn't have to. If he was smart, the guy wouldn't let her. It didn't matter if the call lasted only long enough for a hello and good-bye. All he needed were a series of clicks, and he would have the number, and Cole's, the reverse directory, would point him dead aim on the target.

28

"I've got some news," Melissa said. She had arrived home later than usual, had seemed distracted as they were dressing for the evening at Donatello's.

"Good or bad?"

"Depends," she said. He waited. "I had a call from that agent this morning."

"I didn't know you'd signed with her."

"I haven't, not yet. But she's acting like I already have, or that there isn't any question that I will."

"She called you at work?"

"Yes. She's submitted me for a film."

"And?"

"She sent them the tape of that soap I did a couple of months ago. She said they liked it. She said they were excited, only that's probably agent talk, or Hollywood talk. Anyway, they want to fly me out to California to audition and do a test."

"Are you going?"

"I think so."

"When?"

"Probably in a week or ten days, something like that. I'll be out there a couple of days, that's all. Back for the holidays."

"And if you get it?"

"I'm not counting on it. But if I do, yes, I'll take it. For chrissake, Ben, don't look at me like that."

"How am I looking at you?" He knew how. He could feel it in the turning of his stomach, like everything was spinning and sinking.

"We always knew something like this might happen. It's not like we never talked about it. I thought you wanted it for me."

"I do," he said. "But, Jesus, I'll miss you."

"It probably will come to nothing, of course, but if it does happen, I won't be gone forever. It would only be for a couple of months and then I'd be back."

"Sure. That's what they all say. But they never come back."

"I'll come back," she said. She looked straight at him. "Depend on it. I'm in love with you." She turned away and went back to dressing. He watched her. This time, she wore a beige silk skirt that swirled around her, and a matching blouse. Another bargain at the thrift shop. If it all came true, she wouldn't have to shop there anymore.

"Something else," she said, turning back toward him. "Nikki called me this morning and asked me to have lunch with her."

He turned and stared. "Did you go?"

"Sure. She came downtown and took me to a place in Little Italy. The food was marvelous. So was the ambience. I mean, there were people you only read about. Maybe not you, but me."

"Who?"

"Well, there were four movie stars and two directors. I recognized them right away. A couple of writers. I'd seen their pictures on book jackets. And there was Generoso Ruggieri. I recognized him from the newspapers. Nikki said he ate there all the time. He was all alone in the booth and they treated him like he was royalty. The waiters, the owner, everybody came up to him and bowed and scraped like they were his courtiers. Anyway, Nikki and I had a good talk. Ben, she's in love with that guy."

"Ruggieri?" He grinned at her.

"No, dumbhead. Gene Donatello. She met him during the summer. She was up in Boston visiting her family and he was up there on business. Her father's in stocks and bonds, and he and Gene were apparently meeting about some big deal. Anyway, her father brought Gene home to dinner and that's how they met. She was really surprised they hadn't met before, because her father had known him for twenty years, maybe more. She said she took one look at him and that was it. It didn't matter that he was as old as her father. He was kind of mysterious, she said, and he was so confident that you just knew that this was one powerful man. He called her when she got back to New York, and it just took off from there. Now, she says, her father's really pissed off at Gene about something, and he's told her not to have anything more to do with him. But she doesn't care. She's in love with Gene and that's all that matters."

"Yeah," he said. "That's why she asked you to lunch, to tell you she was in love with the guy?"

"That, and, I guess, to warn me about tonight. She said the other people who are going to be there are all old friends of Gene's, so they're his age, and so are their wives. When she's around them, they make her feel like a kid. So when she saw me the other night, she thought for once she was going to have somebody her age there so she'd have somebody she could talk to."

"I see," he said. "When she asked, I wondered about it."

"One more thing," she said. "She told me to tell you that one of the people who'll be there is your boss. Bill Dolan. He and Gene grew up together."

The cab let them off in front of the building a few minutes after seven-thirty. The doorman stepped out, opened the cab door for them, then held the apartment-house door. The concierge looked them over, smiled, rang Donatello to announce them, and then directed them to the elevators to the right.

A man in a morning suit opened the apartment door on the fifteenth floor when they rang. He took their coats and pointed the way into the living room. It was a big room with a view at one end over Central Park, to the shimmering lights in the windows on Central Park West, and beyond to a glimpse of the wide, dark Hudson River, even to the lights on the distant Jersey side. The furniture in the room was massive, dark carved wood, Italian Renaissance, straight-backed chairs and sofas. It didn't look comfortable. On the floor was a huge Persian rug. Donatello was obviously a collector. Small Renaissance icons were on display in glass cases and on the mantel above the massive fireplace, and there was Renaissance art on the walls.

They were the first to arrive. The living room was empty. Nikki appeared from somewhere, saw them and hurried across the room. "God," she said, "am I glad to see you. These things can be deadly. Everyone reminiscing about the old days like they hadn't seen each other in thirty years. And wait'll you get a load of their wives. You know that old saying about you can take the kid out of the country but you can't take the country out of the kid? That's them. Only, in their case, it's not the country, but the West Side, like, you know, Hell's Kitchen before it became fashionable. It is fashionable these days, isn't it?"

"Not yet." Rogers grinned. "Someday, maybe, We're early?"

She laughed. "Never. Everybody else is late. It's the thing."

Donatello strolled into the room, saw them, paused just an instant, and then came across, hand outstretched. Donatello turned toward Melissa, smiled appreciatively, and bowed his head. "I'm glad you could make it," he said.

"Melissa's going to Hollywood," Nikki said.

Donatello looked at her. "True?" he asked.

"Just for an audition and a screen test," she said. "No offer or anything like that. Just a maybe."

"I know some people out there," he said. "Perhaps I could help."

"Not unless you own the studio," she said.

He laughed. He looked over at Rogers and noticed Rogers studying the paintings on the walls. He smiled.

"They look like they ought to be across the street," Rogers said. "On the second floor."

"Hardly," Donatello said. "Maybe the icons, but not the paintings. They're just 'school of' works, not by the masters themselves. I may have money, but not that much."

In the distance there was the melodious chiming of the doorbell. Donatello turned, murmured something, and stepped toward the entrance. A minute or so later, Frank Tremanti appeared, his wife at his side. She was a short, plump woman, a little dumpy, with a wide, red friendly face. Her clothes were designer originals, and might have looked fashionable on someone else.

Donatello greeted them, took Tremanti by the elbow and led him toward Nikki, Melissa, and Rogers. His wife hung back, hovering, almost as though she were afraid to enter the room. "I know you," Tremanti said to Melissa and Rogers. "Right?"

"You met them the other night," Nikki said. "At the restaurant. Remember?"

"That's right," Tremanti said. He grinned at Rogers. "You're one of Billy Dolan's boys, right?"

"Right."

Tremanti beckoned his wife. "For chrissake, Teresa, don't be a mouse all your life." She sidled across the floor to them and smiled uncertainly. "Say hello to these nice people," Tremanti ordered. He looked as though he was trying to remember the name.

"Ben Rogers."

"That's right. I'm terrible about names." Tremanti laughed. He looked at Melissa. "And this is . . . hey, I never did get your name. How the hell did that happen?"

"Melissa Redburn," she said.

"You ought to be in the movies," Tremanti said. "I mean it."

"She is," Nikki said.

"Not quite," Melissa said.

Tremanti looked again. Melissa explained. "I could help," he said. "All kinds of movie people, they hang out in my joint. I could pass the word."

Melissa laughed.

Suddenly, the room filled. The doorbell kept chiming and Donatello moved easily back and forth between the room and the entryway, welcoming his guests. Bill Dolan stepped into the room, his wife, Patricia, beside him.

Congressman Michael Benedetto arrived a minute later with his wife, Renata, a handsome, statuesque woman with an air and style that proclaimed she was somebody.

Peter McIntyre, the Assistant DA, was next, with his wife, Rosemary, nearly as tall as he.

The last to arrive was Bishop Dennis Molloy, dressed as usual in his clerical garb. He looked a little harried, a little distressed, but in an instant the expression changed, his mouth curling up in a smile, as though pleased to be with his friends.

A young woman served hors d'oeuvres. A young man took drink orders. The men gathered in a group at one side of the room, near the windows; the women formed another group, around one of the sofas. Only Nikki, Melissa, and Rogers didn't join them, creating, instead, their own separate group.

"It's always like this," Nikki said. "It's like those guys don't have a thing to say to their wives. You know, like out of an old TV sitcom where the little woman stays home and cooks and knits and raises the kids, keeps her mouth shut and never offers an opinion because she doesn't have the brains to have one."

Rogers felt eyes watching him. He looked up. Patricia Dolan moved away from the other women and toward him. "Ben Rogers, isn't it?" she asked.

"That's me," he said.

"It's been a long time," she said. "You don't go to department affairs any longer?"

"No," he said. "I'm not welcome. Kind of a leper these days."

"I can't believe that," she said.

"Believe it," he said. "Who wants Internal Affairs around to throw a wet blanket over the fun?"

Rogers felt more eyes watching him. The group near the windows had turned toward him. Dolan stepped out, moving toward him, waving, appearing surprised. "Ben," he said. "What the hell are you doing here? Nobody told me you knew Gene. Come on over and meet some people."

Rogers grinned at Melissa, Nikki, and Patricia Dolan. "I'm just another guy out of the old school," he said. He moved toward Dolan. Together they entered the group.

"Ben, do you know these guys?" Dolan said. The way he said it, the way he seemed to dominate the group, left an impression that it was his party, that he was the man the others looked to, rather than Donatello. Dolan gestured to the tall, thin man wearing a clerical collar. "Do you know Dennis Molloy?"

They nodded to each other. "We met briefly," Molloy said.

"You introduced us," Rogers said. "A couple of weeks ago."

"At your cathedral." Molloy smiled. "When you had us all in for the briefing about the holidays."

"That's right," Dolan said. "There were so many people around that day, it went right out of my head." He turned then to a silver-haired, florid-faced man with a very professional smile. "How about Mike Benedetto? Do you know him, too?"

Benedetto put out his hand. Rogers took it. The grip was

firm, held just an instant too long, the politician's pressing of the flesh. "I don't think we've met," Benedetto said. "Nice to know you."

"You must know Pete McIntyre," Dolan said.

They nodded to each other. "Of course," McIntyre said. "Rogers has turned over some good cases to us. I think we may have helped him a little now and again, too. In fact, weren't you over our way just a couple of weeks ago?"

Rogers knew what was coming. He had expected it ever since he saw McIntyre enter the room. He'd been turning over what he would say when the Assistant District Attorney brought it up. He moved his head a little. "Yeah. Just before the election," he said.

"I could have sworn it was after," McIntyre said. "But, what the hell, it was sometime around then. Something about a case you were on, wasn't that it?"

"Right. Just to get some background. It was kind of a wild shot."

McIntyre looked up toward the high ceiling, thinking, then looked back. "I remember now," he said. "You were with Pamela Turner. You were interested in, what was his name?" He looked over at Donatello. "That guy from your bank, Gene. The one you handed to us for embezzlement."

Donatello was now watching Rogers closely. "Rosenblatt," he said. "Werner Rosenblatt."

"That was the name," McIntyre said. "Son of a bitch committed suicide about then, right?"

"What was this all about?" Dolan asked. "I never heard anything about it."

"An Internal Affairs thing," Rogers said. "You remember the case. We thought some of our guys were into diverting weapons to the wrong people. I got a tip from one of my street people that somebody was laundering the profits for them, and the guy was a banker. He thought the guy's name was something like Rosenblatt, some foreign name. The ADA filled me in on him. It didn't look like his kind of thing, and before I could follow it up, the guy killed himself. End of story."

"When was all this?" Dolan said.

"End of October, beginning of November, something around then," Rogers said.

"How come it never came across my desk?"

"Maybe it did," Rogers said, "and it didn't make an impression. It was strictly small potatoes."

"Did you resolve it?" Dolan asked.

"Beats me. It's out of my hands," Rogers said. "Somebody else took it on."

"When was that?"

"When I went on special assignment," Rogers said.

Dolan looked at the others. "Ben," he said, "is doing some-kind of job for the about-to-be mayor. So secret nobody tells me what it's all about. Morrison said don't ask, so I don't ask."

"You're working for Morrison?" Donatello said.

"Temporarily," Rogers said. "I think I told you I worked with him when he was at Justice and we got along. So he asked me to look into a few things for him before he takes over."

"What kind of things?" Donatello persisted.

Rogers smiled at him. "Strictly hush-hush. Like the chief said, I'm not supposed to talk about it."

Donatello studied him, the expression frozen. Just then, the man in the white jacket appeared in the doorway and announced that dinner was served. Rogers turned away quickly and headed for Melissa and Nikki.

It was one of those dinners where nobody sat next to the person he'd come with. Donatello sat in an ornately carved chair at one end of a long white damask-covered table, tapers burning in sterling candlesticks, the places set with ornate sterling and Spode china. On either side of him he had seated Nikki and Melissa. Molloy was at the far end of the table. Rogers sat about halfway down, with Rosemary McIntyre on one side of him and Patricia Dolan on the other.

"Gene, you should have gotten a dinner partner for Dennis," Benedetto said when they were all seated.

"How so?" Donatello said.

"Thirteen at the table," Benedetto said. "Unlucky, you know, like the Last Supper."

There were smiles. "But who," Molloy said from the end of the table, "would we appoint as the messiah, our savior?"

"Who else but Gene," McIntyre said. It wasn't a question.

Dinner was lavish and complicated, many courses, each accompanied by a different wine. Before they were finished, they had been served clear consommé, coquilles in oyster shells, salad of endive and four different kinds of lettuce, medallions of venison in a rich wine sauce—the game shot in the fall during the hunting season, Donatello explained—fresh fruits, and a variety of cheeses.

In the middle of the dinner, a half-dozen conversations going on simultaneously, Rogers turned to Patricia Dolan. "Does he always serve dinners like this?"

"Once a month," she said.

He looked at her. "You really do this once a month?"

"We always get together the first Thursday of the month," she said. "It's a tradition. The guys call themselves the Thursday Club. In the old days, we used to alternate. Now Gene insists that we come to his place."

"You all cooked like this?"

"Don't be silly," she said. "In those days, it was strictly pot luck. It was fun. We were all just starting out. It was right after the boys got back from Vietnam and Bill and I were the first ones to get married. He was pounding a beat then, and Gene, Peter, and Mike had gone back to school, Dennis hadn't entered the seminary yet, and Frank was tending bar at a little place in the neighborhood. I don't think we had ten dollars among us. But we made do. Now . . ." she spread her hands.

"Why Thursday?"

"I don't know. It just happened, right after Bill and I got married, I think it was when we got back from our honeymoon. We got together and we've just kept it up. We all grew up together on the West Side, you know, and the boys went to school together. It was just natural that we didn't want to lose touch. So, it became our tradition. That's how come the Thursday Club. We get together for dinner, then the boys go off by themselves for cigars and brandy and talk about whatever they talk about, and we women have a little hen party until they get back."

He studied her for a moment. "You know," he said, "I can't help it, but you look a lot like Peter McIntyre."

She laughed. "I should," she said. "He's my brother. And he was Bill's best man. All the others were ushers, and the girls were all my bridesmaids. That's how close we were then, and we still are."

Suddenly, the table went silent. Donatello was leaning toward Nikki, his voice rising, angry and disturbed. "You went where?" he demanded.

"Oh, Gene," she said, "I took Melissa to lunch. It was broad daylight, for goodness' sake."

"I told you, I don't want you going to places like that. It could be dangerous."

"You're being silly. What could have happened? The restaurant was packed, as always. I mean, there were celebrities all over the place. I mean, you could have cast one of those gangster movies without even leaving the restaurant. The only one who was missing was Marlon Brando. But there was a real live godfather there anyway. Generoso Ruggieri. He didn't look very dangerous to me. He just looks like a nice old man."

"He may be seventy, but he's no pussycat," Dolan said.

"And he probably had twenty of his wiseguys posted around the room," McIntyre said.

"What could happen?" she said. "With all those people around? It's probably safer than a million other places."

"I don't want you going there again. Do you hear me?" Donatello said.

"I'm a big girl, Gene. I can take care of myself."

"Sometimes I wonder," he said.

"I was doing it before I met you," she said. "I'm still doing it. Now, can we please change the subject?"

"Ah, the overprotective male," Patricia Dolan whispered to Rogers. "Gene's in love for the first time, and I think he wants to wrap her in cotton wool and keep her safe from the world."

"Can you blame him?" Rogers said.

"You men are all alike," she sighed. "Don't you know times have changed?"

He laughed. "I hear that every day."

"It's the truth," she said. She looked around the table. "I only wish Bill believed it. He thinks, they all do, that we can't take care of ourselves, and they can't ever discuss anything important around us because we have no heads for business. They think women are just little porcelain dolls to keep up on a shelf. They'll never change." She shook her head. She seemed more philosophical and accepting than angry.

The dinner finally ended. Donatello and the other men rose.

"Here we go," Patricia Dolan sighed, "men in one direction, women in the other." She looked at Rogers. "And which direction do you go in, Ben?"

He looked around uncertainly. "Beats me," he said. He

waited for some kind of signal to join the male congregation. Donatello and Dolan exchanged looks. Donatello looked over at him. "Ben, I hope you'll excuse us." he said. "We have some private matters to discuss." The men disappeared down a hall, and he was left with the women.

"One rooster with all the hens," Patricia Dolan said. "You might as well come with us and have coffee in the living room while they talk business."

He shrugged. "Good company, nevertheless," he said. Then, "What kind of business?"

"God knows," she said. "Stocks and bonds, probably, and how to make more money. What else are men interested in?"

"Even your husband?"

"Especially my husband. Try bringing up five children on a policeman's salary, even when you're a chief."

"And Bishop Molloy? I thought priests were above that kind of thing."

She laughed. "Didn't you know? That's what he does for the church."

An hour later, the cigars had been smoked, the brandy drunk, and the men were back in the living room. None of them seemed particularly elated, Molloy more depressed than the others, a gloomier look on his face than when he had first appeared that evening. Whatever business they had been talking about apparently had not been settled to anyone's satisfaction.

A few minutes later, the goodnights said, the guests were on the street, the doorman hailing cabs. As they rode downtown, Melissa said, "You and Mrs. Dolan hit it off."

"I met her before, back when I was just a plain cop. She's a nice lady. Smart."

"None of them is exactly stupid," Melissa said.

"Except Mrs. Tremanti?"

She laughed. "Not as dumb as she acts. She's just learned what he thinks her place ought to be."

"Knows which side her bread is buttered on, right?"

"That's one way of putting it. The men off to the study for brandy and cigars, the women to the living room for coffee, and never the twain shall meet."

"Not just brandy and cigars," he said. "Stocks and bonds and how to make more money."

She looked over at him through the dim interior of the cab.

"Did you say more? More money?"

"That's the way Patricia Dolan put it. I imagine Donatello advises them where to put what they have."

"If they listen to him," she said, "they all must have plenty. They certainly dress it."

"I wonder," Rogers said slowly, "if he ever makes a mistake."

"If he does," she said, "he's not telling anyone."

"Except his friends, when the chips are down and he doesn't have a choice. I just wonder," he said.

She looked closely at him. "Why?"

"I don't know," he said. "But when they came out of that little session with the cigars and brandy, there wasn't one of them that looked happy. And if what they were talking about was money and investments, then maybe that was the reason. Maybe Donatello gave them a bum steer and they all took a bath."

29

A little after nine on Friday morning, Rogers called Morton Solomon. The lawyer was already at his desk.

"I wondered if you'd call again," Solomon said. "What can I do for you this time?"

"You can tell me exactly what Werner Rosenblatt did at the bank. What his job was."

Solomon sighed. "I have a client in about fifteen minutes. Why don't you come in about eleven? I'll make some time for you."

At eleven, Rogers was back in Solomon's office, back in the same chair, enjoying the same view.

Solomon watched him, a little smile turning his lips upward, making his face not so forbidding. "I don't suppose you could have called Mr. Donatello or somebody at the bank and asked them," he said. "No, of course not. To answer your question, Werner's activities at the bank ran the gamut. He handled a number of accounts for private customers and his job was to make money for them and safeguard what they had. Among other things, he was an arbitrageur."

"Isn't that what Boesky did? But I was never really sure exactly what it meant."

"It's not as esoteric as it seems. Simply put, it's a way of playing the different closing times of the world's stock markets against each other. They all trade during regular business hours and are open according to local time, naturally. The arbitrageur buys at a going price on one market as it's closing and then sells a few hours later at a slightly higher price on another market in a different part of the world. The difference in the price on each share may not be much, but he's dealing in thousands, in tens of thousands of shares, and that adds up. He also does the same thing in the value of one currency against another."

"That was Rosenblatt's specialty?"

"Not exclusively. It was merely one of his tools, as it is with any international bank. Werner was expert in it, certainly, but he was also an expert in a lot of other areas. He had to be if he was going to make money for his clients and for his bank. So he had to know about investments, buying and selling stocks and bonds, he had to know the ins and outs of underwriting corporate issues, about loans and mortgages. In other words, he had to know all there was to know about finance.

"But the thing you have to understand is that a bank like Fidelity is not a simple commercial bank. You don't walk in off the street, fill out some forms and some days later pick up a check for your loan. Fidelity does not write small loans for the man in the street. Its loans, mortgages, what have you, are large, and those who borrow are corporations and people of means. It will not, for example, help you finance the purchase of your house or apartment. If, however, you were planning to erect an office tower, a luxury apartment building, a large shopping center, an industrial park or office complex, a major addition to your current factory, a ski resort, inside the United States or abroad, then you might turn to someone like Fidelity, which would advance you the funds from its own resources, or find other sources willing to assume some of the mortgages.

"Now, Werner managed a number of large accounts. Those accounts had varied interests. So he had to know how to be able to provide all the services those accounts demanded."

"And, naturally, he had a lot of money to play around with."

"Access, yes. But strictly controlled, Mr. Rogers. There were auditors looking over his shoulder constantly. There were account summaries examined by his superiors, especially by Mr. Donatello. He couldn't just operate on his own hook. He had to get approval before he could make any major move. And there was his personality. Werner just didn't make major decisions easily. He was not a man to rush pell-mell into a situation before giving it painstaking thought and then looking for authorization from someone on a higher level. Access, yes, but the ability to manipulate it, no."

"Even knowing all he did, I suppose there were plenty of risks?"

"Of course there were risks. There's risk in walking across the street. There's risk in everything. There are no sure things in life."

"But some of the things he was doing were riskier than others, right?"

"Of course. You can lose your shirt—and pants—arbitraging if the market doesn't move the way you hope and expect. Loans, even the best of them to the most secure clients, can sometimes be defaulted. During a real estate slump, the value of mortgages is not what it once was, and the value of stocks declines during a recession. A securities offering may find no takers at the offered price and so either must be withdrawn or sold at a reduced price. The stocks in which you've invested your client's money, or the bank's, may decline instead of rise. In all these cases, the bank may be left with its funds tied up in paper it cannot unload, or sell only at a loss."

"But if everything went right, you could make a killing."

"If everything went right, yes."

"Especially if you knew about something before anybody else did," Rogers said.

"That, Mr. Rogers," Solomon said, "is called insider trading. It is strictly illegal. Men go to prison for doing that. Mr. Boesky went to prison, Mr. Milken went to prison, others have gone to prison within recent memory for insider trading, for using confidential information not available to the general investor to rig the markets and so enrich themselves and their friends."

"But it's been done."

"It's been done."

"And they've made a killing if the information they had was right."

"And," Solomon said, "some have lost everything, which was no less than they deserved, when the information misfired."

"Then," Rogers said, "I imagine they'd be desperate to find a way to recoup. Especially if they'd been playing with other people's money. And if they couldn't, then they'd look for a place to run and hide."

"If you're thinking of Werner Rosenblatt, you couldn't be more mistaken. Even if he aspired to it, he was not in a position, financial or otherwise, to do so. Make a killing or run? Hardly likely. Not his way."

"I wasn't," Rogers said slowly, "thinking of Werner Rosenblatt."

Solomon nodded. "I see." He looked away for a moment, down at his desk. He reached for a file folder and opened it. "As it happens," he said, "if you hadn't called me, I was going to call you."

Rogers waited.

Solomon took some slips of paper from the folder and held them out. "Sophie brought these to me the other day. She was going through Werner's clothes, getting them ready to give away, and she found these in the pocket of one of his suits. She has no idea what they mean, but she thought I ought to have them. I think you might find them interesting."

Rogers took the papers. There were names written on them, and a lot of figures. He looked back at Solomon.

"The names," Solomon said, "are corporations. The figures are the prices their stocks sold at, highs and lows. If you look, you can't miss the fact that most seemed to have been tied to a skyrocket. There's one, though, that went the other way, right through the floor."

Rogers looked back at the papers, skimming through them. He looked up. "What the hell is Centex? And what the hell happened to it?"

Solomon shrugged. "I think you might want to find out," he said, "and if you do, you might learn why Werner had that list."

30

He called the Securities and Exchange Commission from a phone booth in the lobby of Solomon's building. It took about thirty seconds before he was connected to George Fielding in the enforcement office.

"What can I do for you, Ben?" Fielding said.

"I want to meet."

"Can we make it Monday? How's three?"

"I was hoping for now."

"No can do. I've got to make the one o'clock shuttle."

"If it has to be Monday, then Monday it will be."

He took the subway uptown and then walked the few blocks to Janice Palmer's. He rang a few bells, waited for an unwary buzzer, and when it sounded, went through the door and back down to the basement. In the storage closet, he took a look at the tape recorder. The tape had spun a little way on the reel. She had made at least one call. It took him less than five minutes to disconnect the wires, pack up everything, and be back on the street and heading for the subway downtown.

In the silence of his own apartment, he turned the recorder

on, rewound the tape and let it play. First, there was the series of clicks. He noted them. He had the number she'd dialed.

Then the voices came through, clear and distinct.

"Hello?"

"Tommy?"

"Yeah."

"There was a cop here a little while ago."

"So?"

"He knows. They're . . ."

"You dumb bitch! Hang up! Now!"

There was something about that voice that stirred something in his memory. For the moment, he couldn't make the connection. He let the tape run on. The only sound was the whirring of the recorder. From her own phone, she had made only that one call, and had not received any.

He took his volume of Cole's, ran down the list and got the name. The guy she called was named Thomas Littlejohn. Now Rogers remembered. He had known him, and so had Palmieri, back when they were partners in Homicide. Littlejohn was strictly bad news, a former cop who was lucky not to be wearing prison gray. He'd been a narcotics cop who had a vicious sideline. He'd pocket about half of whatever he happened to seize during a bust and then sell it back to the boys he'd taken it from. The thing was that after a while Littlejohn got greedy and the boys objected to his price. Then, one night, there was a little trouble in a dark alley, and by the time the backup got there, a lowlife pusher was sprawled in the garbage, face bashed in, bullet in his brains. Littlejohn was bending over him with a hot revolver in one hand, bloody knuckles on the other. According to Littlejohn, he'd caught the lowlife just as a sale was going down, chased him into the alley, and when the guy pulled on him, he'd had no choice.

It was a good story and a plausible one. There was just one thing wrong. Littlejohn was a couple of inches over six feet, weighed about two hundred forty pounds, and, with his beer belly, was in no shape to run even a twenty-yard dash. Also, Littlejohn had a reputation as a blowhard and a coward, a guy who'd never chase anybody into an alley, who avoided trouble whenever possible, who always found an excuse to run the other way. Plus, the pusher was a runt, a foot shorter than Littlejohn and more than a hundred pounds lighter, and people who knew him said he had never been in a fight in his life. He'd been busted half a dozen times in the past, and if he couldn't buy his way out, he'd always given up without an objection. Palmieri and Rogers drew the case. The more they looked into it, the dirtier Littlejohn looked. But of course he was a cop, and the dead guy had been a pusher, which meant that nobody really cared. So he walked on the homicide, putting on a show, laughing at Palmieri and Rogers when he did, and adding a few sour words about what he intended to do to them if he ever had the opportunity.

But it hadn't ended there. They'd put together enough evidence to tie him in with the narcotics swindle. Littlejohn was brought up on departmental charges. He didn't go to the slammer, though. All the department did was take his badge and boot him over the blue wall. He hadn't gone gladly, swearing he'd get back at the guys who framed him, meaning Palmieri and Rogers, Rogers in particular because it had been Rogers who had been the main witness against him. Nobody paid any attention to the threats, of course. Littlejohn was always making threats. So Rogers remembered Littlejohn very well. That bust was the last one he and Palmieri had made together before he got his promotion and was transferred to IAD.

Rogers called Carlos Rodriguez. "Carlos," he said when they were connected, "you want that good collar?"

"You know it. You got it, right?"

"I got it."

A little after ten on Saturday morning he reached the converted brownstone. Rodriguez was waiting for him, sitting in his car, double parked just outside the building, official sign in the window to keep away the ticket writers.

"It's your deal," Rogers said. "I'm just along for the ride."

Rodriguez smiled happily.

They went up the steps, into the entryway, and rang Janice Palmer's buzzer. No answer. They rang the super's buzzer, and identified themselves when he responded. He appeared behind the glass pane in the door and stared at them. Rodriguez flashed his shield. The super opened the door and led them to the elevator. He rode up with them and stepped aside as they rang the bell. Nobody answered.

"You got a key?" Rodriguez demanded.

"I got a key," the super answered. He didn't reach for it. "Open it up," Rodriguez said.

"You got a warrant? I can't do it unless you got a warrant."

"Don't worry your head about it," Rodriguez said. The super looked at him for a moment, shrugged, pulled out a large ring full of keys, tried a couple in the lock before he found the one that fit, turned it, and opened the door.

The smell wasn't too bad yet. They caught just a whiff of it. Rodriguez's face froze as he looked at Rogers. "Shit," he said.

They went quickly along the brick-walled hall toward the living room. The super hesitated, then followed. Some of the framed posters that had hung on the wall were on the floor, the glass broken. The living room was a disaster. Books and records were scattered everywhere, more posters had been torn from the walls, the television was smashed, the stereo scattered, the wires torn from the components. Chairs were overturned, cushions pulled from the sofa. There was blood on the walls, blood on the sofa, blood all over the white flokati rug. In the middle of everything was something that must once have been Janice Palmer, only it would have been hard to tell, because there was hardly much face left, only a bloody mass. Somebody had worked her over with a club or with a fistful of nickels. Her clothes had been ripped off. Whoever had killed her had a good time with her, either before or after.

It was early afternoon before they left the apartment. The body had been taken away by then, the place was crawling with cops from the precinct, cops from Homicide, fingerprint experts spewing powder everywhere, police photographers taking a million pictures. Rodriguez had spent the hours filling them in, and then he and Rogers moved on, leaving the premises to the others, and went back out to the street.

Rodriguez got behind the wheel of his car and they headed for a quiet tree-lined street on the border of Forest Hills in Queens. It was a street of ivy-covered duplex garden apartments, probably condos, a couple of blocks from the subway entrance and the elevated railroad tracks.

"The son of a bitch has come up in the world," Rodriguez

said as they walked toward one of the buildings. "He must really be raking it in these days."

"Full time," Rogers said. "In the old days, it was just a sideline."

Rodriguez looked at him. "You think maybe he had it in for Felix, for what you and him done to him back then?"

Rogers shrugged. They reached the door and Rodriguez pushed the bell. Somebody approached the door from inside, but didn't open it. "Yes? Who's there?"

"Thomas Littlejohn?" Rodriguez said, putting on an official voice. "Police. We'd like to have a word with you. Open up."

There was a pause. "What do you want?"

"If you'll let us in, we'll explain."

"I got nothin' to talk to you about."

They could hear movement. Whoever was behind the door was moving away, fast. A door slammed somewhere inside.

"Carlos," Rogers said sharply, "get around back. The bastard's running."

Rodriguez turned and sprinted across the lawn, looking for an opening between the buildings. His gun was in his hand now. He found a gap about fifty feet down and disappeared through it. Rogers waited just a moment, listening, making sure whoever was inside was not going to come back. He heard only silence. He drew his gun and started after Rodriguez, moving rapidly through the gap, emerging at the rear of the apartments into an area of small backyards and garages. Rodriguez was just ahead, racing toward one of the garages.

A tall, heavy man was lumbering into the garage. He was still in shirt sleeves despite the cold. A car door opened and slammed shut. An engine turned over, caught, and a car started to back out. "Hold it right there," Rodriguez shouted. The car kept backing, accelerating, was about half out when Rodriguez aimed and fired at the rear tire. The tire blew. The car swerved, its front end smashing into the open garage door.

Rodriguez and Rogers moved quickly toward the car, approaching the driver's side. The big fat guy with the overgrown belly was slumped over the wheel, stunned. Rogers pulled open the door, grabbed him by the collar and yanked him out, thrust him against the side of the car, holding him erect. Rodriguez ran his hands down across him, pulled a pistol from a shoulder holster, threw it a few feet away, pulled another from the waistband of the trousers, threw that one, pulled another from an ankle holster, added that one to the litter, found a switchblade knife in a back pocket, dropped that.

"The son of a bitch is a walking arsenal," Rodriguez said. He gathered the weapons and put them into a pile.

Littlejohn shook his head groggily, and tried to pull free. Rogers shoved him harder against the car, pulled out a pair of handcuffs and shackled Littlejohn's hands behind his back. "Carlos," he said, "read the motherfucker his rights."

Rodriguez went through the Miranda ritual.

"What the fuck do you guys want?" Littlejohn said, coming back from wherever his mind had been.

"Where do you want to begin? How about a couple of murders for starters?"

"Fuck off!" He swiveled his head a little and saw Rogers. "You!" he said. "Damn you to hell!"

"No walks this time, Tommy," Rogers said.

"Fuck you!"

Rogers looked at Rodriguez. "You've still got the mouth, Tommy. I'll bet you still haven't got anything to go with it. Carlos, let's take him inside."

Rodriguez stepped forward, grabbed the cuffed hands, twisted Littlejohn away from the car, and shoved him forward. Littlejohn stiffened, trying to hold back. Rodriguez pulled the cuffed hands higher up the back, bringing a yelp of pain. He pulled back his fist and punched hard into the middle of the back. Littlejohn crumpled forward. Holding onto the cuffs, Rodriguez kept him from falling, shoving him ahead. "Now move your ass, you son of a bitch."

Littlejohn gave up and moved. Rodriguez marched him through the back door of the apartment. Once inside the living room, he pitched Littlejohn onto the sofa, then stood over him.

Rogers watched for a moment, then began to search the apartment. In a bedroom closet he found a police uniform. On a shelf there were three Uzis, an AK-47, and six pistols with bores big enough to send out slugs that could blow a hole in a cement wall. One drawer in the dresser was filled with pills of all kinds and shapes, enough to supply the needs of a couple of hospitals for at least a week. He piled everything onto the bed and then went back into the living room, standing just inside the door and looking at Littlejohn.

"You're going away, Tommy," he said. "For a long, long time. You'll be an old man before you breathe fresh air again."

"Fuck you!"

"Can't you think of anything else to say?"

"Yeah. I want to see my lawyer."

"All in good time. Let's talk a little first."

"I got nothin' to say. Like I told you the other time, you'll make nothin' stick."

"Pure Teflon, that's you. Only not this time."

"Bullshit."

"Really? The crap in your bedroom will do for starters. I'm really interested in how you'll explain all those bottles with the hospital labels still on them. You got a license for the guns Carlos took off you, and for that arsenal you got stacked in your closet? I sincerely doubt it. And then, you dumb fucker, you left your prints all over the broad's apartment."

"You're full of shit. I don't know what you're talkin' about."

"No? It seems to me I heard that song before."

"Yeah? Well, that time, you and that other cocksucker couldn't prove a thing."

"What cocksucker was that, Tommy?"

"Palmieri, that bastard."

"Oh, yes, Felix. That's another little matter. How about if we add him to the list?"

"What the fuck are you talkin' about?"

"Haven't you heard? Felix Palmieri got himself killed."

"Big deal. Tell me somethin' I don't know. What's it got to do with me?"

"I think you did it, Tommy," Rogers said.

Littlejohn went white. He tried to sit up straighter. He stared at Rogers. Fear washed through his eyes. "You can't pin that on me," he said.

"Oh, I think maybe we can," Rogers said. "I'll bet Ballistics can tie one of your guns to the bullet that got Felix. You had it in for him. Remember what you said when you walked back then? You're our boy, Tommy. No doubt about it. You know what you can get in this state for killing a cop?"

"For chrissake, Rogers," Littlejohn shouted, "I didn't do it.

Honest to Christ, it wasn't me. I can prove it. I was someplace else."

"Sure. You're as pure as the driven snow, only you know what the snow looks like in the city," Rogers said.

"I want a lawyer."

"We heard you the first time. Right, Carlos?"

"I'm havin' a little trouble with my ears." Rodriguez said. "You know, ever since this creep cracked me when he was resistin' arrest." Rodriguez started to advance on Littlejohn, his hand balling into a fist and rising. "I think maybe we ought to work him over a little. Like he did with the dame. Maybe he'd see the light."

Littlejohn shrank back. "I got cuffs on," he said. "You wouldn't do that."

"I wouldn't?" Rodriguez said.

"Jesus," Littlejohn said. "Give me a break." Rogers remembered that people who knew him said that despite his size, Littlejohn was afraid of getting hit. He was a coward. Only this time he had no place to run and hide.

"Like the one you gave Felix?" Rogers said.

"Honest to God, I had nothin' to do with that. You gotta believe me."

"Why?"

Rodriguez doubled his hand into a fist, pulled it back and slugged Littlejohn in his fat belly. The air went out of him. He doubled over, gasping. His eyes filled with tears. Rodriguez hit him again in the same place.

"Oh, Jesus. No more, please, you guys, no more, don't hit me again."

Rodriguez stood over him. His arm drew back again. He glanced over at Rogers. "In the belly it don't leave no marks."

"Please," Littlejohn begged. "Ask me anything. I'll give you anything. Don't hit me. I can't take it no more. Jesus."

"You got a tape recorder, Carlos?" Rogers asked.

"In my pocket," Rodriguez said. He pulled out a microrecorder, turned it on, tested it, nodded. "It's okay." He started it running.

Rogers looked down at Littlejohn. "You understand you're being recorded?"

"Yeah," Littlejohn said.

"You understand anything you say may be used against you in a court of law?"

Littlejohn nodded.

"Say it," Rogers demanded.

"I understand, yeah."

"You are not required to make a statement without a lawyer being present. Do you understand that?"

"Yeah."

"Do you want a lawyer?"

Littlejohn hesitated. Rodriguez drew back his arm. Littlejohn looked at him and fear ran through him. "No," he muttered, "I don't want a lawyer."

"We are now going to ask you some questions. You are prepared to answer of your own free will?"

Rogers nodded to Rodriguez. "The pills, Littlejohn," Rodriguez said. "You were stealing them from the hospitals?"

"Yeah. I had a nice thing going. I had these nurses and they were getting the stuff for me."

"You were pretending to be an officer in order to get the narcotics out of the hospitals?"

"Yeah."

"How many hospitals?"

"Half a dozen."

"Give us the names of the nurses who were supplying you."

Littlejohn rattled off a list.

"You raped and murdered Jenny Mendoza, is that correct?"

"I didn't rape the little bitch. She wanted it. I was givin' it to her regular. Part of her pay. I didn't have to rape her."

"But you murdered her?"

"It was an accident. I didn't mean to waste her. She was holdin' out on me and I just wanted to teach the dumb bitch a lesson."

"Sure," Rodriguez said. "Some lesson. You also raped and murdered Janice Palmer, is that correct?"

Littlejohn hesitated.

"Is that correct?" Rodriguez demanded.

"She was goin' to go to you guys," Littlejohn said. "Goin' to turn me in. I couldn't let her do that."

"So you murdered her to stop her? And then you raped her after she was dead?"

"No, no," Littlejohn said, pleading. "It didn't happen that way. We were arguing, I got carried away, it was an accident, that's what it was, an accident."

"Oh, yeah," Rodriguez said. "We believe you. We sure as hell do. We'll let that pass for now. We'll come back to it later. One more thing. You called Detective Palmieri out and you met him in an alley and you shot him. Is that correct?"

"No! No! I never killed Palmieri. I swear to God, I done a lot of things. You got me on 'em. But I never did Palmieri."

"I think you did," Rodriguez said.

"Honest to Christ, I didn't. You gotta believe me. They say he got it from the front. You think he would have let me walk up to him and give it to him? Jesus, you guys knew him. You know, not in a million years. Why would I lie about that? Ask yourselves. You got me on the others, so what have I got to lose? If I done it, I'd tell you. It's the truth, so help me. I got nothin' against Palmieri. You, you bastard, you was the one who sang about me. If I was to get anybody, it'd of been you, and you're still walkin' around."

Rodriguez studied him. He snapped off the recorder and motioned for Rogers to follow him into the bedroom. "You believe him?"

"About Felix?" Rogers nodded slowly. "Yeah, I believe him. He's right. There's no way Felix would have let him come at him from the front, no way Felix would ever have agreed to meet him in the first place, and certainly not in an alley in Little Italy in the middle of the night. No, it wasn't Littlejohn."

"Yeah. What do we do now? Take him in, right?"

"Right. You got yourself a good collar, Carlos."

"For that I'm grateful. I won't forget. You ever need anything else, you call me."

"Sure."

"You got any other leads who did Felix?"

"A couple."

"An' you're not about to let go?"

Rogers shook his head.

"You need some help, I'll be there," Rodriguez said. "Don't forget, Felix was my partner, too. I liked the guy. He shouldn't ought to have gone that way."

31

George Fielding examined the world with pale blue eyes obscured behind thick rimless glasses. His view was skeptical. With his narrow pale face and thin tight lips, Fielding looked like an accountant. Looks are deceiving, or, at least, they tell only part of the story. He was an accountant, but he was also a man who could see hidden truths lurking in a column of numbers. When Rogers first met him, he'd been with the FBI, an agent who could track the money backward and forward and lay it out so that even a schoolboy could follow the trail. He was still doing the same thing, but now for the Security and Exchange Commission.

He was buried behind a mountain of ledgers in his small office overlooking Federal Plaza in lower Manhattan when Rogers appeared at one o'clock that Monday afternoon. Though they'd talked now and then, they hadn't seen each other in nearly five years, and for the first few minutes they reminisced a little about the days when they'd worked together down in Washington for John Morrison.

"Enough bullshit, Ben," Fielding said finally. "What brings you to these environs?"

"Insider trading," Rogers told him. "Not old stuff. New. Like in the last six months or so."

"Since when is Internal Affairs interested in insider trading? I didn't think cops had those kind of contacts."

"Some do, some don't, but this doesn't have anything to do with cops. I'm doing something for Morrison."

"The old elephant never forgets who fed him the peanuts," Fielding said. "What do you want to know?"

"What have you got that doesn't smell right?"

"You want to know about facts, or just rumors and the like?"

"Probably the rumors."

"I'd let you see my files, only it would take you a week, and you still wouldn't know anything. You must have something in particular in mind. Or somebody."

"What I have in mind is a deal that went sour."

"Tell me some more and maybe I can help you."

"It had to be something that didn't stir up the nest while it was going on. Like some little outfit nobody ever heard of and nobody gave diddly-squat about. Only somebody knew something was going to break that was going to turn that company into a gold mine. It had to be stuff that nobody else knew. So they started buying in, not big, and not all of a sudden, but slowly and quietly. The money was probably untraceable, like from offshore accounts, that kind of thing. Maybe they were looking for control or maybe just to make a killing, but whatever, I think they saw it as the end of the rainbow. Then something happened, and the whole thing fell apart. The dough's gone and they can't talk about it because if they do, their ticket's going to be punched. But they're bleeding real blood."

"My heart goes out to them," Fielding said.

"Sure. The way I see it, George, it's your kind of thing. You keep track. You know what's going on in every corner."

"I only wish," Fielding said. "You're throwing me something I haven't heard word one about." He leaned back, took a pipe from a rack on his desk, filled it, packed it, lit it, drew on it, let the smoke drift out. "It's way out," he said after a while.

"Maybe," Rogers said. "But you have to leave tracks behind before the snow drifts in and covers them."

"They've probably got light feet. Besides, what the hell do you care? They got incinerated. Tough shit."

"I care because I think they're looking for a way to recoup, and maybe they've found a surefire one."

Fielding studied him. "You're working for Morrison?"

"Right."

"And he's got somebody he wants for his administration, only he's not so sure. Right?"

"Right."

"I get the drift." He turned and stared out the window, then turned back. "You're probably talking military," he said finally.

"I am?"

"You are. Has to be. The whole thing has to revolve around a military contract that didn't gel though your guy thought it was a sure thing. Military contracts can run into nine, ten figures. You hit it right, you're on a rocket to the moon and beyond. The thing is, military contracts tend to be classified top secret, not even a whisper, until the last minute when the company XYZ gets the award. Nobody's supposed to know, not the public and not even the company itself. All the company knows is that its proposal is under consideration, but just how much consideration nobody says. All they got is hope, but that ain't much when ninety-nine out of hundred times their blueprint ends up in the trash can. Otherwise, you'd get a run-up on the market like you wouldn't believe, ten, twenty, thirty points overnight just on a rumor.

"I'd be willing to bet that what you're talking about is R and D, you know, a research-and-development deal. Some little guy came up with an idea, spent a lot of time and money laying it out, and then threw it into the hopper. It's his and nobody else's, so there's no competition, like there is when a couple of big boys are bidding against each other. The odds against are about ten thousand to one, maybe more. But if you get the prize in the Cracker Jack box, it can turn a pygmy into a giant. The contracts start small, but if they work out, and you get a production contract down the road, you couldn't begin to count the profits.

"Now, suppose somebody got a very private leak that if Congress gives the okay, the Pentagon's going to give our little pygmy, Company XYZ, a R and D contract. If it's the way you laid it out, the leak went to somebody outside the company. What did your outsider do? He started buying up the stock, quietly and in small lots so he wouldn't create a stir and start a run that'd shoot the price up. He probably picked up a hundred shares here, a hundred there, never more than a thousand at a time, if that, and all under different dummy accounts, and he may even have bought a controlling interest, although he'd be a fool to try to exercise it, at least right away. He figured he could just sit back and watch his money grow—geometrically, once the contract was let. That's what you're talking about."

"Where would he get the leak?"

"From one of two places, and only them. The Pentagon itself or the congressional military subcommittee handling this stuff."

"George, the goddamn deal must have fallen apart. I'm sure of it. What the hell happened?"

"Don't you read the papers, Ben? They cut the Pentagon's budget. And in the process, they wrote *finito* on Buck Rogers and the space cadets." He smiled briefly. "How much you figure your pigeon is out?"

"No idea. Probably in the multiples of millions."

"You know who he is?"

"Yeah. At least I think so."

"All his own money?"

"His, and some other people's."

"You have any idea what he was into?"

"You ever hear of a company called Centex?"

Fielding leaned back and examined Rogers. His face was expressionless. "I heard," he said at last. "Its stock went up, and then it went down. It didn't only go down, it deep-sixed. They had a stock issue pending. They had to withdraw. That's what your guy was into?"

"I think so."

"He took a bath. And now he's looking to recoup? How?"

"You wouldn't believe it if I told you."

He walked slowly north from Federal Plaza toward the Village and home. A cold front had blown in during the last hours and an icy gale howled through the city's canyons. Rogers was oblivious to the weather, whatever the fury nature was creating less than the turmoil in his mind. He did not like what he was thinking, but he could not turn away from it. Too many separate pieces that had seemed to have no relationship to one another were beginning to come together, and the picture they made was one he did not want and could not accept. Again he remembered what Robert Penn Warren had written—that man is conceived in sin and born in corruption, so there's always something on everybody, and if you look hard enough you'll find it. John Morrison had set him looking, and he had found that something, at least that's how it seemed. And so now he was being forced to look in a way he had never done before at a man above suspicion, a man he almost idolized, even, in a way, loved. Maybe he was wrong, he kept telling himself. Maybe being old friends and always in need of money, Dolan and the others, the priest and the Assistant District Attorney especially, had simply trusted Donatello, had followed his advice without thinking or considering what it was based on beyond what he might know from his position, and so had given him their money to invest, hoping he would make it work and earn. Maybe that was the explanation. He hoped so.

He was in a lousy mood when he walked into the apartment. He wanted to strike out, start a fight, anything to take his mind off what was ripping him apart. Melissa was in the bedroom. A suitcase was open on the bed, some of her clothes piled alongside it.

"What the hell is going on?" he said.

She turned and looked at him. "I'm packing," she said. "Helen called today. They're flying me out to the Coast day after tomorrow."

"Aren't we full of good news."

She stopped and stared at him. "What the hell is wrong with you?"

"Not a goddamn thing. What am I supposed to do, break into a dance in celebration?"

"Are you looking for a fight?"

"If you give me enough time, I'll come up with a reason."

She sighed and turned away. "I haven't got time," she said. "There's a bar down the street. I'm sure you'll find someone there to oblige you."

She went back to sorting clothes, putting some in her suitcase. He watched for a moment, then turned and left the room. He made himself a drink and downed it quickly, then poured another and carried it to the chair by the telephone. He dialed Morrison's private number. The voice that answered said the mayor-elect was in conference. Rogers left his name and said it was important.

He sat by the phone, sipping his drink, waiting. A couple of times Melissa appeared in the doorway and stood there for a moment, studying him. He looked away.

About a half-hour later, the phone rang. He picked it up before the first ring ended. It was Morrison. "I have to see you," Rogers said.

"You have something?"

"Yeah."

Morrison paused. There was something in the tone of that single word. "Come up right away," he said. "I'll make some time."

"Not now," Rogers said. "I have to go to Boston first."

"When?"

"In the morning. I may need to make a deal. I hope not, but it could be necessary. I need your backing."

"What kind of deal?"

"Immunity for information."

"How can I authorize that? I'm just a private citizen until January first."

"You know everybody. You can pull the strings if you want to. In order to get this guy to talk, I have to be ready to offer him an out."

"What's he got that's worth immunity?"

"At the very least, I think he can nail Donatello to the wall. Maybe a few others, too. I won't know for sure until I talk with him."

There was a pause. He could imagine Morrison's mind considering the options. The mayor-to-be had wanted Donatello, had believed in the man, maybe he still did, but now it was turning out the banker's mask covered a different face, and it was a face not many people had ever seen. Morrison had to know just what that face looked like, what was revealed when the mask was stripped away, and now Rogers was on his way to see somebody who could do the stripping, and he was asking for the means to persuade him. Rogers heard the sigh. "You don't give me much choice," Morrison said. "If you have to, but use it only as a last resort. I'll back you."

"Can I say you've talked to Washington and they'll buy?"

"In for a penny, in for a pound," Morrison said. "What the

hell. Tell him whatever you want. I'll do what I have to do. But call me the minute you get back. Hell, call me from Boston."

"I'll try," Rogers said. He hung up and looked around. Melissa was watching him carefully from the doorway. "What's wrong?" she asked.

He shook his head. "You name it, it's wrong."

"It's not just me going away? I'll be back at the beginning of the week."

"I know that. No, it's not that."

"Then what?"

"Everything else. Too much money and not enough. Good guys who turned out to be greedy bastards. People I like and I'm going to have to hurt. People I ought to hate and I can't. My fucking job. Everything."

She nodded slowly and moved toward him. "Don't say any more," she said. She knelt and put her arms around him. "Just come to bed."

"All your stuff is there."

"So? We'll throw it on the floor."

32

It was snowing in Boston, which meant that the plane had to circle for a while. The woman in the seat next to Rogers was swearing under her breath, cursing Trump and threatening to sue him for all he was worth if she missed her meeting and lost that contract. Rogers thought about pointing out that she'd have to stand in line, and the line went all the way from the Trump Tower to Atlantic City, and, besides the shuttle wasn't The Donald's any longer.

But he didn't say anything. He kept his silence. He had other things on his mind. He had called ahead, identified himself as a New York City police lieutenant, and the guy had agreed to see him whenever he arrived. No questions, no hesitation, nothing except "Yes, come ahead," as though the guy had been waiting for the call, as though he had known it was coming.

The plane finally stopped circling and began to descend. Fifteen minutes later, they were on the ground. The snow was still falling, and the cab ride in from Logan was slow and slippery, but Rogers was in no rush. Once they were through the Sumner Tunnel, it took only another fifteen minutes before the cab pulled up in front of a Federal style townhouse facing the Common.

The small brass plaque beside the door read: "Wellstone & Farley." No mention of the stocks and bonds they dealt in. Just the name. The reception room was furnished with antiques, the walls decorated with portraits of somebody's colonial ancestors. The receptionist, a woman in her fifties with gray hair and a stout body, looked up as he approached.

"I have an appointment with Mr. Wellstone. I called last night. The name is Rogers."

After a moment on a house phone, the woman told Rogers that Mr. Wellstone would be with him shortly. She motioned toward some uncomfortable straight-back chairs.

Time passed as Rogers tried to find something of interest to read in *Fortune*. About a half-hour later, he was directed to Mr. Wellstone's office.

Matthew Wellstone was standing in his office doorway watching, as Rogers approached. The resemblance to his daughter was unmistakable. It was there especially in the patrician face, and in his manner, the way he held his body. He exuded probity. If you asked him to invest your money, you could be sure he would make the right decisions. Or that, at least, was what the manner proclaimed.

"Mr. Rogers? Come in. I wondered if you'd make it in this weather." He didn't offer to shake hands. He turned and went into his office. More antiques. He motioned Rogers into a chair across from him. In another chair, at right angles to the desk, perched another man, mid-fifties, about the same age as Wellstone. Otherwise he was much less imposing. He studied Rogers intently.

Wellstone looked at Rogers. "What is this all about, Mr. Rogers? I must say, I was hesitant when you called last night. I don't know you, and you refused to explain why it was essential that we meet this morning. I'm a busy man. But you said it was a matter involving my safety and my future, and if I agreed to see you, you would explain then. All right. You're here. Now, precisely who are you and what is this all about?"

Rogers took his time. "Eugene Donatello," he said.

Wellstone looked across at the other man.

"Mr. Wellstone," the small man said, "has nothing to say about Mr. Donatello."

Rogers looked at him. "Can't he speak for himself?"

"My name," the small man said, "is Jonathan Cabot. I am

Mr. Wellstone's attorney. Under the circumstances, I think it better if I speak for him. Now, Mr. Rogers, who are you?"

"I'm a New York police officer," Rogers said. "I'm on special assignment for the new mayor, John Morrison."

Cabot said, "I think you're on a fool's errand. Had you informed Mr. Wellstone last night of the purpose of your visit, he would have advised you to stay home. He would have told you that you would be wasting your time flying up here, especially in this weather."

Rogers shook his head and smiled. "Oh, I think Mr. Wellstone knew precisely why I wanted to see him, or if he didn't know, he suspected. Why else are you here, sir?"

"You have no jurisdiction in Boston, Mr. Rogers, and Mr. Wellstone is under no obligation to respond to any of your inquiries."

"I know that," Rogers said. "But I'm not here in an official capacity. This is purely informal. Anything I ask is only to gain information to help Mayor Morrison, not to incriminate Mr. Wellstone. Is it all right with you if I ask Mr. Wellstone a question?"

"That would depend on the question. I reserve the right to advise him not to answer."

"I understand." Rogers looked at Wellstone. "Sir, do you know a Eugene Donatello?"

"Mr. Wellstone knows many people," Cabot said. "Mr. Donatello is a prominent man in financial circles. It would be only natural for Mr. Wellstone to know him."

"Mr. Wellstone," Rogers said, looking at him and not at Cabot, "have you ever done business with Mr. Donatello?"

"I think," Cabot said, "I would advise Mr. Wellstone not to answer that question."

Rogers turned to Cabot. "Do you think there's something incriminating about admitting he's done business with Donatello?"

Cabot gave a short laugh. "Come, young man. No tricks. There might even be something incriminating about admitting that it's snowing outside. It all depends on your purpose."

"My purpose is to confirm what I already know about Donatello. Mr. Wellstone can provide the confirmation. I don't need him, but I can use him."

Cabot's eyes narrowed. He pursed his thin lips. "To the contrary," he said," I think you need him. Very much."

Except for his eyes, which kept moving between Cabot and Rogers, Wellstone had sat silent and motionless behind his desk. Now he suddenly said, "Just what do you know?"

Cabot turned to him. "Matthew," he said sharply.

"No, Jonathan," Wellstone said. "Let's hear just what this police officer thinks he knows. I think he's bluffing."

Rogers leaned back. He took his time. If he didn't make this persuasive enough to convince Wellstone—and Cabot—he might as well walk out of the office and take the next shuttle back to New York. "How far back do you want me to go?" he said.

Wellstone straightened. He said nothing.

"How about if we just talk about a little deal the two of you were in last summer? Do you want me to lay it out? It goes like this. Donatello came up here and told you he had inside dope that a little company was going to get a big military research and development contract that was going to turn it into a giant overnight. The source was impeccable. Couldn't be better. Did he tell you it was straight from the congressional committee that was going to approve the contract? Maybe. Maybe not. But that's where it came from. That's where a lot of inside stuff he passed to you over the years came from. Strictly illegal, of course. Using it was breaking the law. Using it could end you up in a prison cell. But what the hell, you'd made plenty over the years buying and selling for Donatello on the basis of that kind of secret information. Only, this time, the deal went sour, because Congress decided maybe it was time to give peace a chance, as the saying goes, so the contract didn't happen. Donatello lost his shirt, and you lost your shirt, and so did some other people. The thing is, you not only lost your shirt on this deal, you're probably going to go to Allenwood or Lompoc or some other federal pen as well. It'll be the talk of Boston. Matthew Wellstone of Back Bay and Plymouth Rock and all the rest in prison gray."

"Pure speculation," Cabot said. "I doubt whether you could prove anything."

"No? Don't bet on it."

"Mr. Wellstone admits nothing."

"I don't expect him to. At least, not right away. You wanted to know what I know. I gave you the outline. If you want, I'll fill in the details. I'd just like to hear his side."

Cabot pursed his lips. He looked at Wellstone and gave a brief nod. He turned to Rogers. "Would you excuse us for a moment, Mr. Rogers? I'd like to talk with Mr. Wellstone in private."

Rogers nodded in assent and left the office, taking a seat in the outer office. The door closed behind him. After about five minutes, the door opened again and Cabot gestured to Rogers to return.

"What are you prepared to give in exchange for Mr. Wellstone's cooperation?" Cabot asked.

"What do you want?"

"Immunity from prosecution. Are you in a position to make such a promise?"

"It's a possibility."

"We have to take your word?"

"Pick up the phone. Call Morrison. Ask him. I'll give you his private number." Rogers reached into his pocket, pulled out a pen and a small notebook, flipped to a blank page, scribbled the number on it, tore it off and handed it to Cabot. Cabot studied it, folded it, slipped it into his pocket.

"I assume Mr. Wellstone would be expected to testify before a federal grand jury and in open court at trial?"

"That would be up to the Justice Department," Rogers said. "Morrison has been in touch with them. He'd know better than I would what they intend."

"Nothing Mr. Wellstone says can be used against him."

"Naturally."

"Mr. Wellstone will not go to trial and will not go to prison."

"That would be up to the Justice Department."

"Not good enough. We want a guarantee that the most Mr. Wellstone will receive is a suspended sentence and, perhaps, a fine."

"If what he says is good enough, Morrison could probably put in the word. I'm not in a position to promise that."

"We must have that promise."

"Call Morrison. But I can tell you right now, if Mr. Wellstone doesn't cooperate, he's going to be in a cell adjoining Donatello's. No ifs, ands, or buts. The government will come down hard on him."

"Excuse us again, Mr. Rogers," Cabot said. He reached for the phone, waited until Rogers rose and left the office. Once again, Rogers waited outside. Twenty minutes later, Cabot opened the door and motioned for Rogers to return.

"I've talked with Mr. Morrison," Cabot said. "He has promised to do his best. We had a conference call with an Assistant Attorney General in Washington. Mr. Morrison obviously still has a lot of influence."

"And he uses it when he has to. I don't think you have much choice."

"It's up to Mr. Wellstone. I have advised him that his best course is to cooperate."

Rogers looked at Wellstone. His skin had assumed a gray tone. Beads of sweat stood out on his forehead. He took a deep breath and swiveled his chair so he could look through the window behind him. In a few moments, he looked back. "I suppose," he said, "I have to do this. He looked back at Rogers. "Yes, I know Donatello."

"Have you done business with him?"

"Yes," he said. "I've done business with that man, to my everlasting regret."

"Recently?"

"Yes. Recently, and for the last twenty years."

"Involving the purchase of stock?"

"In for a penny, in for a pound," he sighed. "Yes. I arranged the purchase of shares for him. Not for the first time."

"But not in his name?"

"Never in his name. Always in street names, dummy names that he gave me, anything but his own name."

"How did Donatello pay for these purchases?"

"Do you mean, did he walk in here with an attaché case filled with cash? Don't be ridiculous. He paid by check, the checks drawn on various banks."

"Banks in this country?"

"No. Always from offshore banks, on numbered accounts. Some were in the Bahamas, some in Panama, some in Switzerland and a few other places where numbered accounts are legal and common, and the laws very strict about revealing the identity of the owners of those accounts."

"Didn't that make you suspicious that there might be something illegal going on, laundering or something else?"

"Suspicious? Young man, I knew from the first time Gene Donatello walked into this office that the entire enterprise smelled to high heaven."

"And yet you agreed to cooperate with him?"

"I doubt whether I can make you understand. Twenty years ago, the situation here was very difficult, almost impossible. My father had invested unwisely and spent foolishly and so there was little left of the business when I began. We were having trouble making ends meet. And then, one morning Gene Donatello appeared. It wasn't exactly out of the blue. We'd met casually a few times at conventions and other affairs. We'd had a few drinks together and engaged in some general conversations. This day he appeared with a proposition. He said he had received confidential information that an offer was to be made for the purchase of a certain company. The proposed purchase price was to be about forty dollars a share higher than the then market price. He had access to a virtually unlimited amount of money to invest. However, for reasons he couldn't discuss, he was not in a position to buy the shares in his own name, and further, he did not want a run-up on the stock through major block purchases. He proposed that we buy the stock in small lots, using a number of street names, over a period of a few months before the announcement. And, so as not to arouse any undue suspicion, that we farm out some of the purchases to other brokers around the country, whose names he would supply. If we would agree to do what he asked, he would pay us twice the normal commission. And, if we so desired, he had no objection to our taking advantage of this information by purchasing some shares for ourselves, though he warned us to be extremely cautious so as not to raise an alarm.

"We were so close to going under at the time that I didn't stop to consider the implications or the legality or the morality or the consequences. It just seemed a way out. So I put on the blinders and agreed. We did as he directed and bought the shares. I would estimate that the investment was in the neighborhood of ten million dollars. As he had predicted, or, rather, knew, the announcement was forthcoming, and the price of the stock rose about fifty points in a matter of days.

"That was the beginning. Since then, Gene Donatello has come to us with similar propositions once or twice a year. He was never wrong, and as a result we have become extremely wealthy, far beyond our expectations. And so has Donatello and so have the people he represents.

"I have never speculated on where he gets his information or the original sources of those offshore funds. I've never wanted to know. I persuaded myself that if I didn't know, I could always plead ignorance, always claim that I was merely doing what my client wanted. My heritage, my upbringing, the moral code that was instilled in me by my parents aside, it was not a difficult thing to do because it was extremely profitable. It has turned us from a firm barely able to keep our heads above water into a very successful one, with the concomitant personal rewards. We now have a great many clients in addition to Gene Donatello. We deal with them according to the highest standards of our profession, and they trust us implicitly, and with reason. That, I understand, does not excuse our dealings with him. It is hardly even mitigation. But it is true, nevertheless."

"You mentioned," Rogers said, "that Donatello was always right. I gather this last time that wasn't so."

"You gather correctly," Wellstone said. "For the first time, his information was not just faulty, it was disastrous. He came to me this past summer and said he had received information that a small Texas company named Centex Research was going to be awarded a major research and development contract by the Pentagon, a contract that would eventually turn the company into a billion-dollar military enterprise. The stock was selling for about ten dollars a share. Employing our usual methods, he wanted to buy every available share of the company's stock, a purchase that would entail an outlay in the neighborhood of a hundred million dollars. We proceeded to do as he asked. Then Congress cut the military appropriations bill, and the contract was not approved. Centex, which apparently had been tooling up in expectation, went into Chapter Eleven, from which, I fear, it will never emerge, and its shares are good only for papering bathroom walls, if that."

"You invested your own money in it?" Rogers asked.

"Sadly, yes." He took a deep breath and shook his head. "Now, Mr. Rogers," he said, "I have a question for you. How did you find out about me?"

"Your daughter, sir."

"My daughter? Nicole? I ordered her to stop seeing that man. But she was never one to obey orders, even when she was a child. You know her?"

"I've met her a couple of times. She went to college with a friend of mine."

"I see." He sighed. "How sharper than a serpent's tooth it is to have a thankless child," he quoted. "Not really. She's a good girl. She sees the best in everyone. Just how she's going to see this, just how everyone, my friends, my family, my associates, are going to see it, God only knows. I'm going to lose everything, I suppose. That, and the disgrace."

"You should have thought of that a long time ago, sir," Rogers said.

"You're right, of course, I should have. Well, I'll have the distinction of being the first in my family to be a convicted felon, since they didn't convict people for dealing in slaves in the old days."

"It's not that hopeless, Matthew," Cabot said.

"What do you think, Mr. Rogers?" Wellstone said.

"The government helps those who help it."

Wellstone gave a short laugh. "What do they call it? Becoming a stool pigeon? Well, beggars can't be choosers." He looked away for a moment, then turned back. "Now, Mr. Rogers, the condemned man has one last wish. Will you let me buy you dinner at Locke-Ober's, across the Common?"

"I wish I could accept. But I want to make the shuttle back to New York."

"Of course. Another time, then. Though I doubt if there will be another time."

33

The weather in New York was a lot better than in Boston. The snow line had stopped somewhere in Connecticut, and though the weather in the city was arctic, the sky was clear, the city lights sparkling brightly. The trip in from La Guardia was quick, and he reached the apartment just after seven.

Melissa was somewhere in the other room when he walked through the door. Her suitcase rested beside it. He glanced at it, then looked away, trying to ignore the implication. He called to her. She came from the bedroom, moved quickly and embraced him, holding tightly. "How did it go?" she asked.

"Okay, I guess," he said. "I got what I was after. And a lot more. Wellstone laid it all out in spades; hearts, clubs, and diamonds, too."

"Poor Nikki," she said.

"She's a big girl," he said. "She can take it."

"It won't be easy. I mean, to find out that both your father and the man you love are . . . what would you call them, crooks?"

"At the least. I see you're ready."

She nodded. "It wasn't easy to decide what to take," she said. "Here we are freezing half to death and out there they're walking around in shorts. It's just hard to believe."

"You'll be back when?"

"Sunday at the latest. Maybe earlier, if they hate me."

"They won't. Have you eaten?"

"I was waiting for you."

She retrieved a heavy sheepskin coat from the closet, and they went out into the cold, wandering for a while through the Village until they decided on a small Mexican restaurant they came to often.

Over dinner, as they toyed with the food, he asked, "What time's your plane?"

"Nine," she said. "Tomorrow morning."

"I'll drive you out," he said.

"You don't have to," she said. "They're sending a limo."

"Cancel it," he said. "I want to drive you."

She nodded slowly. "I was hoping you would say that."

They rode in silence through the early morning traffic. Once they reached JFK, he dropped her off at the terminal, then parked the car. He joined her inside near the security checkpoint leading to the gates. They kept looking at each other, not talking.

"I guess it's time for me to go," she said as the loudspeaker announced that the flight to Los Angeles was beginning to board.

"I guess so," he said. He handed her a small package he had been holding. "Here."

"What's this?"

"A little something to remember me by, and to help you pass the time."

She studied his face. "Can I open it now?"

"Sure."

She unwrapped the package and looked at the book that had been inside, the one he had bought the night Sully died. "Wherever did you find this? I've been looking for it for years."

"In a secondhand place one night a couple of weeks ago. It was going to be a Christmas present, one of them, anyway. Make it early Christmas."

She moved quickly against him, holding him as though she

wouldn't let go. Then she broke free and moved quickly through
the electronic barrier, not looking back as she headed toward
the gate.

Rogers watched until he could no longer see her.

The ride back into the city was slow, the traffic heavy, a
mixture of commuters and Christmas shoppers. It was well after ten before he found a parking place near Morrison's Fifth
Avenue apartment.

Morrison was waiting for him. He led Rogers into the living
room. "Coffee?" he asked.

"Coffee," Rogers said.

"Anything else?"

"Just coffee."

Morrison poured him a cup and watched impatiently as Rogers took a sip. "Okay," he said. "Tell me. I hope you can make
it fast. I've put off one meeting already and I've others scheduled all day. I did what you asked when that lawyer called from
Boston. Your man will have his immunity, if he's really got the
goods."

"He's got them. I'll make this as fast as I can," Rogers said.
"To begin with, Donatello's strictly bad news. Get out of it while
you still have time."

"Facts," Morrison demanded. "Details."

"Everything the letter writer said, it's true. Did I tell you
his name was Werner Rosenblatt? He's supposed to have shot
himself. But I doubt it."

Morrison sat up at that and stared. "What do you mean?"

"His widow and his lawyer think somebody got to him. At
first I thought it was the usual widow and best friend pipe
dream. Now I'm not so sure."

"Find out," Morrison ordered.

"I intend to. To continue, Rosenblatt didn't have the half of
it." Rogers proceeded to lay out what Wellstone had told him,
what Solomon had known and what he thought, and everything
else he had learned and surmised.

"I assume," Morrison said, "you learned most of the details
yesterday in Boston?"

"Some of it," Rogers said. "Some from the lawyer. Some on
my own hook. The guy in Boston put a lot of it together from the
beginning, or at least from when he was roped in."

"The man in Boston? The lawyer said his name's Wellstone. Who is he?"

Rogers considered. He shrugged. "He was Donatello's broker, his front man. If all you're going to do is dump Donatello, there's no need to bring him in any further. If you or somebody decides to indict, that'll be another story. Meanwhile, let him sweat, let him wonder when the floor's going to cave in. It'll do him good."

"He told you he thought Donatello was a front for other people. Correct?"

"Right."

"Who?"

"Facts or speculation?"

"You know me. I want facts. Anybody can speculate. You can't prosecute on speculation. Theories are worth the paper they're written on, and not much more."

"Then I don't know. I can guess, but I don't know for sure."

"Find out. Was anyone else involved? I mean, in addition to Donatello and the people behind him?"

"I think so."

"Who?"

"Again, I can speculate, that's all."

"Find out. I'm going to tell Chief Dolan that I want you with me for a while longer because there are other things I want to do. Maybe I'll even take you on my staff permanently. We'll see, after January first. Meanwhile I want you to nail this down solid."

"What are you going to do about Donatello?"

Morrison laughed sarcastically. "Drop him, of course. Gently, though. I've become a politician now, Ben. I've learned about tact. He's got a lot of friends, and I can't afford to alienate them. I may need them in the future. So I'll tell him that I've given his generous offer of public service a great deal of consideration, but I realize I can't ask him to make the sacrifices, financial and personal, that would be required if he took a city job. It would be asking just too much of a man in his position. And so I've decided to appoint someone else. In fact, I'll call him as soon as you leave, and I'll announce the name of the new man this afternoon. I've already sounded somebody out, and he's agreed to come on board if I wanted him. Now, just get to work on this whole thing. Put it all together for me. I want to nail that bastard's hide to the wall, and everyone who was in this with him. Take over the city, for God's sake. We'll see who takes over what."

He drove through the heavy Christmastime traffic downtown to the garage near Hudson Street where he and Melissa parked and shared the two hundred a month fee. If Melissa got the part and moved out west, he thought, he'd have to give up the garage and join the alternate-side parking lottery. Or maybe just give up the car altogether. Being without her was a thought that he tried to resist, a thought he tried to shove as far away as possible. She had, over the past year, become an essential part of his life. He didn't want to think what it would be like if she were gone. He'd have to make do somehow.

From the garage, he walked slowly home to the empty apartment. As he turned the corner onto his street, moving east, he noticed a big man step out from the shelter of a basement passage and start toward him. The sun was in his eyes, blinding, obscuring the figure. His mind was on other things and he didn't pay much attention. The big guy kept coming toward him, and suddenly he noticed that the man had a baseball bat clutched in one hand. He had one of those stray thoughts: it's a little late, or a little early, for the baseball season. It lasted only a moment before he understood.

The man with the baseball bat was right in front of him. The bat rose high over his head. Rogers suddenly recognized him. Ding-Dong Faranulli. Rogers tried to move, to turn, but he wasn't quick enough. His leg, still not totally healed, buckled. He raised an arm to try to protect himself, lunged at Ding-Dong, and tried to grapple with him. The bat came down and the world went away.

34

He kept drifting in and out. Once, he came near the surface. His eyes were closed, yet the light blinded him; he tried to seal them tighter, only it didn't work. His head felt like somebody was playing handball inside, against the walls of his skull. If I'm dead, he thought, I went to the wrong place. He heard voices and tried to blot them out, pushing them away, sinking back toward oblivion.

There were always voices around him, strange voices, men's voices, women's voices. They seemed to be shouting in his ears, trying to tell him something, trying to get him to do something, but he couldn't make out the words, and whatever it was they wanted him to do he didn't know or care. He tried to tell them to go away and leave him alone, but he couldn't form the words. He slipped back into the place where there was no feeling, where there was nothing.

There were people poking him, prodding him, moving and shifting him. He wanted to tell them to stop, but the words were only in his mind, and they got no further. He wanted to tell them to go away and leave him alone, just let him die if that was what was going to happen. But nothing came out.

Images passed in and out in a jerky rhythm like some old

movie not quite in synch, moving at not quite the right speed. Images, pictures, memories—they kept floating in and out of his mind in jumbled order, blending, and making no sense.

One time, he didn't know whether it was day or night, and he didn't care, he thought he heard his grandmother's voice, heard his grandmother crying. He wondered what she was doing here. She almost never left her neighborhood. He drifted away again, sliding down an old coal chute, brittle chunks abrading his skin, his lungs filling and choking on coal dust, a huge dark form catching him as he reached bottom, holding him against an unyielding chest, the coal dust in his nose changing to the sweet aroma of grapes, the pungent odor of smoke, and then the blackness of nothing.

Another time, he thought he could make out Chief Dolan's voice, Dolan talking, but not to him, and then another voice, Morrison's. He didn't even wonder about that.

He was sure he sensed Melissa somewhere nearby, was sure he could catch her distinct aroma, that mixture of perfume and her. His mind told him it wasn't possible. She was in California.

Then finally it became not quite so easy to let go, and the pain wasn't quite so bad when he came back. He hovered around the edges for a while, not really awake, and then he opened his eyes. The blinds were closed, the room dim, but there was a hint of sunlight outside. He moved a little, and it hurt. He stopped. He moved his hand, felt wrappings around his chest, moved it higher, felt his head wrapped in something. He moved his head a little, and it didn't hurt so much. There was a needle stuck in his arm, taped to the forearm, tubing dangling from it, connected to a bottle on a metal stanchion, dripping fluid.

The door opened and somebody wearing white came in. She moved toward him slowly. He watched her. She noticed that his eyes were open. "You're awake," she said.

"I'm awake." He tried to say it, but the words were a croak out of a dry mouth. He swallowed, licked his lips, said it again, and this time the words came out, just a whisper. It hurt his throat. "Water," he mumbled.

The woman in white ignored that, turned, and hurried out. In a minute, there were others in the room, bending over him, telling him not to try to talk, doing things to him, some that hurt, some that didn't. He asked for water again and somebody brought a glass with a straw and told him to take one sip and no more. He did. He started to take another, and the glass was removed.

He drifted away again.

When he came back, Melissa was sitting in a chair by the bed, watching him. At first, she didn't notice his eyes opening. Then she did. "Ben," she said. "Oh, God, Ben." She reached out and took his hand and held it. She started to cry.

He tried to say something, only he couldn't form words. He swallowed and tried again. "I thought," he began, stopped, began again, "you're supposed to be in California."

She began to laugh. "Oh, God," she said. "My God."

"Water," he said. She reached for a glass with a straw on the table by the bed and brought it to him, held it while he sipped. Water going down had never felt so good. She took it away. "What happened?" he said. "Why aren't you in California?"

"I was," she said. "Do you know what today is?"

He thought about that. "No."

"Christmas Eve," she said.

The baseball bat had been more than two weeks before. It took him time to accept that.

"We thought you were going to die," she said.

"I thought I already had," he said. He felt himself drifting down again, and he looked at her, trying to memorize her face. Then he was gone.

When he woke again, it was dark outside. A nurse was doing something around the room, being very quiet. He watched her for a while, then, "Hi."

She turned. "You're awake," she said. "Good. Oh, Merry Christmas."

"Is it indeed?"

"Indeed it is," she said. She went to the door, disappeared, then returned with a doctor. The name on the tag attached to his greens read, "Albert Lowenthall, M.D."

Lowenthall bent over him, poked and probed, around the ribs, around the head. "Everything's healing," he said. "You're going to recover. Merry Christmas. Do you know how lucky you are?"

"No. How lucky?"

"Nobody thought you were going to make it when they brought you in. Seven fractured ribs, fractured skull, internal injuries, God knows what else. You were lucky some guy came along while you were being worked over. What the hell did he use?"

"A baseball bat," Rogers said.

Lowenthall turned that over. "A baseball bat? It's a wonder he didn't kill you. He must really have had it in for you."

"He did."

"Do you know who he was?"

"I know."

Lowenthall nodded but didn't follow up. The name would have meant nothing to him. He completed his examination and left. A half-hour later, the door opened again and two guys in plainclothes walked in. They didn't have to wear uniforms or have their shields pinned to their lapels to label them cops. They introduced themselves: Detective Stevens and Detective O'Brien, from downtown. Chief Dolan had assigned them to the case, they said. He was personally interested. They had been waiting, hoping that Rogers would come to and they'd get to talk to him, hoping he wouldn't die so that then it would go to Homicide, even if he was an IAD rat, though they didn't quite say rat. They even wished him a Merry Christmas, though not necessarily a Happy New Year. Did Rogers know, they asked, who had come after him?

"Dinardo Faranulli," he said. "They call him Ding Dong. He's a wiseguy."

"Good enough," O'Brien said. "We'll pick him up."

Fat chance, Rogers thought. He didn't say it. But it was true.

Melissa arrived with presents and announced she wasn't leaving until they threw her out, that day and every day until they let him go home. Even then she wasn't sure what she could do. She was just part-time at police headquarters anyway, and they could make do without her until he was better. His grandmother came with presents, sat there silently looking at him, tears in her eyes. Somebody installed a small tree on a table by the window, with colored balls hanging from its branches, tinsel draped across it. It glistened in the sunlight coming through the partly opened slats in the blinds. The light didn't bother him so much anymore.

Chief Dolan dropped by to see how he was, his wife, Patricia, with him. When he was out of the hospital and feeling better, she wanted him and Melissa to come to dinner. Dolan told him he was to do nothing and think of nothing until he was completely well. Morrison had told him he wanted to keep Rogers, but to hell with Morrison. Morrison could wait until Rogers was not just on his feet, but completely back to speed. Then they'd decide about that.

Morrison stopped by. It was just a week until his inauguration, but he took the time. Melissa was still there. Morrison told him the important thing was to get well. He still wanted Rogers to do that job, but it could wait. There was no particular rush now.

"What do you mean?" Rogers asked. "I thought you wanted it done and done fast."

"I did," Morrison said. "But events have a way of playing themselves out without our intervention. I don't suppose you've heard? No, of course not. You've been out for quite a while. Nobody has to worry about Gene Donatello anymore."

Rogers stared at him. "I don't get it," he said.

"He went up to his hunting lodge in the Adirondacks a couple of days after I talked with him. I could tell he didn't like my decision not to go with him, but he said he understood. He said he had been willing to make the sacrifice, and he was still willing, but if that was my decision, he would abide by it. He even wished me well and if I ever needed his service in the future, he would do whatever he could. What a hypocrite. Of course, one shouldn't speak ill of the dead. Still and all . . ."

"What do you mean?" Rogers demanded.

"You wouldn't have heard. He had a hunting accident. He was out in the woods and the story is that apparently he tripped over something in the snow and his shotgun went off. Blew his head away. The caretaker at his place went out looking for him when he didn't return to his lodge and found him. He'd been dead for a couple of hours. I wonder, though, if he suspected everything was about to come down around him. It would have eventually you can be sure."

"Suicide, you mean?" Rogers said. "Not Donatello. No way.

He would have been sure he could put the fix in. You can bet on that."

Morrison slowly nodded. "So it was probably just an accident. A fortuitous one."

"An accident?" Rogers said. "Maybe. Maybe not."

Morrison stared at him. "Why not?"

"Just a hunch. Maybe nothing to it. When I can, I'll look into it."

"You'll look into nothing until you're fit."

"I know that. Still . . ." He let that hang.

When Morrison left, Rogers turned to Melissa. "How's Nikki taking it?"

"Not good," she said. "I've seen her a lot. She cries all the time. She doesn't know what he was and I can't tell her, of course. Not about him or her father. She went home to Boston for the holidays."

"Good idea," Rogers said. "Her father's not such a bad guy, really. He got mixed up and he didn't know how to get out. It'll haunt him for the rest of his life. Still, it shouldn't be such a bad holiday for him. He's got his daughter around, and I think he knows he's off the hook for the time being. With Donatello gone, nobody needs him as a witness because he didn't know anybody else. And unless something turns up when they get around to Donatello's records, which I doubt, there won't be anything to show what he did. That must be a relief."

In another few days they had him up and walking the hospital halls, though he needed help at first. His legs felt like jelly, and the rest of him ached unbearably at every step. He had almost no strength. Somebody had once told him that it took two days to recover for every day you were in bed. He was beginning to think it was more like a week, maybe a year. They had him eating, but the hospital food was unappetizing in appearance and worse in taste. It wasn't helping his recovery, he was sure.

It didn't take long for the word to spread that Rogers was on the way back. Over the next days, guys from Internal Affairs were in and out, Melissa was in and out, his grandmother was in and out, even some guys from the department came to see him. Carlos Rodriguez appeared a few times and told him he was making it a personal thing to get this guy Faranulli. Everybody was out looking for him, but Ding-Dong seemed to have vanished from the face of the earth.

"Actually," Rogers said, "if you get him, he's another good collar for you, Carlos."

"How so? I mean, you're still breathing air, even if it ain't fresh."

"Remember the Arab?"

"How could I forget?"

"Ding-Dong rang his bell," Rogers said. "Him and a partner of his, name of Gino Santucci."

"Well, what d'ya know? You sure?"

"No proof, but sure as sure. Proof you can get."

"Proof I'll get."

"He did one more, Carlos. If you get him, I'll appreciate it."

"Felix?" Rodriguez stared at him.

Rogers shook his head. "It's possible. But I wasn't thinking of Felix."

"Who then?"

"Little guy people called Sully. His real name was Sean Sullivan."

"Who was he?"

"Just a little guy who never hurt anybody and who liked Chinese food, hot, the hotter the better."

"He was one of your stoolies, right?"

"Right. I think maybe it was Ding-Dong that cut out his tongue and strung him up."

"I heard about that," Rodriguez said. He stayed a few minutes longer and then left. "I'll be back," he promised. "With good news."

A couple of mornings later, just before the new year began, a huge arrangement of long-stemmed red roses was brought into the room by an admiring nurse. Melissa was there. She stared at the roses, then at Rogers. "Somebody loves you," she said. "A whole lot."

"You?"

"I love you a whole lot," she said. "But I couldn't afford this."

"Not even when you're a big important movie star?" It was

the first time in weeks he had even thought about that. Now he did, and he stared a question at her.

She laughed. "Never," she said. "We'll talk about all that another time. Not now."

"Is there a card?" he asked.

She found a small white envelope nestled among the roses. She pulled it out and held it toward him.

"Read it to me," he said.

She opened it, read it, looked at him strangely. Then she read it aloud, slowly. "Be well. Mend quickly. The assassin will do evil no more." There was no signature.

"Do you know who sent this?" she asked.

He nodded slowly. "I think so," he said. "Somebody I want no favors from."

Late that afternoon, he was sitting in a chair in his room when Carlos Rodriguez walked in. His face was expressionless. He said, "I got news."

Rogers looked at him. "You got Ding-Dong?"

Rodriguez shook his head. "No such luck. Better, maybe. Only not for him. Some cop walking over by the river found him this afternoon, right under the same bridge where they did your guy Sully. What they did to him you wouldn't wish on your worst enemy, which maybe he was. It must of taken 'em a couple of days. I figure they wanted him to feel it. Jesus. There was blood everywhere. And he was burned like from top to bottom. They cut off his balls an' shoved 'em in his mouth an' then sewed the mouth shut, an' I figure they done that while he was still alive. They left just enough so we made a positive ID. Ding-Dong Faranulli an' no mistake. The bastard ain't gonna ring no more bells." He laughed. It was a nasty sound with no humor. "Oh, one more thing. We can't touch his partner, Gino Santucci."

Rogers stared at him. "Why not?"

"He bought his way out. He run to the feds an' now he's in the witness program. They got him over on Governors Island, all nice an' safe and sound, an' I hear he's spillin' his guts."

JANUARY

35

They sent Rogers home from the hospital at the end of the first week in January. Everything was healing nicely, they said, and though he still felt weak and tended to have dizzy spells if he tried to do too much, he was able to get around on his own. He'd be able to get back to his old routine in another couple of weeks, they told him. He just shouldn't try to hurry things. He should relax, take it easy and recuperate.

When they were back in the apartment, he wandered a bit, looking at things he'd thought he'd never see again and which had taken on an added importance. He tired quickly, and Melissa tried to get him to go to bed, but he refused.

"Are you going to be a bad patient?" she asked.

"A lousy one," he said. "That's why they threw me out of the joint so fast."

"At least sit down," she insisted.

He sat in an old overstuffed chair and leaned back, suddenly glad to be off his feet, suddenly realizing how tired and weak he really was. He closed his eyes, listening to the sounds Melissa made as she moved about. Then he slept.

When he woke, Melissa had drawn a chair next to his and

was sitting, watching him. She saw his eyes open. "You're awake," she said.

He nodded.

"Would you like something to eat?"

"I suppose so," he said. "It'll be good to eat real food for a change."

She smiled and started to rise and move toward the kitchen. "It won't take long," she said.

He stopped her. "Before you go," he said, "there's something I have to ask. What happened?"

"I thought you knew," she said.

"Not about me," he said. "You. You haven't said a word."

"They offered me the part."

"I hope you took it."

"I did."

"Then what are you doing here?"

"Taking care of you."

"Seriously."

"The picture's on hold. They've had trouble with the leading man, the director, and the script. You know what they say, if something can go wrong, it will. So they're doing some recasting and rewriting. They're not going to want me until sometime in February."

"In the meantime?"

"I'm going to take care of you."

"No way. We'll just get on each other's nerves if we're cooped up together without a break twenty-four hours a day."

"You need somebody."

"Like hell. Give me a few days and I'll be fine. I can take care of myself."

"No. You need somebody, at least for now."

"Then make a call. They'll send a nurse or somebody a couple of hours a day. I want you to go back to work."

"At One Police Plaza?"

"Exactly. There you can be my eyes and ears. I'm going to need someone to do some things since I can't do them myself for a while."

She thought for a moment, then slowly nodded. She turned away. "Now let me make dinner. It may not be Tremanti's, but it'll be prime Redburn."

"Who could ask for more? Or better?"

*   *   *

Over the next days, they established a routine. Melissa rose at her usual time, fixed breakfast for him, and then left for work. Rogers slept late, rose, ate breakfast, took walks in the morning, a little longer every day, feeling himself growing stronger. At noon the nurse arrived, checked him over, made lunch, insisted he rest afterward, did things around the apartment, and then left about four.

In the afternoons, following his nap, Rogers tried to organize his thoughts, to put together disparate and seemingly unconnected facts and ideas. He made notes, putting down what he had discovered and what he had surmised. He read slowly through all Felix Palmieri's papers, all his notes, trying to see what he had missed. He was sure there was something somewhere. He was sure, too, that Felix had left clues about all that unfinished business. Maybe it was in the papers; maybe it had been in something he had said in that last conversation arranging the meeting that never came off. He just couldn't bring it back. He had trouble concentrating too long; his mind wasn't working right yet.

About five-thirty each day, Melissa arrived home. She made dinner. In the evening, they listened to music or watched television, or read some. Then they went to bed early.

Slowly his strength returned, and with it a growing impatience with the weakness that still remained, a mounting need to get out and start taking care of unfinished business. Little things began to set him off. Nothing pleased him, nothing satisfied him. He was short-tempered with Melissa, finding fault, yet knowing he was being irrational and unreasonable, and forcing himself to apologize. People telephoned, but Rogers invariably cut the conversation short, sometimes hanging up after a few words, often just turning on the answering machine when he woke so he wouldn't have to pick up the phone when it rang, monitoring the messages and rarely returning them. He railed at the nurse, finally sending her away one afternoon and telling her not to come back. The apartment felt like a jail cell.

He had to do something. The last week in January, he called Morrison. The new mayor, trying to make order out of the city's chaos, was busy, his secretary said. She took a message and said she'd pass it on when Morrison was free.

Late that afternoon, Morrison returned the call. He sounded harassed, but he also sounded pleased to hear from Rogers. Was Rogers feeling better? he asked. He'd been meaning to call, but he didn't want to bother Rogers until he was sure he was fit, and besides, he had hardly a free minute. When he'd agreed to run for mayor he had no idea of the complexity of the job, of the million and one decisions that had to be made every day.

They talked for a while, Morrison not hurrying him. Finally Rogers said, "I need a favor."

"Ask and it will be done," Morrison said. "As long as you don't want the keys to the treasury. Not that you'd find much there. Hardly enough to pay for those dinners and that parking ticket and the rest of the money you spent."

"I never sent you a bill," Rogers said.

"Melissa did," Morrison said. "While you were in the hospital. Don't worry. I took care of them. Now, what can I do?"

"I want to get onto Governors Island."

Morrison laughed. "There's a ferry," he said. "You need an in with the Coast Guard to take it. I can do that. But why?"

"I want to get to a guy who's in the witness program. They're holding him there."

"Who's holding him?"

"The federal marshals."

There was a pause. "Does this have anything to do with our problem?"

He couldn't tell Morrison he thought that was a wild shot, an improbable one, that there was little likelihood that Gino Santucci knew anything about Donatello or anyone else involved with his schemes. But Santucci knew about the Arab, and he might know about other things, and if Rogers was going to clear away the fog that shrouded Felix Palmieri's last cases, he had to talk to him. So he hedged, saying, "Maybe. Maybe not. I won't know until I talk to him."

"I see. What's his name?"

"Gino Santucci. And I want to talk to him alone. No feds around. Just the two of us."

"You're asking a lot. I'll see what I can do and get back to you," Morrison said.

Morrison called the next afternoon. Rogers had the machine on. When he heard that it was Morrison, he picked up.

"It wasn't easy," the mayor said. "I had to go to the Attorney General directly and practically beg. But you're in. Go out there tomorrow. Ask for Sergeant Hartnett. He'll be expecting you. They'll have a private room set aside for you and this Santucci. Call me when you're finished."

Rogers stood on the deck of the Coast Guard ferry, enjoying the January cold, the bite of the wind against his face, feeling the icy fingers of salt spray. It was good to be out, good to be on the water, good to be working again. He felt strong and able. He felt content for the first time in six weeks.

It was a quick trip to Governors Island. Once there, Rogers went as directed to the special barracks reserved for special guests. There was no guest register, no public list of who was there, for among them were those who had sought the government's protection in return for telling all they knew about people and things the government wanted to know about. Once their song was sung, they would get a new name and a new life in some distant place. Until then, they were guarded on this secure island, their presence and even their existence known only to their protectors.

Because of the sensitivity of the situation, and the extreme security precautions, it was highly unusual for someone not directly involved to be allowed admission. Certainly Rogers's escort, Sergeant Hartnett, was not pleased. "Strictly against regulations," he said. "You shouldn't be here."

Rogers smiled a little. "But I am."

"That doesn't make it right," Hartnett said. "I'm responsible for the safety of these people. No one but authorized personnel is supposed to even know about them."

"I'm sure you do a good job," Rogers said. "But I know."

Rogers was escorted into one of the barracks, then into a small, windowless cubicle. It contained a single green metal table and two hard metal chairs and a metal ashtray.

"Make yourself comfortable," Hartnett said. "I'll have the prisoner brought down." Rogers walked in. Hartnett spun, slammed the door shut as he left, and locked it.

Ten minutes later, the key grated in the lock again. The door opened. Hartnett was back. This time he had Gino Santucci with him. Gino wasn't wearing a fashionably cut Italian-tailored suit this time. He was wearing Army fatigues. They matched the pallor of his face. He tried to assume his usual arrogant manner, but it wasn't working. Gino Santucci was one scared former wiseguy, protection or not.

Gino looked at Rogers. The look turned to a glare. "What the hell is this?" he demanded. "They didn't tell me nothin'. All they said was some guy wanted to see me. They didn't say who."

"I want to talk to you," Rogers said.

"Fuck off," Gino said. "I only talk to the feds. You city cops can take a flyin' fuck."

"The feds say you should talk to me."

"Bullshit."

"If they didn't, would I be here, just you and me all alone for a nice private tête-à-tête?"

Gino thought about that for a moment. He shrugged. "Okay. So, what the fuck do you want?"

"I want to talk about an Arab."

"Talk to the feds. I already told 'em about that."

"Tell *me*."

"The bastard welched. He got what was comin' to him."

"He welched on what? The bread he owed you or the junk he wouldn't carry in his pouch?"

"Both. I told 'em. Who cares about the fuckin' Arab anyway? Why wouldn't I tell 'em? They can't touch me. I got immunity from everythin'."

"Did you tell them that Ding-Dong was in it with you?"

"Fuck Ding-Dong. He can look out for hisself."

"What made you run to the feds, Gino?"

"I got religion."

"I believe you. You sure it wasn't because you were afraid you'd get what Ding-Dong got?"

"Ding-Dong's got rocks where his brains oughtta be." He stopped and stared at Rogers. "What about Ding-Dong?"

"You haven't heard?"

"I hear nothin'. They don't let me read the papers. They don't even let me watch the news on the TV. It's like ain't nothin' goin' on out there as far as I'm concerned. One big blank. What about Ding-Dong?"

Rogers told him.

"Jesus Christ," Gino said. "I didn't know. Poor bastard. Jesus Christ." He started to sweat. It wasn't hot in the room, but the sweat stood out on his face; it stained the armpits of his shirt. He looked like somebody had turned on a faucet. He shook his head, trying to regain control. "What the fuck," he said. "I warned the stupid bastard. I told him . . . Shit, I got nothin' to worry about. Nobody can get at me in here."

"Who would want to get at you, Gino?"

"You kiddin'? Everybody, for chrissake."

"I can see," Rogers said, "why they'd want to get you, especially if they know what you're doing. But why would somebody do that to Ding-Dong? Not just waste him, but burn him, cut off his balls, all the rest."

"A million reasons," Gino said.

"Give me two."

"Maybe they was worried he'd do what I done. Like come on in."

"What 'they' are you talking about?"

"Shit. Do I gotta spell it out?"

"The Don? Ruggieri?"

Gino sweated some more. Rogers wondered if he was pissing in his pants. It was probably a sure bet, the way he was shifting around on the chair. "Maybe," Gino mumbled.

"What did Ding-Dong know?"

"Ding-Dong didn't know shit."

"And you do?"

"Nobody knows what Ruggieri don't want him to know, an' he didn't want me to know that much. I was strictly a gofer. Gino, go for this. Gino, carry that there. Gino, pick up that. That kind of shit. You see him, you tell him that."

"Why would I be likely to see him?"

"He sent for you that time. I figure you must have somethin' he wants. So maybe he'll send for you again."

"What did you tell them about Ruggieri?"

"Nothin' they can use. Believe me, they asked me a zillion questions about him. They pumped the well until there wasn't no more water left in it. I told 'em what I know, but about Ruggieri it was strictly zilch." He laughed a little. "I think they was disappointed. Other stuff, they loved. They couldn't get enough."

"But Ruggieri knew what you and Ding-Dong were doing, didn't he? I mean, you were a gofer with a few sidelines."

"I guess he knew. What the hell, the old man didn't give a

shit about a little shylockin', a little of this an' a little of that. He just looked the other way."

"So long as it wasn't junk?"

"No way, man. Ruggieri don't like that crap. He got a fuckin' hair up his ass about it for some reason. I never could figure. Some of the other big guys, they don't care so long as they get their cut, or they play with the stuff themselves. Not Ruggieri. He'd cut off your balls if he found out you were doin' it."

"Which is what he did to Ding-Dong."

Gino nodded slowly. He took out a pack of cigarettes and lit one, drew on it nervously, trying to collect himself. "Christ, he wasn't supposed to know. We thought we was covered. Somebody must of ratted on us."

"Is that why you ran?"

"One reason, yeah."

"If it wasn't Ruggieri, Gino, who was bankrolling you? The kind of operation you must have been running, I think the Arab was just a little part. It couldn't have been cheap. Who was putting up the bread?"

Gino laughed. "You wouldn't believe. The feds couldn't believe when I told them. You wanna know? A big fuckin' Wall Street banker, that's who."

"His name couldn't have been Donatello?"

Gino stared at him. "The feds told you," he said accusingly.

"It's hard to believe," Rogers said.

"Bullshit," Gino said. "Believe it, 'cause it's true."

"How would you ever meet a guy like that?"

"Easy. The old man used to give me packages. Gino, take this there. Gino, deliver this. I done what he said. One time, I got a look. The packages was money. Big money, big bills. So I take 'em where he said an' I drop 'em off. One day, it was like sometime last summer, there's this big guy in the place. He took the package. Next time, he was there again, only that time he asked if maybe I'd like to do a little work for him on the side, make some dough on my own besides what the old man was payin' an' what I was pickin' up doin' other things. So I says, sure, what d'ya got in mind? What he had in mind was bringin' junk in. Which sure as hell surprised me. I mean, he didn't look like the kind, especially since he was workin' with Ruggieri. I dunno, maybe he was desperate or somethin', like he figured he had to make a big score. I guess he was buyin' it over there an' he wanted guys to set things up to get it over here safe. I don't know how, but he knew that there was some of these diplomats who was into us for plenty an' wasn't payin' up. The fuckin' Arab wasn't the only one. So he come up with the idea of puttin' the pressure on 'em to use their diplomatic pouches to carry the stuff. Which is what we done. Most of 'em couldn't of been more cooperative. The fuckin' Arab was the only one gave us trouble."

Leave it to the feds, Rogers thought. They knew about Donatello and drugs and God knows what else, all the time Morrison was considering turning the city's finances over to Donatello's care, and they hadn't said one goddamn word. They would have let it happen, they would have let the city go down the tube without a word of warning, and if anybody ever caught wise, they would have said they couldn't tell the new mayor because it would have compromised one of their ongoing investigations. They loved that phrase: "compromised an ongoing investigation." It excused everything. Bullshit.

"What else did you do for Donatello, Gino?" Rogers asked.

"A little of this an' a little of that. He asked an' we did. Simple as that. You know, one hand washes the other."

"Like what?"

"What the hell. I already told the feds. Lot of stuff. Like, a couple of months back, he asked us to do a little job. No sweat an' good pay. He wanted some old guy knocked off. Make it look like he killed himself, he said, an' then burn all his papers, like that was what he was doin' before. He gives us an address an' he tells us nobody but the old guy's gonna be home this particular night. A cinch. So Ding-Dong an' me, we go up to this place by the river, in Riverdale, you know, an' the place is like Swiss cheese. You just waltz in, doors ain't locked, nobody checks nothin'. Up we go. Guy don't even lock the door to his apartment. We go in an' would you believe it, he's asleep in a chair. So, Ding-Dong walks up to him an' puts a piece we brought along special against his head, an' it's goodnight, Irene. It took us a fuckin' hour to burn all the shit he had lyin' around, an' stir up the ashes so nobody could put the stuff together. You know, we never even found out the guy's name. What the hell. A job's a job. We owed him one anyway."

Not goodnight, Irene, Rogers thought. Goodnight, Werner Rosenblatt. So, the widow and Morton Solomon were right, after all. And, Rogers thought, though he didn't say it, it was more likely Gino himself who'd put the gun against Rosenblatt's temple than Ding-Dong. Maybe Ding-Dong hadn't even been there. Maybe it had been a solo for Gino Santucci. It was hardly credible that Donatello would have trusted Ding-Dong even to go to the corner for a pack of cigarettes. Gino was something else. Besides, Ding-Dong's thing wasn't guns. It was baseball bats. But, what the hell, it didn't matter. Let Gino have his little lie, if it was the only one.

"You guys didn't happen to do another little job for him, did you? Like try to run me down late one night on my street?"

Gino looked blank. "When was that?"

Rogers told him.

Gino shook his head. "No way. I was out of town then. Couldn't of been me."

"What about Ding-Dong?"

"No way, man. The son of a bitch didn't know which end of a car made it go. I mean, you put him behind a wheel, which nobody ever done, an' the only thing he could do was make it run backwards. Somebody tried to run you down, which it's too bad they didn't succeed, it wasn't me, an' it sure as hell wasn't Ding-Dong."

"I'll buy that. Still, there's something else I can't figure, Gino. Why did you and Ding-Dong waste Felix Palmieri?"

Gino stared at him, shook his head, sweated some more. He reached for the pack of cigarettes, lit another, puffed on it nervously. "I done a lot of things," he said, his voice hoarse. "But you gotta believe me, I never killed a cop. So help me. Not on my life. Not on my mother's eyes."

"I don't believe you. Palmieri got it on the turf. Palmieri was looking into a rub-out of the Arab. Palmieri was also looking into the rub-out of one of your competition. So you had two reasons to take him down. What could be more natural?"

"Honest to God, I never. I swear. No matter what the motherfucker was lookin' into, we was protected when it come to the Arab. An' Sal Ianucci, that was strictly a intramural thing, nobody gave a fuck except his own guys. What'd the cops care? What d'you guys say, let 'em kill each other an' who gives a fuck? Let me tell you, I had nothin' to do with Palmieri. Why would I lie about somethin' like that? I got immunity. They can't do nothin' to me even if I done it, which I didn't. What's one more thing? Why wouldn't I say if I done it?"

He pressed, but Gino Santucci held his ground. Rogers turned to a few other areas, to extraneous matters that had nothing to do with anything he cared about then, and the answers always jibed with what he already knew. But whenever it got around to Felix Palmieri, Santucci always had the same answer: he hadn't done it, he didn't know who had done it, he didn't even know why it was done. Sure, people talked about it when it happened, but even among the wiseguys it was a mystery.

When he left Governors Island, Rogers had a lot of answers. Some of them had been unexpected. He hadn't thought Donatello was into drugs as well as other things. But maybe he shouldn't have been so surprised. Was there anything that Donatello wouldn't have done, or didn't do? He didn't think so. And the guy must have been desperate during the summer when the Centex deal fell apart, looking for anything, any way to recoup.

He knew, too, who had supplied the money, or a lot of it, that went into Donatello's scheme. That didn't surprise him, either. He had thought it would have to be someone like Ruggieri. He only wondered how long the two had worked together and what else they had done. Maybe he could find out, although more likely he'd never know. Just as it was unlikely that, unless Donatello had left records behind, anything would happen to Ruggieri.

For weeks, his mind had been playing with the sense behind Ding-Dong Faranulli's attack on him, trying to find a reasonable answer, if reason lay behind anything that gorilla ever did. He had considered, then discarded, the idea that the attack had grown out of a desire for revenge for that long-ago confrontation, a desire intensified by their recent meeting on the street. That scenario was just beyond the realm of the possible. Gino had given him the reason. The attack had come hard upon that dinner at Donatello's, that dinner during which the banker had discovered that Rogers was working for Morrison on something secret. Donatello had not been slow to deduce the tie between that job and the long delay in his appointment. He had errand boys to clear away such impediments. Thus Ding-Dong and his baseball bat.

Or maybe, Rogers suddenly thought, Donatello had suspected something before that. That first attack, the hit-and-run on Melissa's opening night, had come not long after he had gone up to Rosenblatt's apartment and interviewed the widow. He had the impression then that someone was following him, but he had dismissed it. Maybe it all fit together. And maybe Donatello had not tried again because from all indications Rogers was onto something else, wasn't following up on Rosenblatt. Maybe. It was possible. Anything was possible now. He thought back over the hit-and-run, remembering the list of cars he had checked out. None of them seemed likely then, but now one did. He remembered that Donatello owned a hunting lodge in the Adirondacks, that he had died there. And he remembered, too, that one of the cars was owned by a guy who was a caretaker at a lodge in those mountain forests.

About the murder of Felix Palmieri—if he could now eliminate some possibilities, he wondered where that left him. He could rule out the Arab and he could probably rule out Sal Ianucci as the reasons why, and Ding-Dong Faranulli and Gino Santucci as the killers. The killer was someone else and the reason lay in another direction. But where? He still didn't know which way to go. He would go back and once more study what remained of Felix's papers, and he would press his memory. Or what was left of it.

36

Rogers went from Governors Island to City Hall. He needed to see the mayor.

His honor was, of course, in a meeting, but Rogers said he would wait. The mayor's secretary was not encouraging, but after about an hour, she picked up the intercom, listened, looked surprised, and gestured toward Rogers. "The mayor will see you now," she said.

Morrison was alone in the vast office that seemed too big for just one man. As Rogers came through the door, he rose from behind his desk and hurried toward him. He looked worried.

"Are you all right, Ben?" he asked.

"Fine," Rogers said. "Not a hundred percent yet, but fine."

Morrison motioned toward a sofa and led the way there. "You saw this Santucci?"

"Just came from there."

"I hope you learned something," Morrison said. "I trust you. I trust your instincts. But are you really certain of everything?"

"I'm certain. Why?"

"As soon as I moved in here, I asked federal auditors to go through Fidelity's records, something they agreed to do only as a favor. The bank's got branches all over the world, so it's impossible to get all the records. But the auditors looked at what they could, and they found nothing. I mean absolutely nothing that could tie Gene Donatello to criminal behavior, even irregular behavior that might not be criminal. There were funds missing, of course, and not a few hundred thousand dollars, but more like ten million. But all those funds had been diverted from the accounts handled by that man Rosenblatt. There was nothing irregular in any of the accounts that were directly under Donatello's control."

"I'm not surprised," Rogers said. "The guy was too smart. I'd bet he always had things ready so the auditors would never find anything, at least not here."

"It's not just the bank," Morrison said. "I put people to work on his estate. They hunted high and low, and what they came away with was nothing incriminating, nothing that would cast a shadow over his reputation. There were no huge bank accounts, no excessive amounts of stocks and bonds and other investments, nothing he couldn't have acquired honestly over the years."

"Naturally," Rogers said. "Like I said, he wasn't stupid. He wouldn't leave anything out in the open where anybody could find it. I'd bet anything there must be a dozen safety-deposit boxes scattered around that you'll never come across, and just as many numbered accounts in safe places outside the country. Maybe nobody will ever find them and what's in them will rot. Or maybe somebody else has access, which wouldn't surprise me. But, Jack, I don't care what your damn auditors found or didn't find. The son of a bitch was dirty. You have no idea how dirty."

Morrison stared at him. "You'd better explain."

Rogers did.

Morrison digested it and nodded.

"Okay. I believe you. But the goddamn Department of Justice—they had that bastard there on the island. They listened to him. They knew what the hell he was saying. And they never said a word to me? They would have stood by and let me swing in the wind?"

"They would, indeed. They've done it before. You ought to know. Just because you used to be one of them doesn't mean they wouldn't do it to you. After all, you're a local these days, on the outside looking in, and you know what they think of locals."

"I'm going to have a long talk with the A.G. about this," Morrison said. "Not that it will do any good." He shook his head. "I don't suppose we can get that man Ruggieri?"

"On this? I doubt it, not unless the feds have something besides Santucci and decide to share it, which they'll never do until they're damn good and ready, which could be never."

The mayor thought for a moment. He studied Rogers. "It's not over, is it?"

"No."

"I didn't think so." He sighed. "Who else was in it beside Ruggieri?"

Rogers considered. "The congressman, Benedetto. That's for sure. That's where the inside stuff was coming from. Some others."

"Who?"

"You always said you wanted proof. I haven't got that yet. Just suspicion."

"Give."

He shook his head slowly. "Not yet. Not until I nail it down, not until there are no holes. Just don't trust anybody, Jack. Not a goddamn soul, no matter how high up."

Morrison studied him. "For God's sake, Ben, keep on it until you've got it. And stay in touch. This door will always be open."

37

He didn't tell Melissa that he was going to make a little trip. If everything worked out, he'd be back in the evening, and he could explain it then. This was something he had to do for himself, to tie off some loose ends.

He waited until Melissa had gone to work and then took a cab out to La Guardia and grabbed a plane for Albany. In the state capital he rented a car and drove north into the Adirondack region, reaching Au Sable Fork just before noon. There were deep banks of snow piled alongside the roads but the sky was clear and there seemed no immediate threat of more snow.

He drove straight to the local police station, identified himself and asked to talk to whoever was in charge. He was taken to the chief, a grizzled, middle-aged man who looked like he spent most of his time outdoors.

"What can we do for you, Lieutenant?" the chief asked.

"About a month ago," Rogers said, "a guy named Eugene Donatello had an accident at his hunting lodge up around here. They say he tripped and his shotgun went off, blew his head to pieces."

"That's right," the chief said. "He was a popular fellow

around here. Nice man. Generous. It was a shame. I don't know how it could have happened. He was an expert hunter, a crack shot. In fact, I went out with him a few times. He really knew his way around the woods."

"What I was wondering," Rogers said, "was anybody up here with him at the time?"

The chief studied him. "Why?"

Rogers shrugged. "I've been doing some work for Mayor Morrison. He was considering Donatello for an appointment when this thing happened. So, naturally, he was curious and he asked me to look into it."

"You certainly took your time about it," the chief said. "More than a month now since it happened."

"There were some other things to take care of," Rogers explained. "This is the first chance I've had."

"Well," the chief said, "it wasn't our case. The state police took it on, seeing that he was such an important man, and, anyway, it was out in the country."

"They must have filled you in."

"They did. Nothing suspicious about the thing at all. Everything said it happened just the way it was reported. But to answer your question, yes, there were other people about. The caretaker, Frank Vernon, to name one. A surly cuss, but I guess he did his job all right. A couple of other people, too, friends of Donatello from down your way. In fact, one of them was a cop from what I hear, one of the top cops in your department. And a few others. Most of them have been up here with him more than once. They were all back in the lodge when it happened, from what they said. It was snowing and Donatello went out on his own. When he didn't come back after a couple of hours, they went out to look for him. And they found him. That's the story they all have and there's no reason not to believe them."

"I don't see why you shouldn't. Still, I'd like to take a look at the place on my own—not that I'll find anything, but it'll make Morrison happy."

The chief shook his head. "Mayors are always sending people on wild-goose chases. You know how to get there?"

Rogers said he didn't, and the chief gave him directions. "If you want, I'll send somebody with you."

"No need. I like to do things on my own."

"Your choice," the chief said. "When you get out there, see Vernon. If he's sober, maybe he can help you. You find anything out of the ordinary, you'll let me know."

"Naturally."

From the town, he headed northeast toward Lake George, found the small side road the chief had mentioned, and turned onto it. A plow had merely skimmed the surface, leaving behind a hard-packed crust of snow that made the driving slippery and treacherous. A dozen miles along, he nearly missed what he was looking for, a narrow lane between two stone pillars. A chain blocked the entrance. A sign hung from it: Private—No Trespassing.

The chain was easy enough to remove, but the driving was much more difficult. No plow had passed this way and the snow was deep. But there was a groove cut by a car since the last snow, and he held his wheels in it.

The lodge was a half mile from the entrance, a sprawling building made of rough-hewn logs. Rogers parked and started walking toward the lodge, following a narrow path.

There was smoke drifting from the chimney of a small cottage about fifty yards to one side of the main lodge. A car was parked in front of it. The car was black under a coating of grimy snow and slush. It was a Ford, about 1987. The last two digits on the license plate were 83. He moved around to the front of the car. The glass in the right headlight was cracked, and there was a dent in the fender.

The door to the cottage opened. A squat man with a bullet head and a face that had been created out of too many brawls in the local bars, stood in the entrance, staring out. He was dressed in shabby jeans and a red flannel hunting shirt.

"What're you doin' here?" he demanded. "Can't you read signs? No trespassing. This is private property."

"Is your name Frank Vernon? Somebody down in the village mentioned that the place was for sale and if I was interested I ought to drive up and ask you and you'd show me around," Rogers said mildly.

"My name's Vernon, all right, but they told you wrong."

"They must have. Sorry."

The guy kept staring at Rogers. "I know you," he said suddenly.

"I doubt it," Rogers said. "We've never met."

"No, I know you. I seen you somewhere."

"Not likely. I've never been up this way before." Rogers turned and started to walk back toward the car, moving as fast as he could through the deep snow. Behind him the guy kept staring, recognition finally coming to his face. Vernon turned abruptly and stepped quickly into the house. Rogers glanced back over his shoulder and began to move faster. The guy was in the doorway again. Only this time he was holding a rifle, and the rifle was starting to rise.

Seeing shelter in the evergreens off to the side, Rogers sprinted toward them, gasping after just a few steps, realizing just how weak he still was. He strained, reached them, ducking low to avoid the branches just as the first shot came. It passed over his head, tearing loose a branch, showering him with needles.

Rogers dropped into the snow, burrowing for shelter, for protection. He pulled his own gun from its shoulder holster. Vernon had a rifle; he had only a pistol. The odds were stacked, but it was better than nothing. Rogers was a good shot, but not at this distance. Vernon would have to get a lot closer to him if he was to have a chance at hitting him.

It wasn't playing out the way he had hoped. He hadn't come up here looking for trouble. Not this kind of trouble, anyway. He had hoped to satisfy himself about the hit-and-run without arousing any suspicion on Vernon's part, and then maybe hand it to the locals.

Another shot hit one of the branches, lower, but still over his head. The evergreens were so dense he didn't think Vernon could see him, that he was shooting blind. He raised his head a little and peered through the snow-covered green. He could make out Vernon standing just outside the doorway of the cottage, holding the rifle, eyes narrowed and straining to see. He must have heard something because he brought the rifle up again and snapped off another shot. It passed well to the right.

Now Vernon began to move, bending low, rifle ready, sliding toward the tree line. Rogers held his fire. Vernon was still too far away.

Vernon vanished into the trees. He was trying to move quietly, but the growth was too thick and Rogers could hear him brushing against pine needles. Rogers remained where he was, moving only his head to follow the direction of Vernon's passage.

The sounds grew fainter, stopped altogether. Then he heard another shot. He waited. The rustle of branches started again, coming his way now, drawing closer.

He waited. His gun came up, shifting toward the sounds. Closer still. He caught sight of a red shirt. He started to aim. The shirt disappeared behind the foliage. He held. The rustling came closer. He saw the shirt again. It was close enough to risk it. He gripped the pistol in one hand, holding that hand in the other to steady his aim, squeezed the trigger, and the blast erupted in his ears. A puff exploded from the middle of the red shirt. He fired twice more in rapid succession. Then the shirt was gone.

Rogers waited. There was no sound. Still, he didn't move. He held his gun in both hands, ready. He let time pass. Then, slowly, carefully, he rose and edged his way through the trees toward where he had seen the shirt. He reached the spot. Vernon was sprawled on his back, the rifle a few feet from his hand. The stain in the center of the shirt was redder than the shirt. Vernon's eyes were half open. But they weren't seeing anything. And they never would see anything again.

38

He didn't get back to New York until the next morning. There were too many questions to answer from the local cops and from the state police. It was impossible for Rogers to explain everything, but he tried to sketch it out as succinctly as circumstances allowed. He hadn't wanted any trouble with the guy, he kept saying. He'd just come here to try and answer a few questions for himself, like, Was it Vernon who had tried to run him down? But trouble had come, and Vernon hadn't given him much choice.

He might be a cop himself, but he was a city cop up in the northern wilds and so he not only had no standing but everything about him seemed to brand him in the eyes of his listeners as some kind of alien creature to be viewed with suspicion and skepticism. Besides, Frank Vernon had been a local, and a reclusive one who had never made trouble, if you didn't count a few bar brawls as trouble.

From the troopers' barracks, surrounded by the state cops, the locals, and the local prosecutor, Rogers reached out to Morrison for help, and finally got to him late in the day. Morrison listened as Rogers sketched the outlines, saying little as Rogers told him that Vernon had been one of Donatello's enforcers. He became noticeably more interested when Rogers suggested that maybe a search of the lodge might turn up things the mayor's auditors might have missed.

Rogers put the county prosecutor on the line, a guy who used to be with the Department of Justice in Washington, and fortunately knew Morrison, had even worked under him for a time. The mayor convinced him that Rogers was up in his territory on the mayor's business, that whatever he had done was only because he had no choice, and the whole thing should be kept under wraps for a couple of days.

Rogers went back to the lodge with the troopers and helped with the first search. It would be something that would take days before it was done. Inside its rough-hewn log walls, the lodge was vast, consisting of a half-dozen bedrooms, kitchen, study, and a main room with a huge stone fireplace. He had no desire or intention to stay around for the whole search. The first hours didn't turn up much, mainly a lot of weapons, of the hunting variety. In a wall safe, which a local locksmith managed to crack, they found a stack of papers with numbers on them, but they didn't mean anything unless you knew what they stood for. Rogers thought maybe the numbers had to do with bank accounts, but it was only a guess, and there probably was no way of ever knowing for sure.

By the time they locked the lodge and returned to the barracks, the troopers were his friends. It was dark by then, and it had begun to snow. He called Melissa and told her only where he was, and that he wouldn't be home until the next day. She was, for the first time since he had met her, nearly inarticulate with concern and anger, because he had gone without letting her know, and because he was in no condition to be doing whatever he was doing. He didn't mention Vernon and the shooting.

A couple of troopers took him into town for dinner, where they were joined by some of the local cops. They didn't talk much, just watched him pick at the food, and then got him drunk which they understood was a necessary thing. Felix Palmieri had done that when they'd worked together and Rogers had to kill a guy who was about to shoot Felix in the back. That was the first time he'd ever killed. This was the second. Sometimes, Felix had said, a cop has to kill because there isn't any other way. For most cops, it's a terrible thing. Maybe the guy was all bad, maybe he had it coming, but dead is dead, and whatever might have been there that could have been changed was gone forever. He'd have dreams, nightmares about it for a long time, Felix had said, and that was all right, too. There was nothing you could do about that. You just have to get through it and come out whole and changed as little as possible.

Rogers finally got drunk enough to sleep. In the morning, one of the troopers drove him down to the airport in Albany, another trooper returning the car to the rental place. He was home by noon. Melissa was waiting for him. The anger that had been building in her through the night had evaporated, leaving only the concern.

"Oh, Ben, what happened?" she said when she saw his face.

"I had to kill a guy," he said.

She had been around cops at One Police Plaza long enough to know what that meant, what killing actually did to a man. She didn't ask anything else, just came to him and put her arms around him and held him.

He said one more thing, so she would understand: "He was the guy who tried to run us down that night." It was explanation enough.

He immediately immersed himself in work. He went back to Felix Palmieri's files. On most of them he could now stamp "Closed." There was just the one, based on some scribbled, disjointed notes on odd scraps of paper about a long-dead hooker. It certainly seemed like nothing. What he ought to do, he thought, was at least get a look at the autopsy report. The next day he'd go across town and find out who had worked on the corpse, and get a copy, and tap the doctor for anything else he might remember.

In the morning, he went to Bellevue, to the medical examiner's office. In the corridor, he ran into Sadowsky, the doctor who had cut Sully. Rogers asked if Sadowsky remembered anything about a body that had been brought in from the Staten Island dump, maybe around September.

"Who the hell could forget?" Sadowsky said. "Thank God, I didn't get her. It was Kaplan." He motioned down the corridor. "His office is down there."

Rogers found Dr. George Kaplan behind his desk, reading a medical journal. Rogers identified himself.

"What can I do for you?" Kaplan asked.

"I understand you got the body from the Staten Island dump last fall."

"Correct. Worst thing I've ever had to do. Christ, she just about fell apart at the touch. Are you looking into that? I thought it'd be dead and buried by now." He laughed sarcastically.

"You know," Rogers said, "nothing's dead and buried until it's dead and buried with a marker over it. What I'd like to see is your autopsy report."

"I sent it along at the time," Kaplan said. "Right into channels. Copies here, copies there, copies everywhere."

"Well," Rogers said, "I guess they're all somewhere in the stacks, because nobody seems to know where they are."

Kaplan sighed. "If you really want to read it, I'll get one for you." He picked up the phone, pressed a couple of buttons, and told whoever answered to tap the computer for the report and run off a copy. "Ten minutes," he said to Rogers, and went back to his journal.

Ten minutes later Rogers walked out with the report and headed back to the apartment. Settling into a chair, he began to read. He read it a couple of times, looking for something, anything.

In life, she had been a hooker. There was little doubt about that. She had been dead maybe twenty-five years. The condition of the body said that, and so did that damn Piel's Beer coaster in the plastic bag. Rogers remembered having seen the old Harry and Bert Piel commercials on TV when he was a kid, but the beer itself had gone the way of a lot of other forgotten brands by the time he had his first brew. What else? A lot of stab wounds in the chest. Why more than one, unless the guy loved to use a knife? Or unless a bunch of guys took turns? And one of those wounds was right over a bullet hole, so at first Kaplan almost missed it, and he probably would have if the slug hadn't been there. Why? Was the stabbing a deliberate effort to hide the bullet wound? Was there something special about the bullet that the guy wanted to hide? He kept looking for it but he couldn't see it, not unless there was something about the grooves that would point to a specific gun, but that gun must have vanished long ago.

When Melissa arrived home, he made her a drink, pointed to a chair, and waited until she was settled. She looked at him with a puzzled expression. He tossed her the reports. "Read these," he said. "See if anything strikes you."

He watched as she read slowly, finished, went back and read again. She looked up at him. "What did you want me to find?" she asked.

"I'm not sure," he said. "It's just a feeling, something that Felix must have got that I missed. It has to be in there somewhere."

"The thing about the stab wounds, so many of them? Why would they do that when she must already have been dead from the bullet?"

"I got that."

"Something about the bullet itself?"

"Yeah. But what?"

She looked back at the report, read that part of it slowly, looked back at him. "I've never heard of police using a bullet like the one he describes," she said. "Is that it?"

He stared at her, took the report from her, and read Kaplan's description of the bullet: "A soft flat-nosed lead variety that exploded and shattered on impact." That had to be it. He grinned at her. "You're a goddamn genius," he said. Nobody used bullets like that anymore. Nobody had used them in all the time he'd been a cop—not the cops, not the punks on the street. You probably couldn't even find one unless some dealer had an old lot in the back someplace, and by now they'd be useless.

Then he remembered that Felix had once told him something about bullets like that, may even had shown him one. There was something else that Felix had said that last time they'd talked. Rogers remembered it clearly, hearing Felix's voice in his ear once more, saying, "It could be your kind of thing. *Capeesh?* Only you got to be an old hairbag like me to get it." Could he have been talking about the bullet?

Think like Felix, he told himself. What would Felix do? As Melissa watched, he picked up the phone and dialed the number on Varick Street, got through to Charlie, the gnomelike keeper of the old records. "Charlie," he said, "this is Ben Rogers. From Internal Affairs."

"I know who you are," Charlie said. Charlie knew who everybody was, just as Charlie knew everything there was to know and knew where everything was. "You were a buddy of Felix Palmieri, poor bastard."

"Charlie," Rogers said, "a question and a favor."

"Ask me the question first, then I'll decide about the favor."

"What do you know about soft-nosed lead bullets that ex-plode and shatter on impact?"

Charlie laughed. "Jesus, ask me something hard. Nobody's used that crap since the sixties. They issued a mess of the slugs to some of the guys back then. They were supposed to be extra special, like they'd stop an elephant in his tracks no matter where they hit. The problem was, they'd do more than just stop the bastard. They'd mess him up real bad so maybe they couldn't put him back together again. You know anything about the Civil War? They used what they called mini-balls back then. You get hit with one, it wouldn't just make a nice little hole, it'd blow your fucking arm or leg off, and if you got hit in the stomach, it'd mess up your insides so the liver'd be where the kidneys was supposed to be, only you wouldn't be able to tell one from the other. Those soft-nosed babies were like that. So what happened was, after maybe a year or so, the Civil Liberties people were screaming bloody blue murder, and the department saw the problem, and they pulled those things back. Okay? Now, what's the favor?"

"I want to send someone over, and I'd appreciate it if you'd let her take a look at some old missing persons files."

"How old?"

"Maybe twenty-five years back, mid- to late sixties."

"They couldn't be the same ones Palmieri was interested in right before he got it?"

Rogers took a deep breath. "The same ones. Can you dig them out?"

"Don't have to. The last time the poor bastard was here, when he left I put them aside because he said he'd be back later to look at them again. They're still there. I never got around to putting them back. You can't come yourself?"

"No," Rogers said.

"Who do I look for?"

He glanced at Melissa. She was watching him carefully. She nodded. "Her name's Melissa Redburn. She works at One Police Plaza. I'll try to have her there sometime tomorrow."

"I'll be here," Charlie said.

39

Melissa offered no objections to Rogers's plan. She would do whatever he asked. Still, he felt he had to explain. "I don't want to put my nose anywhere that has anything remotely to do with the department right now," he said. "I just have this feeling, that's all."

"You don't have to explain," she said.

"I do," he said. "Go there. Charlie will show you these files. Look through them."

"What am I supposed to be looking for? I mean, besides an old missing persons report on a prostitute, if anybody ever reported her missing."

"Somebody must have, otherwise Charlie wouldn't have kept the files in his desk. He'd have put them back. Look for anything that sounds familiar. A name. A place. Anything at all."

After she left, there was a call to make. He dialed Homicide and left a message for Carlos Rodriguez. An hour later, Rodriguez called back.

"Carlos," Rogers said, "do you remember when you and Felix drew the Arab?"

"Sure. How could I forget?"

"You told me you got called off right at the beginning. Who called you off?"

"The captain, of course. He got us in an' he said, drop it. It's diplomatic, is what he said, which we know now just wasn't so, but what the hell, who was to know then, an' so it was out of our jurisdiction. He said orders was we was to forget it."

"Do you know where those orders came from?"

"From on high, I guess. Where else? I figured it must of been the feds, an' they was gonna take it over. I didn't hear no more about it until you showed up and started askin'."

Time passed, the hours dragged as Rogers waited for Melissa to get back. He began to worry. Maybe he had been wrong to send her. People knew they were a pair. If somebody was watching him, they might be watching her, too. He reached for the phone and dialed Varick Street, reached Charlie.

"Charlie, Ben Rogers. Is Melissa Redburn still there?"

"She was. Just left. Nice girl. She read the files and asked if she could make copies. I let her."

"Can you catch her?"

"Well, she's only been gone a couple of minutes. I'll try. What's up?"

"If you catch her, tell her to take a cab. Not to ride the subway. Take a cab."

"I'll see what I can do."

Rogers couldn't just sit around waiting in the apartment. He went down to the street, walked back and forth between the house and the corner, looking for a cab, looking toward the subway a couple of blocks away, willing her to appear.

Then he saw her coming from the subway. She was walking quickly, her large purse slung over her shoulder. He started toward her. She was still more than a block away, but he could see there was a guy behind her dressed in a down coat, keeping pace with her. Rogers quickened his own pace and called out to her. She stopped and waved toward him.

Rogers reached her and passed, approaching the man in the down coat. "Hello, Mickey," he said. "Kind of off your turf, aren't you."

The guy stopped and looked at Rogers. "Hi, Ben," he said. "Long time no see." His name was Mickey Conrad. They had been in the Police Academy together. Conrad worked out of One Police Plaza these days. He was on Chief Dolan's staff. "What're you doing around here?"

"I live a couple of blocks away. You following my girl?"

Conrad looked at him with surprise. "Me?" he said. "Not my kind of thing. I come here all the time. I like to wander the Village. Look at the sights. You know. Kill time."

"Sure," Rogers said.

Conrad shrugged and started to turn away. "See you sometime, Ben." He crossed the street, moving slowly, like he had all the time in the world, like he had nowhere in particular to go. Rogers watched him for a moment and then turned and started back toward Melissa.

She stood on the sidewalk, waiting until he joined her. She looked up at him. "That man," she said. "He was following me."

"I figured," he said.

"I mean, he was standing outside Records when I left, and he followed me to the subway and all the way."

"He didn't try anything?"

"No. He just followed. That's all."

"I think," he said, "I'd better get you out of here, get you someplace safe for a while."

She looked at him closely and nodded slowly.

Once they were back in the apartment, he said, "Charlie told me you copied the files."

"That was just so you could read them if you wanted to," she said. "But you know me. I've got that kind of memory. Something goes in, it writes itself and never goes away."

He looked at her closely. "So you found something?"

Her face sobered. She looked unhappy. "Yes," she said. "You won't like it. I hate it."

"I know," he said.

She looked at him sharply. "You know?"

"Not the details. But, yes, I know. It's been there all the time. I didn't want to know it. I didn't want to see it. So I looked everywhere else until there was nowhere else to look, until I couldn't deny it anymore. Bill Dolan."

She nodded slowly. "Yes. It was twenty-five years ago. The girl's name was Matty Wheeler. On a Wednesday morning—if you want the exact date, I'll give it to you. Anyway, on this particular Wednesday morning a girl named Gerry Maddox filled out a missing persons report on Matty Wheeler at the Midtown North Precinct. They roomed together in some hotel on West Forty-fourth Street. She didn't say, but I gather they worked the area together. Matty had been missing for about a week, and Gerry was starting to get worried that something might have happened to her. She'd last seen Matty just before midnight the previous Thursday. Gerry had gone off with a client and left Matty alone on the street over by the West Side piers. When she got back a couple of hours later, Matty wasn't there, and Gerry said she thought Matty must have gone off with a client of her own, so she wasn't especially concerned. But Matty didn't come home that morning, and she didn't come home over the next few days, not even when Gerry wasn't around. She was positive about that because all of Matty's things were still in their room, nothing was missing. By now she was worried, so she went to the precinct to report it, and she wanted the cops to find her friend. Do you know who was assigned to the case?"

"You don't have to tell me," he said. "Bill Dolan."

"You've just won sixty-four thousand dollars," she said. "I read his reports. He interviewed the local prostitutes. He talked to people who lived in the neighborhood, and some other people. Nobody had seen anything and nobody knew anything, and I gather nobody cared anything. What was one hooker more or less? There was just one thing. One of the people he interviewed was the night bartender at Jim Clancy's, which apparently was a local saloon. He didn't know any more than anybody else, which meant he didn't know anything. The thing is, the bartender's name was Frank Tremanti." She took a deep breath. "That's it," she said. "Case closed. Matty Wheeler never turned up, as far as I could discover, and nobody looked for her after Bill Dolan closed the case, and the only one who ever cared was Gerry Maddox."

"You done good," he said. "I'll take you out and buy you a good dinner."

"On Morrison?"

"On me, this time. And then you're going to pack some things and I'll drive you out to my grandmother's. I want you to stay there until this thing is wrapped up. You can call in sick."

"I'd rather stay here with you," she said. "I can take care of myself."

"Sure," he said. "I know that. But I'd be happier the other

way. I've got enough to think about with having to worry about you here alone."

"You wouldn't have to worry."

"I'd worry."

"Because of that guy who followed me?"

"Yeah. It means that Dolan knows somebody's looking into the past, and now he knows it's you. And I figure he knows what you found."

"And you," she said.

"Both of us."

She nodded slowly.

40

His grandmother offered no objections to taking Melissa in for a few days. Rogers was her grandson and she would do what he asked without asking for reasons. Besides, the days ahead would give her the opportunity to press her case for marriage on Melissa.

The next morning he called the archdiocese and asked for Bishop Dennis Molloy. There was a pause, followed by a "Just a moment, please," and then another pause, and finally the phone was answered by a male voice that wasn't Molloy's.

"I wonder if I could speak to Bishop Molloy?" Rogers asked.

"I'm sorry," the voice said. "Bishop Molloy is no longer at this office."

"I thought he worked out of the archdiocese."

"He did. But several weeks ago, the bishop asked the cardinal to relieve him of his duties. He wanted to return to a parish and serve the needs of the poor. The cardinal acceded to his wishes. Much to everyone's regret."

Rogers kept his voice expressionless. He didn't say what he was thinking, which was that the church must have done an audit of its resources and discovered that Bishop Molloy had made some very bad investments. But the church, like the Police Department, was surrounded by a wall to protect its own. The Department threw them over the wall when it had to. Maybe the church only sent them back to a parish to atone. "Could you tell me which parish he's in?"

"He's at St. Joseph's, on the West Side."

Rogers knew the church, west of Times Square, in an area of Manhattan that hadn't yet been gentrified. He took the subway uptown and walked west until he reached it. St. Joseph's was old, plain, and run-down, nothing gracious or grandiose about the architecture, a strictly utilitarian structure for ministering to the spiritual needs of the neighborhood poor.

He went inside. A couple of parishioners were kneeling and praying, a couple more were waiting near the confessional. On the altar, a priest was moving about, lighting candles, arranging sacraments. Rogers knelt and crossed himself at the head of the aisle, and then took a seat in a rear pew. Another priest came through a side door and ascended to the altar. Rogers watched him. Bishop Molloy. The bishop spoke to the other priest, made a few adjustments, did a few other things, and then started to descend. Rogers rose and moved quickly toward him.

"Bishop Molloy," he said when he was within a few feet.

Molloy turned. "Lieutenant Rogers," he said. "What a surprise." He didn't look terribly surprised. "I didn't know you belonged to this parish."

"I don't."

"Then what brings you here? I heard you had a dreadful accident. I hope you've fully recovered."

"I'm fine now," Rogers said. "If you have a few minutes, I'd like a word with you."

"Confession?" Molloy asked.

"Not mine," Rogers said. "Is there somewhere we can talk in private?"

"Certainly. Just follow me." Molloy led Rogers through a door, down a dim and dingy corridor and then into a small battered office. "Now, what is it you wish to talk about?"

Rogers looked about. "Quite a change from the powerhouse, isn't it?"

"My choice," Molloy said. "I felt I'd gotten out of touch with what the church is really about. Indeed, I had. Here, I'm rediscovering my faith and my vocation. I should have done it years ago." The remark sounded rehearsed. He became silent, looked at Rogers, and waited.

"I want to ask you," Rogers said finally, "about the Thursday night before Chief Dolan married Patricia McIntyre."

Molloy looked at him steadily, his face blank. "That Thursday night? I don't quite follow you."

"But you do," Rogers said. "If you want, I can tell you all about it. Do you want me to give you the gory details about a black hooker who used to hang out in front of Clancy's saloon until she was given a permanent home in the Staten Island dump?"

Molloy said nothing. He stared directly at Rogers, his face a blank. Then slowly he lowered his eyes and took a deep breath. "So you know," he said. "I had a premonition when I first saw you that you were our nemesis. I've been waiting twenty-five years for someone to come along and ask me that question— waiting for it, and dreading the moment. I've been anticipating, with growing apprehension, and resignation, that it would happen at any moment, ever since Bill called me last fall to ask if I had seen the story in the papers about the discovery of a woman's body in the dump on Staten Island. I knew that when the question was asked, I would tell the truth. There was no other course for me to take. Did you know that Bill and Patty were married in this church?"

"I didn't, but I'm not surprised. You all used to live around here, didn't you?"

"Within a few blocks."

"And Jim Clancy's was just down the street?"

"Jim Clancy's? Oh, yes, only a block from here. It's gone now, of course. As are so many other things from the time when we were young. The way of the world, constantly changing and constantly remaining the same."

"But Jim Clancy's was still around that Thursday night, wasn't it?"

Molloy sighed. "Yes, it was."

"And Frank Tremanti was the bartender."

"He was. We were all young then, just back from the war, and just starting out. Frank was the bartender, Bill just a rookie on the police force, the others back in college, and I—I was uncertain of my vocation. I was torn between the spiritual and the secular. I was still trying to find my way."

"That Thursday night?"

"That night. Yes." He shook his head, looked down at his hands, looked back at Rogers. "It was all so stupid, and so unforgivable, and in the end, so appalling. I don't suppose I can make you understand how it was and how it happened."

"People keep saying that to me," Rogers said. "Try."

"Yes. I've held it in too long. We should be in the confessional, only you should be the confessor and I the confessee seeking absolution. Where do I begin? At the beginning, that terrible Thursday, though it didn't start out that way. Bill and Patty were to be married on Saturday. We, that is, Peter, Eugene, Michael, Frank, and I, thought we should all get together one last time as young and free bachelors and throw a party for Bill, to celebrate and commiserate, that is how one of us put it. We agreed to meet at Clancy's about eleven, and since Frank was the bartender, he would make sure we had the back room to ourselves. It was not supposed to be anything more than some food and some drinks and remembering the past, growing up in the neighborhood, going off to the war together, that sort of thing. We all drank too much, much too much, especially after the bar closed about one and we had the place to ourselves. We lost track of time. I don't remember when, but at some point Eugene, Michael, and Frank went off to a corner and began to talk. They were laughing very loudly. Eugene went out and came back a few minutes later. He had this black girl with him. What men see in such women is beyond me. I suppose she was attractive in her way, pretty enough, and she had a very good figure. Eugene brought her into the back room. If we'd only known then how truly evil Eugene was, maybe none of this would ever have happened. But after this night it was too late. He spun his web, and we were all caught, unable ever after to free ourselves. This woman obviously knew what she was there for; she was very matter-of-fact about it. She climbed up on a table and pulled up her skirt. She was not wearing undergarments. She lay back and spread her legs and asked who was going to be first. Eugene pushed Bill forward. The guest of honor must naturally take the lead, he said. Bill feigned reluctance for a few minutes, then went aboard. He was followed by

Eugene, and then Michael, and then Peter, and then Frank. And then they all turned to me. I hung back. I had never been with a woman like that before; in fact, I had never been with any woman before that night. And I have never been with a woman since. I was repelled, I didn't want to do it. They insisted, finally pulling down my pants, having the woman stimulate me. It was disgusting. I felt as though I had been dipped in a sewer and that nothing could ever cleanse me. When everyone was finished, the woman demanded her pay. I think she asked for a hundred dollars. They laughed at her. Bill pulled out his badge and told her he was a police officer. He said she ought to give them a discount because he was a cop. She laughed and then she got angry. An argument started. They started pushing her and she fought back. We were all so drunk. I remember I was just sitting on the floor, watching, almost unable to move. Everything got louder, her yelling for her money, them laughing. Then from somewhere, she pulled a knife and started to run at Bill. He took out his police revolver and shot her in the chest just before she reached him. She fell backward. Bill bent over her. She was dead.

"It was a dreadful moment. The six of us were in that room with a dead woman. We didn't know what to do. We couldn't leave her there. That was obvious. It was also indisputable that her body must not be discovered. She was well known in the neighborhood and there was a bullet in her that could be traced to Bill's gun. Somehow, her body had to disappear.

"Bill said that if she vanished, that would be the end of it. She was just another prostitute, and women like that appear and disappear without a word, that no one cares and no one asks questions. Frank suggested a plan. Behind the bar was a dumpster. The private sanitation crews emptied it out every morning and carried the trash to a dump somewhere. Her body should be placed inside one of those heavy plastic garbage bags, the bag sealed tightly, and then thrown into the dumpster. The sanitation men would come along, take it out to the dump and no one would ever hear of her or see her again, and so the problem would be solved. In retrospect, it was an incredibly naïve plan; it's amazing we weren't found out then.

"Anyway, they all agreed on what to do, except I wanted no part in it. And then Bill said, I remember his words clearly, he said we were all in it together, each one responsible. He picked up the woman's knife and said we were all to stab her with it, each wound to be one that if she were not already dead would be fatal. No one declined. Bill went first. He stabbed her directly over the bullet wound. I don't remember the exact order after that, except I was last. I didn't want to do it, but I couldn't refuse. When my turn came, I closed my eyes and stabbed her somewhere and then dropped the knife.

"Frank went and got the garbage bag. The first one was not strong enough and her body broke open the bottom and slid through. So they doubled up the bags and then threw the knife in with her, and some other trash from the bar. Frank, Eugene, and Bill carried the bag out to the back and threw it into the dumpster. Then nobody said anything for a long time. We just sat in that back room and waited. About five or six in the morning the sanitation truck arrived. We could hear the lift begin to grind as it hooked onto the dumpster, raised it, turned it, and emptied into the truck. Frank whispered that now we had nothing to worry about.

"And that was Thursday night. The worst night of my life." Molloy had been looking at Rogers with pleading eyes, eyes that begged for understanding, perhaps for forgiveness. Now he lowered his head onto the desk, buried it in his folded arms. His body was shaking.

Rogers sat silently, considering how to proceed. Whatever he did, whatever he said, it wouldn't matter. Obviously Molloy was prepared to give him whatever he wanted. He had bottled up the memories too long, and now they would pour out. That was the difference between a priest like Molloy or an aristocrat like Wellstone, who needed only the promise of immunity and the hope that he wouldn't go to jail if he talked, and a Donatello or one of the lowlifes Rogers was so used to dealing with. The slime had no conscience. What they did they considered only their trade, little or no different from the callings of the rest of the world, the legitimate world. When they got caught, there was no remorse, only regret that they got caught. And when they got caught, the first thing they did was try to find some escape. Not a Molloy or a Wellstone. They were imbued with a moral code that left them with an abiding and overwhelming sense of guilt. Still, Rogers felt no compassion for this priest. He was, after all, a priest, a man with a higher calling than most, a commitment beyond that of other men.

Molloy looked up, unable to meet Rogers's eyes.

"A pretty story," Rogers said. Molloy grimaced, as though he had been slapped across the face. "You went on from there, the six of you, to pile up fortunes and power and position and celebrate in your damn Thursday Club."

"It wasn't like that," Molloy said, "not at first."

"How was it?"

"It was Eugene's idea, or Bill's, I'm not sure which. They said we must never lose touch. We were bound together for the rest of our lives by what we had done. We had to remain close. We must never speak about that night outside our circle because if one of us did, we would all go to prison. And so, to make certain, we would meet regularly, we would meet once a month on a Thursday night. It would be a constant reminder. And it has been."

"Yeah," Rogers said. "But it seems to me you guys weren't so full of remorse that it turned you into paragons of virtue. I think it was just the opposite. You guys killed that poor dumb broad, and after that it didn't matter what you did because you'd already done murder. You used that murder to excuse every-thing else along the way. What the hell, they can only hang you once."

Molloy recoiled. "No, no. Since that night, my only aim has been to help the church, to do good, to atone."

"Atone? How?" Rogers asked. "By using inside information to make a fortune? By using government secrets to line your pockets? Help the church with money from drugs and the rack-ets? Do good by God knows how many other murders? Bishop, what the hell are you talking about? For twenty-five years, all you guys have done is break the law, every law of man and God, every day of your lives. And you guys thought you could get away with it. Hell, not just get away with it, but end up ruling the world."

Molloy was stricken. He shook his head, kept shaking it. "Murders?" he said. "Only that poor girl. There haven't been any others. There couldn't have been."

"No? What about a poor old guy up in Riverdale who was supposed to take the rap for that screwed-up deal you guys lost a fortune on last summer, only he came running for help? What about a cop shot down in an alley because he was getting too close to you people? And that's just in the last couple of months.

How many more have there been over the last twenty-five years who got in your way? No other murders? Bullshit. You guys even kill your own, though if anybody deserved it, Donatello sure as hell did."

"Eugene had an accident," Molloy said.

"Some accident," Rogers said. "You were all up there."

"I wasn't," Molloy said. "I heard about it later. They told me it was an accident."

"Sure," Rogers said. "I believe you."

"I didn't know," Molloy pleaded. "They never told me. Oh, God, I should have remained a simple parish priest. It would have been better."

"But you didn't. And now you're in over your head, and you're going to drown. All you guys are, except Donatello, and he's already gone down for the third time."

"Lieutenant Rogers, believe me, I'm drowning now. I was seduced by dreams of power within my world, the power to do good, to atone. By ambition. We were all seduced by our dreams and our aspirations. I realize now I never asked the questions I should have asked. I accepted what they told me. I believed them. I was blind. Vanity of vanities, all is vanity." He looked away, up at the wall, at the crucifix hanging over his head. He stared at it for a long time before turning back. He shook his head. "Are you going to arrest me?"

"Not right now," Rogers said. "Later, maybe. I don't imagine I have to worry that you'll run."

"No need to worry, Lieutenant. No need at all. Even if I were of a mind to, where would I run? Whither shall I flee from Thy presence? Now, if you'll excuse me, I have preparations to make."

Rogers nodded slowly and started to rise. There was no need to ask anything more now. He kept his eyes on Molloy. There was a kind of serenity about the man, as though he had somehow cleansed himself, as though he had come to see himself clearly for the first time in years and had come to a decision.

"Goodbye, Lieutenant," Molloy said. "And thank you."

41

It was after five by the time Rogers reached One Police Plaza. Through much of the afternoon, he had wandered aimlessly about lower Manhattan. The sun had been bright, blinding, as it reflected off car windows and the sheer glass of the soaring towers, and the temperature was mild for the last days of January. The streets were crowded with natives and tourists alike enjoying the respite from the cold.

After an hour of walking, Rogers found himself beneath the Manhattan Bridge, staring up at the crumbling underside, at the brick pillars. It was a place that would forever be imprinted on his mind, with images he could never erase. Later, when he wandered into Little Italy, he found the alley where Palmieri had died. He peered down its dim length, making out a row of garbage cans, the litter spilling out. Another indelible memory was formed in his mind.

He stopped at a phone booth near Foley Square and dialed his own number, to play back the messages off his answering machine. There were four calls from Dolan, all within the last two hours, demanding that he call immediately. There was a call from Molloy, saying in a calm voice that he was in God's hands now and Rogers should not blame himself. There was a call from

Carlos Rodriguez asking how he was and how about a call. There was one from the hospital reminding him he was scheduled for a checkup the next morning. There was a call from somebody who didn't leave his name, hoping that he was well and saying if there was anything he wanted done, he shouldn't hesitate to call. Rogers recognized the voice. He was surprised and he wasn't surprised. Nothing surprised him anymore. There was a call for Melissa from the agent saying everything on the film had been ironed out and they wanted her out on the Coast next week, and please call and confirm.

It was dark, and growing colder, when he passed through the doors of One Police Plaza. The day people were gone, and the lobby was quiet, only a few guys in uniform, and some in plainclothes, wandering about. He rode the elevator up, got off, went down the long corridor. Most of the offices were dark and empty. There was a light radiating from an office at the end, and Chief Dolan's door was open. He entered without knocking. Dolan was behind his desk, his blue uniform still neat and crisp, even after a long day, the stars on his shoulders glittering. The top of the desk was orderly, as it usually was, a stack of papers arranged in a tray at one side, pencils and pens in a cup.

Dolan looked up. He appeared as he always did, the tough, honest cop with the open face that you knew you could trust no matter what. He seemed to have been expecting his visitor. "Hello, Ben," he said.

"Chief," Rogers said.

"Dennis said you'd be along. I expected you earlier."

"I had some thinking to do."

"I imagine you did. I see you've recovered."

"Just about."

"Still, you haven't been idle, have you? You and that girl of yours. You've both been doing some visiting, and asking a lot of questions."

"Some."

"For the mayor, or just on your own?"

"A little of both. They overlap."

"Have you found what you were looking for?"

"Yes."

Dolan nodded slowly. He sighed. "I liked you, Ben. You're a good cop. In a lot of ways you remind me of myself when I was your age."

"I doubt that," Rogers said.

"It's true, nevertheless," Dolan said. "Like you, I used to see everything in black and white, never in shades of gray."

"There's good and there's bad," Rogers said. "We're supposed to know the difference."

"Nothing in between?"

"Maybe for other people. Not when you're a cop."

"Someday you'll learn. You have to if you're going to survive."

"I hope not."

"It must be nice to be so certain."

"My God, Chief, you were my hero. You were the cop's cop, the man everyone on the force wanted to be like."

"Ben, are you just now discovering that all heroes have feet of clay?" His eyes went over Rogers. "Are you wired?"

"No?"

"Can I believe you?"

"You'll have to, unless you want to shake me down."

"No," Dolan said, "that won't be necessary. You've never learned to lie easily. Maybe out in the street, but not with me." He paused. "So tell me, why did you come? What did you think it would accomplish? Haven't you got it all? From Dennis? From everything else?"

"Probably. I think I just wanted to look at you."

"What do you see? Do I look any different? Have I changed?"

"No," Rogers said. "You look the same. On the outside."

"But not inside?"

"I never really got a good look inside you before. I don't think anyone did, except maybe those friends of yours. Certainly Felix never did."

"Is that it? Felix Palmieri?"

"Poor Felix. He was your friend. He trusted you. He even trusted you with his life. Look what that got him."

"I liked Felix. You wouldn't understand, but I really liked him."

"No, I wouldn't understand. You liked him and you shot him down in an alley like he was a piece of garbage you could just throw away. You called him out in the middle of the night. Something important, you must have said. We have to meet right away. You told him where. Poor Felix. He believed you.

He thought you were straight, and he went. Right into that alley for a private conversation, and when he turned around, there you were, and you pulled your gun and shot him. It took me a long time to figure that one, because I kept rejecting it. I didn't want to believe it. I kept looking for something else, for someone else, but it was there all the time. There wasn't another guy alive who could have called Felix out like that and had him come. And there wasn't another guy who could have shot Felix straight on from the front without Felix pulling his own gun. It had to be you. It couldn't have been anyone else."

"Just theory," Dolan said.

"More than theory," Rogers said. "The truth. I suppose you're planning the same thing for me."

"Why in the world would you think that?" Dolan said.

"I'm an impediment, Chief," he said. "I've been screwing up all your plans. The thing I wonder is when you began to suspect it. Was it right at the beginning, when Morrison asked for me and wouldn't say why? Maybe, but you weren't positive until that night at Donatello's. But it was too late by then. I'd already told Morrison what I knew."

"Even if all this were true, what do you think you could do about it, Ben?"

Rogers took a deep breath. He shook his head. "I'm not sure."

"You know, there's really not much you can do. I don't think you can prove anything. Gene's dead, and so is Dennis. I don't imagine you know that. It's true, though. Not long after you left him. I suppose the church will call it a heart attack. In a way, it was. Like Gene's accident. Who else is there? The man up in Boston only knows about Gene. And you can be sure none of the others is going to say anything. Unlike Dennis, they're not priests who worry about the hereafter. All you can do is create a scandal, make things very uncomfortable for a little while. But in the end it would be just your word against mine—against ours, men like Mike Benedetto and Pete McIntyre and Frank Tremanti. We're a very powerful group. We have reputations beyond reproach. We have friends in very high places. Who do you think would be believed? You'd be discredited as a disgruntled cop that nobody had any use for anyway. People would start looking into your affairs, and, you know something, I'd just bet they'd find that you'd been on the take for years, that you'd squirreled away a large bank account somewhere. The next thing you knew you'd be over the wall. You wouldn't have any protection. It would be a pretty uncomfortable place."

"Don't bet on it," Rogers said.

"Ben, I only bet on sure things. You don't really think we'd be sitting here talking like this if I thought there was any risk? I'm not a complete fool."

"You know, Molloy said that Donatello was an evil man, that he was the one bad guy who roped you all in. I think Molloy was wrong. I think you make Donatello look like a minor leaguer. He was out front, but I'll bet he was only a puppet, and you were behind the scenes, pulling the strings all the time."

Dolan laughed. "Don't make yourself look more ridiculous than you already are, Ben. Now, get out of here and stop wasting my time."

"I'm going," Rogers said. "But there are a few things you ought to remember. The records are still there on Varick Street. The bullet must be somewhere down in ballistics. People may not believe me at first, but somebody's going to start looking and asking questions that should have been asked years ago, and when they do, you can write, End of story."

"You're a dreamer," Dolan said. "Things have a way of disappearing. And questions? We have all the right answers."

"Not all," Rogers said. He turned and walked out of Dolan's office, back the way he had come along the corridor toward the elevators.

What had he thought would happen in that office? It had been so easy with Wellstone and Molloy. They had been waiting for him with fear and dread, waiting to let the dam burst. Had he really thought that Dolan would collapse as they had? If he had really considered what he knew of the chief, he should have realized that would not happen. Dolan was right, of course. In a direct clash between them, Dolan was certain to win.

42

As he walked uptown from headquarters, Rogers considered his options. The truth was, he didn't have many, maybe none at all.

Felix had always said there was no such thing as a dead end, a blind alley. Felix had always said that if you looked hard enough, you could find a way out of any situation, no matter how hopeless things looked. Well, Felix had gone into a blind alley and there'd been no way out for him. Now maybe Rogers had walked into the same kind of alley, with the same conviction of his own invincibility. He thought he had figured it all out; now everything was falling apart. He was suddenly all alone, with no way out. Within days, Melissa would be going to California, maybe even leaving him for good. He would have to deal with Dolan alone. He knew Dolan well, knew enough about him now to be sure it would be only a matter of days, maybe not even that long, before Dolan would bring the sword down across his head. If Dolan had his way, it would be end of story for Rogers. He had the power to do just about anything he wanted.

Dolan would come up with something, and he'd have McIntyre's help and Benedetto's, too, and everything would be neatly arranged so that Rogers would be caught like a fish in a net. Dolan would set him up. Dolan would destroy him. And even Morrison wouldn't be able to rescue him. Morrison would have to dump him, walk away, to save his own neck.

From a phone booth near the apartment he dialed his grandmother's number. She answered. She was glad to hear from him. He assured her he was just fine, and that he hoped everything would be settled in a couple of days.

When Melissa came on the phone, her voice sounded tight as she said his name. She was all right, she said, just missing him. A lot.

He told her about Molloy and Dolan.

She listened without comment. When he was through, she said, "What are you going to do now?"

"Maybe they need an extra on that picture of yours."

"Be serious."

"I'm not sure," he said. "Keep at it. Let it play itself out."

He was up early the next morning. It was before seven when he dialed Morrison's private number. "The mayor said to inform you that he's very busy at the moment," a voice said. The line went dead.

He looked at the phone. He put it down, rose, went to the closet and got his coat and started out of the apartment. At the corner, he caught a cab, rode it across town and up the East Side. He was at Gracie Mansion by seven-thirty. "Tell the mayor it's very important," he told two guards at the gate. "Tell him I have to see him."

Word came back to let him through. Morrison and his wife were in the small dining room, in the middle of breakfast. When Rogers entered, Morrison turned to her. "Janet," he said, "would you leave us alone for a while?" The mayor looked unhappy.

She rose without acknowledging Rogers, which was unusual. He was motioned into a chair. "Would you like coffee?" The mayor was always polite.

"I'd like some," Rogers said.

Morrison gestured toward a sideboard. Rogers poured some coffee and returned to the table. Morrison watched his every move. "I had a call about you first thing this morning," he said. "From Chief Dolan."

"He moves fast," Rogers said.

"You've been suspended."

Rogers felt his stomach sink. He expected it, but still it hurt.

"He's bringing you up on charges. When you called, I wasn't ready to talk to you. At least not until I had a chance to consider the implications. He's got me in a corner. I can't afford you now, any more than I could afford Donatello, though, of course, there's no comparison. Then I thought I'd hear what you had to say."

"My word against Dolan's," he said.

"The way it has to be, in public anyway. Chief Dolan said he has proof that you've been taking graft from the Mafia. From Generoso Ruggieri."

"Not true."

"He said he has proof that you have a large account in an offshore bank."

"The same bank where Werner Rosenblatt had his account, I suppose."

"Do you know Generoso Ruggieri?"

"Yes."

"Have you been in his office?"

"Yes."

"In his private office, alone with him?"

"Yes."

"Have you had lunch with him?"

"Yes."

"Have you been in his home?"

"No."

"Are you receiving money from him?"

"No."

"From anyone in that organization?"

"No."

"Have you done favors for him or anyone in that organization?"

"No."

"Why have you met with Generoso Ruggieri?"

"The first time, he sent some boys to pick me up. He wanted

to talk to me. God knows what about. He talked in riddles. We were together about fifteen minutes and that was it. The other times were by accident. I ran into him and he asked me to have lunch. I figured maybe I could learn something. I didn't. That's the extent of it."

"Your word against Chief Dolan's."

"Precisely."

"Why would Chief Dolan lie about you?"

"Don't you know? You wanted me to tell you who else was in this thing beside Donatello. I told you I wanted to be sure, I wanted proof before I gave you the names. I haven't the proof, at least not all of it, but Dolan's involved. He's been up to his ass in it for years. And he knows I know it. Dolan ran Donatello. Dolan ran Benedetto and McIntyre and Tremanti and Bishop Molloy. They were all part of it."

"There's never been a word against any of them until now," Morrison said.

"There's more," Rogers said. "Dolan killed Felix Palmieri, personally. I think it was Dolan killed Donatello. Personally. You want the whole thing in detail, I'll lay it out for you in detail."

"Chief Dolan said you'd start making accusations if I confronted you. Where's your proof?"

"Like I said, no proof. Not yet, anyway. But I'll get it. It has to be out there somewhere, and I'll find it."

"I believe you, Ben. You've always been honest with me. You've always been on the mark in anything I've asked you to do. You've never given me a reason to question your honesty or your commitment. But you were right; I've got to have proof. When the press and the politicians on the other side find out about this, and you can bet they will, do you have any idea what's going to happen? Especially if they learn you've been working for me? The goddamn shit will hit the fan."

"I understand," Rogers said. "You'll have to throw me to the wolves. I'd probably do the same thing if I were in your place."

"My God," Morrison said. "The whole thing is absolutely devastating. A congressman, the chief Assistant District Attorney, Dolan."

"I told you not to trust anybody," Rogers said.

"You told me. But I didn't think it went this high. I hoped

not, anyway. Dammit, Ben, you'd better come up with the proof. I'm depending on you, and I'm not the only one. Do you understand?"

"I understand," Rogers said.

"Until then, I've got to stay clear of you. But, for God's sake, go out and get it, and get it fast."

43

He walked slowly south from the mayor's official residence, through John Jay Park, along the esplanades by the river, hardly feeling the biting winter wind slashing at his face, cutting through his coat. Desperation took hold. He had told Morrison he would find the necessary proof and that he would be back. But he knew that had been little more than a wild boast. There wasn't a man in the department to whom he could turn for help now. Even guys like Rodriguez would be afraid to be seen with him, would be afraid to try to help him. Dolan had made sure of that.

It was nearly noon before he turned the corner onto his block. There was a small crowd outside the building, among them a couple of guys with cameras. So Dolan had put out the word and the press was in ambush. He turned back and went down the next block. He went into the courtyard behind his building, getting to his apartment the back way.

When he opened the apartment door he was confronted by a long white envelope lying just inside. In the upper left-hand corner was the seal of the Police Department. This made it official. The letter notified him that as of that date, he was suspended from active duty without pay. Charges were being

filed against him alleging official misconduct. He had the right to
an attorney. He would be notified when formal hearings would
be held.

The light on the answering machine was flickering. There
were lots of nessages, mostly from the papers and the television
and radio stations, asking him to call this reporter or that one,
asking for a statement, asking for an interview, asking for an
explanation. They would go unanswered.

Late that afternoon, he called George Fielding at the SEC and
told him what he'd learned about Centex. Fielding thanked him
and said he'd follow it up. Then Fielding said, "I hear you're in
a little trouble."

"Word sure gets around fast."

"It does, doesn't it. Christ, it's the lead in the tabloids.
Internal Affairs cop charged with corruption. The pictures don't
do you justice."

"I didn't know there were any," he said.

"Things from the police academy when you were a rookie."

"Jesus. I wouldn't recognize myself."

"Nobody else would, either. Look, Ben, in a showdown, my
money's on you."

The phone call was at least a start. Maybe Fielding would
turn up something, but probably it would be only about Donatello and Wellstone, and about Benedetto feeding Donatello
things that weren't supposed to leak. That would take care of
the congressman. But Dolan had covered himself too well. Fielding would find nothing about the chief, Rogers was sure of that,
and unless somebody did, the noose would keep on tightening.

He would need a lawyer; maybe Solomon could help. He
called, but Solomon was out of town, in Chicago, and he wouldn't
be back until Monday. Rogers left his name and asked that
Solomon call him when he returned.

He felt as though he were trapped in one of those sealed
rooms whose walls kept sliding gradually inward, closer and
closer together, until they finally crushed you.

Maybe this room had an exit, though. It would be a long
shot, and not something he wanted to do. It went against everything he believed in, everything he valued, everything he'd
worked to achieve. But the more he thought about his situation,

the more he searched for some other way out, the more he understood that this was his only hope.

He took a deep breath, steeling himself against what lay ahead. He went back out of his building the way he had come. As he passed, he took a quick glance down his street. The crowd outside his apartment had grown. He moved on.

44

It was a little after seven when he turned the corner of Mulberry Street in Little Italy and found himself outside the small building whose brass plaque said that Parnassus Associates had its office inside.

The door was locked. He rang the small bell under the plaque. A voice asked who was there and what he wanted. Rogers gave his name, said he wanted to speak with Mr. Ruggieri. There was silence. He waited. A buzzer sounded. He pushed the door open and mounted the stairs. He rang again outside the office. There was a clicking and the door opened. He walked inside.

A clone of Gino Santucci was standing just inside the entrance, watching him. He said nothing, merely gestured toward Ruggieri's private office. The door was slightly ajar.

Ruggieri was alone, sitting on the sofa, a glass of white wine in his hand, an uncorked bottle on the table before him. He rose. "Lieutenant Rogers," he said. "I was not expecting you."

"Mr. Ruggieri," Rogers said.

"You will join me in a glass of wine, and then later, you will be my guest for dinner?"

"Why not?"

Ruggieri reached for another glass, poured wine into it, and added some to his own glass. "Sit, my young friend. Here, next to me." He patted a place on the sofa. Ruggieri handed him the glass. "We will drink a toast," he said. "I will not propose it. It should be a silent one, to each his most desired wish." He raised his glass and took a sip. Rogers sipped his. "Do you like it?" Ruggieri asked. "It is bottled especially for me in a vineyard I own in Sicily."

"It's very good," Rogers said. It was.

"Now, what brings you to me at this hour? It must be very important."

"I wanted to thank you for the roses."

Ruggieri shrugged. He smiled a little. "The message was for you," he said. "The roses were not. They were for your friend. I have seen her. She is very beautiful. She is also a lady. She deserves only the best."

Rogers tried to conceal his surprise. "I also have a message for you," Rogers said. "From Gino Santucci. He said to tell you that he's told the feds absolutely nothing about you."

"There was nothing he could tell. He knows nothing."

"That's what he said."

"But that's not why you came here," Ruggieri said.

"No," Rogers said. "Not really."

"Tell me. I've been reading about you today. My young friend, you are in a lot of trouble. I would say somebody has stacked the deck and you're holding a dead hand."

"It looks that way," Rogers said. "You left a message for me the other day. You said if there was anything you could ever do for me, I shouldn't hesitate to call on you. I don't know why you should, but I'm not going to ask why. Not now. I'm in a corner, and I need your help."

"So, you decided to take me up on my offer. What is it you want me to do?"

"Let me tell you a story. For a lot of years, you were working with a guy named Gene Donatello, a banker. Maybe he was working for you, I don't know, but one way or another, you were in some things together. And not just the two of you— some very close friends of Donatello's as well. In fact, I think one of them was even closer to you than Donatello, but we'll come to that later."

Ruggieri said nothing. He watched Rogers closely.

"Last summer," Rogers went on, "Donatello put a lot of your money, and a lot of other people's money, into a company called Centex. About fifty million dollars, from what I understand. It was a sure thing. You couldn't lose. You were going to make a fortune. Only he was wrong; the company went bust. From what I hear about you, I'd say you gave Donatello an ultimatum: to pay back what you'd lost, and maybe even the profits he'd guaranteed. Donatello was desperate. He and his friends had a plan, but it was going to take time. The condition the city was in, Jack Morrison was a shoo-in to be elected mayor, and Donatello figured if he backed him all the way, in exchange Morrison would put him in charge of the city's finances, which would put him in a position to funnel a lot of things in your direction, not just money, but city contracts and a lot more, and before he was through, you'd all end up even better than you'd hoped.

"But a little guy in Donatello's bank sent a letter to Morrison putting the finger on his boss, and Morrison asked me to look into it. What I found was enough to keep Donatello from getting the job, and you didn't get what you thought you were supposed to get, and I guess you must have been pretty pissed off. I don't blame you. And you really must have been even more pissed off when you found out that Donatello was into drugs with Gino Santucci and his partner, Ding-Dong Faranulli, because, according to Gino, that was breaking your rules, and he said if you ever found out that any of your people were into garbage, you'd cut their balls off. So, before you know it, Gino was running to the feds, Ding-Dong went bye-bye, and Donatello had a little accident, which I guess put a paid in full on all his accounts with you.

"Meanwhile, a friend of mine got killed in an alley near here. I think you didn't have anything to do with that. But when I started looking into it, along with some other things, it led back to the murder of a hooker twenty-five years ago, and that led me straight to Donatello again, and to his five buddies. A couple of days ago, I talked to one of them, a priest. You've probably heard about what happened to him after he laid it out for me.

"That leaves the other four. I don't give a crap right now about three of them—Mike Benedetto, McIntyre, and Tremanti. They'll get theirs. Which leaves the last one, Chief William Dolan. I think you know him very well. I think he's very close to you, or at least he was. I think you know what he's been doing all these years. In fact, the more I've thought about it, the surer I am that one of the reasons Dolan made all those spectacular busts of guys in the families, all the families except yours, and managed to come up with evidence nobody else could find, and climbed straight to the top without a detour, was because he had a pipeline, not to somebody up there, but straight to you. And one hand washes the other, right? So all these years you've been helping Dolan, and he's been doing the same for you. A real team, the two of you."

"An interesting story," Ruggieri said. "You have a vivid imagination. But you didn't come here just to tell me your theories. You want something."

"I want Dolan's head on a platter. He thinks he's safe. He thinks he's got nothing to worry about. He thinks he's covered his tracks so nobody can ever do anything to him. Maybe he's right. I don't think so. And I want his head."

"Do you have any idea what you're asking? Even if it were within my power, it would be impossible. And how would his death help you?"

"I don't want him killed. That's too easy. I want to throw him over the wall. I want to throw him to the wolves and watch them eat him alive. So, I need information, facts, details, stuff that I can use to blow him right off his perch. Without that, as he says, it's just my word against his. I need proof to go along with what I already know. You told me once that a bad cop was bad for everyone. Well, Dolan's a bad cop, the worst there is. And even if I can't prove a damn thing right now, I will, eventually. I won't give up. Maybe in the end nobody will believe me, but a thousand-watt spotlight's going to be shining on him through the whole thing. No matter what he's done for you up to now, by the time I get finished, he's going to be useless. Less than useless. He'll try to drag you down with him."

"What you ask is still impossible."

"Not impossible, Mr. Ruggieri. Not for you. You can do it in a way that would keep you in the clear. I'm sure of that."

Ruggieri sipped his wine, then put the glass on the table and rose, walking slowly around the room. He turned and looked at Rogers. He smiled without humor. "This is truly amazing, my young friend. One policeman asks me to supply information that will destroy another policeman. Asks me, Generoso Ruggieri. The irony is beyond belief."

"But you can do it."

Ruggieri shrugged.

"Mr. Ruggieri, do you think I'd be here, asking for a favor, asking for this favor, if there was any other way? And one more thing. You said you saw my girl. You said you thought she was beautiful and a lady. She is. She's a lot more, too. She's special. I don't know whether you know it, but Dolan sent somebody after her."

Ruggieri stood very still. He looked at Rogers carefully. "She was hurt?"

"No. The guy was just following her. But she knows too much. She knows what I know. I think Dolan's desperate. God knows what he'll do next."

Ruggieri sighed deeply. "I think we'll postpone our dinner together until another time," he said. "Now, Lieutenant, I bid you goodnight." He went to the door and held it open. Rogers rose and walked through it. Ruggieri stood in the doorway watching him, his face impassive. As Rogers started through the door to the outside, he noticed Ruggieri make a small gesture to the clone.

45

It had been a gamble, a long shot, but Rogers was sure he had no other cards to play. He wouldn't know for a few days whether Ruggieri would grant his request, and he still had no idea why the Mafia boss had been so open to him, why he had even made an offer to help in the first place. Perhaps the answer lay somewhere in the past, back when Ruggieri had known his grandmother. One day, he would make her tell him about the man, persuade her to talk about her memories without the bitterness and hatred that had filled her voice that other time. In the meantime, he would not ask questions, would accept whatever Ruggieri was willing to give, and pray that he would not ask things in return that Rogers could never grant.

He stayed home the next couple of days going out only to buy groceries and to pick up the papers, so he could read the stuff about the crooked cop whose job had been to protect the city from crooked cops and who had turned out to be twisted himself. Fielding was right, the photographs with the story were all old ones.

He called Melissa from a pay phone, trying to reassure her and his grandmother, promising them that it would come out all right in the end, that he was working on it. He could tell they weren't convinced.

At home, he never used the phone, letting his machine handle all incoming calls, most of them from the press. About noon on the third day, when the phone rang, as always, he didn't answer, listening to the monitor, expecting it to be another reporter calling for an interview. Then he heard his grandmother's voice. He picked up the phone.

"Nonna?"

"Benito," she said, "I must talk with you."

He didn't like the edge in her voice. "About what you read in the papers?" he said. "Forget it. It'll work out."

"That I know," she said. "I believe in you. It is not that. About Melissa."

He sat up. "What about Melissa?"

"That man was here. I will not say his name, but you know who I mean. He has not changed."

He understood. "When?" he asked. "What did he want?"

"He has just left. He took Melissa with him."

"Took her?"

"He did not force her, if that is what you mean. No, he talked to her and she went with him."

"Where?"

"He would not say. He said only that I was not to worry, that no harm would come to her and you would hear soon."

"Jesus," he said. "Do you believe him?

"For all the things he did, to me he never lied," she said.

For the next three hours Rogers paced the apartment, waiting. He called Melissa's agent. The agent hadn't heard from her that day. They'd talked a few times in last couple of days, because the people on the Coast wanted Melissa in a week, and there were things to discuss. But that day, no, they hadn't talked.

The phone rang again. The machine picked up. He listened to the monitor. A voice he didn't recognize came through. It didn't identify itself, and said only a few sentences. They were enough. "We think you should make a trip. To a place upstate that you know. Your friend is waiting for you." The line went dead.

He didn't hesitate. He grabbed his coat, headed out the

door, down the stairs and out the back, moving fast toward the garage where they parked the car. It had to be a trap, a way to get him out of the city, alone. He didn't care. He would deal with that possibility when he had to. Melissa was what was important, and if there was even a chance that she needed him and that he could help her, he had to go to her.

46

He didn't have to stop in town this time to ask directions. He knew the way. It was late, after ten at night, by the time he reached the turnoff. The chain-link fence was fastened between the stone pillars, guarding the access. As he got out of the car, someone huddled into a dark overcoat stepped out of the darkness. Another Gino clone. He flashed a light in Roger's face, nodded, gestured him back to his car, unhitched the chain, and waved Rogers through.

He drove up the long lane, still deep in unplowed snow, following in the ruts made by earlier cars. Another car followed just behind. There were lights in the lodge, blazing out into the darkness. Two cars were parked outside, a Cadillac stretch limo and a new BMW. He pulled up behind them, turned off the engine, and started to get out. The other car pulled alongside. The driver opened the door. "Just leave the keys in the ignition," he said. Rogers shrugged and did as he was told.

The door to the lodge opened. A young guy watched Rogers approach, then stepped toward him. "Just a minute," he said. He ran his hands expertly across Rogers's body, retrieving a pistol from a holster clipped to his belt, and another from an ankle holster. He stepped aside then and let him pass.

It was warm inside, with a roaring fire burning in the massive fireplace. Ruggieri stood to one side of the fireplace, with Dolan across from him. Melissa sat on a sofa facing them. If others were there, Rogers couldn't see them, but he was sure there were more, probably just behind the closed doors. The three people in the room turned and watched him as he stepped inside. Melissa started to rise. "Ben," she said.

"Are you all right?" he asked.

"Yes," she said.

"You're sure?"

"Yes."

"Nobody has harmed the young lady," Ruggieri said. "I brought her here myself. She was treated with the greatest courtesy."

Rogers looked at Melissa. She nodded. "Mr. Ruggieri was very polite," she said. "We had a nice talk on the way here. I learned a lot."

"Why the hell is she here?" he asked Ruggieri.

"It was one way to get you here. The best way. Without trouble."

—"Okay, so I'm here. What now?"

Dolan laughed, the sound grating on the ears. "What was it you said, Ben? You've become an impediment. Both of you."

"And you have to deal with impediments?"

"You're so right."

"Why go to all the trouble of bringing me up here? I thought you were doing a pretty good job as it was."

"A start," Dolan said. "Just a start."

Rogers nodded slowly. "A setup," he said.

"Of course," Dolan said. "You're a pariah now. Everybody knows that. You can read all about it every day in the papers. So you ran, you disappeared, you and your girl together. We'll have a big manhunt. They'll be looking for you in all the lower forty-eight, maybe in Alaska and Hawaii, too. But they'll never find you. End of story."

"I know too much."

"You know too much. As long as you're around, you're a danger. I can get you sent away. But you could always stir up the garbage, set people asking the wrong questions. You understand."

"Sweet reasonableness, aren't we?" Rogers looked toward

Melissa. She was watching them, her eyes intent, studying, not believing what she was hearing. "Me I can understand," he said. "But why her?"

"She knows what you know."

Rogers turned toward Ruggieri. The don's face was impassive. "I was a goddamn idiot," Rogers said.

"Business is business," Ruggieri responded. "I regret what has become necessary, but Chief Dolan has been my partner for many years. As you yourself said, he is what he is because I made him."

"Sure," Rogers said. "But he's going down, and he's going to take you with him. Talk about impediments—he's the damn impediment. You can bet your ass on that."

"Big talk, Ben," Dolan said. "But it's nothing but hot air. You're not around, nobody's going to ask questions. Hell, they wouldn't know where to look or what to ask."

"Don't be so sure," Rogers said. "Morrison knows what I know."

"Which is why he threw you to the lions?" Dolan said. "Don't make me laugh. Even if you said anything, what the fuck can he do?"

"Don't underestimate him," Rogers said.

"I underestimate nobody," Dolan said. "Which is why I'm where I am." He turned toward Ruggieri. "We're wasting time," he said.

"You're in a hurry?" Ruggieri said mildly. But there was something in the eyes, something about the manner, as though he were coiled.

"I want to get back to the city," Dolan said. "I've got things to do."

"We all have things to do," Ruggieri said. He looked at Rogers. "How much does the mayor know?"

"Most of it."

"What you told me?"

"Yeah. Most of it."

"Anybody else?"

"A few guys, bits and pieces. Here and there."

Ruggieri nodded. "But not the proof."

"If they look, they'll find it."

"Undoubtedly. Not right away, but someday. I'm sure you left markers, like a trailblazer in the woods," Ruggieri said.

"Goddamnit, Ruggieri," Dolan said.

"He's right, of course," Ruggieri said. He was watching Dolan closely. The chief didn't seem to notice.

"Bullshit," Dolan said. "Rogers is strictly a one-man show. Like that fucking Palmieri. They keep things under their hat."

"You're so sure?"

"On my life."

"It's not a bet I'd be willing to take," Ruggieri said.

"Listen, you bastard," Dolan said, "I go down, you go down. Plain and simple. Only I'm not about to go down."

"You think so?"

"I know so. You're the one had better worry. What I know about you could send you away for a thousand years, with no parole."

"My friend," Ruggieri said, "I do not like threats."

"It's no threat. It's the goddamn facts."

"A policeman's word against that of a man like me. Is that what you're saying?"

"Damn right. Only not just a cop. A chief. And not just my word. You think I haven't been piling stuff up all these years?"

"I'm sure you have," Ruggieri said.

"You can bet on it. It's all in a nice safe place and there's not a damn thing to implicate me. I'm in the clear."

"Naturally," Ruggieri said.

"You'd better believe it. Now, let's get this fucking show on the road."

"Billy, Billy," Ruggieri said sadly, "I always liked you. I remember when you were just a young cop on the beat and Eugene brought you to me. You were a nice kid then, ambitious, yes, but you knew your place, you knew what was expected of you. You knew that I could make you a very rich man. You knew that I could do things for you that would get you where you wanted to go. You would not have talked to me like that in those days."

"Those days were those days," Dolan said. "These days are these days. Times change."

Ruggieri nodded. "They do. And not for the better."

Rogers had overcome his sense of disorientation enough to realize that these words had double meanings. He glanced at Melissa, and he saw that she had caught it, too. And he saw something else—that she knew something he didn't.

"Look, you son of a bitch," Dolan said, "I've protected you

all these years. You're still walking around breathing fresh air because of me. Now, I'm going to start calling the shots."

"I see," Ruggieri said. His expression was impassive, but the muscles in his neck tightened. "Now *you* are the boss of all bosses, as people say."

"You'd better believe it."

"And you are giving me orders?"

"Damn right. Now, let's get it over with."

"Of course," Ruggieri said. He turned to Rogers, looked at him, then at Melissa. "What Chief Dolan wants," he said, "is for me to kill you. Both of you."

"That's obvious," Rogers said. He started to reach inside his jacket, then remembered that the guy outside had taken his guns. He was defenseless. Melissa rose from the couch and came to him. He put his arm around her.

Ruggieri watched them. He shook his head. "Benito," he said. "Young lady. There is something I'd like you to do."

"I don't think so," Rogers said. "Maybe we don't have a chance, but I'm going to make some trouble before I go." He started toward Ruggieri. Then he stopped and stared. What had Ruggieri called him?

Ruggieri put up his hand. Two of his people came out from behind doors. They had guns pointed at Rogers. "Don't be foolish," Ruggieri said. "It won't help. And it's not necessary."

Ruggieri turned toward Dolan, motioned toward his people. Their guns moved. They were pointing at Dolan now. "Billy," Ruggieri said, "the thing about partnerships is that each partner has to know his place, has to be willing to accept it. We were partners for a long time because we both knew the rules. Unfortunately, you've forgotten them, and when that happens, the partnership comes to an end. Sad but true. I will miss you, the way you used to be." He looked away, back at Rogers and Melissa. "Take your young lady," he said, "and go through that door, get in your car and drive away. Don't stop and don't look back, just drive back to the city. Once you are far away, you might want to look on the backseat. And once you are far away, ask your young lady to tell you what she knows. Now, go."

Rogers stared at him. Ruggieri made a peremptory gesture and turned back toward Dolan. The chief was staring at Ruggieri. He was sweating. Rogers looked away, took Melissa by the arm, and started toward the door. The guy who had frisked

Rogers was still just outside. They passed him. He looked at them, and then went into the lodge.

They reached the car, expecting to hear something behind them, but there was only silence. They drove slowly to the main road, maintaining silence, as though to speak would shatter the spell which had allowed them to escape. They drove for a while on the highway, then Rogers pulled the car over to the side of the road and stopped. He took Melissa in his arms and held her, and she held him, not wanting to let go. After a few minutes, he drew away, and looked into her face. He shook his head. "My God," he said.

"We're alive," she said.

"We're alive," he said.

"I didn't think it was possible," she said.

He nodded. "On the backseat," he said. "What's there?"

They both turned and looked. On the backseat was a large packing carton. Rogers leaned way over and pulled it open. Inside were stacks of papers and documents inside dozens of file folders, a pile of photo transparencies, tape recordings, and a lot more. He picked up one of the transparencies, turned on the overhead light and held it up. He could make out Dolan and Donatello. They were at a table somewhere. There was a third man with them. Rogers recognized him. Sal Ianucci, the mob boss who had been shot down a couple of months before. No friend of Ruggieri's. He picked up a couple of other transparencies and looked quickly at them. Dolan, Donatello, Benedetto, McIntyre, all of them, singly, together, in pairs and more, some on the street, some in rooms, and always with an identifiable mob boss, but never Ruggieri.

He stared at them, then back at Melissa. "The son of a bitch," he said. Dolan wasn't the only one who had piled up some memorabilia for future protection.

He started to laugh. He grinned at Melissa. "Is this what he meant by your knowing something?"

"No, that's not what he meant."

"What?"

She studied him for a moment. "Don't you really know?" she said. "Haven't you guessed who he is? Your grandmother knows. I saw it when he came into the house. I knew it then. He didn't have to tell me."

"What?"

"He's your grandfather, of course."